Constructing
Mark Twain

Mark Twain and His Circle Series
Tom Quirk, Editor

Constructing
Mark Twain

New Directions in Scholarship

Edited with an Introduction by

Laura E. Skandera Trombley
and Michael J. Kiskis

UNIVERSITY OF MISSOURI PRESS   COLUMBIA AND LONDON

Copyright © 2001 by
The Curators of the University of Missouri
University of Missouri Press, Columbia, Missouri 65201
Printed and bound in the United States of America
5 4 3 2 1   05 04 03 02 01

Library of Congress Cataloging-in-Publication Data

Constructing Mark Twain : new directions in scholarship / edited with an introduction by Laura E. Skandera Trombley and Michael J. Kiskis.

   p.   cm. — (Mark Twain and his circle series)
   Includes bibliographical references and index.
   ISBN 0-8262-1377-4 (alk. paper)
   1. Twain, Mark, 1835–1910—Criticism and interpretation—History—20th century.
2. Criticism—United States—History—20th century.   I. Skandera-Trombley, Laura E.
II. Kiskis, Michael J.   III. Series.

PS1337.3.C66   2002
813'.4—dc21

                                                              2001040996

Text Design: Stephanie Foley
Jacket Design: Kristie Lee
Typesetter: BOOKCOMP, Inc.
Printer and Binder: Thomson-Shore, Inc.
Typefaces: Indy Italic, Minion, and Myriad

Previously unpublished words of Mark Twain and his family are © 1998 by Chemical Bank as Trustee of the Mark Twain Foundation, which reserves all reproduction or dramatization rights in every medium. Quotation is made with the permission of Robert H. Hirst, Gene Hirst, general editor of the Mark Twain Project.

To my beloved parents, John and Mary Skandera,
who taught me laughter is as powerful as love.

Laura E. Skandera Trombley

To the memory of my mother, Frances E. Kiskis,
who would be not a little surprised (but neverthe-
less pleased) that I have managed to make a life
reading and writing. As Sam Clemens wrote of his
mother, I can say of mine: "Technically speaking,
she had no career; but she had a character, and it
was of a fine and striking and lovable sort."

Michael J. Kiskis

Contents

Acknowledgments

We would like to thank all the people in Mark Twain studies who over the past decade have laughed at our jokes, read our work, listened to our stories, and bought us drinks. Bless you all.

Laura: I am grateful to Jennifer Archibald, assistant to the dean of the faculty, who prepared the manuscript for publication, and to Doris Gitzy, administrative assistant to the academic dean, who organizes my days (and occasionally my life). I am fortunate to count William Flanagan, Cap'n Bill and Linda, and Michael Kiskis as confidants and partners in crime. Finally, my deepest love to Nelson and Sparkey, who constitute the sun and moon in my personal cosmos.

Michael: I want to acknowledge the help and affection of friends both local and distant—Leah Glasser, Denise Knight, Scott Minar, Robin Milliken, Charlie Mitchell, John McLaughlin, and Laura Skandera Trombley. Thank you for caring enough to support me when I am right and caring enough not to celebrate (at least not too loudly) when I am wrong. I am a better reader and writer and teacher and person because of you.

Constructing
Mark Twain

Introduction

LAURA E. SKANDERA TROMBLEY AND MICHAEL J. KISKIS

> I believe that the trade of critic, in literature, music, and the
> drama, is the most degraded of all trades, and that it has
> no real value—certainly no large value.... However, let it go.
> It is the will of God that we must have critics, and mission-
> aries, and congressmen, and humorists, and we must bear
> the burden.
>
> Mark Twain, *Mark Twain's Own Autobiography*

If there is such a thing as a nonregulated and free literary marketplace, Samuel L. Clemens–Mark Twain has been and remains one of its hot commodities.[1] Over the past eighty years there has been an avalanche of scholarship about Clemens's life and work. Indeed, if one wishes to become familiar with the body of criticism, the task would take the better part of a decade. The sheer mass of criticism published concerning Clemens (either as primary subject or supporting character) suggests that writing about him has become a rite of passage for the novice and a career capstone for the distinguished scholar-biographer specializing in American literature. Clemens himself, if he were inclined toward honesty, would be taken aback by his ability to conjure an audience, both popular and academic (especially academic), so long after his death. Hundreds of gallons of ink have been spilled in tribute to the writer and to his literary alter ego.

From Clemens's ever-so-careful attempts to use the press to create and fine-tune his public persona to the thousands of pages of academic analysis that have been generated since the early criticism of William Dean Howells

---

1. Twain, *Mark Twain's Own Autobiography*, will hereafter be referred to as *AU*.

1

and Brander Matthews, Clemens has held a spotlight all his own within American literary studies. That spotlight has rarely, if ever, dimmed. Even if the intensity of the light and angle of the beam have been adjusted by subsequent generations of readers and critics, his reputation has not suffered the typical dark corners that speckle the literary stage—the spirits of Herman Melville, Ernest Hemingway, F. Scott Fitzgerald, and T. S. Eliot must all look on with a mixture of awe and chagrin. Clemens himself tried to explain his staying power by claiming that his books were not fine wine for the elite but clear water for the common reader; "everybody," he wrote, "likes water."[2] As we have moved through the twentieth century, critics have, in fact, performed the literary equivalent of the miracle at Cana as they have pronounced Clemens's proletarian water among the finest of elite American wines.

Still greater attention will soon be aimed at Clemens: the one hundredth anniversary of his death is now in sight (a mere nine years from this writing). That anniversary is worth pointing to as an indicator of Clemens's staying power. As prelude to what will no doubt be the equivalent to a scholarly frenzy, we thought it especially timely to take an extended look at Clemens's life and work and, perhaps, provide several hints for the major reevaluation that is sure to come. As readers and teachers and commentators on the life and career of Samuel Clemens, we considered it important to reflect on the rapid changes now under way in how we understand Clemens within the confines of his own time as well as his value to our own. Critics have not been shy in their attempts to construct, deconstruct, and reconstruct Clemens. He is amazingly plastic, but critics are all too ready to morph him to suit their purposes. They—we—dab him with color and stretch his figure using our own interpretive prism. We are deliberately pausing here for a moment to wonder what he would think of all this and to identify and judge our complicity in the continuing work to transport Clemens so completely and so intimately (and, at times, so inappropriately) into our own time. We are now at a point where the accumulation and breadth of scholarly interpretation compel us to look back over the territory that has been explored to see how our own ideas have been shaped by the work

---

2. Twain to William Dean Howells, Feb. 15, 1887, Mark Twain Papers.

of our predecessors. That foundation built of past scholarship gives us a clearer view of what is in store for the future of Twain studies. It also suggests that there is a good deal of meaning still in the notion of a community of writers and its influence on creating an identity (both for its subject and for itself).

Of course, Clemens's fecundity as a writer remains at the center of our work. The sheer volume of his writing urges us to recalibrate his value as a contributor to American life and culture. He was, in all, a supremely confident author who used the whole range of life as his pallet. We are still coming to terms with his range, with the expanse of his thinking and reactions, with his successes and failures, and with his abilities, inabilities, and biases as we read his work and read for its connection to his life. No doubt, and in significant measure because of his mongrel and plastic nature, American culture has adopted Clemens as a premier spokesperson; his commentary is constantly adopted and freely adapted to fit our needs. As apprentice or expert marketers, some critics have been and are shameless, in fact, in how quickly they co-opt him as sage or huckster, often with a dismaying sloppiness, and disconnect Clemens from his own time in order to grasp him firmly as our contemporary, as one of us, and to embed him within the shocks and quakes of our time. As we prepared this collection of essays, we shuddered to imagine how soon advances in computer animation will treat us to a walking, talking Clemens shilling (what else!) cigars and scotch, reducing him to what he and his family feared the most—a mere caricature. Indeed, although Clemens has been dead for ninety years, in some fairly significant ways one scarcely notices it. Impersonators roam the countryside performing Mark Twain before schoolchildren, paying audiences, and gatherings of scholars. New editions of *Adventures of Huckleberry Finn* are continually being published along with scholarly volumes of his letters. New films are under production, and two documentaries of his life are in the pre- and postproduction stages. Scholars gather at conferences and endlessly argue about Clemens's life, legacy, and sometimes even his literature. The weary traveler can spend the night at the Huck Finn Motel and relax while watching Twain visit the folks on *Bonanza* or *Star Trek* and snacking on Mark Twain macadamia nuts. In New Orleans the Mark Twain Pizzeria features Twain gazing through the glass front window—Mark Twain and pizza? The same traveler can pack clothes in luggage endorsed by Twain's great-great-great-nephew (an impostor), and even pay their bills with Mark Twain cyber bucks issued by the Mark Twain Bank.

But perhaps it is not as bad as all that. There is a strength at the center of Clemens's character, a strength that assigned him an essential poise as events and ideas swirled around him. His was an essentially modern consciousness that reveled in and was repelled by change. He was keenly sensitive to the mutability of life and the play of ideas that affect national or cultural definition. He understood that a culture is not a collection of immutable artifacts (literary or otherwise) but a dynamic conversation that courses within, through, and around those artifacts. Clemens would, we believe, agree that R. W. B. Lewis had it just right in his preface to *The American Adam:*

> [A] culture achieves identity not so much through the ascendancy
> of one particular set of convictions as through the emergence
> of its peculiar and distinctive dialogue. (Similarly, a culture is
> on the decline when it submits to intellectual martial law, and
> fresh understanding is denied in a denial of further controversy.)
> Intellectual history, properly conducted, exposes not only the
> dominant ideas of a period, or of a nation, but more important,
> the dominant clashes of ideas. Or to put it more austerely: the
> historian looks not only for the major terms of discourse, but also for
> major pairs of opposed terms which, by their very opposition, carry
> discourse forward. The historian looks, too, for the coloration or
> discoloration of ideas received from the sometimes bruising contact
> of opposites.[3]

Clemens might have thought of himself as such an historian. He talked of such a "bruising contact of opposites" years earlier as he described his autobiographical method, "a form and method whereby the past and the present are constantly brought face to face, resulting in contrasts which newly fire up the interest all along, like contact of flint with steel" (*AU,* 3).

---

3. Lewis, *The American Adam: Innocence, Tragedy, and Tradition in the Nineteenth Century,* 2.

The contact that Clemens generated as he composed his fiction or as he re-created his life grew out of a sustained effort to place characters as well as himself at odds with others and with the very communities and times in which they and he lived. In an innately dialogic vision, he saw himself as an outsider (perhaps as the quintessential or iconic outsider) and his writings, ultimately, as artifacts, as composites of the ideas and trends and values accumulated from the society with and within which he traveled. The tension and conversation that resulted from the clash of ideas and perspectives were tinder for the fire of his imagination. And despite the still too often categorizing of Clemens as funny man, the reality is that he pushed active interpretation, not passive entertainment; in a variation of the call and response, he presented many of his stories in forms that left the final reaction and response open to his readers. They too, demanded Clemens, must participate in the dialogue.

In all, Clemens was both a participant in and an instigator of the dialogue that is recognized as American culture. His novels, stories, travel writings, essays, letters, quips, and maxims are, at the very least, a multilayered monologue that inspires and exhorts comment. Clemens swam in the current of his increasingly modern culture by reading and writing. And, like him, we swim in the currents of his and our cultures by reading and writing— about him. Like him, we engage in a supremely self-conscious act: we read and write in order to find some tie to the world around us, something that takes us to a new understanding of ourselves and takes us to a deeper appreciation of the aesthetic and ethical demands that are placed upon us by our own lives. We explore and create culture to make sense of the world; Clemens's writings and his life offer seemingly inexhaustible resources for such prospecting. He provides an array of materials most useful to our own work of cultural alchemy.

As alchemists, then, we read and interpret and write. Hence, this collection. Surely, some will yawn or exclaim and complain, "No! Not ANOTHER edition of essays on Mark Twain! What more can be said?" That complaint is more than likely seasoned with assumptions about Samuel Clemens–Mark Twain as established literary and cultural icon and about unwavering allegiance to critical precedent. Our intention, instead, is to treat Clemens and established critical ideas with a dash of skepticism and with a sense, so valuable to our understanding, of the ways we shape and reshape, use and (perhaps) abuse icons. Not challenging the scholarship that created the icon suggests an unwillingness to reconsider the history of critical traditions and the way those traditions have been and are tied to time-bound perspectives, beliefs, agendas, and biases. Icons—even secular icons—simplify mystery and solidify certainty. Protecting them displays a reluctance to plane the gilt off the public image to find the complexity of the human being that is the kernel of the image.

This work of literary carpentry is the drive behind this series of essays. Typical analogies of restoration or reclamation do not fit here. Both intimate a return to some original state or pristine condition, an unaffected, untarnished, untrammeled image. To think that possible with an immensely complicated Samuel Clemens and his potent ego-supplement Mark Twain turns away from the weight of biographical and literary material that has come our way during the past century. This is especially true of the post–World War II years in which Twain studies flourished as part of a movement to ensure the dominance of U.S. culture and during the last decade of the cultural wars that has seen the firings of multiple canons, each aimed at shaking the literary status quo. Participants in both movements are often unwilling to admit that each has been highly selective, perhaps even exclusionary, in their approach to Clemens. One of the basic tenets of writing is that authors choose what they put in or leave out of their story. Even granting the progress in locating new biographical evidence, the narrative produced by writers and scholars about Samuel Clemens has been marked by its creators' recurring predilection to include or exclude (or ignore or misrepresent) often pertinent bits and pieces of his life and times. Worse has been a seemingly deliberate (though never fully or consciously admitted) push to practice pathography. It is one thing to remove the gilt to see the man; it is another thing to toss gobs of agenda-laden muck with the hope of forging a critical and literary identity not for the subject but for the biographer and critic.

Until recently, studies of Samuel Clemens have offered incomplete renderings of important areas of his life and, at times, simplistic formulas of how his life and times and relationships influenced his writing. For example, one area that has been virtually ignored until the publication of *Mark Twain in the Company of Women* has been the pivotal influence, indeed formative influence, of the women surrounding Clemens and, perhaps even more important, his wife, Olivia Langdon.[4] Also, questions of Clemens's approach to family life have taken on new power as scholars have come to see personal context as a valuable source for insights into Clemens's creativity. Few recent observers see Clemens's talent as unaffected by, as standing firm against, the microsociety of family or the macrosociety of nineteenth-century America. Biographical evidence can also lead to a reassessment of Clemens's literary ties to the domestic fiction of the nineteenth century. Still another example is the dominance of the Clemens-Twain personality split in the critical tradition. Biographers have long accepted the notion of a division within Clemens—the question, once oversimplified to allow an easier categorization, became who was Samuel Clemens and who was Mark Twain and how do we tell the difference? Again, until recently, there has been no clear explanation of why (or even if) such a dichotomy exists, and we have come to wonder whether such a dichotomy was present in the historical Clemens (which becomes at times a quest like that for the historical Jesus) or whether it is a product of the critical interpretations handed down to us in an ongoing attempt to atomize a complex personality into pieces more easily categorized and then described. Certainly, the fault in such work—if we decide to concentrate on fault at all—grows out of the critical and cultural perspectives that have influenced such studies. Reflecting on the sequence of scholarship on Clemens-Twain can help us all better understand our own place in the critical parade. Critics do not work in a vacuum. Samuel Clemens did not. None of us do.

There has been, fortunately, a move in some recent scholarship to complicate our understanding of Clemens, especially as questions related to race and gender and class have become more pronounced. As we move further away from the times within which Clemens lived and wrote, we are better able to gain needed perspective on the myriad influences that shaped him as a man and writer. Such has been the case in work that has begun to unpack the generative power of Clemens's literary and personal associations: What voices did he hear? What voices did he tend? How did those voices blend into his fiction and into his life? We are also more apt to hear questions

4. Skandera Trombley, *Mark Twain in the Company of Women.* Hereafter referred to as *MTW.*

related to Clemens's legacy and to the symbiosis between that legacy and the evolution of critical traditions. There is an expanding critical interest in placing Clemens within a broad scheme of literary influences, influences that suggest he is not so much the end product of one specific literary tradition (for example, the literary humor of the old Southwest) but a hybrid shaped by a multivocal, multiracial, and cross-gendered consortium of male and female writers. Such questions should prompt us to interrogate how the tradition of critical judgment on Clemens has been influenced as individual critics work within paradigms contemporary to their own working lives.

All of this leads to a more complex understanding of Clemens: a complexity that demonstrates that simplified dichotomies manage only to obscure human personalities and relationships. Clemens's personality has never been thought simple; his relationships (all of them) were nothing if not complex. And the relationship between him and the critics and commentators who have worked off of his life and writings remains among the most complex of all. Over the past ten years there has been a flurry of biographies and critical studies of Samuel Clemens. In one sense this activity can be seen as generational, a new crop of junior faculty working their way to tenure and choosing Clemens as their topic. This, though, is unusual in today's academic climate: studies of individual authors have fallen out of critical favor and have been set aside for the involved and theoretical maze of broad cultural studies. Interestingly, work in Clemens-Twain has, in fact, become an entry for solid work that blends the tradition of the single-author study with contemporary cultural and theory-based criticism. Such work deserves closer reading and considerable contemplation. Because of it Clemens has emerged as a contested literary icon. Indeed, it is possible to read recent and various studies and biographies as texts that test the limits of theory and the boundaries of the canon. It appears that we are experiencing a Kuhn-like paradigm shift here: the new supplants the old; the skepticism that informs new approaches displaces or at least rattles the steel tradition. This critical equivalent to Clemens's autobiographical contact of "flint to steel" crosses generations. To put it more directly, Clemens's life and works are being inscribed both by those who come recently from graduate school and by those who have lifelong investments in the figure they have, in many cases, helped to create. The essays chosen for this collection underscore the strains and shifts within the epistemology of criticism that focuses on

Samuel Clemens. In 1974 Hamlin Hill, in his incendiary essay "Who Killed Mark Twain?" identified the areas of Twain scholarship he thought had been neglected and called for "spice and flavor, zestful prose, scholarly self-respect, and the courage to offer untraditional perspectives on [Mark Twain's] life and works."[5] We believe the essays selected here provide the qualities Hill deemed essential and in sum represent a generation's work in Twain studies.

The collection opens with two essays that place Samuel Clemens–Mark Twain immediately within a domestic scene. Michael J. Kiskis sets the stage by discussing Twain's ties to the "Other American Tradition," namely, literary domesticity. Using examples from *Adventures of Huckleberry Finn,* "The Death of Jean," and the *Autobiography,* Kiskis interprets these disparate texts as evidence of Twain's concern with familial relationships. In Kiskis's view Twain consistently chose the home as the location to debate issues of morality. Vic Doyno wrestles with the issue of defining Twain's success as paterfamilias in his illuminating essay, "Samuel Clemens as Family Man and Father." Noting that nineteenth-century norms are decidedly different from contemporary ones, Doyno discusses Twain's parents as well as his middle-child placement within the family. He also points out Twain's interest in family dynamics and parental discipline. On a related topic, the role Mary Mason Fairbanks played in guiding the development of Twain's social skills and, more critically, his writing is thoughtfully investigated in J. D. Stahl's "'To his preferred friends he revealed his true character': Mary Mason Fairbanks's Disguised Debate with Sam Clemens." Fairbanks, a professional writer for the *Cleveland Herald,* was an active and equal participant in Twain's role playing and consented to the "game of mutual self-creation." Stahl notes that Fairbanks's role in Twain's development was wrongly minimized by earlier critics because of the movement to reject any "domesticating influence," that is, literary domesticity.

Mark Twain's creation of himself as a writer is the subject of Jeffrey Steinbrink's and Robert Sattelmeyer's essays. In "Mark Twain's Mechanical Marvels," Steinbrink demonstrates how Twain's love of technology was a lifelong obsession that influenced his "construction of mechanistic metaphors

5. Hill, "Who Killed Mark Twain?"

for the creative process." He follows the influence of technology on Twain's writing process from *The Innocents Abroad* to the *Autobiography*. Robert Sattelmeyer traces Twain's prose distortions of his early life in "Steamboats, Cocaine, and Paper Money: Mark Twain Rewriting Himself." In "The Turning Point of My Life," Twain shatters the myth of a bucolic boyhood that he in part, Sattelmeyer argues, helped create. Twain's rewriting late in life was to try to make sense of his present circumstances, circumstances that contained a "darkening vision of human nature." Twain's later writings are also featured in Jennifer L. Zaccara's "Mark Twain, Isabel Lyon, and the 'Talking Cure': Negotiating Nostalgia and Nihilism in the *Autobiography*." Zaccara recognizes Twain's penchant for working throughout his writing career in an autobiographical mode, yet she views this writing as a precursor for the kind of experimentation he would attempt when he turned to his autobiography. She connects Twain's dictations with the popular "talking cure," a method espoused by the emerging psychological movement. Zaccara contends that Isabel Lyon's role in the "cure" was to assist Twain in his dictations by serving as his warm-up audience and acting as his "pseudo-analyst."

Several contributors have written provocative essays dealing with questions of ethnicity and race within Twain's works. Twain's "problematic" turn-of-the-century writings are the focus of Henry B. Wonham's "Minstrel and the Detective: The Functions of Ethnic Caricature in Mark Twain's Writings of the 1890s." Wonham views the rise of racial stereotyping during this period as affecting Twain's writing in the sense that despite trying to resist the prevailing culture, his "ethnic caricatures . . . dismantle the paradox of Jim's complex identity." Jim Leonard's "Huck, Jim, and the 'Black-and-White' Fallacy" finds Twain's use of logic in *Adventures of Huckleberry Finn* highlighted when writing about racial issues. Naturally, Huck's decision to "go to hell" is featured, as is the "logically fallacious structure" that forms the basis for Huck's decision. The ways in which Twain includes logical fallacies in the narrative, Leonard claims, deconstructs the "black-and-white" "false dilemma." David L. Smith contends, in "Humor, Sentimentality, and Mark Twain's Black Characters," that one of the most controversial issues in Twain criticism has been the interpretation of representations of race. To assist in framing his discussion, Smith reviews Tom Quirk's *Coming to Grips with Huckleberry Finn* as well as his own earlier publication "Huck, Jim, and

American Racial Discourse" and Shelley Fisher Fishkin's *Was Huck Black?*
Twain's use of dialect, Smith argues, provides readers with more than "sociolinguistic verisimilitude," and exchanges about dialect are by their nature
"politically charged." Ann Ryan takes issue with critics and popular culture
in her essay, "Black Genes and White Lies: Twain and the Romance of Race."
She examines Jonathan Arac's view that *Adventures of Huckleberry Finn* enjoys a misbegotten reputation as an iconic American novel examining race.
The text is not to blame for this deification, Ryan argues; instead we need to
examine America's penchant for interpreting the narrative as a tale of how
racism was resolved.

Questions of space and metaphor come to the fore in Tom Quirk's "Mark
Twain in Large and Small: The Infinite and the Infinitesimal in Twain's Late
Writing" and John Bird's "Mark Twain Studies and the Myth of Metaphor."
Quirk ventures that one of Twain's strengths was his willingness to become
lost. The concept of a limitless space, instead of frightening Twain, appeared
to intrigue him and served as the subject for his essay "Was the World Made
for Man?" Twain was also fascinated with the infinitesimal and wrote about
it, most notably in "Three Thousand Years among the Microbes." Quirk
observes that in his examination of the infinite and infinitesimal, "Twain
extended the reach of his fundamentally democratic imagination outward
to the fringes of the universe and inward to a single-celled world." Bird looks
to the imagination and metaphor building that critics have undertaken as
he revisits the book-length critical studies published over the past ten years.
He relies on the theories of Colin Turbayne and Roman Jakobson to assist
him in identifying the ideas present in Twain scholarship (the metaphor
of twinness comes immediately to mind). Bird's intention is to predict the
future direction of Twain studies by revealing "some of its distortions, past
and present."

Finally, a direct reply to Hill's essay and a status quo check comes from
Laura E. Skandera Trombley and Gary Scharnhorst in their piece, "'Who
Killed Mark Twain?' Long Live Samuel Clemens!" Trombley and Scharnhorst comment on whether Hill was justified in his attack on Twain critics
and identify recently published works that have, at times substantially, challenged well-established approaches to Clemens-Twain and that have pushed
the boundaries of the field.

In the end, a change in theory or perspective or emphasis does more than alter scholarship about Clemens-Twain; it has the potential to change significantly the figure, the man, the icon, the canon, the text. There is much at stake here for scholars: reputations have been built on particular interpretations, and that prior scholarship has been used, at times, to claim exclusive prospecting rights. Who will stake a lasting claim for the Samuel Clemens of the coming century, and what theoretical perspective(s) will dominate? To whom will Clemens belong? But scholars are not the only ones who have a stake in Samuel Clemens. The broad population of interested readers also has a claim, and the criticism published today will shape public perceptions. The symbiosis between reader and critic has always played a role in the public conception of Clemens-Twain. How will future readers come to know him? Will they gaze on the icon or come to understand the man? Which icon? Which man? This collection confronts these questions and offers a series of observations that point to riches still to be mined by twenty-first-century readers.

Mark Twain and the Tradition of Literary Domesticity

MICHAEL J. KISKIS

When I ask students what they know about Mark Twain, they invariably respond with a host of established images—white suit, white hair, frontier born and raised, westerner, southerner, the river. Many have read either *The Adventures of Tom Sawyer* or *Adventures of Huckleberry Finn;* few have moved beyond the party line of Twain as American classic. Fewer still know him as the author of *The Prince and the Pauper* or *Personal Recollections of Joan of Arc;* some have been touched by the controversy of race and have come to see the debate over racism in his works as the only issue worthy of attention or scorn; all tend to think that he emerged fully formed amid Mississippi sandbars and small towns constrained by solid family and community values. All are surprised by his attachment to his family.

For a good long time, Twain scholars, like my students, have been operating within exclusionary readings and tightly wrapped and carefully marketed icons. When I was introduced to Mark Twain's writing in 1981 during my first semester of doctoral study, the theme of the seminar was Mark Twain as Artist (emphasis, in fact, on failed artist). That focus on and interpretation of Twain were clearly tied to the debate begun more than sixty years earlier by Van Wyck Brooks and Bernard DeVoto: the two camps divide over Twain as frustrated and failed artist (Brooks) or Twain as essential proponent of American individualism and of the innate power of the vernacular and folk mind (DeVoto). Twain studies is still held hostage to that debate.

The relative ease of an interpretation based in such dualism has created a cottage industry in Twain studies. We continue to squeeze and mold Twain into prepackaged notions of who and what he was or should be—we apply current theoretical approaches and constructs to his works in a display of intellectual gymnastics rather than a concentrated and open-minded exploration. We do not often admit that the prism through which we read Twain conjures specific images and interpretations. Though we make noises about understanding the affect of interpretive paradigms on our work, we do not always view those paradigms with a skepticism that allows entry to opposing views or that allows us to appreciate a more (or less) complex understanding of Twain's humanity. It is a classic case of what Annette Kolodny describes as the challenge facing feminist scholars: "Insofar as we are taught how to read, what we engage are not texts but paradigms."[1] My point is that for too long we have kept to one interpretive paradigm when reading the works of Mark Twain. We have focused mainly on his supposedly unambiguous support for individual—even iconoclastic—freedom.

In her introduction to *Domestic Individualism: Imagining Self in Nineteenth-Century America*, Gillian Brown argues that we need to complicate our reading of American literature by blending the mythic criticism that focuses on the growth of a peculiarly American individualism (which takes explicit form with Emerson) with an understanding of nineteenth-century American women writers' focus on domestic images and experiences of home and hearth that they used both to challenge a market controlled by male writers and to build their own literary tradition:

> Individualism and domesticity have both long figured as thematics of nineteenth-century American culture, but as distinct and oppositional trajectories. Thus two disparate literary movements seem to emerge in the 1850s: on the one hand the American Renaissance, represented by the "classic works" of Emerson, Whitman, Hawthorne, Melville, and Poe; and on the other hand the Other American Renaissance, inscribed in the works of Stowe and such writers as Susan Warner, Fanny Fern, Harriet Wilson, and Elizabeth Stuart Phelps.
>
> This gender division has persisted with remarkable neatness and clarity throughout American literary criticism. Recall how myths of the origins of American culture describe second-generation Adamic and oedipal stories: new Edens, sons in exile, estrangement from

---

1. Kolodny, "Dancing through the Minefield: Some Observations on the Theory, Practice, and Politics of a Feminist Literary Criticism," 280.

women. . . . In this androcentric, if not misogynistic, account of
American culture, literature records the battle between the masculine
desire for freedom and the feminine will toward civilization: the
runaway Huck Finn versus the "sivilizing" Widow Douglas. The
paradigm of the dreamer's flight from the shrew defines the domestic
as a pole from which the individual must escape in order to establish
and preserve his identity. Huck lights out for the territory in order
to avoid what Ann Douglas calls "the feminization of American
culture," to flee from the widow's sentimental values that epitomize,
in Henry Nash Smith's words, "an ethos of conformity."[2]

Brown begins a useful reappraisal of the validity of parallel literary movements. She also points to a way to set Mark Twain and his literary creations
within a much broader and, I think, more accurate tradition in American
letters. Taking Brown's comments as my lead, I intend to examine Twain's
tie to the "Other American tradition" of literary domesticity—to the definition of home, the boundaries of home, and the freedom to be gained by
belonging. Mark Twain never wanted to escape the "domestic"; in fact, his
identity depended heavily upon values embedded in home and hearth. For
evidence, I will look to *Adventures of Huckleberry Finn,* "The Death of Jean,"
and the *Autobiography.*

My experience as a reader of *Adventures of Huckleberry Finn* during the
past fifteen years has introduced me to a variety of critical judgments ranging from the complaints against Huck's obstinate ignorance to a celebration
of his archetypal quest for freedom, to applause for his ability to transcend
both religious and racial prejudice, to disappointment with the final third
of his story, to a sophisticated response to the final adventures that argues
for the unified whole. It fascinates me that each of these approaches is still
in play; none has been effectively calmed. I now have a sense that we have
recently turned a critical corner and face still another—and compelling—
approach: the next interpretive battle may be over Huck's influence on how
we see and understand family relationships.

This places *Adventures of Huckleberry Finn* at the center of the swirl over
domestic concerns in the mid- to late nineteenth century. Huck's runaway

---

2. Brown, *Domestic Individualism,* 5. Hereafter referred to as *DI.*

status, his being essentially an orphan, places him at the side of young Ellen Montgomery of Susan Warner's *Wide, Wide World* (1850), Sylvy of Sarah Orne Jewett's "White Heron" (1886), or, later, even young Lily of Mary Wilkins Freeman's "Old Woman Magoun" (1891). These writers place their characters in a struggle for moral action—most often within households and communities shaped, perhaps exclusively, by women. In our own time, Huck is placed within the drive by social conservatives to highlight William Bennett's praise for supposedly conservative-owned virtues—Self-discipline, Compassion, Responsibility, Friendship, Work, Courage, Perseverance, Honesty, Loyalty, and Faith—and for stories that speak "without hesitation, without embarrassment, to the inner part of the individual, to the moral sense."[3]

Twain, I think, would be ambivalent. He saw the moral sense as no key to appropriate behavior; it is too easily shaped by external authority, too quickly transformed from an interest in compassion into the slave of a conscience like that which Twain's narrator battles in "The Recent Carnival of Crime in Connecticut," or like that which Huck battles as he runs for his life. Yet, issues of morality are deeply embedded in Twain's domestic fiction, especially the question of how to teach morality—by the voice of authority or by the resilience of tradition. In *Adventures of Huckleberry Finn* the debate is manifest in the conflict between the narrow blasts of Miss Watson and Pap on one side and the steady perseverance of the Widow Douglas and Jim on the other.

Twain insisted that the arena for this consideration of morality is the home. I recently taught a graduate class called "Mark Twain and Social Justice." Our discussion of the constellation of social issues in *Adventures of Huckleberry Finn* quickly focused on the profound absence of the "traditional" family and social networks within the tale. As we worked through Twain's writings, one student became more apprehensive: finally, looking very uncomfortable, he announced that he felt that he would have substantial problems bringing *Adventures of Huckleberry Finn* to his students. The questions of aesthetics were not the problem, nor did he feel the questions of race insurmountable. His prime concern became how to introduce a story

---

3. Bennett, ed., *The Book of Virtues: A Treasury of Moral Stories*, 14.

about an abused child of an alcoholic parent to a group of students whose home lives were so much a mirror image of Huck's. "This story," he said, "is too close to their real lives." Twain's consideration of home—or absence of home—fostered his uncanny ability to look into the dark corners of human life and paint a picture that may, in fact, be more accurate in 2000 than it was in 1886 or 1846.

Clearly, just as the increased consciousness of civil rights since the 1950s inspired readers to consider the role that race plays in *Adventures of Huckleberry Finn,* our contemporary concerns ignite questions related to family issues, social and legal protections, and values. Consider that the new judge brought in to rule on the matter of Huck's custody (a battle between Pap and Judge Thatcher and the Widow Douglas) decides in Pap's favor based on an assumption that biology trumps compassion and overrides legal protection: "[H]e said courts mustn't interfere and separate families if they could help it; said he'd druther not take a child away from its father. So Judge Thatcher and the widow had to quit the business."[4] Four paragraphs later, however, that new judge is full of regrets after Pap's short-lived reform and "reckoned a body could reform the old man with a shot-gun, maybe, but he didn't know no other way" (*Case,* 49). The whole next chapter (chapter 6) presents a haunting picture of an abduction, frequent cowhidings and beatings ("But by-and-by pap got too handy with his hick'ry, and I couldn't stand it. I was all over welts"), psychological abuse, and, most troubling of all, attempted murder and Huck's contemplation of patricide:

> By-and-by he rolled out an jumped up on his feet looking wild, and he see me and went for me. He chased me round and round the place, with a clasp-knife, calling me the Angel of Death and saying he would kill me and then I couldn't come for him no more. I begged and told him I was only Huck, and he laughed *such* a screechy laugh, and roared and cussed, and kept on chasing me up. Once when I turned short and dodged under his arm he made a grab and got me by the jacket between my shoulders, and I thought I was gone; but I slid out of the jacket quick as lightning, and saved myself. Pretty soon he was all tired out, and dropped down with his back against

---

4. Twain, *"Adventures of Huckleberry Finn": A Case Study in Critical Controversy,* 48. Hereafter referred to as *Case.*

the door, and said he would rest a minute and then kill me. He put his knife under him, and said he would sleep and get strong, and then he would see who was who.

So he dozed off, pretty soon. By-and-by I got the old split-bottom chair and clumb up, as easy as I could, not to make any noise, and got down the gun. I slipped the ramrod down it to make sure it was loaded, and then I laid it across the turnip barrel, pointing towards pap, and set down behind it to wait for him to stir. And how slow and still the time did drag along. (*Case,* 54–55)

The choreography and pacing of the scene inspire terror. The experience itself motivates Huck to get the hell away. The disagreeable idea of being dragged from place to place by Pap to avoid another custody battle is replaced with a deliberate choice of homelessness and wandering and, what is worse for Huck, loneliness.

All of this takes place prior to Huck's coming upon Jim on Jackson's Island. Whether that reunion is part of Twain's initial plan or not (Vic Doyno has suggested that it was *not* part of Twain's early intention), the first seven chapters offer troubling images of an adolescent struggling at the furthest margins of small-town life. Huck's character is set. His actions and reactions for the rest of the tale remain consistent with what we know from these first episodes. We know that Huck, as the child of an alcoholic, as a young boy torn between loyalty and fear, as a student of violence and loneliness, will do what he can to survive, to get along. He will be reactive not proactive. He will allow others to set the agenda (even his stories take their cue from the individuals he meets) and will choose to remain quiet: his refrain, whether to Miss Watson's complaints or to the later felonies of the Duke and King, is to keep still; speaking up "would only make trouble, and wouldn't do no good" (*Case,* 33). Huck's behavior in the final section of the tale is consistent, which, in fact, helps to resolve at least part of the critical discomfort generated by Huck's reluctance to challenge Tom Sawyer's crazy actions toward Jim.

What, then, *does* the story offer if its teller's primary consistency is expedient behavior and reactions sparked by fear? At its heart, *Adventures of Huckleberry Finn* is the story of two survivors, each of whom is reluctant to act alone or to speak out: both Huck and Jim, though for different reasons, are robbed of their options and of their voices by the social system that reigns over them. Only when they are separated from that system are they able to consider choices and offer even tentative commentary on their lives; only when they loosen themselves from the constraints are they able to talk. And it takes a good deal of time before they can talk to each other on a human level rather than through the disguises they inherit from their social caste. (Compare, for example, Huck's attempt to explain the French language [chapter 14] to Jim to the later exchange after their separation in the fog when Huck is shamed into apologizing to Jim [chapter 15] or, still later, Jim's story about his deaf daughter [chapter 23].) Their increasingly intimate talk reinforces both their alienation from the society at large and, perhaps more important, their exile from any semblance of family.

And where does that lead us? If the whole of Huck's story is about the disintegration of human bonds and the eventual breakdown of even the most tentative of human connections, we will have grave problems making a case for its value as a moral tale. *Adventures of Huckleberry Finn* presents us with nagging questions: How do we deal with the dizzying array of possible—and very often ambiguous—lessons that push through the narrative? Do we pick and choose to make the text more palatable as moral instruction? Do we, for example, opt for an optimistic interpretation in order to demonstrate that Huck, in the end, has managed to grow into a critical but loyal member of the society? Do we present his rejection of society—all society—at the end of the novel when he decides to "light out for the Territory *ahead of the rest*" in order to escape the community to which he has recently returned as a positive step? Is self-exile an option to be applauded? Has his experience made him more or less suspicious of allegiances—not to mention relationships— with other individuals or groups? After all, staying very much in character, Huck decides to turn and run rather than confront the demands of community membership. He runs from the possibility of family. He turns to irresponsibility with relish and anticipation. That is not a moral lesson.

I would like to make a different argument. The key to the immorality of Huck's tale is not in *his* slouching toward irresponsibility and expediency but in *our* own ease in ignoring the whole of Huck's life or (worse) cheapening it with a condescending chuckle and a quickened step so that we push him from our view. Perhaps we decide that he gains sensitivity because it is safer for us if he does so. Huck, after all, is the homeless child on the street. The immigrant shut out from our schools. The child who, because of a self-destructive belief in his own corruption and worthlessness, grows up to be his pap. Mark Twain's moral lesson is *not* that Huck gains a sense of his own humanity by transcending the constraints and stereotypes placed on him and on Jim by the authority of school and church and home but that Huck fails. The stout heart does not win over the deformed conscience. Huck's failure is our lesson. Midpoint in the composing process, Mark Twain added the admonishment that "persons attempting to find a moral . . . will be banished" (*Case,* 27). Huck tried. And he was banished. Huck—and Mark Twain, and Samuel Clemens—left a story to us steeped in domestic concerns in the hopes that we would come to understand the primacy of home and the value of compassion.

Compassion is, however, a difficult emotion to pin on Mark Twain. At least it has been that way within our established interpretive paradigm. After our look at Twain's building a case for compassion in *Adventures of Huckleberry Finn,* let's turn now to his autobiographical writing to consider an even more profound description of the value of human relation.

In December 1909, Mark Twain penned what he called "the final chapter of my autobiography." The essay, published posthumously in 1911 as "The Death of Jean," has received only quick mention by biographers and has been passed off as highly sentimentalized, yet it is one of the more affective pieces in Twain's canon (frankly, I have found no piece so likely to destroy conventional notions of Mark Twain). Critics have been content to slip the piece among those works considered extraordinary not because it hints at a genuine domestic foundation in Twain's emotional life (though this *is* a valuable and neglected aspect of Twain's life and writing) but because it does not conform to established, comfortable ideas of Twain as misanthropic social philosopher. It challenges the established paradigm and is, therefore, relegated to the ash heap of sentimentalism. Mark Twain, it seems, is not allowed to express real and troubling emotion. And we, as critics, are made uncomfortable by that emotion and must look away before we admit that Twain had (and maybe that we have) an emotional life.

Some biographical background may be helpful here. In the summer of 1909, Jean Clemens, Twain's youngest daughter, arrived in Redding, Connecticut, to rejoin the Clemens household (to reconstitute that household may be a more accurate description since Clara would marry in October and later move to Europe). The aging Twain, who by this time had watched the procession of the dead as a genuinely interested bystander, was pleased with the potential for reconnecting with Jean, who had been shuttled back and forth between a maze of sanatoriums and cures since her diagnosis with epilepsy in the 1890s. Their relationship had been a difficult one. And while all Twain's relationships were difficult, none bore so tragic a tint as those with his children.

With a potential reconciliation in sight, Jean dies on the morning of Christmas Eve. She seems to have suffered a seizure and drowned in her bath. She is found by the household's servant, Katy Leary. Twain begins:

> Jean is dead!
> Has anyone ever tried to put upon paper all the little happenings connected with a dear one—happenings of the twenty-four hours preceding the sudden and unexpected death of that dear one? Would a book contain them? Would two books contain them? I think not. They pour into the mind in a flood. They are little things that have been always happening every day, and were always so unimportant and easily forgettable before—but now! Now, how different! how precious they are, how dear, how unforgettable, how pathetic, how sacred, how clothed with dignity! (*AU*, 245–46)

Twain's calm is extremely affective here. Throughout his career he was haunted by a tendency to burlesque and melodramatic pathos at moments of personal stress; however, here there are no histrionics, no melodramatic expression of grief. The grief is there. And it is deep. But it is present not in the specific experience of Jean's death but in the catalog of deaths that Twain creates as he replays his past:

> In England thirteen years ago, my wife and I were stabbed to the heart with a cablegram which said, "Susy was mercifully released today." I had to send a like shock to Clara, in Berlin, this morning. . . .
> I lost Susy thirteen years ago; I lost her mother—her incompara-ble mother!—five and a half years ago; Clara has gone away to life in Europe; and now I have lost Jean. How poor I am, who was once so rich! Seven months ago Mr. Rogers died—one of the best friends I ever had, and the nearest perfect, as a man and a gentleman, I have ever yet met among my race; within the last six weeks Gilder has

passed away, and Laffan—old, old friends of mine. Jean lies yonder, I sit here; we are strangers under our own roof; we kissed hands good-bye at the door last night—and it was forever, we never suspecting it. She lies there, and I sit here—writing, busying myself, to keep my heart from breaking. How dazzling the sunshine is flooding the hills around! It is like a mockery. (*AU*, 246–47)

Twain's narrative distance is deceiving, and it is troubling. He mentions his losses to build to the climactic conflict between the glory of the world that surrounds an abundance of death. Most fascinating is his willingness to chronicle not only the names of his blessed but also the process that he uses to calm his hurt: writing acts as a restorative, as a balm that allows him to sit as a companion to Jean though her death is the final reminder of his own mortality. The contrast between her death and his life is too obvious. The final mockery may not be the shining sun, but his being alive to notice it and to gain some aesthetic thrill at the spectacle. The bitterness that supposedly wraps his thoughts and impressions is here nowhere to be found. Instead we have a sadness and a profound expression of emotional numbness and the dull recognition that longevity is more a cure than a blessing: "Would I bring her back if I could do it? I would not. If a word would do it, I would beg for the strength to withhold the word. And I would have the strength; I am sure of it. In her loss I am almost bankrupt, and my life is a bitterness, but I am content; for she has been enriched with the most precious of all gifts—that gift which makes all the other gifts mean and poor—death" (*AU*, 249). Twain echoes the message to which he returned so often in his fiction—the gift of death. It is, after all, the feigned death that allows Huck to escape an abusive and homicidal father; it is the release for Joan of Arc; it is the gift that Satan brings in "The Mysterious Stranger." Death prompts Twain to rejoice in the destruction of Eden in the diaries of Adam and Eve; it is the last, the most potent, of "The Five Boons of Life"; and it is the final release that he has evaded for so long.

Twain finally faces the image of his own death as he transports himself to the site of Jean's arrival and burial in Elmira. He did not make the funeral journey, but he imagines the scene:

2:30 P.M.—It is the time appointed. The funeral has begun. Four hundred miles away, but I can see it all, just as if I were there. The

scene is the library, in the Langdon homestead. Jean's coffin stands
where her mother and I stood, forty years ago, and were married;
and where Susy's coffin stood thirteen years ago; where her mother's
stood, five years and a half ago; and where mine will stand, after a
little time. (*AU*, 252)

The deadpan voice that Twain used so expertly in his humor is here trans-
lated into a mechanism to relate emotional fullness and the exhaustion
that is companion to grief. There is resignation and, as he has said earlier,
contentment in the realization of his coming participation in the family
pageant. Bitterness, anger, frustration have been put aside so that he can
focus on reclaiming family attachment. Four months later Twain died of
congestive heart failure. His coffin did stand in that same room.

But how does this evaluation of Twain's emotional tie to family enter
into the established critical tradition within Twain studies? It doesn't. At this
point, Twain is, by most accounts, bitter, cynical, railing against God and the
universe, and taking every opportunity available to hoot and toss epithets
at the possibility of human redemption. Critics, biographers, and scholars
have taken an odd form (a perverse form?) of delight in perpetuating this
sour image of Mark Twain. Yes, his comments carried strong indictments of
human foolishness and folly. Yes, he saw the worst in humans, and especially
saw the worst in himself. But there is much more to Twain than that, and
this is not particularly good news to those still embedded in the Brooks-
DeVoto argument or those who insist on Twain's exclusive title as definer
of American individualism. The duality that resides in the opposing images
of the writer who after Emerson is seen as most responsible for defining
the character of American self-reliance and the carping, vituperative, and
godless philosophical gadfly is too convenient. It is time we moved past that.
But toward what?

Since most of my time is spent rummaging around in the attic that is
Mark Twain's autobiographical dictations and writings, let me start there.
The autobiography is very much a domestic tale. Looking especially at the
portion of material that Twain published during his lifetime (principally in
the *North American Review* in 1906 and 1907), we face a Mark Twain who
is deeply involved in the tradition of literary domesticity. His concerns are
with hearth and home. With family. With the absence of family and the

need to locate and develop emotional ties within an extended community of friends and acquaintances. In scenes that echo the writings of Caroline Kirkland, Mary E. Wilkins Freeman, Sarah Orne Jewett, and, later, Willa Cather, Twain offers haunting descriptions of basic domestic life:

> I can see the farm yet, with perfect clearness. I can see all its belongings, all its details; the family room of the house, with a "trundle" bed in one corner and a spinning-wheel in another—a wheel whose rising and falling wail, heard from a distance, was the mournfulest of all sounds to me, and made me homesick and low-spirited, and filled my atmosphere with the wandering spirits of the dead; the vast fireplace, piled high, on winter nights, with flaming hickory logs from whose ends a surgary sap bubbled out but did not go to waste, for we scraped it off and ate it; the lazy cat spread out on the rough hearthstones, the drowsy dogs braced against the jambs and blinking; my aunt in one chimney-corner knitting, my uncle in the other smoking his corn-cob pipe; the slick and carpetless oak floor faintly mirroring the dancing flame-tongues and freckled with black indentations where fire-coals had popped out and died a leisurely death; half a dozen children romping in the background twilight; "split"-bottomed chairs here and there, some with rockers; *a cradle—out of service, but waiting, with confidence;* in the early cold mornings a snuggle of children, in shirts and chemises, occupying the hearthstone and procrastinating—they could not bear to leave that comfortable place and go out on the wind-swept floorspace between the house and kitchen where the general tin basin stood, and wash. (*AU*, 116–17; emphasis added)

In the background we hear the voice of Huck Finn—it resonates with deep emotional upset and loneliness. The forlorn cry of the spinning wheel, the uneasy spirits abroad in the night. And we have the signal image of home—the patient, confident cradle.

Embedded in this passage is, I think, a new understanding of Mark Twain. His interest in domestic life was neither shallow nor fleeting. It resonates throughout his major and minor works. Yet, we continue to skid past domesticity on the way to other topics and concerns. We consider Tom Sawyer's home life only to introduce the ironies of community leadership and values; we look at the dilemma of the prince and the pauper and see criticism of the arbitrary nature of royalty; we proclaim Huck's aloneness as a path to reinventing a moral consciousness; we watch Hank Morgan destroy Camelot and tie his actions to the failure of American imperialism or American reconstruction. Each of these readings furthers the agenda of the icon builders. Icons limit our appreciation of complexity. They limit our choices.

Clearly, then, I am arguing for a more complex reading of Mark Twain's work and an acknowledgment of and an appreciation for his connection to literary domesticity. Tom Sawyer, Huck Finn, Hank Morgan, Joan of Arc, Roxy, and Adam and Eve: all suffer the most domestic of ills—the inability to negotiate human relationships. And no matter how we turn away from this to find more seductive, more broadly political, more socially sophisticated readings, we still must face the reality at the heart of Twain's stories—that pain is at the center of home and grows out of the search for home.

At the end of *The Adventures of Tom Sawyer,* Twain offers an exchange between Huck and Tom that epitomizes that pain. Huck is considering escape from his newly assigned place in the home of Widow Douglas. Tom, however, will have none of that:

> " . . . Huck, we can't let you in the gang if you ain't respectable, you know."
>
> Huck's joy was quenched.
>
> "Can't let me in, Tom? Didn't you let me go for a pirate?"
>
> "Yes, but that's different. A robber is more high-toned than what a pirate is—as a general thing. In most countries they're awful high up in the nobility—dukes and such."
>
> "Now Tom, hain't you always been friendly to me? You wouldn't shet me out, would you, Tom? You wouldn't do that, now, would you, Tom?"
>
> "Huck, I wouldn't want to, and I don't want to—but what would people say? Why they'd say, 'Mph! Tom Sawyer's Gang! pretty low characters in it!' *They'd mean you, Huck.* You wouldn't like that, and I wouldn't."[5]

Of course, Huck caves in to this pressure. Despite Tom's condescension, despite what we might, I think rightly, interpret as Tom's deep ambivalence

---

5. Twain, *Adventures of Tom Sawyer,* 235. Hereafter referred to as *ATS*.

(I am tempted to say hatred) toward the desperate boy, Huck gives in. He needs to belong. To someone. To something. And so does Twain. Once more to the end of "The Death of Jean":

> It is all over.
> When Clara went away two weeks ago to live in Europe, it was hard, but I could bear it, for I had Jean left. I said we would be a family. We said we would be close comrades and happy—just we two. That fair dream was in my mind when Jean met me at the steamer last Monday; it was in my mind when she received me at the door last Tuesday evening. We were together; we were a family! The dream had come true—oh, preciously true, contentedly true, satisfyingly true! and remained true two whole days.
> And now? Now Jean is in her grave!
> In the grave—if I can believe it. God rest her sweet spirit!
> (*AU*, 252)

Ultimately, Twain's work recounts the struggle of the human heart to find a place in this world, to find peace, to find a place to lie comfortably content with our mortality. To find a home. To hear the whine of the spinning wheel and think not of the mournfulest sound but of the peace of your own bed.

Mark Twain eventually left behind the hoax, joke, and tall tale for the more powerful images of community and home. In fact, he sought out the dilemmas of personal relationships as the basis for his storytelling. Whereas power, the lust for it and the failure to achieve it, is a focal point in many of Mark Twain's tales, he is at his best in those pieces that focus on domestic relationships: the childhood bluster at the opening to *The Adventures of Tom Sawyer*; the raft episodes in *Adventures of Huckleberry Finn*; the memories of an old and disappointed lover in *Personal Recollections of Joan of Arc*; the domestic fiction in the McWilliams short stories, the animal tales, the stories of the good and bad boys; and the anecdotes that creep into his speeches and his autobiography. This argues for complexity; however, we often continue to focus on "The Notorious Jumping Frog of Calaveras County," "Grandfather's Old Ram," "Dick Baker's Cat," along with a host of tales that fit our expectation of Twain's frontier roots, even those in *Innocents Abroad*. There is much more to Twain. Two of his more notable stories, "The Facts behind the Recent Carnival of Crime in Connecticut" and "The Man That

Corrupted Hadleyburg," center their deep irony within a domestic environment. We have rarely—and then barely—dipped into the outrageous diary entries of Adam and Eve or the quirkiness of Captain Stormfield's visit to heaven, each of which depends on the conflicts that inhabit domestic scenes lighted by parochial attitudes that underscore contrasts between expectations and reality. And Twain's "Chapters from My Autobiography" is best seen as an examination of domestic relationships in an extended family.

Gillian Brown's notion of combining the two now parallel traditions will help us understand Mark Twain, for in the end, his strength is demonstrated in his ability to incorporate the broader focus and social irony that comes through his literary mothers. Twain scholars would now do well to see that the humor of the old Southwest is only one of the influences and, perhaps, not a dominant influence after all. The frontier boast was an effective tool for Twain. But he had a good deal more success when he set aside the wool and furs of the frontier for the homespun and silk of the household.

Samuel Clemens as Family Man and Father

VICTOR A. DOYNO

Was Sam Clemens a good family man? Was this famous author a good father? We can begin to answer these interrelated questions, but it is necessary to keep in mind the norms of nineteenth-century American living, because it would be unfair simply to measure Sam Clemens against the ideas of 2001. While exploring this topic I wish to make explicit many contrasts and comparisons of nineteenth-century norms and our current standards in this first decade of the twenty-first century. Moreover, I wish to be explicit that when I think, infer, and write about this necessarily complex topic, I draw upon my life experiences as a relatively optimistic, monogamous, sixty-year-old American male who, with my wife, has helped create, grow, and launch three young people into independent adult life.[1]

For obvious reasons, this exploration will be roughly chronological; Sam Clemens had to learn to be a husband and a father. While he was learning, and while his children were maturing, this country and his cultural context were gradually changing and developing new attitudes toward children. Put in the crudest possible terms, children were, in general, much less valued earlier in that century; many people, including some parents, seemed to regard children approximately as selfish, intrusive, disobedient, disruptive small adults who must be broken or disciplined into less-sinful behavior for their own good. Lloyd DeMause's essay in the *History of Childhood* and

1. I am grateful to the trustees and librarians for the Clifton Waller Barrett Collection at the University of Virginia for their help and to the Mark Twain Foundation for their permission to quote previously unpublished material.

Viviana A. Zelizer's *Pricing the Priceless Child* illustrate the range of completely different attitudes toward children, attitudes that now may seem to us appalling but can easily still be replicated in some Third World countries. I have come to believe that Sam Clemens, in his real life and in his activities as Mark Twain, American author-commentator, helped shape the newly emerging, more humane American attitudes toward children. For example, his literary decision to use Huck Finn's own voice and point of view to tell the child's story certainly helped adults realize that a child—even an ignorant, low-status child who speaks a nonstandard dialect—could have opinions, feelings, and values that could engage adults' minds and command adults' sympathies. I speculate that, after 1885, people who have been fully, imaginatively, engaged with Huck's voice and point of view might be far less likely to give a twelve-year-old child a severe beating.

Let us begin with the shaping of Sam Clemens's values and personality. Sam's parents, Jane Lampton Clemens and John Marshall Clemens, were in all likelihood positive influences. His mother's quick, fresh wit and free-flowing sympathy may indicate that she was a relatively indulgent parent. Neither Aunt Polly nor the Widow Douglas, who have been taken as fictional, partial replicas of Jane Clemens, would be considered mean, depriving, or harsh disciplinarians. Although they might be ineffective, every perceptive boy would realize that these loving maternal figures are well intentioned. The somewhat distant figure of John Marshall Clemens may have served as a judgmental standard. Perhaps the combination of an immediate witty, clever, maternal warmth and an elevated, stern, restrained paternal morality contributed to Sam's unique personality.

His family placement as a younger middle child may have influenced young Sam to be a perceptive, mediating caretaker. Such a family placement probably helped young Sam learn how to "read" faces, personalities, or clues and learn how to infer the attitudes of many older, more powerful, semiparental siblings. The fact that Orion was relatively erratic or foolish and that Pamela was relatively simple perhaps encouraged Sam's independence and trust in his own opinion. With such proximate siblings, Sam could have relatively little need to develop deceit. Moreover, Sam probably learned, both at home and during his summer visits to the Quarles's farm, to be comfortable with the constant high levels of activity, the ebb, flow, and crosscurrents of many personalities. In similar circumstances some modern children learn to be sensitive to other points of view and learn how to deflect criticism with quick wit.

Certainly he had learned to be a caretaker, to feel responsible, by the time of his younger brother Henry's death after a steamboat explosion. According to Sam's memory, he and Henry had earlier discussed what to do in the event of a boating accident, including the hypothetical professional duty to attempt to rescue passengers. In Sam's mind, after the actual explosion, Henry apparently was thrown clear but bravely and self-destructively decided to swim back into the live steam to attempt to help. The resulting damage to his lungs was then—and probably now—untreatable. When Sam arrived at the primitive emergency medical site, he learned that someone had made the necessary triage decision that placed Henry in the death ward. Sam attended Henry, waiting and administering morphine. Later Sam blamed himself for Henry's death, thinking that Henry's injury was influenced by their talk and that his death was caused by too large a dose of the morphine. (Combat doctors learn that when gradually built up, very large doses of morphine are not fatal, but are often a blessing. Now morphine probably would not be given for such a terminal injury because of its suppressive effect. But Sam did not pick the opiate; he administered what he was given, providing pain relief and sedation in a terrible situation.) Sam had to bring Henry's body home to his mother and family. That trip and arrival could not have been easy.

In many of the family letters Sam is presented as the family stalwart, able to gain success, able to solve problems, able to care for and provide for the others, especially for his older brother Orion and his family, and for their mother, Jane. Among the harshly negative experiences of Sam's childhood, youth, and early manhood, we would have to include the breaking apart of families, the separations of parents and children, either by deaths or by slave sales. Of course, nineteenth-century medical practices were, by modern American standards, quite primitive. The mortality tables and Twain's fiction indicate that there was no shortage of widows, orphans, and "friendless" children. These breakups of familial coherence and happiness were real and, in all likelihood, substantially more threatening ruptures than abandonment, divorce, and impoverishment are to our current "civilization."

Of course, in those days of nonexistent or ineffective contraception, childbirth usually proceeded without episiotomy or antiseptic procedures and accordingly led to many deaths of mothers and infants. If a mother was lucky enough to avoid hemorrhage and puerperal infection, she usually faced a long, painful healing process, with the constant threat of staph or *E. coli* infections or other "complications." Even healthy women often had a quite reasonable fear of pregnancy. Child mortality was high. I believe that the norms were approximately as follows: for every four live births, one infant dies in the first six months, one child dies before five years, and one person dies before age twenty-one, leaving one adult with a probable life expectancy of about forty-five to fifty-one years.

Judged against these norms Jane and John Marshall Clemens were relatively successful parents. Pleasant Hannibal lived for about three months, Margaret lived for more than nine years before a fever took her, Benjamin (two years older than Sam) also died at more than nine years, and Henry died at almost twenty-one years. Folk wisdom of the time said "Small coffin, great sorrow," but Orion, Pamela, and Sam survived into adulthood. Similarly, Sam and Livy Clemens were, theoretically, relatively fortunate, although we know that each loss of a child was devastating. Their firstborn, only son, Langdon, lived for sixteen months; Susie, a gifted, perceptive, quite-valued child, their "darling," lived to age twenty-five; Clara survived to a full adulthood; Jean, their last child, died after an epileptic seizure in a bathtub at age twenty-nine, on Christmas Eve morning, 1909. Although they had some warning of the seriousness of Langdon's illness, the other two deaths were utterly unexpected, shattering losses that left those who survived without any preparation to think or say "good-bye." Similar levels of sorrow were visited upon the black individuals whom young Sam knew and liked. Repeatedly in Sam's life and in Mark Twain's fiction we come across the emotional devastation of a slave family that is destroyed or scattered by a sale: Aunty Cord, renamed in "A True Story" as Aunt Rachel (with obvious biblical allusion), the young slave boy whose whistling irritated Sam but reassured Jane Clemens; Jim's crying about his separation from little Johnny and 'Lisabeth; and Roxy's dilemma.

In my life experience the normal life cycle is that we, as adults, bury our parents, and, in turn, we are buried by our children. When that pattern is broken, when the order is reversed and the parents have to bury the children, whether because of war, disease, or accident, the loss seems to have an enormous, long, depressive impact upon the parents, who become almost inconsolable because the child will become a dark hole in the heart, a vacuum, a valued potential personality and a cherished love that will never be seen. Sam and Livy observed anniversaries of Susie's death in a silence that would, in my opinion, also cast a pall on Christmas and make some other annual holidays, such as Easter, unbearable. Sam and Livy buried children together twice, and after Sam buried Livy he endured the process alone once more. Just as Dr. Samuel Johnson could not bear to reread the ending of Shakespeare's *King Lear,* I still cannot reread Sam Clemens's letters to William Dean Howells about the deaths of Susie or Livy with dry eyes. Sam could not bring himself, at age seventy-four, to travel to Jean's burial at the family grave site in Elmira.

Against these harrowing sadnesses Sam must have had great happinesses, uncountable moments of daily acts of kindness and of love that strengthened him, tempered him. We can, of course, never learn all the details of their lives nor conduct a perfect double-blind study; if we could compare two or more Clemens families we might see exactly the same characteristics but with different events. Instead we must rely on mixtures of evidence and inference with our own sense of multiple causations and multiple effects. Also, we have the problematic advantage of retrospection, and accordingly we can recognize the patterns and sequences, the supposed causations. To answer any resulting sense of biographical certainty, determinism, or inevitability, I would whisper that most people live their lives and die their deaths step by step, day by day, uncertainly, as if they were walking down an unlit hallway in a stranger's house. Moreover, we who know most of the narrative of Sam's life, from 1835 to 1910, may think—almost subconsciously—that many choices were deliberate and reasoned. But many choices probably were accidental, the results of drift, inaction, nonchoices. The whims and the daily confusions of interactions among five family members with strong personalities, plus relatives, helpers, and friends, defy precise calculations.

It would be a modernist, sentimentalist mistake to infer that Sam Clemens was a perfect modern husband and father, as if he was or should be expected to be a wonderful combination of Alan Alda and Leo Buscaglia. Undoubtedly Sam was occasionally or frequently forgetful; he was impulsive; he was moody. Moreover, he had very poor financial judgment and misinvested and thereby lost great sums of money. He traveled a great deal and left a disproportionate amount of responsibility to Livy. Among his flaws we should note that he would impulsively and expansively invite acquaintances to visit at the Hartford home, letting the burden of hostessing and entertaining fall on Livy's shoulders. However, I suggest, with firm conviction and a moderate tone, that Sam Clemens, judged within a realistic context of his own era, was an extraordinarily good husband and father.

In one letter acquired by the Hartford Memorial we find some evidence of Livy's attempt to modify his behavior. She seems to speak to Sam frankly, directly, considerately, with qualification and gradations of tonality she apparently trusted him to perceive:

> One thing I want to caution you against, and it may seem disagreeable when I do it, but it may put you a little on your guard. Don't be too ready and cordial to invite people to visit you. Of course, I don't mean people like Mr. Cable that we are all so much interested in but others, those that you casually meet. If we could give them a dinner or luncheon as they do you, it would be well enough, but when people come they generally come for 24 hours.[2]

In this letter I do not hear unreasonable scolding, but patient, reasonable explanation. In general, Livy's letters to Sam reveal her intelligence, her polite, well-mannered wisdom, and her utterly unconditional love for her husband. A relatively unbiased observer who spent five weeks and four days with Sam and Livy, James B. Pond, offers this assessment of Sam's responsiveness to Livy's suggestions: "Her influence is always instantaneous."[3]

How did they become so close, so mutually respectful, as a couple? We know, from the famous letter to Will Bowen, that Sam, who had grown up in a relatively emotionally restrained home (he claimed he saw his mother and father kiss only near a child's deathbed), felt that his marriage was an emotional release, a transformation to real ecstasy. But the first year of their marriage was saddened by the death of Livy's father, Jervis Langdon. Sam and Livy had a new son, Langdon, who apparently cried a great deal. And I know Buffalo has long, hard winters, with many overcast, dark days. During

---

2. *Hartford Courant,* Apr. 1, 1992, A8.
3. Alan Gribben and Nick Karanovich, eds., *Overland with Mark Twain,* 7.

the obligatory mourning period the young couple probably grew closer, depending on each other—for they were visited only by David Gray and his wife, a human kindness that made Sam value Gray's friendship through the subsequent years.

Livy apparently had a difficult time at little Langdon's birth, and the baby seemed quite demanding. He cried a lot. When he wished to be picked up he reached out, but instead of having his palms outward, as most children do, he turned his palms inward. I think he did not walk before sixteen months, and family remarks indicate that he had unusually flabby muscle tone. A bust of the child reveals that he had a remarkably high, somewhat narrow, bony forehead. These details have led a modern pediatric neurologist, Dr. Thomas Langan of Buffalo, to suggest that the child might have had a "bossed forehead," indicative of a hydrocephalic condition. Nowadays a relatively easy operation to install a shunt would relieve the internal pressure and pain that could have caused almost constant, almost inconsolable, crying. Probably the family did not understand this condition; I hope the inexperienced parents did not blame themselves. But Sam characteristically did blame himself for the boy's death, thinking that his own inattentiveness to a displaced blanket killed the child. In all likelihood, whatever disability or germs (perhaps diphtheria) ended Langdon's young life would not have been prevented by a mere blanket. (A friend has reminded me that years later Twain would write in *Extract from Captain Stormfield's Visit to Heaven* about a young mother searching in heaven for the baby she had mistakenly thought would remain at the age of death. I infer that such wrenching, deeply emotional, irreparable family wounds do not disappear, but linger and continue to hurt.)

These experiences probably combined with Livy's experience of partial paralysis as a teenager, which Laura Skandera Trombley has attributed to Pott's disease (spinal tuberculosis), to make both parents especially watchful, worried, and anxious about medical matters when Susie, Clara, and Jean were born and in the crucial years while they grew up (*MTW*, 82–83). We moderns need only imagine how we would feel as parents if we were suddenly without penicillin, tetracycline, and sulfa drugs, without all the miraculous cures of modern pediatricians. Sam and Livy's attentiveness, caution, and fearfulness seem, even at this temporal distance, to be quite reasonable and rational responses to their lived reality.

We have a great many resources to draw upon to learn about their many years of fervent, devoted parenting. The Clemenses' family life is reflected prismatically in many fictional works, such as the McWilliams stories and in some explicitly thematic stories and occasional essays. But there is also a wealth of direct information. Kate Leary's adoring opinions may seem uncritical, but they do capture the daily life of a witty, loving family. We have numerous letters from Sam to Livy, and some from Livy to Sam; we have Susie's incomplete biography of her father, with many observations about familial life from a perceptive child's own point of view. Because these resources are relatively well known, I shall discuss two little-known—perhaps almost unknown—accounts of actual family life, the unpublished private journal Sam Clemens kept about the children's growing up, "A Record of Small Foolishness," and a response titled "What Ought He to Have Done?" on child rearing and familial discipline that Sam wrote for the *Christian Union* in 1885 in response to a specific, terrible situation.[4] While reading this relatively unknown material, consider how many nineteenth-century American fathers would think this intelligently or write this perceptively about their children? How many twenty-first-century American men are now this sensitive to tone and nuance, to the individuality of the children, or to the wisdom, integrity, and character of the mother? I do not claim that Sam Clemens was perfect, an ideal husband and father, but I do suggest that he was extraordinarily devoted, perceptive, and attentive.

In August 1876 Sam decided to begin keeping a private journal of the remarks his children made as they were growing up. The notebook also contains many observations about the daily concerns of their family life. The mottled cardboard covers are well worn, rubbed away in the places where Sam held it in his left hand. Sam placed a biblical quotation on the title page, "And Mary treasured these sayings in her heart." I believe that this prefatory allusion conveys his attitude of almost religious devotion to his wife and family. The first several pages of the journal deal with Susie's and Clara's births and differing characters. His decision to start the journal and his commitment to writing in it certainly prove his desire to understand his children's points of view; it was an ideal training discipline for a sensitive parent.

---

4. Twain, "A Record of Small Foolishness," 7; hereafter referred to as RSF. Twain, "What Ought He to Have Done?"; hereafter referred to as WOD.

The journal tells us that at age two years, two months, and a few days Susie named her baby sister by saying about the one-hour-and-four-minute-old infant, "Dat bay got boofu' hair." And the two adoring parents honored that naming observation for years. What verbal power is greater than the ability to name? Sam noted an incident from February 1877:

> The other evening while we were at dinner the children came down from the nursery as usual to spend the hour between six and seven. They were in the library and the folding doors were open. Presently I heard Susie tell the Bay to lie down on the rug before the fire—which the Bay did. Then Susie came into the dining room, turned, ran back, hovered over Bay and said—
>
> "Now, Bay, you are a little dead baby, you know, and I am an angel come down to take you up to heaven. Come, now, get up—give me your hand—now we'll run—that's to pretend to be flying, you know! Ready, now—now we're flying."
>
> When they came flying by the dinner table something there attracted the Bay's attention and she suddenly stopped, but Susy ran on, full of enthusiasm. She brought up behind a chair by a door and cried out—
>
> "Come on, Bay—here's heaven!" then put her hand on the door knob and said,—"See! *here's* Jesus!" (RSF, 14–15 and repeated on 26–27)

Such an incident, along with Susie's inquiry about how little Langdon would be able to recognize them in heaven because he had died so young, would make most parents wince, take a sharp breath, and vow to protect the children. Sometime after April 1877, Sam noted:

> Susie has always had a good deal of womanly dignity. One day Livy and Mrs. Lilly Warner were talking earnestly in the library; Susie interrupted them several times; finally Livy said, very sharply, "Susie, if you interrupt again, I will send you instantly to the nursery!" Five minutes later, Livy saw Mrs. Warner to the front door; on her way back she saw Susie on the stairs, and said, "Where are you going, Susie?" "To the nursery, Momma." "What are you going up there for, dear?—don't you want to stay with me in the library?" "You did not speak to me right, Momma." Livy was surprised; she had forgotten that remark. She pushed her inquiries further; Susy steadily said,

with a gentle dignity that carried its own reproach, "You didn't speak
to me right, Momma." She had been humiliated in the presence of
an outsider. Livy felt condemned. She carried Susie to the library,
and argued the case with her. Susie hadn't a fault to find with the
justice of the rebuke, but she held out steadily against the manner
of it, saying gently, once or twice, "But you didn't speak to me right,
Momma." She won her cause; her mother had to confess that she
hadn't spoken to her "right."

We require courteous speech from the children at all times and in
all circumstances; we owe them the same courtesy in return; when we
fail of it we deserve correction. (RSF, 27–28)

The rooms devoted to the children in the Hartford home offer mute
evidence of the parents' attention to the children. And Sam's sensitivity to
tone and nuance reveals his values. One is glad that Sam Clemens never had
to hear how many modern, "civilized" people now speak to and discipline
children in supermarkets.

The daily life of the family included quite a bit of good humor, and the
children were fully included: "One day in Paris Susie watched her momma
make her toilet for a swell affair at the Embassy, and it was plain that her soul
was full of applause, though none of it escaped in words till the last touch
was put on and the marvel was completed; then she said, with a burst of
envying admiration, 'I wish *I* could have crooked teeth and spectacles, like
momma!'" (RSF, 37). The child's naive, loving compliment was taken with
humor, not with reproach. The family apparently was even able to perceive
humor in stressful situations, a sign of familial resilience. Sam remembered:

> [W]hen Bay was three years old, Susie was taken down to the town,
> one day, and was taken with a vomiting when she got back in the
> evening. Bay, off in the corner in her crib—totally neglected—
> observed the coddling and attention which Susie was receiving as
> long as she could reasonably stand it; then sat up and said gravely and
> simply: "Well, some time I'll be dressed up and go downtown and
> come back and throw up, too." (RSF, 75–87)

Humor, perceptive observation, verbal precision, imaginative sympathy,
mutual consideration, and loving attitudes seem to combine to help form
the children into strong individuals:

> July, 1882. Susie 10 years old—came to momma's room and asked
> if she should ring for the nurse: Jean, in the nursery was crying.
> Momma asked "Is she crying hard?" (meaning, cross or ugly.) "Well,
> no—it's a weary, lonesome cry."
>
> She is growing steadily into an admirably discriminating
> habit of language. Yes, and into the use of pretty large words, too,
> sometimes—as witness: The night before, I referred to some pref-
> erence expressed by Jean. Susie wanted at once to know *how* she
> expressed it—in as much as Jean knows only about a dozen words. I
> said, "Why she spoke up with marked asperity, and exclaimed, 'Well,
> Mr. Clemens, you may support that fallacy, if native perversity, and
> a fatuous imagination so move you: but the exact opposite is my
> distinct and decided preference.'"
>
> Susie's grave eyes stood wide open during this speech; she was
> silent a moment to let it soak home, then said in a tone of absolute
> conviction, "Well, papa, that *is* an exaggeration!" (RSF, 38)

Such good-humored joshing indicates a witty, warmhearted inclusion of the
child and a pride in the child's intelligent independence. As Susie and Clara
grew more mature, Sam was able to make quite acute observations in the
journal about the differences between their personalities.

We can use portions of two previously unknown letters to gauge the
quality of the daily interactions, the probable effects of Sam Clemens within
the family. On July 19, 1877, he wrote to Clara, aged three:

> I have bought two bath tubs and two dolls . . . for you and Susie. One
> of the dolls is named Hosannah Mariah and she is in very delicate
> health. She belongs to you.—She was out driving and got rained on
> and caught a very severe cold . . . she had partially recovered . . .
> caught a new cold, which paralyzed the sounding-board of her
> ears and the wobbling nerve of her tongue. She has never spoken
> since. I have consulted the best physicians. They say constant and
> complicated bathing will fetch her. . . .

The same day he wrote Susie, letting her know her doll was named Hallelu-
juh Jennings: "She suffered from a stroke of some sort and since that day
all her efforts . . . have failed to take the stiffening out of her legs. They say
incessant bathing is the only thing that can give her eventual relief."

From this evidence I infer that Clemens respected his children's imaginations. He recognized the doll bathing that seems to fascinate children. And he seems to have some differentiation in how the girls are treated: they are each given a separate letter; they are regarded as individuals. Sam probably thought that Livy would be involved in reading each letter to each child, while the other listened and absorbed how her sister was addressed. Moreover, I infer that Sam and Livy were raising these children to be caretakers, and we should recognize in the creation of maladies for the dolls that Sam's imagination includes medical disasters. Few moderns would think to give a child or grandchild a doll with a debilitating medical history, but Sam's era, experience, and psychological balance of good and evil apparently led him to create fictional histories so that the dolls would "need" the children and engage the children's sympathetic attention.

Evidence of a similar considerateness occurs in a letter Sam wrote in October 1881 to a friend after the family dog had died. Any modern, non-sentimental realist could easily mock even mentioning the dog's death as inexcusably maudlin, bathetic dullness. But many family members who have had to console children would disagree. Clemens says,

> [P]oor Rab was an expense to nobody . . . his soul is stainless, both
> of the crime and of the intent. The servants who only had to feed
> and pet Rab were inconsolable over his loss, none but the coachman
> and the gardener desired his departure. It was these whom he kept
> busy dragging him away from vehicles. But all five agreed in wanting
> a pup of Rab's breed and they promise that they will train that pup
> to respect the passing horse and be a joy and a solace to the whole
> household.[5]

Not many modern people wealthy enough to employ five domestic servants would think to consult them about a puppy's breed.

Sam and Livy provided a home that gave a great deal of attention and love to their children; seemingly minor family energies, such as Sam's work on a private journal that records Jean's baby talk or the loving attention of their aunt Susan Crane and many attentive family friends, probably led the children to feel slightly more appreciated or valued and more self-confident

5. *The Victor and Irene Muir Jacobs Collection.*

than a hypothetical average American child of that era. Also, by choosing the extraordinarily comfortable locations in Elmira and Hartford, Sam and Livy placed and grew their family in the most supportive, enabling, and pleasant places possible. Their friends and neighbors were, in general, intelligent, well educated, sophisticated, enlightened, advanced in social attitudes, and advantaged in worldly goods. The Clemens family's social circle included respectful, considerate friends who were well traveled and well connected. The norms and expectations of Nook Farm were, in fact, high and constructive, appropriate for the lives that Sam and Livy probably imagined for their children.

As the years went by Sam seemed to develop an even greater appreciation for his wife's skills as a mother and child nurturer. Confirmation of Sam's deference to Livy and of his loving, intelligent appreciation of her can be found in another amusing, relatively unknown source. In 1885 Sam read an article about a disobedient, defiant child in the *Christian Union*. The article writer sought advice about what should be done. Sam, apparently upset by the article, wrote out his opinion of what his wife would do, swore Susie and Clara to secrecy, and read his account to them. They agreed with his version of what "Momma" would do. Sam then sent the account to the magazine. But he later began to get "cold feet," realizing that Livy might be embarrassed or chagrined by this revelation of internal family matters. I have chosen to include the entire article, which sets forth the problem— in elevated but effective language—and Sam's complete response because we, as moderns, need to know fully the nature of the conflicts about child rearing in 1885. The father who disciplined his child probably was certain he was acting for the child's good. The magazine query "What Ought He to Have Done?" and Sam's reply follow:

> The following incident is so suggestive of the difficulties attending the wise government of children that we reprint it entire from the May issue of "Babyhood," and commend it to fathers and mothers for thoughtful consideration:
> *To the Editor of "Babyhood"*: "John, senior, is Papa, about thirty. John, junior, usually addressed without the prefix, was two years old December 13, 1884. Visitors exclaim over him as a "love of a child": his mother believes him to be perfectly beautiful; mulatto Sally, who has nursed him from birth, pronounces him "a *cheruphim*, if ever

there was one on earth." Since a certain day that month John, senior, considers him "a handful."

On that day Junior, who had hitherto been obedient to the ukase prohibiting him from touching anything on his father's writing-table, entered the library, where that personage was at work, snatched an open letter from under the busy fingers, and threw it upon the floor.

"Now! 'ook papa!" ejaculated the cheruphim, locking his fists at his back, and putting out his lower lip in a defiant pout that made him into the loveliest picture the mother had ever looked upon.

"Junior is a naughty boy!" said the father judicially. "No, mama!"—for she stooped to recover the paper—"Junior must pick it up and put it back on the table."

"Ont!" uttered the angel, smilingly.

"My lamb!" (deprecating) from the mother.

"Pick it up, sir!" (magisterial) from the father.

Both Johns have bright brown eyes. They met now with a danger-ous flash, as when two rapiers strike full on the edges of the blades.

"Junior—'ont—pick—it—up!" The pout was angry; a small heel rang sharply on the hearth.

John, senior, pulled open the drawer and took therefrom a strip of whalebone that might have been tossed there after the Fall dressmaking was over. Mother and child had seen it once before, on a dreadful November afternoon neither had forgotten. They recognized it immediately, the one with paling, the other with reddening cheeks. A sibilant sigh cut the awful hush that fell upon the three at its appearance. The father answered it:

"My dear," (in ominous composure), "I am going to see this thing through. You had better leave the room."

"John dear, I am sure the darling will—"

"Obey me? So am I. It is a mere question of time. For your sake—and his—you would do well to leave us. He thinks you sympathize with him."

Did she? Her anguished gaze devoured him, standing erect before the parent transformed into judge and lector. The beautiful eyes were wide and ablaze; the baby feet were planted firmly and far apart on the floor; the baby mouth was shut in a hard line. She fell on her knees beside him, gathered him into her arms; her wail was out of the depths of a wrung heart:

"O my boy! do what papa tells you to do! Pick up that paper for mamma!"

Then (will she ever forget it?) he twisted himself loose from her embrace and struck her full in the face, his own inflamed with rage.

"Go 'way, bad mamma! Junior ont!"

Weeping aloud as she went, the mother flew to the remotest recesses of the house, shutting the doors behind her, not to hear the pursuing shrieks.

"Now," persisted the father, suspending the punishment and speaking with slow distinctions, "pick up that paper and lay it on the table! Do you hear?"

A mighty breath of relief escaped him as the child moved toward the letter.

"A sharp fight, but a short one!" he murmured. Junior put out— not his hand but a little foot, catching the toe under the edge of the paper. He pushed it along to his father's chair, there gave it a dexterous flirt that nearly landed it on the senior's knee, and, delighted at the exploit, laughed out gleefully, the tears arrested at the fount.

John, senior, put the paper back on the very spot where it had lain before.

"That won't do, young-man! Take it up with your fingers!"

Again brown eyes struck fire against brown eyes. The chubby hands clutched one another behind the stiffened spine, and between locked teeth came:

"Junior *thay he 'ont!*"

The mother, through all the closed doors, heard the outcries that ensued, then the stern tone of command intermitting the ground-swell of sobs.

"Papa" (the blood welling unseen with every stab the parent dealt himself) will-whip-his-boy-until-he-picks-that-paper-up-with-his-hands-and-lays-it-on-the-table!"

Victory at last! Down dropped the boy on his hands and knees, crawled up to the hateful object of contention, deliberately bent his head, picked up the letter with his teeth, crept in the same dog-like fashion to his father, and laid the prize on his boot! May the writer submit a question to the readers of this true story? What ought John Senior to have done?

Clearly this narrative provoked Sam Clemens–Mark Twain because he responded immediately, angrily, and at length:

"What Ought He to Have Done?"
Mark Twain's Opinion.

Editor Christian Union: I have just finished reading the admirably told tale entitled "What Ought He to Have Done?" in your No. 24, and I wish to take a chance at that question myself before I cool off. What a happy literary gift that mother has!—and yet, with all her brains, she manifestly thinks there is a difficult conundrum concealed in that question of hers. It makes a body's blood boil to read her story!

I am a fortunate person, who has been for thirteen years accustomed, daily and hourly, to the charming companionship of thoroughly well-behaved, well-trained, well-governed children. Never mind about taking my word; ask Mrs. Harriet Beecher Stowe, or Charles Dudley Warner, or any other near neighbor of mine, if this is not the exact and unexaggerated truth. Very well, then, I am quite competent to answer that question of "What ought he to have done?" and I will proceed to do it by stating what he *would* have done, and what would have followed, if "John Senior" had been me, and his wife had been my wife, and the cub our mutual property. To wit:

When John Junior "entered the library, marched audaciously up to the desk, snatched an open letter from under his father's busy fingers, threw it on the floor," and struck the ill-mannered attitude described in the succeeding paragraph, his mother would have been a good deal surprised, and also grieved; surprised that her patient training of her child to never insult any one—even a parent—should so suddenly and strangely have fallen to ruin; and grieved that she must witness the shameful thing.

At this point John Senior—meaning me—would not have said, either "judicially" or otherwise, "Junior is a naughty boy." No; he would have known more than this John Senior knew—for he would have known enough to keep still. He wouldn't have aggravated a case which was already bad enough, by making any such stupid remark— stupid, unhelpful, undignified. He would have known and felt that there was one present who was quite able to deal with the case, in any stage it might assume, without any assistance from him. Yes, and there is another thing which he would have known, and does at this present writing know: that in an emergency of the sort which we are considering, he is always likely to be as thorough-going and ludicrous an ass as this John Senior proved himself to be in the little tale.

No—he would have kept still. Then the mother would have led the little boy to a private place, and taken him on her lap, and reasoned with him, and loved him out of his wrong mood, and shown him that he had mistreated one of the best and most loving friends he had in the world; and in no very long time the child would be convinced, and be sorry, and would run with eager sincerity and ask the father's pardon. And that would be the end of the matter.

But, granting that it did not turn out in just this way, but that the child grew stubborn, and stood out against reasoning and affection. In that case, a whipping would be promised. That would have a prompt effect upon the child's state of mind; for it would know, with its mature two years' experience, that no promise of any kind was ever made to a child in our house and not rigidly kept. So this child would quiet down at this point, become repentant, loving, reasonable; in a word, its own charming self again; and would go and apologize to the father, receive his caresses, and bound away to its play, light-hearted and happy again, although well aware that at the proper time it was going to get that whipping, sure.

The "proper time" referred to is any time after both mother and child have got the sting of the original difficulty clear out of their minds and hearts, and are prepared to give and take a whipping on purely business principles—disciplinary principles—and with hearts totally free from temper. For whippings are not given in our house for revenge; they are not given for spite, nor ever in anger; they are given partly for punishment, but mainly by way of impressive reminder, and protector against a repetition of the offense. The interval between the promise of a whipping and its infliction is usually on [sic] hour or two. By that time both parties are calm, and the one is judicial, the other receptive. The child never goes from the scene of punishment until it has been loved back into happy-heartedness and a joyful spirit. The spanking is never a cruel one, but it is always an honest one. It hurts. If it hurts the child, imagine how it must hurt the mother. Her spirit is serene, tranquil. She has not the support which is afforded by anger. Every blow she strikes the child bruises her own heart. The mother of my children adores them—there is no milder term for it; and they worship her; they even worship anything which the touch of her hand has made sacred. They know her for the best and truest friend they have ever had, or ever shall have; they know her for one who never did them a wrong, and cannot do them a wrong; who never told them a lie, nor the shadow of one; who never deceived them by even an ambiguous gesture; who never gave them an unreasonable command, nor ever contented herself with anything short of a perfect obedience; who has always treated them as politely and considerately as she would the best and oldest in the land, and has always required of them gentle speech and courteous conduct toward all, of whatsoever degree, with whom they chanced to come in contact; they know her for one whose promise, whether of reward or punishment, is gold, and always worth its face, to the uttermost farthing. In a word, they know her, and I know her, for the best and dearest mother that lives—and by a long, long way the wisest.

You perceive that I have never got *down* to where the mother in the tale really asks her question. For the reason that I can not realize the situation. The spectacle of that treacherously-reared boy, and that wordy, namby-pamby father, and that weak, namby-pamby mother, is enough to make one ashamed of his species. And if I could cry, I would cry for the fate of that poor little boy—a fate which cruelly placed him in the hands and at the mercy of a pair of grown-up children, to have his disposition ruined, to come up ungovernable, and be a nuisance to himself and everybody about him, in the process, instead of being the solacer of care, the disseminator of happiness, the glory and honor and joy of the house, the welcomest face in all the world to them that gave him being—as he ought to be, but for the hard fortune that flung him into the clutches of these paltering incapables.

In all my life I have never made a single reference to my wife in print before, as far as I can remember, except once in a dedication of a book; and, so, after these fifteen years of silence, perhaps I may unseal my lips this one time without impropriety or indelicacy. I will institute one other novelty. I will send this manuscript to the press without her knowledge, and without asking her to edit it. This will save it from getting edited into the stove.

Mark Twain

Sam's indignation about the whipping and about the damaging effects of inconsistent parenting reveals how far his opinions were in advance of his culture's norms. In 2001 how many children have been trained by their parents' random rewards to wheedle and whine? Now how many parents punish only in anger, and punish inconsistently? Now how many fathers are this attentive and respectful of the mother's actions? (Four of the six women whom I have asked to read the *Christian Union* letter have remarked, within two minutes of conversation, to the effect that "I wish that my husband would say something like that about me.")

Certainly the way that Sam thought of and treated Livy would have the effect of shaping each girl's expectations and preconceptions about what it would be like to be an adult woman and what personal characteristics are to be valued. Again, Sam was not a perfect father; he was irascible to outsiders, and probably moody or unpredictable. Moreover, he was often away, reluctantly traveling a lot, attempting to make his living and do his many jobs. Although there were advantages such as food, shelter, and travel along with attentive domestic servants, undoubtedly it was difficult for Susie, Clara, and Jean to be the children of such a famous man. The financial disasters must have been destabilizing. The girls were, of course, likely to receive attention from "gold diggers," fortune hunters, or people who simply wanted to have some association with a celebrity. Often a daughter in such a situation learns to distrust or to be skeptical about whether she is being valued as a friend or enjoyed as a person, only for her own sake. Accordingly, the development of friendships, one of the normal methods of developing positive self-esteem, can actually become problematic. These complexities, added to the conventional, largely unquestioned sexism of that age and social class, undoubtedly restricted the girls.

Moreover, as the girls grew another aspect of Sam's personality grew more important. He knew many men well and knew male lust and was always penetrating about character flaws. Accordingly, Sam Clemens was a very watchful, chaperoning father, quite unwilling or reluctant to have his beloved daughters become involved in any inappropriate relationship or become sexually active or exploitable. The unspoken command "No cads need apply" probably applied to almost any man who could even resemble a suitor. The husband whom Livy had called "Youth" and the man whom a secretary called "King" was willful enough to resent anyone who might "harm" or would seek to divert or divide the love and devotion of his princesses for their father.

Jean's affliction with epilepsy must have tortured the family. Medical relief was almost impossible; in addition, for much of Jean's life many ignorant people would regard her disease as perhaps a personal or moral failing. (In that age tuberculosis and epilepsy were considered by some people as possible evidence of some unmentionable moral failing, perhaps related to uncontrolled "unhealthy" desires.) The poor child and her family faced and endured such reactions. It must have saddened Livy and Sam to know that in that society Jean's epilepsy greatly reduced or ended the likelihood of her marriage. And neither Livy nor Sam ever knew the quiet, less demanding, fulfilling life joy of hugging a grandchild.

Toward the latter part of Sam's life he made two similar attempts to regain or restore an earlier condition of happiness. For a number of years he created a series of paternal, avuncular, or grandfatherly relationships with bright, prepubescent young girls. Probably they reminded him of Susie, Clara, and Jean, of earlier days, of his children's intelligence and innocence. Or perhaps he treated them as imagined grandchildren, as links to a future he knew he would not see. Undoubtedly he liked their wit, innocent enthusiasm, and devotion.

In his fiction, Mark Twain also tried repeatedly, pathetically, to create stories in which a once happy family faces great dangers, suffers the loss of one or more children, but somehow the family is restored to the earlier complete condition. Some of these stories and manuscript fragments, when read sympathetically, with knowledge of Sam's actual biography, could make a stone cry. He tried to do imaginatively what he could not do in reality, and he tried repeatedly.

Mark Twain's sensitivity to and appreciation of children add depth, empathy, and philosophical probing to his work. Most readers already value the major novels such as *The Adventures of Tom Sawyer* and *Adventures of Huckleberry Finn*. But we can also turn to the rewarding, lesser-known pieces, ranging from the early "Those Blasted Children" or "Miss Clapp's School" (both 1864) all the way to the late humor based on the naïveté of "Little Nellie Tells a Story Out of Her Own Head" (1907) or the philosophical, wrenching "Little Bessie" (1908). Twain continued to explore this material—pondering how our world, our morality, and our mortality can be perceived by children. As late as December 1909 Twain persisted, writing in *Harper's Bazaar* about his long-term fascination with "Marjorie Fleming, the Wonder Child." His sensitivity to his own family enabled him to explore, appreciate, and dramatize the real and the fictional children's minds.

The influence of Twain's perceiving, sympathetic, respectful attitude toward children seems formative, pervasive, incalculable.

Remembered love and remembered joy could, in theory, be consoling or somehow compensatory for some people. But Sam Clemens had a Lear-like emotional intensity. After Susie's death from spinal meningitis, Sam tried repeatedly to interpret what she had said in her final delirium. And he even tried to contact her through spiritualism, in which he did not ordinarily believe. His late letters, particularly those to Howells about Susie's death and about Livy's death, lead me to believe that in his later years his dominant private emotions were rage, sorrow, and anguish—mixed with public restraint and some bemused forbearance.

As a single parent to Clara and to Jean, he had to maintain a paternal presence. As Hamlin Hill and others have indicated, the later years were not his best. The latter parts of parenting, the deliberate, nonobstructive "letting go" of the child, are in my experience the hardest stages of parenting. The parent's instincts are protective, yet the young adult actually needs freedom and independence. The parent almost automatically attempts to revert to earlier times, when the parent was needed and was so important to the child. I suspect that whereas this process is certainly hard for a married father, it would be immensely more difficult for a widowed male, who might be lonely, frightened of his unfamiliar responsibility, and uncertain about what his wife would have done at this stage about courtship or preliminary displays of affection or intimacy. There was, perhaps, after Livy's death, a Lear-like moodiness, truculence, reluctance, and obstinacy.

When elderly men suffer from angina, indicative of congestive heart failure and cardiac insufficiency, as Sam did, they usually do not get enough oxygen to the brain and accordingly may become confused and behave erratically, without normal inhibitions. Without pharmacological relief, congestive heart failure and angina can be painful, frightening, and disorienting. Mental confusion often accompanies cardiac subfunction, systemic depressants such as alcohol are actually not the person's friend, and the chest pain reminds the person in lucid moments that he is dying.

A Shakespearean sonnet ends, "For thy sweet love remembered such wealth brings / That then I'd scorn to change my place with kings," but that consolation apparently was not usually available to Sam. I wish it had been. He knew the heights and depths of human emotions. Perhaps for those of us younger than Sam Clemens's seventy-four years the best concluding commentary to this account of Sam Clemens–Mark Twain's familial life can be found in lines at the end of *King Lear:*

KENT:	Vex not his ghost, O let him pass, he hates him
	That would upon the rack of this tough world
	Stretch him out longer.
EDGAR:	He is gone indeed.
KENT:	The wonder is, he hath endured so long:
	He but usurpt his life.
ALBANY:	Bear them from hence. Our present business
	Is general woe. Friends of my soul, you twain
	Rule in this realm, and the gored state sustain.
KENT:	I have a journey, Sir, shortly to go;
	My master calls me,—I must not say no.
EDGAR:	The weight of this sad time we must obey;
	Speak what we feel, not what we ought to say.
	The oldest hath borne most: we that are young
	Shall never see so much, nor live so long.

"To his preferred friends he revealed his true character"

Mary Mason Fairbanks's Disguised Debate with Sam Clemens

J. D. STAHL

Samuel Clemens so successfully dramatized and staged his relationship with Mary Mason Fairbanks that biographers have had difficulty getting past the smoke screen of his enactments. In his comic performances enacted in his letters, he was her naughty "cub," she his alternately indulgent and strict "Mother," reproaching him for his bad habits, curing him of misbehavior, and weeding his prose of "slang." Critics have used the elements of Samuel Clemens's "psychodrama" as the basis for various misguided interpretations of the gender conflicts Clemens was bound up in, interpretations that were themselves part of a kind of psychodrama of American literary criticism. Though it is impossible to discover the "essence" of Samuel Clemens's and Mary Mason Fairbanks's relationship behind the games and the rhetoric, it is possible to reinterpret some features of their friendship a bit more sanely and accurately. In the context of critical debate about the role of Mary Mason Fairbanks in the shaping of *The Innocents Abroad,* the examination of their relationship contributes new insight into the changing nature of critical assumptions in American literary history. The recovery of Fairbanks's own voice as a writer and as a woman is a significant dimension of a close scrutiny of her self-representations and her (often humorously disguised, but fundamentally serious) arguments with Clemens, within the constraints and codes of nineteenth-century American language about gender, aspiration, and professionalism.

In June 1867, aboard the steamship *Quaker City,* which was then anchored in Gravesend Bay off Brooklyn because of rough weather, Samuel Clemens, thirty-one years old, made the acquaintance of Mary Mason Fairbanks, thirty-nine. Mary Mason was born in Perry, Ohio; had attended the Norwich Academy and Emma Willard's Female Seminary in Troy, New York; and taught school in New York, Kentucky, and South Carolina. In 1852, she had married Abel Fairbanks of Cleveland, Ohio, coowner of the *Cleveland Herald.* Abel Fairbanks, whose first wife, Alice Holmes, died in 1849, had two children from his first marriage, who in 1867 were twenty and twenty-two. Mary and Abel Fairbanks also had two children of their own, Charles Mason, born in 1855, and Mary Paine, born in 1856. Aboard the *Quaker City,* bound for Europe and Palestine, Mary Mason Fairbanks was writing letters, using the anagram Myra as her pseudonym, reporting on the trip for the *Cleveland Herald.*

A "semiprofessional writer,"[1] Mary Mason Fairbanks was the dominant figure of a social circle aboard ship that included seventeen-year-old Charles Jervis Langdon, son of the wealthy coal merchant Jervis Langdon and his wife, Olivia Lewis Langdon of Elmira, New York; Julius Moulton, also known as Lucius, twenty-two, an assistant engineer on the North Missouri Railroad, whose father, Jonathan Benjamin Moulton, was chief engineer of that railroad; Dr. Abraham Reeves Jackson, forty, from Philadelphia, a witty man who in the Civil War had served as assistant medical director of the United States Army of Virginia and who later became a prominent gynecologist in Chicago; and Emily and Solon Severance, she thirty-seven and he forty-three. Emily was the daughter of a noted physician; Solon was a prosperous Cleveland banker who had risen from messenger to teller to cashier, vice president, and finally president of the Euclid Avenue National Bank.[2] Many of the members of this circle were, like Sam Clemens and Mary Fairbanks, writing letters reporting on the excursion for publication in various newspapers back home. Aboard ship, Sam was playfully flirting with Emma Beach, the seventeen-year-old daughter of Moses Beach, editor of the *New York Sun* and neighbor of Henry Ward Beecher, probably the most

1. Justin Kaplan, *Mr. Clemens and Mark Twain: A Biography,* 44. Hereafter referred to as *MC&MT.*

2. Twain, *Mark Twain's Letters,* vol. 2, *1867–1868,* 63–67. Hereafter referred to as *MTL2.*

prominent minister of the day. In this socially well-connected circle, Sam Clemens the westerner, perceived as crude, stood out for his wit, drawling speech, and uncouth manners.

The matronly, accomplished, well-educated Mary Mason Fairbanks, whom Kaplan describes as "full-faced" and having a "rounded figure," befriended the younger humorist and writer, saw his potential, and developed a relationship with him in which she nurtured his talent and mentored him in social affairs and courtship. For his part, the temperamental Sam Clemens selected her as one of his few lifelong friends, among whom were Joseph Twichell and William Dean Howells, to whom his loyalty remained unwavering. What did Clemens and Fairbanks see in each other, and what did they make of each other, in both metaphorical senses of that phrase?

Her first impressions of him were mixed. On June 9 she wrote:

> There is one table from which is sure to come a peal of contagious laughter, and all eyes are turned toward "Mark Twain," whose face is perfectly mirth-provoking, sitting lazily at table; scarcely genteel in appearance, there is nevertheless a something, I know not what, that interests and attracts. I saw today at dinner, venerable divines and sage looking men, convulsed with laughter at his drolleries and quaint original manners. To my mind, however, he can never win the laurels that were destined to deck the brow of our poor friend who sleeps at "Kensal Green." (*MTL2*, 66)

She was referring to Artemus Ward, the humorist who had worked as a local editor for the *Toledo Commercial* and the *Cleveland Plain Dealer* and would thus have been known to her as a fellow Ohio resident and a writer active in Ohio journalism. Ward had been buried in London in March of the same year. In spite of her regional loyalties, which may have prejudiced her in favor of Ward, she did not hesitate to recognize Clemens's talents.

This woman, who was passably fluent in French (as suggested by her English version of "je ne sais quoi"), who admired the established school of landscape and portrait painting as well as the Old Masters, and who regularly admonished the social group aboard ship to attend prayer meetings, had a keen sense of Sam Clemens's talents. If, like several other women and men in his life, she was wary of the vulgarity and crassness that animated much of American humor, and, like Emma Beach, wished that he would write something dignified for the *Atlantic Monthly,* she was seeking to elevate and channel a force of genius that she recognized and respected. Recent critics have begun to acknowledge the positive nature of Fairbanks's influence on Clemens, as Jeffrey Steinbrink does when he contends: "While she could be merely censorious or conventional in her criticism, Mary Fairbanks often served Clemens valuably by prodding him to allow his audience the chance to appreciate the seriousness and complexity of his character in his work. When he drifted toward the simple-minded buffoonery of the literary comedian, as he did in some *Express* pieces, she was often there to check him."[3]

Sam Clemens's first impressions of Mary Mason Fairbanks are not recorded, but we do have his first description of her to his family, a letter curious to consider when we keep in mind that in it Sam was introducing to his own mother, Jane Lampton Clemens, the other woman whom for the rest of her life he was to address as "Mother." Included here are words and phrases that Clemens canceled out but that are still legible.

> Inclosed is a letter to me from [the wife of the editor of the *Cleveland Herald,*] one of our fellow-passengers. She was the most refined, intelligent, [educated] & cultivated lady in the ship, & altogether the kindest and best.[4] She sewed my buttons on, kept my clothes in presentable trim, fed me on Egyptian jam, [& cured] (when I behaved), lectured me awfully on the quarter-deck on moon-lit promenading evenings, & cured me of several bad habits. I am under lasting obligations to her. She looks young, because she is so good—but she had a grown son & daughter at home. I wrote her, the other day, that my buttons were all off, again. She had another pup under her charge, younger than myself, whom I [called] always called "the cub." Hence her reference to cubs and bears. Lucius Moulton was another cub of hers. We all called her "mother" & kept her in hot water all the time about her brood. I always abused the sea-sick people—I said nobody but almighty mean people ever got sea-sick—& she thought I was in earnest. She never got sick herself. She always drummed us up for prayer meeting, with her monitory "Seven bells,

3. Steinbrink, *Getting to Be Mark Twain,* 59. Hereafter referred to as *GBMT.*
4. The square brackets throughout indicate words or phrases that were canceled in the original but are still legible.

my boys—you know what it is time for." We always went, but we
liked [six] four bells best, because it meant hash—dinner, I should
say. (*MTL2,* 130, Dec. 10, 1867)

The letter is, as is characteristic of Mark Twain, a mixture of reporting and
shrewd performance. It seems tactfully to soften the blow of introducing
a rival for his filial affection by stressing the general sharing of Mary Mason Fairbanks's maternal supervision of her "cubs." It also introduces the
central pleasurable tension that Clemens enacted in his relationship with
"Mother" Fairbanks, namely, his playful, deadpan teasing of her and his
partially pretended, partially real reluctance to submit to her magisterial
moral and social authority and to her efforts to refine him.

Nonetheless, we should not miss the genuine and substantial acknowl-
edgments Clemens made that help to account for the permanence and influence of their friendship: he respected her intelligence, he cherished her
attentions (which he defined as maternal), and he loved to tease her. That
there was also an element of social aspiration in his attraction to her refining
influence is undeniable. When one considers the question of why Samuel
Clemens should have felt the need to adopt a surrogate mother when in fact
he had a perfectly good one of his own in the witty, vivacious, and loving
Jane Lampton Clemens, and why he should choose Mary Mason Fairbanks
in particular as that surrogate mother, the answer has to lie in part in the
Fairbanks's social position. In a very real sense, Sam Clemens was trading
on his genius for the sake of entry into membership in the propertied class:
through friendship and through marriage, the Fairbankses and the Lang-
dons offered an entrance into the wealthy class that the fabled Clemens
Tennessee land never could or did. But it would be too simple to say that
because Clemens traded on his talent, he sold it out. For the gentility and
respectability he ambivalently desired and rebelled against were as much a
part of his complex personality as his uncouth, vernacular style. What he
sometimes projected with glee onto his surrogate mothers and mentors in
respectability was drawn as much from within himself as it was imposed
upon him from without.

But there is a second part to this psychological and social equation that is
often forgotten: in the midst of all his role playing and playful yet purposeful
invention, he was dealing with a real counterpart, a genuine person, whose

consent was needed for their game of mutual self-creation, and whose respect he retained and prized as much as he in turn respected her. That respect was based in part on literary collaboration. It is remarkable how much her efforts to reform his character flow into her efforts to reform Mark Twain as a writer, and vice versa, as Sam Clemens represents it. In fact, one could say that a significant part of Sam Clemens becoming Mark Twain in *The Innocents Abroad* and beyond is the story of the struggle between Sam the "cub" and "Mother" Fairbanks. James M. Cox accurately points out, "[H]ow much of a mother she actually was during the voyage is difficult to say because the relation is projected almost entirely through the magnifying lens of his imagination."[5] It is a noteworthy peculiarity, demanding some explanation, that Mary Mason Fairbanks never appears in the 651 pages of *The Innocents Abroad*, when she was so obviously a major part of his experience on the tour. The "boys" make prominent appearances—"boys" obviously being an irreverent and partially misleading characterization itself—and so do the "Pilgrims," but no kindly if censorious "Mother," much less a fellow professional or semiprofessional woman writer. There is a sense in which the male writer is excluding the female writer here, relegating her to the editorial hearth, but then he is also excluding much else, including, much of the time, Samuel Clemens of Hannibal, Missouri. There is another sense in which Mary Mason Fairbanks is everywhere present in this book—and to reduce her to a censorious gentility is to exclude her indeed.

The battle over the nature of Mary Mason Fairbanks's influence on Sam Clemens's writing has been fought before. Dewey Ganzel, in *Mark Twain Abroad: The Cruise of the "Quaker City,"* denied the prominent role that Mary Mason Fairbanks played in the writing of *The Innocents Abroad*. Although Ganzel acknowledges that Mary Fairbanks read Clemens's correspondence on the excursion and "that she was a help to him," he also argues that "the nature of [her] assistance has been so misconstrued and its extent so exaggerated that it is difficult to consider in proper perspective. . . . The case for the influence of Mrs. Fairbanks rests finally on the rather sentimental view that Clemens was a victim of feminine domination, that he was always influenced by the women in his life." Ganzel's version has been

5. Cox, *Mark Twain: The Fate of Humor*, 67.

refuted by Leon T. Dickinson, who demonstrated anew, in a review in *Modern Philology*, the significance of Mary Mason Fairbanks's editorial influence, arguing that though Ganzel "wants to limit her help to proofreading and copy editing . . . surely it was more than this" and citing the evidence of Emma Beach and Solon Severance's testimony that Mark Twain "destroyed or rejected manuscripts at Mrs. Fairbanks's suggestion."[6] Ganzel's rejection of Fairbanks's literary influence may be read as part of the movement to refute the myth of destructive female dominance set in motion by Van Wyck Brooks and other early-twentieth-century critics. Recent criticism is more inclined to recognize positive value in Clemens's receptivity to "genteel" influence and the complexity of his internal struggles with the values of gentility stereotypically associated with "women's realm." Laura Skandera Trombley has argued: "In both the personal and literary realms, he was a man voluntarily controlled and influenced by women. Women shaped his life, edited his books, provided models for his fictional characters, and, through their correspondence, heavily influenced his fiction and literary works" (*MTW*, 2).[7]

In a sense, the maternal, not to say the matriarchal, presence is absent in *The Innocents Abroad,* an absence so vast as to become an enveloping presence. When we read Sam Clemens's letters in conjunction with *The Innocents Abroad,* we see at work the process of thesis and antithesis that produced the book. As Susan Gillman has characterized one of Mark Twain's many dualities: "While his humor was often rooted in the impulse to subvert authority, he lived out the most extravagant of Gilded Age social and economic fantasies. . . . Concerning his vocation as an artist, this ambiguity

6. Ganzel, *Mark Twain Abroad,* 272–73; Dickinson, review of *Mark Twain Abroad,* 117–19.

7. See also recent discussions by Peter Stoneley in *Mark Twain and the Feminine Aesthetic,* hereafter referred to as *MTFA,* and J. D. Stahl in *Mark Twain, Culture, and Gender.* Stoneley argues that "Twain felt impelled to establish a compromise between the masculine and the feminine, and this attempted mediation between the two is a strong element throughout his career." However, "his efforts were doomed to failure, because the conditions that produced the masculine aesthetic and its feminine counterpart were borne unequally: as his cynicism regarding female suffrage would suggest, women were to be denied the diversity of opportunity and expression allowed to men" (44). In *Mark Twain, Culture, and Gender,* I argue that, in each of his three "Mysterious Stranger" stories, written late in his career, Twain created "a female figure who is admirable and in many respects superior to other human beings but also representative. . . . [H]e employed female figures with a range of inclusive referentiality to represent humanity, male and female" (156).

continued to torment Twain, suspended as he would remain throughout his life between the roles of humorist and serious writer—roles that were culturally constituted."[8] Part of that ambiguity and torment was the effort to internalize maternal authority. As Justin Kaplan put it, "Mary Fairbanks was the kind of civilizing influence that Huck Finn lit out from, but which Clemens courted for years." As Kaplan phrases it, "Without hypocrisy but with a certain willing suspension of identity—the price of which, he would later learn, was anger and a divided heart—he wanted to experiment with her manners and standards, to imitate and possibly assimilate them" (*MC&MT* 44–45).

The word *courted* to describe Clemens's attraction to what Mary Fairbanks represented to him is apt. For "Mother" Fairbanks was not only midwife to the birth of *The Innocents Abroad*, but also was of invaluable assistance to Sam Clemens in his courtship of Olivia Langdon. Mary Mason Fairbanks was the one who urged Sam to marry. Sam's humorous response to her urging suggests how much he saw financial solvency and marriage intertwined. "A good wife would be a perpetual incentive to progress," Clemens quotes Fairbanks, and responds,

> . . . & so she would—I never thought of that before—progress from house to house because I couldn't pay the rent. The idea is good. I wish I had a chance to try it. But seriously, Madam, you are only just proposing luxuries to Lazarus. That is all. I want a good wife—I want a couple of them if they are particularly good—but where is the wherewithal? It costs [sixty dollars] nearly two letters a week to keep me. If I doubled it, the firm would come to grief the first time anything happened to the senior partner. Manifestly you haven't looked into this thing. I am as good an economist as anybody, but I can't turn an inkstand into Aladdin's lamp. You haven't examined into this thing at all, you see. (*MTL2*, 133–34, Dec. 12, 1867)

This is part of the same letter in which he makes his famous statement: "[I]f I were settled I would quit all nonsense and swindle some [poor] girl into marrying me. But I [don't] wouldn't expect to be *worthy* of her. I wouldn't

---

8. Gillman, *Dark Twins: Imposture and Identity in Mark Twain's America,* 21.

have a girl that [I thought] I was worthy of. *She* wouldn't do. She wouldn't be respectable enough." Mary Mason Fairbanks played a major role in the process whereby Sam Clemens reformed himself to become "worthy" of his worshiped "sister" Olivia, in her eyes and in the eyes of Mrs. Fairbanks. When Sam wrote to Mary to announce his engagement, his exuberance was mixed with a shrewd practical sense of economics: "She isn't my sister any more—but some time in the future she is going to be my wife, & I think we shall live in Cleveland. I think that, because I think you will persuade Mr. Fairbanks to sell me [an in] a living interest in the *Herald* on such a credit as will enable me to pay for it by lecturing & other work—for I have no relatives to borrow money of, & wouldn't do it if I had" (*MTL2*, 284, Nov. 26–27, 1868).

His submission to her maternal authority is linked in Sam's mind to his aspirations in courtship:

> Congratulate me, my darling Mother—(that brings the tears to your eyes & a smile [of] to your lips) because you know you do con-gratulate me, away down in the depths of your loving heart.[)] . . . I touch no more spiritous liquors after this day (though I have made no promises)—I shall do no act which you or Livy might be pained to hear of—I shall seek the society of the good—I shall be a Chris-tian. I shall climb—climb—climb—toward this bright sun that is shining in the heaven of my happiness until all that is gross & unwor-thy is hidden in the mists & the darkness of that lower earth whence you first lifted my [ascend ascen] aspiring feet. Have no fears, my mother. I shall be worthy—yet. Livy believes in me. You believe in me, too, whether you say it or not. I believe in myself. I believe in God—& through the breaking clouds I see the star of Hope rising in the placid blue beyond.
> I bow my reverent head. Thy blessing, mother! (*MTL2*, 284)

It is hard not to see a touch of parody in the final invocation. In fact, not only is the exuberance of Clemens's sincere joy tinged with an undertone of irony, but it is also noteworthy how much Sam tells Mary Fairbanks here what her role is and how to enact it—even telling her, with a certain peremptoriness, what she feels. This proceeding mirrors his courtship of Livy, during which, as Peter Stoneley has discussed, "Twain pointed out precisely the qualities that were necessary to his love; he gave Livy advice on how best to preserve those qualities, and perhaps even informed her that she had them" (*MTFA*, 42).

The financial and emotional alliance Clemens was pressing for may have been a bit too intense and close for several of the participants in this naive scenario of life in an Edenic Cleveland, not least of all for Livy herself.[9] A surrogate mother-in-law with reins on the finances as well as the authorial aspirations of a young husband who idolized even if he manipulated her (his surrogate mother-in-law, that is) might have been a frightening prospect to the young bride. One of the ironies of Sam's relationship with Mary is that he granted her authority over him—authority that she exercised at his behest. The same is true of his relationship with Livy, as Stoneley shrewdly points out: "He imbued her [Livy] with the sanctionary attitude that he would so frequently react against; he can clearly be seen to have engineered his own set of feminine values to kick against" (*MTFA*, 43). But it is important to keep in mind that Mary Mason Fairbanks's authority also had a genuine social dimension not invented by Sam Clemens. It was to Mary Fairbanks that Olivia Langdon, Livy's mother, wrote her long and urgent letter pleading for insight into Sam's character after he asked Livy's parents for their consent to the marriage.

Olivia wrote to Mary that Charlie, her son, had reported that Sam had experienced "a great change." Then she asked:

> The question, the answer to which, would settle a most weaning anxiety, is,—from what standard of conduct,—from what habitual life, did this change, or improvement, or reformation; commence?
>
> Does this change, so desirably commenced make of an immoral man a moral one, as the world looks at men?—or—does this change make of one, who has been entirely a man of the world, different in this regard, that he resolutely aims to enter upon a new, because a Christian life? (*MTL2*, 287, Dec. 1, 1868)

Her question provides a revealing glimpse into the ethical imagination of Olivia Langdon and many pious women of her class. She dreaded "immoral-

---

9. For a more detailed discussion of the negotiations between Sam Clemens and Abel Fairbanks that led to Clemens's change of plans concerning investing in the *Cleveland Herald*, see *GBMT*, 35–40.

ity," but, by implication, appears to have been more ready to accept a "man of the world" who had reformed. Profession of religious faith was one of the forms of self-alteration that Sam Clemens temporarily imposed upon himself as part of the self-transformation of courtship, of becoming "worthy."

It is easy to see through the idolization by which Clemens elevated and idealized Livy in the rapturous language of Victorian feeling, which also sounds so condescending today: "Goodbye, Livy. You are so pure, so great, so good, so beautiful. How can I help loving you? Say, rather, how can I keep from *worshipping* you, you dear little paragon" (*MTL2*, 291). But it is important to keep in mind the shrewder, more perceptive side of his relationship with her, which wrestled with her doubts, fears, and tendencies toward illness with psychological insights he must have gained in struggles with himself:

> Do put all perplexing reflections, all doubts & fears, far from you
> for a little while, Livy, for I dread, dread, dread to hear you are sick.
> No mere ordinary tax upon your powers is likely to make you ill,
> but you must remember that even the most robust nature could
> hardly hold out against the siege of foodless, sleepless days & nights
> which you have just sustained. I am not talking to you as if you
> were a feeble little child, for on the contrary you are a brave, strong-
> willed woman, with no nonsense & no childishness about you—but
> what I am providing against is your liability to indulge in troubled
> thoughts & forebodings. Such thoughts must come, for they are
> natural to people who have brains & feelings & a just appreciation
> of the responsibilities which God places before them, & so you
> must have them,—but as I said before, my dearest Livy, temper
> them, temper them, & be you the mistress & not they. (*MTL2*, 289,
> Nov. 28, 1868)

"You are a brave, strong-willed woman," Sam wrote to Livy, willing her to be what he described her to be. He was contributing to her self-definition as a woman, as Robert Browning helped to define Elizabeth Barrett, within the limits of their culture, but also translating that culture into the particular shape of their lives. Whereas Clemens often relied on conventional Victorian images of women in his fiction, his private life at times shows a more discerning sense of women's personalities. He knew how to manipulate stereotypes of femininity for public effect, but that does not mean that he was entirely deceived by those stereotypes in private.[10]

The definition of woman had been a subject of somewhat indirect debate between Mary Mason Fairbanks and Sam Clemens earlier that year, after Sam gave an after-dinner speech on the subject of "Woman" at the Washington Newspaper Correspondents' Club at Welcker's Restaurant in Washington, D.C., on Saturday, January 11, 1868.[11] Mark Twain's toast had fluctuated between Victorian platitudes and sexual innuendoes. Parts of his speech sounded almost identical to his description of Mary Mason Fairbanks's motherly attentions to him aboard the *Quaker City:* "Human intelligence cannot estimate what we owe to woman, sir. She sews on our buttons, she mends our clothes, she ropes us in at the church fairs— . . . she gives us good advice—and plenty of it—she gives us a piece of her mind, sometimes—and sometimes all of it" (*MTL2,* 155).

But other parts of his toast evoked possibilities for womanhood and sexuality not provided for by Victorian respectability. "Sir, I love the sex," he said. "I love all the women, sir, irrespective of age or color." In a remark reminiscent of his comment to William Dean Howells that he felt, after Howells reviewed *Huck Finn* favorably, like the "mother who has given birth to a white baby when she was awfully afraid it was going to be a mulatto," he said, "she bears our children—ours as a general thing" (*MC&MT,* 149; *MTL2,* 153). When Mary Fairbanks wrote Sam a "scorcher" of a letter (which unfortunately has not survived) reprimanding him for what Sam broadly (and most likely too broadly) characterized as "slang" in his speech, she may have been objecting to his colloquialisms, such as "it is but just and a graceful tribute to woman to say of her that she is a brick." More likely she objected to potential

---

10. Evidence of his ability to distinguish between the image and the reality is to be found in his letters to Livy during their courtship. In response to her anxiety at his idealizations of her, he says, "I shall see you, Livy, as I see you now: a Woman—nothing more & nothing less—a Woman, with the faults, the failings, the weaknesses of her sex and of her race . . . a Woman, Livy, mortal, & so of necessity imperfect—a Woman only—God forbid that you should be an angel. . . . Let your mind be at rest—I know you never can be 'perfect'—& am thankful that it is so" (*MTL2,* 315–16, Dec. 7, 1868). He ascribes his exaggerations to "the overflowings of a strong love" and insists that it is "not deliberate flattery, or self-deception, as you mistake it to be, Livy" (315).

11. This event was attended by thirty-seven journalists and nine guests, including Speaker of the House Schuyler Colfax, who later that year was elected vice president under Grant (*MTL2,* 157 n. 1).

sexual implications, among them, "What, sir, would the peoples of the earth be, without woman? . . . They would be scarce, sir, almighty scarce! Then let us cherish her—let us protect her—let us give her our support, our encouragement, our sympathy—ourselves, if we get a chance" (*MTL2* 156), or his innuendoes about looking at Eve in a state of nature. We can only speculate whether she was objecting to his antisuffragist joke, which had been received with great laughter.

In this speech and elsewhere, Sam Clemens's imagination played on Victorian idealizations of motherhood and was repelled, in proper Victorian fashion, by female cruelty, as suggested by his remarks about Lucretia Borgia, but it was also haunted by the possibility of woman's marital infidelity. In *The Prince and the Pauper*, Miles Hendon, compassionately performing the "womanly" offices of sewing young Edward's clothes, sings a song as he plies the needle. The song tells of a woman who "loved her husband dearilee / But another man he loved she."[12] The syntax and grammar are as awkward as the idea was uncomfortable to Twain's audience and almost certainly to himself. Perhaps the boy whose mother married in a fit of pique because the man she loved married someone else naturally carried with him all his life occasional doubts about whether wives loved their husbands best. But such thoughts, and all their implications, were indelicate and explosive. To acknowledge female sexuality, except within narrow limits, was to threaten the entire construct of Victorian propriety and gender. In the anarchy of humor this issue kept rearing its head. But it was safer to exorcise it with idealizations of motherhood and female virtue, even if he considered, as he did, that Mary Fairbanks was yoked to a creature beneath her. As he put it to Livy, "Do superiors ever love, revere & honor inferiors with the brain's consent? Hardly, I think. Mrs. Brooks and Mrs. Fairbanks, brilliant women both, have married away down below them—& it would be hard to convince me that they did not love first & think afterward" (*MTL2*, 301). Therefore, as Sam Clemens represented matters, Mary Mason Fairbanks looked young "because she [was] so good" and "reformed" a man less than a decade younger than herself as if he were a delinquent boy (*MTL2*, 130). These fictions granted her a socially approved sense of power. Clemens used

---

12. Twain, *The Prince and the Pauper*, 150.

these fictions to cultivate, among other things, a friendship that guided him toward the social position he aspired to, but also that exorcised and contained the demons of sexuality, anxiety, and humor.

As for her part, though we have less evidence of Mary Mason Fairbanks's stake in the relationship, we can reconstruct some elements of her sense of self in relation to Sam Clemens–Mark Twain and the larger social context in which they both existed through the evidence of her own testimony. Though her letters from abroad are dismissively characterized by critics such as Justin Kaplan (he calls them "meticulous and unexciting accounts"), a characterization perhaps encouraged by her frequent self-effacing or apologetic comments about her writing, her newspaper correspondence from the *Quaker City* tour reveals a cultured, perceptive, purposeful woman writer. Her sense of the inadequacy of her abilities appears to be partly conventional, partly sincere, as when she writes: "I almost regret that I have attempted to describe anything in this wonderful city [Paris] to you, so utterly inadequate do I feel; but if you will follow my blind guidance, I will retrace with you some of the pleasant steps which I have already taken. I only wish I could impart to you one-hundredth part of the enjoyment which I have realized amid all these strange and beautiful sights" (*Cleveland Herald*, Aug. 14, 1867).

Yet, she chronicles her travels with honesty, as when she tells of her disappointment in seeing the cathedral of Notre Dame in Paris, partly because it did not live up to her expectations of "more gorgeous decorations and more imposing surroundings" and partly because "the solemnity of the scene is marred by the little stalls and tables which are stationed about the entrance for the sale of rosaries, photographs and medals" (*Cleveland Herald*, Aug. 14, 1867). Her letters also evidence a sense of humor, as she recounts comic episodes in the travels of the "pilgrims."

While her writing often employs conventional Victorian metaphors and stylistic embellishments, and she frequently mentions her yearning for the familiar sights, customs, and people of Ohio as well as her maternal longings for her children, her prose displays an acute eye and descriptive powers that belie her conventional self-depreciation. For example, in Spain she notes: "The road-side is lined with overgrown and ill-kept hedges of the aloe, prickly pear, and bamboo cane. The green lizard glided under the broad leaves, and here and there the towering stalk of the aloe spread out its candelabra of blossoms" (*Cleveland Herald,* July 25, 1867). Though her style ranges from factual to sentimental, many examples of her descriptive talent could be cited. It is not surprising that Clemens consulted her about what title to give his book: when he wrote to thank her for sending her published letters, he said, "I see a good many ideas in your letters that I can steal" (*MTL2*, 166). There are passages in the *Cleveland Herald* letters that may well have influenced Mark Twain's reminiscences as he rewrote and expanded his *Alta California* letters. For instance, in Paris she notes, "The city seems one brilliant garden. The cafés and gardens are thronged with families in holiday attire; the parks and promenades are gorgeous with the gaily dressed crowd who move about with perfect decorum, or sit at their ease under the shade of the trees that one finds everywhere in Paris" (Aug. 3, 1867). Compare that with Twain's passage: "I do envy these Europeans the comfort they take. When the work of the day is done, they forget it. Some of them go, with wife and children, to a beer hall, and sit quietly and genteelly drinking a mug or two of ale and listening to music; others walk the streets, others drive in the avenues; others assemble in the great ornamental squares in the early evening to enjoy the sight and the fragrance of flowers and to hear the military bands play."[13]

Though we unfortunately do not have many of Mary Mason Fairbanks's letters to Sam Clemens, we do have a revealing essay she wrote about twenty-five years after the *Quaker City* tour, after many years of friendship with him. The essay provides some insight into her perspective on him and, by implication, on the nature of their relationship. One can interpret "The Cruise of the 'Quaker City,' with Chance Recollections of Mark Twain" as her act of revising both the meaning of the excursion and the public image of Mark Twain himself. It reveals some of her most firmly held values, delivers a kind of rebuttal to what she regards as a popular misinterpretation of the trip that arose in response to *The Innocents Abroad,* and seeks to show a side of Samuel Clemens that accords with her values.

The theme of her essay is transformations—especially if one considers the materials she quotes at length: Samuel Clemens's letter to a debutante (Mary's daughter Mollie) about the transformation from girlhood

13. Twain, *The Innocents Abroad,* 187.

to womanhood and Oliver Wendell Holmes's poem on the occasion of Clemens's fiftieth birthday celebration, which contrasts the baby Clemens in his cradle with the humorous genius Mark Twain. Her essay concludes, "The *Quaker City* sailed out of New York harbor with no celebrities on board. She brought back the *Great American Humorist*." She describes the importance of the journey to Mark Twain as follows: "What the *Quaker City* excursion has done for him need not be reiterated here. It was the bridge by which he crossed from a restless, wavering, well-nigh purposeless youth, to a new life of growing aspirations, and a national celebrity. He was not inflated with expectations on his embarkation and in the early days of the voyage carried himself as one who was drifting out to sea, quite indifferent to time, place, or circumstance."[14]

Her vision of Clemens's unanticipated transformation from drifting, directionless young man to author of national stature is rooted in her sense of the importance of learning. She suggests that the comic persona Clemens created in *The Innocents Abroad* belied not only his seriousness of purpose and the size of his ambition but also the genuine respect he had for knowledge and culture and his dedication to learning.[15] It is relevant to remind ourselves in this context that Clemens was a self-educated man, with some of the attendant anxieties, which Fairbanks's view of him tended to allay.

The purpose of her article, as she states it, is to defend the value of the expedition against those who, "naturally enough, accepting the 'Innocents Abroad' as faithful chronicles, have the habit of deriding the expedition as an enterprise chiefly disappointing in its outcome." She asserts: "On the contrary, through the perspective of more than two decades . . . it must stand approved as one of the most comprehensive of object lessons, a grand traveling school with classes in geography, history, and classic art." She admits by

14. Fairbanks, "Cruise of the 'Quaker City,' " 430–32. Hereafter referred to as CQC.

15. In June 1876, after reading his "Facts Concerning the Recent Carnival of Crime in Connecticut" in the *Atlantic*, she wrote to him: "I tried to take up my pen . . . to tell you how you pleased me. Do you realize how you have improved? How time and study and conscience have developed the fineness of your nature? I just sit back in my complacence & mentally pat you on the head—not that your well-doing is for me or my approval but because I knew it would be as it is, and I am pleased with my own sagacity. Your late article has some most delicate, metaphysical touches and I never was so sure of your having a live conscience, as since you have proclaimed its death" (Twain, *Mark Twain to Mrs. Fairbanks*, 198; hereafter referred to as *MTMF*).

implication that she did not recognize Clemens's brilliance at once: "Who that listened to his drawling utterances on that occasion, would have forecast for him the brilliant future which has since evolved or believed that the careless speaker was to become the hero of the prospective expedition?" (CQC, 429, 430). She acknowledges the significance of Mark Twain's literary success, but her own version of the tour seeks to refute the impression that it was valueless except as a kind of grand entertainment—thus in a sense arguing with the impression Mark Twain had succeeded in conveying. Her close attention to the social standing of the personages involved in the excursion shows her firm sense of the importance of social position—a sense she shared with Clemens, though he surrounded his representations of social prestige with parody and satire. She in effect forces a concession from Clemens when she states that "Even Mark Twain, [the tour's] chief satirist, will concede this [the educational value of the tour], and also that for not a few of the company it laid the basis of a course of study which has enriched their lives and qualified them to help others" (CQC, 430). She creates her own version of Mark Twain's self-transformation with a sharp eye to the differences between the impressions he liked to create and her own assessment of him:

> "I am like an old, burned-out crater; the fires of my life are all dead within me," he said to a fellow traveler as they walked the deck together. But this was only a youthful cynicism, for he was then little past thirty. He did not know then that he had begun a voyage of discovery by whose circuitous route he was to find his inspiration and his opportunity. He had acquired some local prestige in California and Nevada as a humorous journalist, and was the author of a Gulliver sort of story, "The Jumping Frog," but as yet he had furnished little evidence of superior literary ability.
> At first he lolled about the ship as one committed to utter indolence. His drolleries and moderate movements rendered him conspicuous among the passengers, while from his table would come frequent peals of contagious laughter, in the midst of which his own serious and questioning face and air of injured innocence were thoroughly mirth-provoking. Those who had the good fortune to share with him the adventures with which his remarkable and grotesque narratives have made the public familiar, recall with interest the gradual waking up of this man of genius. His keen eyes discerned the

incongruities of character around him, into which his susceptibility to absurdities gave him quick insight. Here in this goodly company of pilgrims, embracing men of mind and men of manners and their opposites, he put himself at school. With what result, let the unparalleled story of the "Innocents Abroad" bear witness.

It followed that in this journey of months, such a man as Mr. Clemens found his own coterie of congenial friends. With them he studied and discoursed of the strange countries at whose shores they were to anchor. He read their poets with inimitable pathos and he was the ship's oracle upon the Old Masters, whom later he ridiculed in his book.

To his preferred friends he revealed his true character, but, with a perversity on his part induced by the unmerited criticism of some of the company, he exaggerated his faults to others. Hence the conflicting estimates of Mark Twain's character, which often confound those who know him for what he is.

The appearance of The Innocents Abroad, which met with an unparalleled circulation, secured for its author a sudden notoriety. For an American ship to go cruising in foreign seas simply for pleasure was in those days a new departure, and although the witty author did not glorify the American traveler, his book was the event of the year. Its success attested its merit and at once he decided upon his career. It was manifest that he had found his calling, and had mined in a richer lode than California or Nevada could ever have opened to him. (CQC, 430)

Though this is obviously a simplified version of events, Fairbanks demonstrates that she has a keen sense of Clemens's choices as well as of social realities. She goes on to tell a mythic version of his romance and courtship, emphasizing the distance between his melodramatic, despairing self-dramatization of two years earlier and the national fame of his success in courtship. (The privacy of Clemens's wedding to Olivia Langdon on February 2, 1870, had been substantially abridged by the fastidious Mary Fairbanks herself, who excused her apparent lapse of taste in reporting the event in her husband's Cleveland Herald by reasoning that although "the quiet, impressive ceremony with all its beautiful appointments is sacred to the few who witnessed it . . . 'Mark Twain' belongs to the public which has a right to know" [GBMT, 78].) In 1892, she notes that "the humorous author in his rapidly increasing popularity could have received no public endorsement comparable with the cordial surrender to him of this fair daughter of an aristocratic family" with not a word about her own role in bringing about this "cordial surrender" (*MTMF*, 431). She defends him against the charge of being merely a humorist, selects *The Prince and the Pauper* as "the book par excellence of his published works" (which in 1880 she had encouraged him to write, with the admonition that "the time has come for your best book, your best contribution to American Literature"), and quotes at length from the letter to her daughter, identified only as a debutante, in which Mark Twain laments her passage from childhood ("the dearest bud of maidenhood in all the land") to womanhood.[16] He consoles himself in this letter with the anticipated gain of her maturity, defining her "dizzy new elevation" in conventional terms that Mary Fairbanks clearly cherished: "The main thing is to be as sweet as a woman as you were as a maiden; and as good and true, as honest and sincere, as loving, as pure, as genuine, as earnest, as untrivial, as sweetly graced with dignity, and as free from every taint or suggestion of shams, affectations, or pretense in your new estate as you were in the old" (CQC, 432). But Mary Mason Fairbanks also quotes his long postscript, in which he urges the young woman to find a certain book by Thomas Fuller and search out what Twain calls "pemmican sentences," compact sentences that compress elaborate thoughts into brief form. "Do you read? What are you reading? What is your criticism?" he asks of her (CQC, 432).

The implied respect for the young woman's intellect is clearly also something Mary Mason Fairbanks valued, as is confirmed by various remarks in her autobiographical entry in the volume *Emma Willard and Her Pupils*, which she compiled and edited. She there mentions Harriette Dillaye, vice principal at Norwich Academy, "who had the happy gift of inciting intellectual ambition in her pupils."[17] Mary Mason Fairbanks's blend of social pride and love of learning emerges in her entry about herself as Mason, Mary J.:[18]

16. Everett Emerson, *Mark Twain: A Literary Life*, 121; *MTMF*, 431.
17. Fairbanks, *Emma Willard and Her Pupils; or, Fifty Years of Troy Female Seminary, 1822–1872*, 432. Hereafter referred to as *EW*.
18. When Clemens failed to visit her on one of his lecture tours, she expressed her sense of having been slighted by writing: "I come from a proud clan, and henceforth you must find me within my castle walls" (*MTMF*, 161). In later years, their friendship became less active, and long intervals without correspondence and visits led to regretful inquiries and apologetic

> Both parents were natives of New England. Her father was a direct
> descendant of Maj.-Gen. John Mason, who emigrated from England,
> and who commanded a successful expedition against the Pequot
> Indians, near New London.
>
> Her mother, born in Windham, Conn., traced her ancestry
> through the Harrises and Allens, of Rhode Island, to its founder,
> Roger Williams. . . .
>
> The father, a man of rare intellectual endowments, considering a
> thorough knowledge of the elementary branches of vital importance,
> adopted a rigid mental discipline with his daughter, which was
> rendered more tolerable for the young girl by the tactful but not
> less conscientious guidance of her more vivacious mother. (*EW*, 352)

The description of her father's regimen implies a criticism of the strict,
distant, and unbending father (not too unlike John Clemens, Sam Clemens's
father), at least of his methods if not of his goals. The image of the rigid
father is overshadowed in her sketch, however, by her detailed reminiscence
of the impression made on her as a girl by Emma Willard, the head of Troy
Female Seminary:

> Who can forget that stately woman in her trailing black satin, with
> its complement of rich lace, and a most impressive turban, which she
> wore like a crown.
>
> She had the bearing of a queen—a gracious queen withal, and the
> Seminary girls were her reverent and loyal and loving subjects.
>
> No article of the Seminary creed was more thoroughly inculcated
> by the precepts and example of her successors, than the fact that Mrs.
> Emma Willard was the head of the institution. (*EW*, 353)

She describes her "vision" of "a graceful woman in ruby velvet, pale blue
ostrich tips in her coiffure, standing upon a slightly elevated dais, receiving
her guests with a matchless air of good-breeding." This vision is contrasted
with the image of the girl Mary Mason "mischievously peering through
the windows of the great hall" from her "point of vantage on the top of
a treacherous barrel" (*EW*, 353).

---

patching up of their closeness. However, nothing ever altered the fundamental respect and
affection in which they both held each other.

In a larger sense, Mary Mason's "vision" of an authoritative woman, in charge of her social surroundings, undoubtedly a model for her own exercise of social authority on board the *Quaker City,* contrasts starkly with the diffident, apologetic "Myra" who appears intermittently in the *Cleveland Herald* letters obeying other, conflicting demands of feminine decorum. Within the realms of education and of the home, Mary Mason Fairbanks was empowered to exercise authority, but in the broader realm of public life, her awareness of the expectations of gendered identity created self-effacements such as the pseudonym Myra or the formulaic disclaimers about her literary ability. Considering the implicit conflicts contained in these contrasting roles, her concluding self-assessment in the autobiographical sketch in *Emma Willard and Her Pupils* is particularly revealing, for she casts her life choices in terms of career and work, and does so in ways that imply an inner conflict between professionalism and domesticity. Interestingly enough, among many specific events that she narrates from her life, she makes no mention of her friendship with Samuel Clemens: "Although somewhat literary in her tastes, Mrs. Fairbanks chose rather to devote herself to a domestic career. It has been said of her 'that she held the pen of a ready writer.' She has been an occasional contributor to magazines, and a frequent newspaper correspondent, having traveled extensively at home and abroad, but it has been chiefly in the domestic sphere that she has found her work" (*EW,* 354).

Recognition of this conflict and of the particular ways in which Mary Mason Fairbanks chose to harmonize the warring elements of it, such as her almost ritual invocation of homesickness for her children while she was abroad as if to fend off accusations (internal or external) of having abandoned her children, allows us to see ways in which her relationship with Samuel Clemens, and the forms they both chose to give that relationship, enabled her to exercise authority in a realm that was cast in the metaphor of family life but that in fact impinged upon the public life of letters, writing, and the national consciousness. Through their friendship, Sam Clemens gained access to and assurance in the social realm inhabited by Mary Mason Fairbanks. She in turn gained the knowledge that she was helping to educate and shape a writer of national stature. She was empowered to do so through playing a role that, though its nickname was "Mother," allowed her to combine some of the attributes of the queenly Emma Willard with the exercise of the talents of a newspaper correspondent whose signature, Myra, was after all only a reshuffling of the letters of her familiar name, which in retrospect can be interpreted as symbolizing her rearrangement of traditional expectations to suit her own ends.[19]

19. An earlier version of this essay was published as " 'Lasting Oblications': The Friendship of Samuel Clemens and Mary Mason Fairbanks" in the *Mark Twain Journal* 34:2 (fall 1996): 7–16.

Mark Twain's Mechanical Marvels

JEFFREY STEINBRINK

The first summer of the last decade of the nineteenth century had just begun; on the twenty-third of June 1890, nearly the longest day of what was to be his final year in Hartford, Samuel Clemens made his way to a machine shop in the city's Colt Arms Factory. There he would spend an uncharacteristically pensive afternoon in the company of the Paige Compositor, the mechanical marvel that he seriously, even passionately, regarded as a fitting capstone to the Industrial Revolution. As the marvel did its intricate work, composing and automatically justifying lines of print, then breaking them down and remarkably resorting types, Clemens looked on in stunned satisfaction. "I have been sitting by the machine for 2 1/2 hours," he later wrote his friend Joe Goodman, " . . . & my admiration of it towers higher than ever. There is no mistake about it, it is the Big Bonanza." There before Clemens was the massive technological harbinger of a new age, an instrument of such power and complexity as to dwarf the mere humans who brought it into existence even as it bore witness to their genius. At two and one-half tons, with eighteen thousand precisely engineered parts, the Compositor intimated to Clemens that he was confronting something of a scale different from his own and from anything that had gone before. "This machine," he said, "is totally without rival."[1]

Perhaps because Clemens's dalliance with the Paige Compositor was so dramatic and its outcome so catastrophic, we sometimes fail to acknowledge that his interest in technology was lifelong—a chronic, persistent fascination, not just another of the eruptions he experienced in his later years. And

---

1. Typescript in Mark Twain Papers, Berkeley, Calif. Quotations from Clemens's letters dated 1867–1868 are drawn from *MTL2*. Those from letters dated 1870–1871 are drawn from *Mark Twain's Letters*, vol. 4, *1870–1871*; hereafter referred to as *MTL4*.

while contemporary critics have begun to attend to the overall importance of technology in the play of his mind, my purpose here is to begin by shifting that focus squarely to the beginning of Mark Twain's career, when he was negotiating his prerogatives as a writer of books for the first time, and then to consider his lifelong tendency to deal figuratively with writing as a mechanical process.[2] I want in particular to explore two industrially generated marvels that are in some ways as remarkable as the Compositor. The first is Clemens's early attempt to fashion a machine of sorts to do much of the work of writing; the second, his construction of mechanistic metaphors for the creative process, metaphors that I believe so effectively unfettered him as to enable that process to go on.

To imagine Mark Twain's writing machine and the circumstances from which it arose, it may help to look to a scene that took place more than two decades before Clemens's reverie in the Colt Arms Factory and in doing so to move briefly from Hartford, Connecticut, to Newark, New Jersey. There, on January 23, 1868, a machine of an apparently different sort, a wonder of the age known as the Newark Steam Man, was making its debut. According to historian of popular culture Everett F. Bleiler, the Steam Man was a seven-foot automaton

> with a 6 horse-power steam engine in its belly. Its legs were double-jointed, so that the knees could bend backward or forward, and its arms reached down to grasp the shafts of a small carriage that carried fuel, perhaps a passenger or two, and controls. Its feet were spiked with strong springs to retract them at each step. Its head, which had a face and hat, concealed a smoke stack and a whistle. The device was clothed so that it would not frighten the horses.[3]

---

2. For contemporary interpretations of Clemens's attitudes toward technology, see especially Sherwood Cummings, *Mark Twain and Science: Adventures of a Mind.* Also useful are John Lauber, *The Inventions of Mark Twain;* and Jennifer L. Rafferty, "Mark Twain, Labor, and Technology: *A Connecticut Yankee* and *No. 44, the Mysterious Stranger.*" For an informed discussion of Clemens's awareness of scientific and pseudoscientific developments in the early 1870s, see Howard G. Baetzhold, "Mark Twain on Scientific Investigation: Contemporary Allusions in 'Some Learned Fables for Good Old Boys and Girls.' " For an interesting pictorial account of the Paige Compositor debacle, see Judith Yaross Lee, "Anatomy of a Fascinating Failure," 55–60.

3. Bleiler, whose interest in the Steam Man focuses primarily on its role in spawning science fiction, goes on to say that after an initial flurry of interest Dederick's invention was

To a person sitting in the beer garden where it was exhibited that day, the Newark Steam Man might have seemed the Big Bonanza. It, or he, almost certainly did to his inventor, Zadoc P. Dederick, who imagined the Steam Man reaching speeds of sixty miles per hour, an accomplishment that would have made a ride in that carriage of his an outing to remember. The Steam Man was a fitting icon of the time, a time of considerable unfocused and uncritical enthusiasm for technological promise, a time when an even more complex piece of imaginative work, Mark Twain, was about to achieve international celebrity.

It happened that on the very day the Steam Man was lumbering from table to table in that Newark beer garden, Samuel Clemens was in Hartford making a contract with Elisha Bliss for the book he would eventually call *The Innocents Abroad*. This, too, was to be a bonanza. "This great American Publishing Company kept on trying to bargain with me for a book," Clemens bragged the next day in a letter to his family. "But I had my mind made up to *one* thing—I wasn't going to touch a book unless there was *money* in it, & a good deal of it" (*MTL2*, Jan. 24, 1868). "I have a very easy contract," he wrote the same day to his *Quaker City* confidante Mary Fairbanks. "I have from now till the middle of July in which to get the manuscript ready. I shall use nearly all my old letters (revamped,) but still many a chapter will be entirely new" (ibid.).

If the Newark Steam Man literally embodied a generation's expectation that human-seeming machines might soon be doing human work, Clemens's Hartford contract for *The Innocents Abroad* signaled his intention to do some arduous and ancient human work—book writing—as "easily" as he could. *His* labor-saving devices were not (yet) mechanical, or at least not as mechanical as that of Zadoc P. Dederick. They included the cut-and-paste revamping of his own newspaper letters, as he acknowledges to Mary Fairbanks; his willingness to "smouch" freely from contemporary guidebooks and travel literature; and his appropriation of Fairbanks's own newspaper letters—the twenty-seven "Myra" letters she had published in the *Cleveland Herald*—as fodder for his mill. "I am ever so grateful to you

---

apparently ignored by the press. "What happened to the Newark Steam Man?" he asks. "No one knows" ("Dime Novel Science-Fiction").

for sending me those copies of the *Herald*," he told her. "I see a good many ideas in your letters that I can steal" (ibid.).

So the art of writing—at least of book writing—was for Mark Twain in his early career the art of collage. *The Innocents Abroad* could be assembled from parts, he thought, some of them not necessarily of his own making. Even those that were his own were of varying vintage and pedigree, some carefully woven into a larger narrative fabric, some simply tacked on here and there like shabby annexes. This piece-by-piece approach to book building, mechanical in the most rudimentary way, arose pretty clearly out of a nagging doubtfulness on Clemens's part about the sufficiency of his imagination to invent a book from scratch. It saw him through the production of *The Innocents Abroad*, although by no means as blithely as he had suggested to Mary Fairbanks. It was when he turned to writing a second book—by this time a married man, supposedly a "serious" man, living in Buffalo— that the anxieties of authorship became painfully real to him. And so it was in Buffalo, twenty years before sitting reverently by the Compositor on that summer day in Hartford, that his preoccupation with industrial technology gave rise to an invention that, had it worked, would have been even more baffling than Paige's marvel. For in Buffalo, in a frenzy of desperate ingenuity, he contrived to build a Mark Twain Machine—an instance of human engineering that would mine the raw ore of experience, convert it to anecdotal ingots, refine those ingots to running feet of narrative, and finally emblazon that narrative with a texture and finish characteristic of Mark Twain.

During those Buffalo days, it seems, *everybody* was inventing. To read Clemens's letters of the time is to get the impression that dreaming up new gadgets or tinkering with old ones was a thriving cottage industry. As Clemens was moving to the city in 1869, Walt Whitman was writing *Passage to India*, "Singing the strong light works of engineers," singing "a worship new" for "captains, explorers, . . . architects, . . . machinists, noble inventors, . . . scientists," the contemporary heroes who were making a reality of the dream of Columbus. In some of the more sustained nonironic passages of his own *Innocents Abroad*, published that year, Mark Twain joins in praising, for instance, the engineers responsible for the broad, straight highways of France and the sons and daughters of science he finds commemorated in Paris's Père la Chaise cemetery, "illustrious men and women who were born to no titles, but achieved fame by their own energy and their own genius."[4]

Within the next few years Clemens would become more than ever caught up in the developing machine technology of his day, which is saying quite a bit, given that he had come of age in the shadow of the printing press and served his novitiate aboard the Mississippi steamboat—arguably the most charismatic instance of technology of mid-nineteenth-century America.[5] He was particularly distracted by the chronic gadgeteering of his brother Orion, who came in the late 1860s and 1870s to be identified in the Clemens clan as a sort of mechanical prodigy, ever on the verge of cobbling together the contraption that would make his fortune. Even *Mollie* Clemens, Orion's wife and a person not easily distracted from her other maladies, was at one point bitten by the inventing bug. While she was off taking the water cure in Elmira, Orion wrote to her, "Sam is fixing up another invention, and he has me to help him. Sit down . . . and study out yours while you are there. That kind of mental medicine will be best for you."[6]

So in the third quarter of the last century the Buffalo air was thick with the brimstone taste of manufacture, and the sidewalks were crowded with would-be engineers. It was in this atmosphere that Clemens was to try to become a writer of books, and no longer primarily a lecturer or a journalist, or even the editor of the *Buffalo Express*, the mission that had brought him to the city in the first place. And it was in Buffalo that Clemens first came to grips with the awful, fretful agony of trying to write a book from scratch. It was there that he learned to fear that he might never be a writer at all. Ironically, Clemens had come to Buffalo expecting to be happier than he had ever been in his life; settling down there with his bride, Olivia, was to make of Buffalo the next best thing to paradise. He left about a year and a

---

4. Twain, *The Innocents Abroad*, 111. Hereafter referred to as *IA*.

5. The best inventory of Clemens's involvement, early and late, with the machine technology of his day is provided in Thomas Grant, "The Artist of the Beautiful: Mark Twain's Investment in the Machine Inventor." "At one time or another," says Grant, "he pursued such diverse projects as a steam generator, a steam pulley, a railroad steam brake, a cash register, a hand grenade, a carpet design machine, a textile designing machine, a steam-from-coal extracting process, a cure for chilblains and a skimmmed-milk cure-all called Plasmon; also a watch company, a portable mosquito net frame, a spiral hat pin and a bedsheet clamp. Three projects became patented: an adjustable garment strap, a pre-gummed scrapbook, and a history game" (59–60).

6. Sept. 6, 1871, Mark Twain Papers.

half later, loathing the city—to use his own word—his wife so weak with illness and fatigue that she had to be carried off on a mattress. On the eve of escaping he wrote his publisher, "I had rather die twice over than repeat the last six months of my life" (*MTL4*, Mar. 17, 1871).

Many critics, myself among them, have attributed Clemens's misery in Buffalo largely to the personal and family troubles that beset him while he, and then he and Olivia, lived there, altogether from August 1869 to March 1871 (*GBMT*, 113–66). There is much to be said for that argument, not the least of which is that Clemens himself was the first to make it, complaining, for example, as he was about to leave the city that such were his agonies there that he felt, as he said in a letter to Elisha Bliss, "the vials of hellfire bottled up for my benefit must be about emptied" (*MTL4*, Mar. 17, 1871). The personal calamities Clemens suffered in Buffalo were no doubt real and telling, and probably for that reason they have come almost to eclipse our recognition of the professional crisis he experienced there, in my estimation the single most formative crisis of his career.

Clemens's move to Buffalo in the summer of 1869 coincided with the publication of *The Innocents Abroad,* his first real book and one that to his surprise wasted little time becoming a national and then an international best-seller. Again, *The Innocents Abroad* was *not* a scratch-built book, but one whose narrative frame and scaffolding were already in place when Clemens came to "write" it. Only when his anxious and solicitous publisher contracted with him, in July 1870, to write a *second* real book did Clemens's problems begin in earnest. Through that summer and fall, with illnesses and deathbed watches to torment him, Clemens sought to make that second book happen and very largely failed. As the deadline by which he was supposed to hand over the completed manuscript—January 1, 1871—approached, the book was hardly begun. *"I am sitting still with idle hands,"* he wailed to Orion (*MTL4*, Nov. 11, 1870). It was a posture to which his first year in Buffalo had accustomed him.

Clemens was daunted by the idea of producing a six hundred–page book—that is, between eighteen hundred and two thousand manuscript pages—out of his own head, his own imagination. He inventoried his personal history for some set of *Innocents*-like adventures to draw upon, and he hit, not very surprisingly and for his part not very enthusiastically, on the other major excursion of his life, his trip west with Orion in 1861.

Perhaps he wouldn't have to *make up* a book, after all; he could recollect and embellish another narrative out of his own experience. And he could draw upon Orion's experiences, too: it wasn't long before he was writing to offer one thousand dollars in future royalties for the notebook Orion kept during the overland stage journey. "Do you remember any of the scenes, names, incidents or adventures of the coach trip?" he asked his brother, "— for I remember next to *nothing* about the matter" (*MTL4*, July 15, 1870). At his request his family in St. Louis shipped him a trunk full of newspaper clippings from his California days. He was gathering his materials—trying, in effect, to patch together the extant record of his own earlier escapades, to cut and paste his way through his second book much as he had his first.

By one definition or another, all writers can be said to write from experience. At this point in his career, at least in the book form, Clemens was inclined to write very directly and often quite literally from his. This was in part a natural enough consequence of his early training as a journalist, but it was more intimately connected to the unspoken compact that had arisen between him and his audience: whether in his lectures or in his books, that audience expected to be treated to the adventures of Mark Twain. In trying to write this second book a pattern took shape at some level of Clemens's consciousness: his own history was to be excavated for "adventures," the raw narrative material across which the writer would let play the personality of Mark Twain, a kind of superheated and funnier version of himself, thereby producing essentially picaresque episodes that could be assembled into six-hundred-page products to be marketed by Bliss's army of subscription agents.

Perhaps it was only when Clemens thought of his books as coming into being according to this mercantile-industrial model that he could carry on as a writer at all. To think of them otherwise—as the fruits of genius, for instance, or as the results of patient, imaginative labor—was simply too intimidating, too much at odds with his quirky but persistent self-doubt. It was in Buffalo that he developed this mechanistic and ironically liberating way of envisioning his work. And it was in Buffalo that a Mark Twain Machine took tangible form.

Clemens's asking Orion for notes and recollections about the western trip was a tacit acknowledgment on his part that the writer-as-story-processor might be helped at some point in the enterprise by another person. At about the same time he was writing Orion, in the summer of 1870, Clemens struck a bargain that caused that possibility to stand out in higher relief: Olivia's brother Charles was about to embark on a round-the-world tour in the company of Prof. Darius Ford of Elmira College. Clemens proposed that Ford send him descriptive letters from various ports of call along their route, letters that he—or Mark Twain—would then edit, augment, and publish in the *Express* under the title "Around the World." When these pieces appeared in the *Express,* most were accompanied by the following headnote: "These letters are written by Professor D. R. Ford and Mark Twain. The former does the actual traveling, and such facts as escape his notice are supplied by the latter, who remains at home."[7]

So here is a further and more explicit development of the process: as we might imagine it in contemporary terms, Ford was to furnish the play-by-play, Clemens the color commentary. In fact we do have to imagine it because the scheme never came to fruition. Ford was so long in providing his first letter that Clemens started the series without him, writing a cappella about the American West. Ford finally managed to produce just two letters, which Clemens simply published without alteration before dropping the series altogether.

But the basic steps of manufacture had been established: a journeyman correspondent, a surrogate, *could* go into the field and send back accounts of his own adventures to be processed through the Mark Twain mill. The work of adventuring could be subcontracted; the newlywed writer, having forsworn his bachelor wanderlust, could remain at home in Buffalo; and a Mark Twain Machine might be set into almost perpetual motion, since it was no longer limited to the resources of Clemens's own experience for its raw material.

It took the particular desperation of that long first winter in Buffalo to bring this scheme to its manic apotheosis. Sitting with idle hands, the impossible deadline for his second book just a month away, Clemens proposed *another* project to Elisha Bliss, one that would carry surrogacy about as far

---

7. The series of "Around the World" letters ran in the *Buffalo Express,* where Clemens was an editor. Despite his plans for a collaboration with Ford, he published the first eight letters on his own, from Oct. 16, 1869, to Jan. 29, 1870. Two from Ford, with no emendations on the part of Mark Twain, were published on Feb. 12 and Mar. 5, 1870.

as it could go, as far, in fact, as the tip of Africa. "I have put my greedy hands on the best man in America for my purpose," he wrote Bliss, "*& shall start him to the diamond fields of South Africa within a fortnight, at my expense. I shall write a book of his experiences for next spring,* . . . spring of '72, & write it just as if I had been through it all myself" (*MTL4*, Nov. 28, 1870). Clemens's best man in America was John Henry Riley, a friend from his Washington days who was about to become the moving part in the Mark Twain Machine. After three months' adventuring and note taking in the diamond fields Riley was to return to the States for debriefing. "You come to my house at the end of your labors," Clemens wrote him, "& live with me, at $50 a month & board, (I to furnish the cigars,) from 4 to 12 months, till I have pumped you dry." Among the inducements Clemens offered Riley was the prospect of establishing him in the lecture field, another process that he could make sound like being run through a fabricating mill: "I want to 'coach' you, thoroughly, drill you completely (for it took me 3 or 4 years to learn the *dead sure* tricks of the platform, but I could teach them to you in 3 or 4 weeks . . .)" (*MTL4*, Dec. 2, 1870).

Riley went to Africa, to fill himself like a cistern with experiences that Clemens could later tap and eventually "pump dry." "I don't care two cents whether there is a diamond in all Africa or not," Clemens wrote Bliss; "the adventurous narrative & its wild, new fascination is what I want" (*MTL4*, Nov. 28, 1870). Clearly, the work of accumulating this adventurous narrative was to fall entirely to Riley. But the work of writing—the actual composition of the book—was to be partly his as well; the process was to be broken into constituent steps, of which Clemens's was simply the last. Upon his return Riley was to sit with Clemens and "a good, appreciative, genial phonographic reporter who can listen first rate, & enjoy, & even throw in a word, now & then. Then we'll all light our cigars every morning, & with your notes before you, we'll talk & yarn & laugh & weep over your adventures, & the said reporter shall take it *all* down, [until finally] away you go for Africa again & leave me to work up & write out the book at my leisure" (*MTL4*, Jan. 4, 1872). Cigars, laughter, tears, and even a stenographer who throws in an occasional word—once this remarkable apparatus was set in motion, the book would almost write itself.

Not too much later in his career Clemens would in fact begin to talk about books writing themselves. This would change the metaphor a bit, making the writer himself the "tank" or cistern in which, somehow, the elements of a story accumulated. But it shared with the more articulated industrial model—the Mark Twain Machine—a single, salient characteristic: it enormously eased the writer's burden of creative responsibility. Having a book write itself might in fact be taken as an elegant refinement of the industrial model, in which *lots* of people contribute to writing the book, just as lots do to the construction of a steamboat or a dynamo.

Consider the Mark Twain Machine in motion. Imagine yourself sitting by it through a June afternoon; it is the Big Bonanza. Riley spills out his vigorous, raw narrative; it is flecked with diamonds, or at least with diamond hunting. Clemens picks it up here and there, improves on it, adds to it. The phonographic reporter gathers it all in, even contributing a stroke of his own from time to time. Later, at his leisure, Clemens completes the assembly and gives it its final polish.

None of this ever came to pass. The Mark Twain Machine proved to be even more a pipe dream than the Paige Compositor that it preceded by almost two decades: by the time Riley returned, brimful, from the diamond fields in 1871, Clemens had written his way out of the catatonia that had provoked him to contrive the Machine in the first place. "Let the diamond fever swell & sweat," he wrote Riley, putting him off; "we'll try to catch it at the right moment" (*MTL4*, Oct. 9, 1871). But never mind. Riley could throw his energies into trying to patent a diamond-sifting and -washing machine that he had been tinkering with. When Riley died of cancer of the mouth in September 1872, Clemens had occasion to realize that he had never found time to pump him dry.

By that time Clemens and his family were well out of Buffalo, and that second book, which turned out to be *Roughing It*, was not only written but also published. In a way the Mark Twain Machine had done its work, even though only one of its parts had ever been set in motion. For it provided Clemens the myth or metaphor he needed as he gained distance from Buffalo and the failures he had experienced there. Constructing the Machine was a way of asserting that writing was not a lonely, isolated, idiosyncratic undertaking that depended on the vagaries of genius or talent. The myth behind the Machine was that writing could be an ordinary-enough fabricating process, one without much mystery or magic about it, one whose operation was certainly less complicated than that of a good steamboat, one that could in fact be subcontracted and mutually negotiated in a busi-nesslike atmosphere of cigar smoke and stenography. That myth, borne of early misery, proved continuously useful and durable to a writer with vast insecurities about the ability of his unaided imagination to conjure whole books. Because he could never entirely appease the anxieties of authorship, writing remained a conjuring act whose mysteries Clemens respected and preserved in the metaphors, often the mechanical metaphors, he chose to describe it.[8]

In 1888, twenty years after the Steam Man roamed Newark, New Jersey, a minister named George Bainton wrote Clemens, as he had other notable au-thors, for his "personal testimony . . . upon the art of Composition." Bain-ton would go on to compile and publish the results two years later in book form.[9] Clemens responded in a letter to Bainton, circumspectly at first. "I am not sure that I have methods in composition," he said. But as he warmed to his task, he ventured a Lego-like metaphor for the writer's mind:

> Let us guess that whenever we read a sentence & like it, we uncon-sciously store it away in our model-chamber; & it goes, with the myriad of its fellows, to the building, brick by brick, of the eventual edifice which we call our style. . . . If I have subjected myself to any training processes—& no doubt I have—it must have been in this unconscious or half-conscious fashion. I think it unlikely that delib-erate & consciously methodical training is usual with the craft.

The writer is passive here, and fortunate, and trained—as Clemens could claim to have been—"unconsciously," not systematically or expensively or even deliberately. Writers are born, the piece implies, and endowed in particular with "an automatically-working taste—a taste which selects, & rejects, without asking you for any help, & patiently & steadily improves itself without troubling you to approve or applaud; yes, & likely enough, when the structure is at last pretty well up, & attracts attention, *you* feel

---

8. Edgar M. Branch refers perceptively to a number of these metaphors ("Newspaper Reading and the Writer's Creativity," 576–603).

9. The letter is dated Oct. 6, 1888; typescript in Mark Twain Papers. Clemens's response is included in *The Art of Authorship: Literary Reminiscences, Methods of Work, and Advice to Young Beginners,* 85–89.

complimented—whereas you didn't build it, & didn't even consciously superintend."

In this scheme "taste" is a wonderful mechanism, or agency, that works behind the scenes like a mason's apprentice, choosing just the right specimens from the cartloads of style bricks that the writer's unmediated experience dumps at the building site. The writer's conscious, intentional faculties need not be much sharper than those of the Steam Man as he lumbers through the world indiscriminately accumulating bricks.

The attractiveness of such a metaphor for an author anxious about his own powers of invention is obvious; he is responsible for little more than staying awake while he reads as his unconscious and "automatically-working taste" does all the work, the creative work, of style building. The writer's consciousness remains inactive. "Doubtless I have methods," Clemens said finally to Bainton, "but they begot themselves; in which case I am only their proprietor, not their father."

As he gave the matter further thought, Clemens was resourceful in finding ways to outdo even this scheme, minting metaphors that cast even the writer's *un*conscious in a passive role. In the 1895 essay "What Paul Bourget Thinks of Us," Clemens insists that no foreigner, in this case no Paul Bourget, can capture the "interior [of a nation]—its soul, its life, its speech, its thought." Outsiders can only "photograph the exteriors." "I think," Clemens goes on, "that a knowledge of these things is acquirable in only one way; not two or four or six—*absorption;* years and years of unconscious absorption."[10] Now even the writer's *unconscious* has a soft job—certainly a softer job than bricklaying. It soaks in the writer's (and the nation's) experience, accumulating over slow time the flavor of that unfiltered broth. Unlike the (comparatively) hardworking agency of taste, which tirelessly selects the elements of his brick style house, the writer's absorptive unconscious simply steeps.

The writer's conscious, deliberate, intentional efforts have no show against this inert, unhurried karmic sponge. The Paul Bourgets of the world are merely restless gnats, flitting from place to place with only their dutifully and deliberately gathered observations to drive their work. "Observation?"

10. The essay appeared in the January 1895 issue of the *North American Review* and is reprinted in *Mark Twain's Works,* 141–64.

Clemens sneers, "Of what real value is it? One learns peoples through the heart, not the eyes or the intellect. . . . How much of [a writer's] competency is derived from conscious 'observation'? The amount is so slight that it counts for next to nothing in the equipment. Almost the whole capital of the novelist is the slow accumulation of *un*conscious observation—absorption." This last line completes, or extends, the metaphor as the absorptive powers of the writer's unconscious are imagined somehow to distill or refine the raw broth of experience to the point where it becomes precious, becomes in fact the all but exclusive source of the writer's "capital." No amount of work, no discipline or learning or taking charge, can mimic or offset this slow, inexorable accretion of wealth. A writer's sensibilities might do better than another person's at amassing this capital—they might provide a richer distillate—but they do so as a result of no greater effort on the writer's part. As in each of these metaphors, the implication is that they do so without *any* effort on the writer's part.

With only a small caveat the same can be said about the best known of Clemens's metaphorical renderings of the art of writing, a meditation recorded among his autobiographical dictations for 1906: "As long as a book would write itself I was a faithful and interested amanuensis and my industry did not flag, but the minute that the book tried to shift to *my* head the labor of contriving its situations, inventing its adventures and conducting its conversations, I put it away and dropped it out of my mind."[11] The writer does have deliberate work to do here, but only as an amanuensis. In the mix of prerogatives and responsibilities that tumble through the metaphor it is clearly the least creative kind of work. The elements in the mix are just the same as those Clemens proposed to John Henry Riley more than thirty years earlier, but the assignments have changed: the book itself has now by implication assumed Riley's role of providing situations, adventures, and conversations, the raw resources from which stories come. But unlike Riley, who in fact went abroad to experience situations, adventures, and conversations, the book makes them up; it *contrives and invents,* and it is in doing so, in accomplishing the richest and most original imaginative

---

11. These particular dictations are reprinted in Bernard DeVoto, ed., *Mark Twain in Eruption: Hitherto Unpublished Pages about Men and Events by Mark Twain,* under the subtitle "When a Book Gets Tired," 196–97.

work, that it most profoundly "writes itself." Clemens personally will have none of this work. He has taken on only the responsibilities of the "good, appreciative, genial phonographic reporter," the hired hand "who can listen first rate, & enjoy, & even throw in a word, now & then."

The writer's unconscious goes unmentioned in this rendition. All volition rests in the book and not, Clemens stipulates, "in *my* head"—not even in that part of his head of which he is unaware and for which he is not responsible. When the book refused to do its work, he says, "I . . . dropped it out of my mind." Books have minds of their own, minds apparently as given to torpor and distraction as their human counterparts. "A book is pretty sure to get tired, along about the middle," Clemens observes, "and refuse to go on with its work until its powers and its interest should have been refreshed by a rest and its depleted stock of raw materials reinforced by lapse of time." Unlike the Newark Steam Man, the Mark Twain Machine, and the Paige Compositor (in their perfected forms), a book is organic by nature and subject therefore to exhaustion and crotchetiness.

In the middle of writing *Tom Sawyer,* Clemens says, "the story made a sudden and determined halt and refused to proceed another step. Day after day it still refused." On the metaphoric level this is an especially interesting turn for the story to take, for where just a while ago it was contriving situations and inventing adventures, typically the work of human agency, here it behaves more like a Nevada miner's donkey or a Genuine Mexican Plug. One way to resolve this discontinuity, this apparently mixed metaphor, might be to suppose that in 1906, as he was dictating these notions, the differences in Clemens's estimation between the beauties of the human mind and those of the Nevada jackass were not great. But Clemens's own solution is to send the metaphor through yet another twist: the story refused to proceed another step, he says, because "my tank had run dry; it was empty; the stock of materials in it was exhausted; the story could not go on without materials; it could not be wrought out of nothing. . . . When the tank runs dry you've only to leave it alone and it will fill up again in time, while you are asleep—also while you are at work at other things and are quite unaware that this unconscious and profitable cerebration is going on."

The tank here is *my* tank—that is, the writer's tank, not the book's. For all its stand-alone organic willfulness and creativity, the story must depend on the writer, as Clemens had proposed depending on Riley, to provide a "stock of materials." The writer remains as resolutely inert and involuntary and stolid as ever in this scheme of things, and so is appropriately imagined *in*organically, as a cistern. The writer's responsibility, if it can be so called, is to leave the tank alone, perhaps to sleep, and, as ever, to remain "unaware that this unconscious and profitable cerebration is going on." Once the tank had thought its way full, he says, "There was plenty of material . . . , and the book went on and finished itself without any trouble."

In the end Clemens fashioned a better, a more useful, Mark Twain Machine out of metaphors than he did earlier using less-durable and less-dependable human parts. It served him better than the Steam Man did Zadoc P. Dederick in the beer gardens of New Jersey. For it released him from the anxiety of authorship by allowing him to suppose that the art of writing was a gift rather than a job, an endowment rather than a responsibility. Books just happened. Stories flowed effortlessly from reservoirs filled by hidden springs, or they were tapped from rich veins that accreted through long, slow absorption. Stories wrote themselves; a gifted writer was actually a stenographer, allowing the words through. In another time, or another metaphor, he might have been called "possessed" or thought of as recording the music of his muse.

A writer was certainly *not* simply a man or a woman with a pen, a stack of blank paper, and only his or her ingenuity to depend on. A writer was not a conscious artisan who did a great deal of deliberate work. A writer was not accountable for the logic, the continuity, or the implications of his productions. A writer never had to worry about management, discipline, coherence, or details. A writer would not run out of ideas or energy or nerve. A writer was not alone. He had the machinery of metaphor, churning more urgently than a six-horsepower steam engine, to convince him that the books would surely write themselves, that the tank would surely fill.

Steamboats, Cocaine, and Paper Money

Mark Twain Rewriting Himself

ROBERT SATTELMEYER

Instantly recognizable in his white suit and matching halo of wispy white hair, in the first decade of the twentieth century Mark Twain was not only a national institution but also, as he put it only somewhat hyperbolically, the "most conspicuous person on the planet."[1] As fame and adulation increased, though, a succession of family tragedies left him despondent and increasingly pessimistic about the human condition. "Whoever has lived long enough to find out what life is," goes a saying in Pudd'nhead Wilson's Calendar, "knows how deep a debt of gratitude we owe to Adam, the first great benefactor of our race. He brought death into the world."

In our day as well as in his own times, the public has tended to overlook this change, understandably preferring images of boys whitewashing fences or of a raft drifting on the Mississippi to the bitter pill of his late satires on "the damned human race." Twain himself, of course, is partly responsible for this happy misperception by virtue of having created so compelling a myth of his boyhood world. Nowhere is this myth more powerful and more appealing than in "Old Times on the Mississippi," his account of how he became a steamboat pilot. But his darkening vision of human nature gradually affected his remembrance of his own life, and in his final years, in his autobiography and in an essay called "The Turning Point of My Life," Twain returned to this period and remembered it in quite different terms. In these late autobiographical works he changed the familiar picture of his early life and altered its imputed trajectory in unsettling ways.

---

1. Everett Emerson, *Mark Twain: A Literary Life*, 291.

One of Twain's best-known wisecracks describes the unreliability of his memory: "When I was younger I could remember anything, whether it happened or not; but I am getting old, and soon I shall remember only the latter."[2] Since the object of humor is to displace the serious, we should be wary of freighting this remark with too much significance. Yet, it does remind us that memory and imagination are often indistinguishable. In Mark Twain's case the relationship is even more complicated, for he tends not so much to embellish his early life as periodically to reinvent it in order to explain the present. Moreover, his life, or rather his telling of it, sometimes imitates art and actually borrows from his own fiction.

In "Old Times on the Mississippi," the series of sketches about piloting that he wrote for the *Atlantic Monthly* in 1875 and republished with additional material as *Life on the Mississippi* in 1883, Mark Twain first discovered and began to exploit what Henry Nash Smith felicitously called the Matter of the River and the Matter of Hannibal.[3] These memories of his boyhood world were the literary capital that would underwrite his greatest work, *Adventures of Huckleberry Finn,* as well as *The Adventures of Tom Sawyer, Pudd'nhead Wilson,* and *Life on the Mississippi* itself. Set against the background of this romantic and nostalgic evocation of the antebellum Mississippi Valley, he calls his desire to be a steamboat pilot the "one permanent ambition" in his life.[4] He glorifies the pilot as "the only unfettered and entirely independent human being that lived in the earth." Twain's richly detailed account of his apprenticeship amply testifies to the truth of his claim that he "loved the profession far better than any I have followed since" (*MTB,* 162). Small wonder that in popular iconography Twain often appears as the elderly sage with white hair and white suit (his most familiar public pose) anachronistically placed in the pilothouse of a steamboat.

What the opening image of "Old Times"—the sleepy small town, the great river, and the boys' ambitions to be steamboat men—leaves out are the harsh economic facts of the steamboat trade and the complex economic

2. Albert Bigelow Paine, *Mark Twain, a Biography: The Personal and Literary Life of Samuel Langhorne Clemens,* 3:269. Hereafter referred to as *MTB.*

3. H. N. Smith, *Mark Twain: The Development of a Writer,* 72.

4. Twain, *Life on the Mississippi* (Oxford ed.), 62. Hereafter referred to as *LOM.*

realities of his own career, both on and off the river. These realities really drove his decision to enter the trade and gradually came to dominate his later, money-tinged fables about getting his start in the profession. In fact, despite the twin poles of his image as elderly sage and naive youth, one of the truest and most pertinent titles of biographical works about him is *Mark Twain, Business Man,* a study written by his nephew Samuel C. Webster. No other American writer of his century came close to making, losing, and making again as much money as Mark Twain.

Throughout his life, business was the principal river he navigated and upon whose shoals and snags he periodically grounded. Even as a pilot he engaged in speculative business projects, and later, in the West, he traded mining stocks zealously, expecting to make a fortune. He achieved his major financial success as an author through subscription publishing, a low-prestige and especially profit-driven branch of the publishing industry. (Subscription books were sold door-to-door by canvassers carrying display kits of samples of the text and a choice of progressively more expensive bindings.)[5] More so even than most writers, Twain regarded his books as commodities to be marketed, and even had his famous pseudonym registered as a trademark. Eventually he formed his own publishing company, Charles L. Webster and Co., to publish books by other authors as well as his own. He used the income from his books and lecture tours for various investment schemes. Having patented a self-pasting scrapbook and invented a game for improving memory, he was especially attracted to inventions and new technology.

The most notable and unfortunate of these ventures was the Paige typesetter, into which he famously poured and lost more than a quarter million dollars. The failure of this machine led directly to his personal bankruptcy in 1894. He eventually recovered from this loss by new literary and lecturing projects, and by turning his business affairs over to Henry Huttleston Rogers, a vice president and director of the Standard Oil Company trust. Whatever he may have said about the American economic system in satirical works such as *The Gilded Age,* his own practices constituted an uncritical endorsement of it.

5. Hamlin Hill, *Mark Twain and Elisha Bliss,* is the best account of Mark Twain's relationship with the subscription publishing industry.

In this context, what we know from contemporary documents about his decision to take up piloting as a career—as opposed to his later account in "Old Times on the Mississippi" stressing its prestige and romantic appeal—consists mostly of economic information that can be told rather briefly. (It also bears remembering that Twain was not the naive adolescent he portrays in "Old Times" either: he was a widely traveled journeyman printer who had lived and worked at his trade in New York, Philadelphia, St. Louis, and Cincinnati before starting his career on the river.) Through his brother Orion's intercession with a distant cousin, James Clemens Jr., a wealthy St. Louis merchant, he tried unsuccessfully to get a cub pilot's berth in the summer of 1855. The following summer, in Keokuk, Iowa, while working in Orion's print shop, he and two local men began planning—conspiring in secret, actually—to go to South America, inspired by a recent (1853–1854) popular account of a government exploring expedition, *Exploration of the Valley of the Amazon,* by Lt. William Herndon and Lardner Gibbon. He wrote to his younger brother Henry that he hoped to leave in mid-September, travel to New York, and embark for Brazil the following March. He did leave Keokuk in mid-October, but traveled only as far as Cincinnati, where he spent the winter working as a printer. On April 15, 1857, he took passage for New Orleans on the steamboat *Paul Jones,* piloted by Horace Bixby, which was scheduled to switch over to the New Orleans–St. Louis route after this trip. He was probably still motivated by his South American scheme, though he had originally intended to leave from New York. Sometime during the trip downriver or in New Orleans, he arranged to become Bixby's cub. In exchange for learning the river, Twain agreed to pay Bixby five hundred dollars, one hundred dollars down (borrowed from another relative, his brother-in-law Will Moffett in St. Louis), and the balance to be paid when he received his license and began earning wages.[6]

These facts derive from contemporary evidence, principally family letters; almost none of the rich additional details he provided in the later narratives about this period can be corroborated by direct evidence. But the

6. Twain, *Mark Twain's Letters,* vol. 1, *1853–1866,* 58–71. Hereafter referred to as *MTL1.*

facts themselves suggest that Mark Twain's piloting career was less the ful-
fillment of a boyhood dream than a detour from the first (but of course by
no means the last) great strike-it-rich scheme of his life.

He grew up in an economic climate when to Americans, in the words of
Henry Adams's history of the early nineteenth century, "the continent lay
before them like an uncovered ore-bed."[7] He had lived through a decade
in Hannibal when a high percentage of its male population had joined the
rush to California for gold, as he would join the rush for silver in Nevada a
few years later. In the popular imagination he shared, the South American
continent could be thought of as a kind of extension of the West, with Lieutenant Herndon and his partner Lardner Gibbon as a latter-day Lewis and
Clark charting the water routes that would unlock its riches. In retrospect it
may seem preposterous to us, as it later did to Twain himself, that a pioneer-
ing expedition to the sources of the Amazon could be successfully mounted
by three men from Keokuk, Iowa, with no pertinent experience. But every
year of the 1850s saw thousands of men and boys set out on similarly ill-
equipped and half-baked expeditions for gold from California to Panama
and Australia.

To abandon this plan for an arduous, unpaid apprenticeship in the pilothouse of a steamboat was an economic gamble of another kind, as well as a
detour from his pursuit of the big strike, but doubtless what attracted Twain
were his prospective wages. Even in the opening passages of "Old Times on
the Mississippi," which present his boyhood ambition to go on the river
in mostly naive and nostalgic terms, he defines the pilot and his ambition
to become one in economic terms: "Pilot was the grandest position of all.
The pilot, even in those days of trivial wages, had a princely salary—from a
hundred and fifty to two hundred and fifty dollars a month, and no board
to pay." The real index of the pilot's wealth, though, was that "two months
of his wages would pay a preacher's salary for a year." Then he added another curious economic reason for wanting to be a pilot. After having been
snubbed by mates and clerks in his initial attempt to get on the river, he says
he dreamed "of a future when I should be a great and honored pilot, with

---

7. Adams, *History of the United States of America*, 9:173–74.

plenty of money, and could kill some of these mates and clerks and pay for them," as though the supreme value of money was as a medium of exchange for a human life (*LOM*, 68–69).

In a sense, this was true. The steamboat industry on western rivers was a business where profits could be made only if human life was regarded as cheap. In Louis C. Hunter's summation of the economics of the trade in *Steamboats on the Western Rivers,* it was "a branch of business enterprise organized on a small-scale and highly individualistic pattern in a manner characteristic of an age of petty capitalism. . . . The keenly competitive and peculiarly hazardous nature of the enterprise tended to keep the rank and file of steamboat operators much of the time in a precarious marginal position."[8] Boats were profitable to the extent that they ran risks: carrying too much steam, overloading freight or passengers, running dangerous chutes to save time, venturing into rivers at marginal water levels, and so forth. And these were in addition to the ordinary risks of operating powerful, highly incendiary wooden boats without navigational aids or lights on shifting, shallow, snag-infested rivers. Not surprisingly, the life expectancy of a Mississippi steamboat was four to five years.

Even if the boat did not explode, burn, or strike a snag and sink, there were other, more sinister dangers. The loss of life among crew members and deck passengers from accident, disease, neglect, and homicide was frequent. During the mid-1850s, corpses turned up at the levee in St. Louis at the rate of about one per day, and travelers' accounts frequently mention bodies floating in the river. Twain himself missed death by an eyelash at least once, when he was put off the steamboat *Pennsylvania* after a fight with a pilot on the way down to New Orleans. On the upriver trip, the *Pennsylvania*'s boilers exploded, and she burned, killing more than a hundred people, including Twain's younger brother Henry.

Twain painted a convincing picture of the stability and solidarity of the pilots' professional organization in "Old Times," but the economic realities of the pilot's life were minimal job security, berths that were usually transient, wages that fluctuated greatly, and, everywhere above Memphis, rivers that were liable to be shut or made prohibitively dangerous by low water or

8. Hunter, *Steamboats on the Western Rivers,* 389. The summary of the conditions of the steamboat trade that follows is drawn principally from Hunter.

ice much of the year. And, as the 1850s progressed, railroads began to siphon off more and more passenger and freight business, making the competition among steamboats for the remaining trade even fiercer and providing further disincentives for safety.

The expansion of the railroad system into the Mississippi Valley in the late fifties and early sixties signaled the end of the "flush times" of steamboating. Although it was masked by a temporary boom on the upper Mississippi and Missouri Rivers, brought on by the rapid settlement of the northern prairies, the decline of steamboats as the dominant mode of transportation was already under way by 1857 as Twain was just setting out on the river. In that year a rail line from St. Louis to Cincinnati opened. Ironically, when Twain went from Keokuk to Cincinnati in 1857, on the trip that would lead to his pilot career, he went by train. By the outbreak of the war, the railroad had been completed from New Orleans to Cairo, Illinois, at the junction of the Mississippi and the Ohio, where connections could be made to the east-west rail system.

These developments were harbingers of a much larger change, a shift in the prevailing direction of domestic trade from north-south to east-west and from water transportation to land transportation. What had in part made steamboats economically viable was the lack of a cheap and dependable means of conveyance across the Appalachian Mountains. This barrier had meant that transportation between the East Coast and the agricultural heartland was cheaper by water along the coast and up the Mississippi and its major tributaries. The railroads changed all that: they promoted the development of new cities such as Chicago along the east-west axis and marked a shift from an age of individualistic, petty capitalism to an age of large-scale oligopolistic and monopolistic business. Contrary to Twain's assertion and to popular belief, it was not the Civil War that crippled the steamboat trade. In fact, according to Hunter there was actually a revival of trade during the war.[9] The sweeping economic changes augured by the railroads were responsible, and these were already in progress by the time Twain met Horace Bixby.

Against this backdrop, it is not surprising that economic motivations and

9. Ibid., 389, 386.

accidents play an increasingly prominent role in Twain's accounts of how he came to end up on the river during the Indian summer of the steamboat era. In the first published account, "Old Times on the Mississippi," as we have seen, it was Twain's magnificently detailed and nostalgic remembrance of his boyhood on the river, along with his portrait of "the great Mississippi, the majestic, the magnificent Mississippi" itself that gives the romantic tone to his account of piloting. In this earliest version the South American scheme operates merely as a comic plot device to account for his meeting with Horace Bixby. Lieutenant Herndon, Twain wrote, "had not thoroughly explored a part of the country lying about the headwaters, some four thousand miles from the mouth of the river," and it was this little tract that he intended to seek out and explore with the fourteen dollars he had left after paying his passage to New Orleans. He found, he says, when he got to New Orleans, that no boats were likely to leave for the mouth of the Amazon for at least ten or twelve years, so he decided to try his hand at piloting (*LOM,* 64, 70, 79).

In the later accounts in the *Autobiography* and "The Turning Point in My Life," however, Twain reveals a much less quixotic purpose than exploration behind this Amazon scheme. Herndon (actually his partner, Lardner Gibbon) had described the Indians' age-old practice of chewing the leaves of the coca plant for its stimulating effects. According to Twain's version of Lardner and Gibbon in his "Turning Point" essay, this stimulant enabled the natives to "tramp up hill and down all day on a pinch of powdered coca and require no other sustenance." Twain said he was inspired by this account "with a longing to open up a trade in coca with all the world."[10]

The passage in Herndon and Gibbon that Twain refers to actually (if ungrammatically) describes the Indians' coca use as follows:

> The Indian brain, being excited by coca, he travels a long distance without feeling fatigue, while he has plenty of coca, he cares little for food. Therefore, after a journey he is worn out. In the city of Cuzco, where the Indians masticate the best quality of coca, they use it to excess. Their physical condition, compared with those who live far off from the coca market, . . . is thin, weak, and sickly; less cheerful,

10. Twain, "The Turning Point in My Life," 133.

and not so good looking. The chewers also use more brandy and less tamborine and fiddle; seldom dance or sing. Their expression of face is doleful, made hideous by green streaks of juice streaming from each corner of the mouth.[11]

If Twain's ambition in 1856 was really "to open a trade in coca with all the world," his own source told him that the object of his commercial ambitions was a potentially dangerous and debilitating drug. Certainly he knew it even better during the first decade of the twentieth century when he wrote the "Turning Point" essay and dictated essentially the same account for his autobiography. Publicity about the negative effects of cocaine had gradually replaced the praise of its many early enthusiasts (such as Sigmund Freud). The Pure Food and Drug Act of 1906 was the first of a series of increasingly stringent attempts to control its use. Significantly in this context, Twain's memoir describes the Indians' use of the drug—taking a "pinch of powdered coca"—in terms that could have been used only by someone familiar with cocaine, not coca, as a twentieth-century social problem. Herndon and Gibbon's report describes the Indians' chewing of wads of coca leaves, their age-old and only way of ingesting the drug. The chemical process for isolating cocaine from the coca plant was not perfected until around 1880, but by 1900, in addition to its presence in many patent medicines and certain soft drinks, its use in powdered form as a snuff was widespread and becoming cause for concern.

Cocaine, in fact, has been the drug of the eighties and nineties twice. Whereas it was virtually unknown when Twain encountered its description in Herndon and Gibbon in 1856, the 1880s and '90s saw its widespread popularity, use, and endorsement by many prominent people—and not just Freud and the great literary user Sherlock Holmes. No less an august personage than Ulysses S. Grant was given a daily dose of a popular cocaine-laced patent medicine during the last five months of his life while he was suffering from throat cancer and trying to complete his *Memoirs*—during which time, incidentally, he was in regular contact with Mark Twain, whose new company was the publisher of those *Memoirs*. And, as a recent history of the drug puts it, "In the 1890s, although people continued to inject cocaine

11. Herndon and Gibbon, *Exploration of the Valley of the Amazon . . .* , 2:182.

and take it in drinks, sniffing or snorting it in powder form was discovered to be a particularly easy and efficient method of administration."[12]

By the turn of the century, the tide of medical and public opinion had shifted, and there was growing concern about cocaine's negative side effects and addictive properties. It was becoming a scourge then as now among the so-called lower classes and in the black communities, and the "coke fiend" entered the popular literature. A 1908 article in the *New York Times* described "The Growing Menace of Cocaine," and in 1910, the year Twain's "Turning Point in My Life" was published, there was even an article in the journal *Current Literature* called "Influence of Cocaine on Contemporary Style in Literature." The author maintained that abuse of the drug was prevalent not only among "the laboring poor in great cities" but "among the intellectual classes" as well, and ascribes much of the superficial brilliance of contemporary writing to the stimulation of cocaine.

Why did Twain first suppress the motive of "opening a trade in coca with all the world" and then, more than thirty years later, not only disclose it but also make it seem even worse by describing it in terms of contemporary drug abuse? The answer to the first part of this question is relatively simple: suppressing this aspect of the South American scheme in "Old Times on the Mississippi" was consistent with the careful skewing of his actual life in the opening pages of the sketch, where he appears much younger, less experienced, and far more naive than he actually was. Having a wildly impractical scheme to explore the upper reaches of the Amazon is in character for the woefully ignorant soon-to-be cub pilot of "Old Times."

Telling it, on the other hand, was consistent with the autobiographical impulse of his old age, when he was inclined to reinterpret his experience in light of the gospel of determinism and fate and economic necessity that he now favored. The thesis and main thrust of the "Turning Point" essay is that choice and free will play no part in one's life, that there is an inexorable chain of cause and effect that directs our course and over which we have no control. In this essay, he was reimagining and rewriting himself into the sordid stream of nineteenth-century economic history by making his

12. The summary of the history and social dimensions of cocaine use in this section of the essay is drawn from Lester Grinspoon and James B. Bakalar, *Cocaine: A Drug and Its Social Evolution*, 37, 28, 26–27.

youthful naïveté of a different order, portraying himself—more accurately, it may be—as just another antebellum seeker after the big strike.

That it was a strike with decidedly sinister overtones and dangerous consequences underscores Twain's well-known propensity to blame himself and take on guilt for all manner of things, especially such tragedies in his life as the deaths of his brother Henry and his son, Langdon. This compulsion to take responsibility for bad things may seem contradictory to his extreme determinism, which of course denies that there is any such thing as responsibility. But it may actually explain it. The deterministic philosophy was perhaps an intellectual attempt to absolve himself of the guilt he helplessly felt.

In any event, Twain gave an additional pecuniary spin to these late revisions of the story of his pilot years that strongly reinforced this note of economic determinism. In both the *Autobiography* and "The Turning Point in My Life" he tells how he found a fifty-dollar bill on the street in Keokuk, a sum of money that enabled him to begin the voyage to Brazil that in turn led to his becoming a cub pilot:

> One day in the midwinter of 1856 or 1857—I think it was 1856—
> I was coming along the main street of Keokuk in the middle of
> the forenoon. It was bitter weather—so bitter that the street was
> deserted, almost. A light dry snow was blowing here and there on
> the ground and on the pavement, swirling this way and that way
> and making all sorts of beautiful figures, but very chilly to look at.
> The wind blew a piece of paper past me and it lodged against a wall
> of a house. Something about the look of it attracted my attention
> and I gathered it in. It was a fifty-dollar bill, the only one I had ever
> seen, and the largest assemblage of money I had ever encountered
> in one spot. I advertised it in the papers and suffered more than a
> thousand dollars' worth of solicitude and fear and distress during the
> next few days lest the owner should see the advertisement and come
> and take my fortune away. As many as four days went by without an
> application; then I could endure this kind of misery no longer. I felt
> sure that another four could not go by in this safe and secure way. I
> felt that I must take that money out of danger. So I bought a ticket
> for Cincinnati and went to that city. I worked there several months in
> the printing-office of Wrightson and Company. I had been reading
> Lieutenant Herndon's account of his explorations of the Amazon and
> had been mightily attracted by what he said of coca. I made up my

mind that I would go to the head waters of the Amazon and collect
coca and trade in it and make a fortune.[13]

Despite its rich detail, this episode is probably an example of Mark
Twain's ability to remember things that never happened. There is a small dis-
crepancy between this *Autobiography* version and the one in "The Turning
Point," where Twain says he found the bill, "advertised the find, and left for
the Amazon the same day." More tellingly, though, Twain left Keokuk early
in October 1856—he was in St. Louis by the thirteenth and in Cincinnati by
the twenty-fourth—a fact that hardly squares with the midwinter setting of
this episode in the *Autobiography* (*MTL1*, 69). Not surprisingly, Fred Lorch,
a scholar who researched Mark Twain's time in Iowa, was unable to find any
advertisements for lost or found fifty-dollar bills in Keokuk papers during
1856–1857, and none of the surviving contemporary documents mention
the find.[14] Far from finding money on the street, he was actively seeking
to borrow it from a number of people he knew in anticipation of leaving
Keokuk (*MTL1*, 66). If this incident ever did happen to the young Sam
Clemens (and there is always the chance that it did, of course), it did not
enter the life and legend of Mark Twain until the autobiographical dictation
of March 29, 1906.

Finally, however, this fifty-dollar bill, like the "pinch of powdered coca,"
is more interesting for its cultural significance than for its actuality or lack
thereof. To begin with, it was not a fifty-dollar bill as we (or Twain's audience in 1910) would understand it. The government did not begin to issue
paper currency until 1861. Paper money existed in the 1850s, but it was
privately issued by individual banks and was only as good as the bank that
issued it. Particularly in the West, paper money was largely backed by land
speculation. It was negotiable only within a limited region and generally
at a significant discount from face value. One of the features of the business panic (severe depression, in fact) of 1857 was that many of these banks
failed, and paper money became virtually worthless.

The currency system in America just before the Civil War, according to
John Kenneth Galbraith's fascinating account in *Money: Whence It Came,*

13. Twain, *Mark Twain's Autobiography,* 2:289.
14. Lorch, "Mark Twain in Iowa."

Where It Went, was "without rival, the most confusing in the long history of commerce and associated cupidity. . . . An estimated 7,000 different bank notes were in greater or lesser degree of circulation, the issue of some 1,600 different or defunct state banks." At the same time some "5,000 counterfeit issues were currently in circulation," requiring merchants to subscribe to a "counterfeit detector," a weekly bulletin of worthless money.[15]

During the era of the gold standard, when Twain wrote these autobiographical fables, the paper money of the antebellum period represented speculation, instability, and deception, especially in the West. For Twain to ascribe his acquiring the means to set out on his career in terms of finding this fifty-dollar bill is to implicate himself in the whole sorry history of unbacked and often corrupt speculation that he had criticized so caustically in *The Gilded Age.* In fact, one of Colonel Sellers's most outrageous would-be scams in that novel involved buying up "a hundred and thirteen wildcat banks in Ohio, Indiana, Kentucky, Illinois, and Missouri," the average discount on whose notes was "forty-four per cent," and then, having cornered the market, drive the banks' stocks up. "Profit on the speculation not a dollar less than forty millions!" he proclaims.[16]

The fifty-dollar bill brings Mark Twain's life and legend into line not only with his philosophy but also with much of his late fiction, where characters' lives are altered by sums of money that drop unexpectedly into their laps— "The Man That Corrupted Hadleyburg," "The £1,000,000 Bank Note," or "The $30,000 Bequest," for example. So interwoven (or interchangeable, perhaps) are memory and imagination that Twain seems actually to have borrowed from his recent fiction in order to reinterpret his life. This would be a fairly far-fetched suggestion were it not for the fact that he had already practiced this technique earlier in his career. "The Private History of a Campaign That Failed," an 1885 autobiographical essay about his Civil War experiences in a Confederate militia in 1861, ends with an incident in which the young Mark Twain and his comrades fire upon and kill a stranger who rides into their camp one night. Twain is disgusted by the senselessness of this murder and determines to wash his hands of war. And, in real life, he did leave the militia after a few weeks to go to Nevada with his brother

15. Galbraith, *Money,* 90.
16. Twain, *The Gilded Age: A Tale of Today,* 86.

Orion, though no killing took place to prompt his leaving. In *Adventures of Huckleberry Finn,* the novel he completed just before writing "The Private History of a Campaign That Failed," however, his young hero lights out for the territory after witnessing many examples of human cruelty, including an innocent man shot down in the street. It is probable that Huck's experiences provided his creator with a plausible motive for explaining his own flight to the West.

The powdered coca and the fifty-dollar bill are finally anachronisms, representative objects of the twentieth century that show the diminished and degraded results of the unbridled quest for riches and the uncritical faith in self-promotion that held sway in the 1850s. For Twain, looking back from the vantage point of the early 1900s, they were grim reminders of what actually lay both behind and ahead of his youthful optimism. By inserting these incidents into his autobiography Twain changed the whole trajectory of his life, making the pilot years not so much an idyllic formative time spent in the unspoiled Mississippi Valley as a brief deflection from the true course that he would resume in Nevada and California as soon as he left the river, the fateful and ill-fated pursuit of the big strike. The quintessential episode of that period, his decision to become a steamboat pilot, Twain finally came to see as an act that aligned him economically with the young country itself, especially with the corrosive effects of its unbridled speculation and penchant for turning a quick profit whatever the consequences. And, as his life had inspired the richest of his fiction, so his fiction finally came around to help him explain the mystery of his life.

Mark Twain, Isabel Lyon, and the "Talking Cure"

Negotiating Nostalgia and Nihilism in the *Autobiography*

JENNIFER L. ZACCARA

While Mark Twain worked in the autobiographical mode throughout his life—in his fiction, in travel books, and even in the ongoing construction of his literary persona—he began to turn serious attention to the composition of *The Autobiography of Mark Twain* from 1897 to 1906. As a self-conscious master of mining the self for literary production, Twain took great interest in experimenting with form and methodology in his autobiography. After 1904, Twain developed a penchant for dictating as opposed to writing the *Autobiography,* with the privileging of voice over writing. Mark Twain's passion for striking out into fresh and original literary territory rarely faltered, but in the decision to try dictation, Twain revealed his hope that voiced memories might possess the power of psychic resurrection.

As a result of his interest in modern psychology and his two-year residence in Vienna from 1897 to 1899, Twain began to formulate a theory of autobiography that contained many of the tenets of an emerging psychological movement in which talk therapy or the "talking cure" played a decisive role. Working with stream of consciousness, free association, memories, and dreams, Twain aimed to tell stories that would enable him to cope with loss: financial bankruptcy followed by the deaths of his daughter Susy and wife, Livy. Mark Twain's personal assistant, Isabel Lyon, first hired as Livy Clemens's correspondence secretary in 1904, played an important role in the author's design to use talk as therapy; her diaries and journals record how, as the eventual household manager and occasional audience for the autobiography, she attempted to bring Twain through his nihilistic philosophy to a renewed faith in the restorative power of the imagination. Although Mark Twain believed that his autobiography would fill whole volumes—a veritable library of recollection, the system broke down under the weight of nostalgia and nihilism.

Mark Twain had a strong interest in modern psychology even before his arrival in Vienna in 1897. Rest cures, hypnosis, and Christian Science were just a few branches of the mind-cure movement that swept through the United States and Europe in the 1880s and 1890s. In his *Discovery of the Unconscious,* Henri Ellenberger identifies a general "unmasking trend" during these two decades in which individuals searched for unconscious motivations and became obsessed with the psyche.[1] Mark Twain joined the Society for Psychical Research (SPR) in 1884 as a result of his interest in "mental telegraphy." The SPR, founded just two years before in 1882, published a journal called *Proceedings,* containing, among other items, testimonies of people who claimed to have seen ghosts. Much of the material comprised accounts by "percipients" with extrasensory abilities or telepathic powers. The journal appealed to a general audience, yet it also attracted writers such as Henry James and Mark Twain. Both writers may well have found in *Proceedings* source material for their literary endeavors—James for "The Turn of the Screw" and Twain for his late fiction and an essay on mental telegraphy.[2]

In other arenas of popular and emergent psychology, Twain encouraged his wife and daughters to seek mind-cure treatment for psychological stress from such sources as Dr. Whipple and Mrs. E. R. de Wolf in New York. Twain took the cure himself from Dr. Whipple: he walked around the doctor's office smoking while Whipple turned his face to the wall (*MC&MT,* 326). In 1894, Twain wrote to his wife, "the very source, the very centre of hypnotism is Paris. Dr. Charcot's pupils & disciples are right there & ready to your

---

1. Ellenberger, *The Discovery of the Unconscious: The History and Evolution of Dynamic Psychiatry,* 277.

2. Anthony Curtis, introduction to *The Aspern Papers and the Turn of the Screw,* 21–22. Much of the preceding information about the SPR comes from a brief reference to James's affiliation with the society in Curtis's introduction.

hand."[3] Although some of Twain's remarks about hypnotism are made in mocking jest, others reveal his serious interest in mind cure as a treatment for his family. Yet, as a writer, he was deeply interested in the ways in which psychological needs might be symptomatic of broader issues of social disintegration and instability in what Peter Gay would call an "Age of Anxiety."[4]

Clemens and his family were living in an era of destabilization and transformation. The social and cultural landscape was no longer based on a set of commonly held beliefs and values. "Europeans and Americans alike began to recognize that the triumph of modern culture had not produced greater autonomy (which was the official claim) but rather had prompted a spreading sense of moral impotence and spiritual sterility—a feeling that life had become not only overcivilized but also curiously unreal."[5] In the United States and in Europe, writers, psychologists, and intellectuals focused on the problem of "the nature of the individual in a disintegrating society."[6] Karl Marx had forecast this with his now-famous dictum "All that is solid melts into air; all that is holy is profaned." The pervasive sense of "weightlessness" created a psychic crisis that could no longer be cured by religion and faith.[7] A wave of therapies designed to deal with problems of depression, anxiety, and stress crashed on the public and contributed to the sense that society faced a spiritual emptiness. What mind cure proposed was a nonmedical solution to social and psychic maladies. Mark Twain and Livy turned to the mind-cure movement initially to enable them to cope with Jean's epileptic seizures and with general problems related to nervousness and depression, but they eventually looked to mind cure as a means of working through grief after the sudden death of their daughter Susy.

Nearly a year after Susy's shocking death from spinal meningitis in 1896, Samuel Clemens brought his family back to Europe to a place fondly called "the City of Dreams." His reasons for coming to Vienna are arguably more

---

3. Frederick Anderson, William M. Gibson, and Henry Nash Smith, eds., *Selected Mark Twain–Howells Letters, 1872–1910*, 307. Hereafter referred to as *SMTH*.

4. Peter Gay, *Education of the Senses*, 3.

5. T. J. Jackson Lears, *No Place of Grace: Antimodernism and the Transformation of American Culture, 1880–1920*, 4–5.

6. Carl E. Schorske, *Fin-de-Siècle Vienna: Politics and Culture*, 4.

7. This is Lears's term for the spiritual ghostliness of the individual in an emerging modern age *(No Place of Grace)*.

complex than they might seem. Clemens's daughter Clara wished to study piano under the tutelage of the famous Theodor Leschetisky. Upon his arrival, the author told reporters that he was looking for new fictional material.[8] Mark Twain, however, had a strong desire to be involved in the world of discovery and had long imagined what it would mean to be "drifting with the tide of a great popular movement."[9] When Samuel Clemens arrived in Vienna in 1897, he entered the world of an emerging psychoanalytic movement, and he was poised to explore new theories about psychic recovery that would have a profound impact on the experimental phase of his later work.[10]

Vienna served as the site of an emerging modern ethos in the 1890s with its ambitious architectural plans and its established intellectual elite. Fluent in German, Mark Twain immersed himself in popular culture, in politics, and in journalism. He attended the meetings of the Austrian Reichsrat and wrote a heated critique of politics called "Stirring Times in Austria" (1898); he was given the grand tour of the neobaroque Burgtheater with its series of ceiling paintings by Ernst Klimt and Gustav Klimt and their partner, Franz Matsch; he befriended the Zionist Karl Kraus and even considered translating his play *The New Ghetto*. Uppermost on Clemens's mind, however, was the issue of educating himself about psychological discoveries. The Clemenses continually studied the most modern methods of psychiatric treatment: "Clemens's notebook bulged with addresses of prominent Viennese medical doctors, and in his search for remedies for his own and his family's ailments, he constantly toured the consulting rooms of leading members of Vienna's medical fraternity." Samuel Clemens effectively educated himself about everything from mind cure to homeopathy, naturopathy, osteopathy, and allopathy.[11] Twain's fascination with psychological discovery reveals his interest in excavating the complex levels of the mind

8. Carl Dolmetsch, *Our Famous Guest: Mark Twain in Vienna*, 1.

9. Twain, *The Innocents Abroad; or, The New Pilgrims Progress*, 24.

10. In 1895, Breuer and Freud published *Studien Uber Hysterie*, and Freud named his new practice "psychoanalysis" in 1896. Although Freud was working on *The Interpretation of Dreams* (1900) during Mark Twain's years in Vienna, Freud's mentor, Dr. Meynert, was already making news with his use of hypnosis in clinical work and with the emphasis on the psychic excavation of the past.

11. Dolmetsch, *Our Famous Guest*, 263.

and understanding its disabling and enabling capacities. The years in Vienna along with Twain's self-education about psychological discoveries fueled his work on the autobiography by opening up new possibilities of literary construction and confirming the author's instincts.

Unraveling the story of the construction of Mark Twain's *Autobiography* involves working with written sketches, dictations, notebook entries, and letters that reveal the complex and often conflicting aims of a writer who reveled in theorizing about literary production and experimenting with modern forms yet had difficulty putting all of the materials together into an artistic whole. In reading Mark Twain's comments about his process, one hears the popular phrases and terms of the modern movement with its myriad fascinations: exploration of the subconscious and unconscious, breaking barriers between the narrative past and present, pushing the limits of traditional structures and forms. In his introduction to the chapters published in the *North American Review,* Twain states his theory of autobiography by drawing on his knowledge of an emerging modern psychology and on the process of free association for his techniques and terminology: "I intend that this autobiography shall become a model for all future autobiographies . . . because of its form and method—a form and method whereby the past and the present are constantly brought face to face, resulting in contrasts which newly fire up the interest all along, like contact of flint with steel" (*AU,* 3, 4). In his psychological focus and even in his comparison of literary substance with modern building materials, Mark Twain consciously and actively sought to work in a modernist mode. By bringing the past and present into explosive connection, Twain worked with fluid ideas of time and space. Through talk, he hoped to recuperate the "obscure script" in the human mind that linked the present with the past. Perceiving that his autobiography lacked cohesion and chronology, that it was essentially nonlinear, Twain argued that form should occur naturally as a result of a process of free association: "It is a deliberate system, and the law of the system is that I shall talk about the matter which for the moment interests me, and cast it aside and talk about something else the moment its interest for me is exhausted. It is a system which follows no charted course and is not going to follow any such course" (*AU,* 4).

The limitless free play of language would expose Mark Twain's mind to his audience without reservation, and it would leave the job of interpretation and coherence to the reader. Twain concentrated on "common experiences" because they offer opportunities for the reader to see his own life reflected in them. The valuation of the mundane as opposed to the extraordinary allowed for individual interpretation of significance and for natural connections that would occur as stories migrated in the reader's mind to positions of affinity. It was a modern approach, offering a kind of "indiscriminate acceptance of the relevance of every statement" and a "logic of coherence behind contradiction."[12] Twain's commitment to the process of free association came about as a response to his readings in modern psychology and his exposure to the popular "talking cure."

In 1896, one year prior to Mark Twain's arrival in Vienna, Freud named his new practice of psychology "psychoanalysis." In layman's terms, the method became known as the "talking cure." Patients were encouraged to talk out their concerns without attempting to shape their thoughts in any way. By exposing the raw connections between ideas and experiences, Freud hoped to allow the tale to tell itself and thoughts to cohere according to their own logic. Psychoanalysts placed great value on the pure voice sailing through the air unself-consciously and without intervention. As Mark Twain began to develop his new process of autobiographical dictation, he incorporated many of the techniques of psychoanalysis with the full recognition that all of his "talk" would evoke revelations about the self. William Dean Howells, Twain's close friend and literary confidant, wondered if Mark Twain knew the risks of self-revelation: "You always rather bewildered me by your veracity, and I fancy you may tell the truth about yourself. But all of it? The black truth, which we all know of ourselves in our hearts, or only the whity-brown truth of the pericardium, or the nice, whitened truth of the shirtfront? Even you won't tell the black-heart's truth. The man who could do it would be famed to the last day the sun shone on" (*SMTH*, 373). Mark Twain's response to this cautionary note reveals his comprehension of the workings of talk as therapy:

> Yes, I set up the safeguards, in the first day's dictating—taking this
> position: that an *Autobiography* is the truest of all books; for while
> it inevitably consists mainly of extinctions of the truth, shirkings of

---

12. Philip Rieff, *Freud: The Mind of the Moralist*, 82. Hereafter referred to as *Freud*.

the truth, partial revealments of the truth, with hardly an instance
of plain straight truth, the remorseless truth is there, between the
lines, where the author-cat is raking dust upon it which hides from
the disinterested spectator neither it nor its smell (though I didn't
use that figure)—the result being that the reader knows the author in
spite of his wily diligences. (*SMTH*, 374)

Twain places faith in the ability of talk to divulge the truth in spite of
the speaker's attempts to disguise it in his discourse. Freud's terms for the
ways in which individuals consciously or unconsciously subvert important material—displacement, condensation, transference—bear a striking
resemblance to Mark Twain's acknowledgment that the truth is only partially revealed or "shirked," if not deliberately hidden by the speaker's devices. Dreams and narratives never mean what they seem to say but are
"always a substitute for something else which cannot be said," and lead ultimately "to further associations which are in themselves substitutes" (*Freud*,
149). Mark Twain leaves it to the reader to locate the truth beneath all of the
author's concealments.

This becomes something of a game when the reader recognizes that the
Autobiography of Mark Twain is the life story of a persona. The search for the
truth requires the reader to disclose the play between the authentic self of
Samuel Clemens and the persona or mask of Mark Twain. The memories of
Mark Twain incorporate the past of Samuel Clemens. Drawing on memories
of childhood and youth, Twain tells a tale that has a partial placement in
truth, but one that relies on the reconfiguration and embellishment of the
tale from the adult perspective of the Mark Twain persona. In the past, Mark
Twain had enjoyed working with what Tom Sawyer had called "stretchers,"
or lies, as he constructed fiction that was meant to sound like truth. During
his years as a frontier journalist, he made a fine art out of a reportorial style
and tone that conveyed false information. At least some of the success of his
writing depended on how well he could dupe his audience. One could argue
that what Twain was trying to achieve decades later in his autobiography
sprang from the same impulse to take the reader by surprise, to manipulate
material for humorous effect, to distort the relationship between fiction and
reality. But the Vienna experience ultimately shaped these playful, irreverent
impulses in original ways: it afforded him a new vocabulary of psychological

terms, suggested that nostalgia might function in therapeutic ways, and validated a kind of lawlessness in structure that was increasingly attractive to Twain. While Mark Twain did not dictate sections of his autobiography during his stay in Vienna, he gained knowledge that would surface in usable form when he turned to the project in serious form five years later.

After nearly a six-year hiatus in the composition of his autobiography, Mark Twain focused on the project once again in Florence in 1904 where he had taken his wife to convalesce. In Florence, he would bring his theories into practice and reveal the ways in which the Vienna experience had enriched his thinking about the possibilities of talking out his story and finding psychological comfort in resurrecting the past. Increasingly, Mark Twain looked to the past to heal the losses of the present moment. Michael J. Kiskis notes that the dictations from Italy functioned as diversions from the trauma of Livy Clemens's illness: "Livy's illness remained an offstage presence throughout: the material is haunted by it" (*AU*, xxxii). Where the autobiographical material written in Vienna indulged in nostalgia, the Florentine dictations were tied to associations with present traumas. Mark Twain turned to storytelling rather than story writing as a modern experiment in autobiography as well as a means of treating his own depression. Using prospecting terms, Twain wrote William Dean Howells in January 1904, "I've struck it! And I will give it away—to you," suggesting that finding relief from the present pain was tantamount to a miracle:

> You will never know how much enjoyment you have lost until you get to dictating your autobiography; then you will realize, with a pang, that you might have been doing it all your life if you had only had the luck to think of it. And you will be astonished (& charmed) to see how like talk it is, & how real it sounds, & how well & compactly & sequentially it constructs itself, & what a dewy & breezy & woodsy freshness it has, & what darling & worshipful absence of the signs of starch, & flatiron, & labor & fuss & the other artificialities!" (*SMTH*, 371, 373)

In the comments to Howells, Mark Twain gives us a clear idea of his desire to give the autobiography an intimate quality. The dictated autobiography would retain aspects of the original utterance so that the written word would sound like talk. This "talk" would give the reader an illusion of authorial presence and thus of a living document. Twain's terms for the naturalness of this process illustrate how he associated talk with freshness and the written word with formality. Talk is "dewy," "breezy," and "woodsy"; print is all "starch" and "fuss." Howells adds to this diametric opposition between talk and writing when he responds that Twain is "dramatic and unconscious; you count the thing more than yourself; I am cursed with consciousness to the core and I can't say myself out" (*SMTH*, 373). Howells acknowledges that one must be willing and able to let the unconscious freely express itself. He imagines a kind of revelry in the dramatic for someone such as Mark Twain. The passage from Mark Twain's earlier letter to Howells needs to be acknowledged on several levels—for its valuation of natural, spontaneous utterance; for its awareness of the rejuvenative powers of speech; and for its exposure of Mark Twain's knowledge of a building block of the mind-cure movement—talk that could construct itself.

When Mark Twain began dictating in 1904, he required the services of a scribe. The role of the scribe was presumably to be strictly functional. She would simply record Mark Twain's dictations and type them out for later editing. But the relationships between Mark Twain and his stenographers were eventually complicated by his tendency to perceive these listeners as potential censors and by the ways in which they were unable to fulfill Livy's role as muse, audience, and editor. In order to comprehend the role of the censor from a psychoanalytic perspective and in the production of Mark Twain's fiction, we need to understand the importance of Olivia Clemens as Mark Twain's preferred critic.

Livy Clemens, whom Justin Kaplan calls "her husband's vigilant editor," frequently read through Mark Twain's manuscripts, offering suggestions and comments. Mark Twain made Livy into an exacting critic—the very type of Victorian propriety. Twain continually joked that he needed Livy's eye to make things "parlor-mentory." Livy's "blue pencil" made the necessary corrections in diction that curbed the sting of Mark Twain's prose. Twain described Livy as a demanding editor, perhaps even a censor who "gives orders" and designates which material "would pass" (*SMTH*, 363). Yet, as censor and editor, Livy served as the foil for Mark Twain. Where Livy had the manners and the etiquette, Mark Twain possessed the unruliness and disrespect of a "youth."[13]

Mark Twain and Livy Clemens played with their assigned roles of brash author and exacting critic and thereby retold the story of an American culture that remained committed to Victorian censorship and propriety even as it aimed to move lawlessly beyond its own boundaries. Much has been written about the feminization of American culture beginning with the Victorian period and about the influence of the feminine aesthetic on Mark Twain's fiction. In spite of his experience in the raw frontier of America and his image as a writer who focused on male experience, Mark Twain used the world of gentility and Victorian values as a foil for his rugged persona. The genteel world represented the ensconced social system from which his characters hoped to break free. In Samuel Clemens's mind, Livy was the ideal woman who embodied all of the virtues and values of gentility. Having seen her first in the form of an ivory miniature in the possession of Livy's brother Charles, a fellow passenger on the *Quaker City Excursion,* Twain framed her within his mind as the very representative of true womanhood. The productive influence that Livy had over his fiction making and editing results from an authentic and loving relationship, but it also illustrates the ways in which masculine creativity and feminine authority help to shape Mark Twain's compositional process.

Livy Clemens's role as censor proved to be a crucial emotional and structural facet of Mark Twain's work. Having his work pass through Livy's hands became something of a ritual. Even as late as January 1904, just five months before her death, Livy continued her work as audience and critic for Mark Twain's autobiography:

> Mrs. Clemens is an exacting critic, but I have not talked a sentence yet that she has wanted altered. There are little slips here & there, little inexactnesses, & many desertions of a thought before the end of it has been reached, but take away the naturalness of the flow & banish the very thin—the nameless something—which differentiates real narrative from artificial narrative & makes the one so vastly better than the other—the subtle something which makes good talk

13. Livy fondly nicknamed Samuel Clemens "Youth."

so much better than the best imitation of it that can be done with a pen. (*SMTH*, 371)

Trying to find a way to escape the editorial blue pencil and the restrictive opposition that was partially his own mental construction, Mark Twain believed that he could evade his censor through the natural laws of dictation. In the process of dictation, each sentence naturally evolved into the next, creating an illusion of seamless unity and precluding any attempts to place a false form on natural utterance. Much of Twain's humor had required a play between the straight man and the funny man or the voice and image of the deadpan as opposed to the innocent narrator, and Mark Twain's manipulation of Livy's role perpetuated this dichotomy in the process of composition itself. Ironically, just as Mark Twain attempted to escape from the "laws" of propriety at last and allow his voice the lawless expression it desired, Livy's health prevented her from continuing as her husband's foil.

During Livy Clemens's illness in Florence in the winter of 1905, Isabel Lyon started to function as an audience for the rehearsal and dictation of Mark Twain's autobiography. In Florence, the autobiographical dictations worked as therapy since they refocused Twain's gaze away from Livy's illness and allowed the past to function as a restorative. Isabel Lyon's enthusiasm for the dictations contributed to their success. In its early stages, Isabel Lyon's relationship with Mark Twain seemed companionable and productive. Twain wrote Howells, "Miss Lyons [*sic*] does the scribing, & is an inspiration, because she takes so much interest in it" (*SMTH*, 371). Inasmuch as the autobiographical dictations provided Twain with a form of therapy and a means of regenerating himself through confrontation with the past, Isabel's listening ear helped to free Mark Twain from the "Valley of the Shadow" that permeated his life during Livy's illness and after her death. Talk was important to Mark Twain not only as a way of rehearsing and tuning his voice, but also as a method of self-construction and self-renewal. Isabel Lyon was a supportive, nonintrusive auditor who, like a therapist, would allow Mark Twain to tell the stories he needed to tell and wanted to hear.

But if Miss Lyon served as a privileged listener who enabled Twain to recover that "Aladdin's fairy story" of his past, she never possessed the editorial powers of Livy or William Dean Howells. No manuscript bears her hand. Lyon could make her suggestions and express her undying enthusiasm and praise, but she did not have the authority to correct manuscripts or alter authorial intentions. Mark Twain perceived Lyon's role in Florence and during the second wave of dictations in 1906 as that of a silent auditor, diligent scribe, and enthusiastic coach. Lyon's presence did not cause delays in Mark Twain's work or censor his ideas in any way. But in the interim period from 1906 to 1909, gradual transformations in Lyon's role took place, and these changes began to disrupt the flow of Mark Twain's discourse.

Mark Twain originally hired Josephine Hobby as a stenographer who would record the autobiographical dictations. Periodically frustrated with her slow means of recording his dictations in longhand, Mark Twain may have found Isabel Lyon to be a refreshing alternate recorder. Evidence suggests that he used Isabel Lyon as an audience for the rehearsal of his more official autobiographical dictations frequently performed in the presence of his biographer, Albert Bigelow Paine. Paine notes that Mark Twain dictated from his bed, wearing "a handsome silk dressing-gown of rich Persian pattern, propped against great snowy pillows" (*MTB*, 1267). This well-known image of Mark Twain immortalized in numerous photographs conveys a sense of leisure and looseness compatible with the author's theories of autobiographical construction. Paine comments, "[W]e never knew what he was going to talk about, and it was seldom that he knew until the moment of beginning; then he went drifting among episodes, incidents, and periods in his irresponsible fashion; the fashion of table-conversation, as he said, the methodless method of the human mind" (*MTB*, 1268).

This "methodless method," however, was itself rehearsed when Mark Twain called on Isabel Lyon to prepare him for the business of dictation. Lyon notes in her journal: "The morning bed-talks are vastly interesting. I go to Mr. Clemens's room a little before 9, after he has finished his breakfast. I make a good enough audience for him to talk against in order to get himself into his dictating swing."[14] Mark Twain's morning "bed-talks" allowed the author to rehearse his dictations and perhaps even sample some potential topics to see if memory and imagination could "fire up the interest." In these rehearsals, Mark Twain seemed poised in his dictations between

14. Journal, June 3, 1906, Mark Twain Papers. Hereafter referred to as MTP.

sleeping and waking. By allowing his imagination to have a free and un-
inhibited access to his subconscious, he entered the "essential condition of
poetical creation . . . the regimen of mental relaxation" that would weaken
the boundaries between memory of fact and fiction making (*Freud*, 97).
This state of relaxation broke down some of the defenses that the speaker
might use to preserve himself from self-disclosure. It opened Mark Twain
up to the free play of his memories and to the possibility of using his creative
imagination to embellish those memories.

Albert Bigelow Paine acknowledged that it took several weeks before
he "began to realize that these marvelous reminiscences bore only an at-
mospheric relation to history; that they were aspects of biography rather
than its veritable narrative, and built largely—sometimes wholly—from an
imagination that, with age, had dominated memory, creating details, even
reversing them, yet with a perfect sincerity of purpose on the part of the narrator to set down the literal and unvarnished truth." What seems clear, however, is that Mark Twain not only rehearsed his dictations but also included
certain details and structures for "literary effect." Twain shaped his stories
for artistic ends, but the narratives also served the larger purpose of making
the past serve the present. Talk functioned therapeutically to bring meaning
and purpose into a world that seemed dreamlike and unreal. Twain was the
first to acknowledge that "It isn't so astonishing, the number of things that
I can remember, as the number of things I can remember that aren't so"
(*MTB*, 1268). The boundaries between fiction and reality had always been
loosely defined in Mark Twain's experience since he drew so heavily from
his youth to fuel his fiction and readily embellished the past to serve the
purposes of fictional self-construction, but in the years following the Vienna experience, Twain began to feel alienated from reality and disturbed
by the fact that his dreams seemed more real and preferable than actuality.
Dictating the autobiography opened up the reservoir of his creative imagination, allowing it to serve as a mode of escape, of therapeutic release, and
of self-conscious affirmation.

Mark Twain reveled in the freedom of discourse that the autobiography afforded him. In June 1906, he informed Howells, "The dictating goes
lazily & pleasantly on." On the average, he was dictating fifteen hundred
words an hour, and he cheerfully commented, "It's a plenty, & I am satis-
fied" (*SMTH*, 377–80). Finding that it was becoming increasingly difficult

to bring happiness into his life after the death of his Livy, in the autobiography, Twain immersed himself in the past, hoping that nostalgia might "bring it all back and make it as real as it ever was and as blessed" (*AU*, 120). Some of the most memorable passages in the autobiography resonate with the author's desire to preserve the things most sacred to him. The poetic description of Uncle John Quarles's farm, for example, stands out as perhaps Twain's most renowned flight of nostalgia. Twain structures the passage with repetitions of phrases such as "I can call back," "I can see," "I know," and "I remember." Each phrase initiates a recollection tied to some sensual image: "I can call back the solemn twilight and mystery of the deep woods, the earthy smells, and the faint odors of the wild flowers, the sheen of rain-washed foliage. . . . I can call back the prairie, and its loneliness and peace, and a vast hawk hanging motionless in the sky, with his wings spread wide and the blue of the vault showing through the fringe of their end-feathers" (*AU*, 120). This written recollection is superior in quality to some of the dictated sections that are less descriptive and more a catalog of faces from the past. On March 9, 1906, for example, Mark Twain dictated the following passage that begins a series of character sketches of lost or forgotten friends.

> I am talking of a time sixty years ago, and upwards. I remember
> the names of some of those schoolmates, and, by fitful glimpses,
> even their faces rise dimly before me for a moment—only just
> long enough to be recognized; then they vanish. I catch glimpses
> of George Robards, the Latin pupil—slender, pale, studious, bending
> over his book and absorbed in it, his long straight black hair hanging
> down below his jaws like a pair of curtains on the sides of his face.
> (*AU*, 210)

Imaginative acts of resurrection enabled Mark Twain to find temporary solace in the feelings and sensibilities of his youth, yet he would find that nostalgia possessed both restorative and destructive powers.

On August 3, 1906, Isabel Lyon suggested that Mark Twain name his planned estate in Redding, Connecticut, "Autobiography House." Ironically, the *Autobiography*, a "structureless" work, contributed to the construction of Mark Twain's final home because the house, designed by William Dean Howells's son John, was to be built at least partially from the proceeds of the published book. This was the first real home that Mark Twain would have since the Hartford house on Farmington Avenue. Although the estate was eventually christened "Stormfield," the consideration of "Autobiography House" suggests that both Isabel Lyon and Mark Twain recognized the power of nostalgia and recollection to enclose the author in the safe walls of the past.

But Mark Twain's nostalgic flights into the past did not enable the author to live with happiness outside of his work. As potential sources of therapy, the nostalgic exercises in the *Autobiography* failed to provide Mark Twain a way to confront reality in a positive way because they underscored the great distance between present losses and what he once had. As the Viennese psychologists had discovered, "the past is not simply dead weight to be cast off by enlightened minds, but active and engaged, threatening to master the present" (*Freud*, 82). When Mark Twain returned to reality from the composition of his autobiography, he increasingly felt as if he awakened to nightmare. Twain's nihilistic philosophy was in some ways a by-product of the excessive nostalgia that the *Autobiography* afforded him.

Mark Twain's experience in Vienna had stimulated and perhaps even laid the groundwork for his continual vacillations between nostalgia and nihilism. In Vienna, the nostalgic mood had deepened after 1890 when Schubert's songs resurrected proverbial folk types and where one of the favorite Viennese pleasure spots was the fake Roman ruin at Schönbrünn, surveyed by visitors in order to relive their historic past.[15] In Vienna too, philosophical nihilism reached a fever pitch with the publication of Nietzsche's *Will to Power* and *Thus Spake Zarathustra*. While he was in Vienna, Mark Twain would have heard the phrase "therapeutic nihilism" with its remote suggestion that nihilism might lead toward affirmation rather than destruction.[16] It is fair to say that Mark Twain came to a nihilistic vision on his own, based on personal experience and a lack of faith in a benevolent God, and that he nurtured this dark view of the world over the years; yet, the Vienna

15. William M. Johnston, *Vienna: The Golden Age, 1815–1914*, 227.
16. "Therapeutic nihilism" was a popular doctrine in Beidermeir Germany and was based on a refusal to prescribe any therapy that might interfere with nature's process of healing. The term oddly inverted its meaning, and many individuals (including Isabel Lyon who uses this phrase in a positive sense in her journals) took it to mean that nihilism could offer affirming or healing possibilities.

experience deepened and extended his own tendency toward nihilism. On April 2, 1899, Twain had written to Howells from Vienna:

> I suspect that to you there is still dignity in human life, & that Man is not a joke—a poor joke—the poorest that was ever contrived—an April-fool joke, played by a malicious Creator with nothing better to waste his time upon. . . . Man is not to me the respect-worthy person he was before; & so I have lost my pride in him & can't write gaily nor praisefully about him anymore. And I don't intend to try. I mean to go on writing, for that is my best amusement, but I shan't print much. (*SMTH*, 329)

Isabel Lyon recognized the dark aspects of Mark Twain's philosophy of life, but rather than perceiving the dangers of Mark Twain's paradoxical swings between nostalgia and nihilism, Lyon viewed Twain as a writer with a modern sensibility, and she took great pains to reveal a kinship between Twain and Nietzsche. On July 6, 1906, Clemens's daughter Jean and her friend Gerald Thayer grappled with certain philosophical issues. Lyon records: "I had been thinking about moral courage and trying to sift it down, and at dinner we were talking about it. To me it seems to be re-pression of self. [Gerald] said it was a 'repression of pity' too and he's right. Then he said I'd better read Nietzsche's *Also Sprach Zarathustra*." On July 13 Isabel's copy of the book arrived, and on August 8 "the King [Twain]" wanted to see it. Although he would hand it back to Isabel exclaiming, "Oh damn Nietzsche! He couldn't write a lucid sentence to save his soul," Lyon proclaimed that she is "glad that he doesn't like Zarathustra, very, very glad—but I shall be able to quote some passages to him—some telling passages—for Nietzsche is too much like himself" (MTP, journal).

In a later discussion about Nietzsche, we can see Twain's humorous recognition of certain affinities between his own acerbic humor and Nietzsche's irreverence. At first Lyon was received with "Damn Nietzsche!" whenever she offered a quotation, but she notes, "First he damns—but then he approves with his head on one side in his quaint listening attitude." Lyon's persistence in reading Nietzsche bordered on a need to have "the King" acknowledge a kindred spirit. On August 27 she commented, "But Mr. Clemens, Nietzsche calls the acts of God, 'divine kicks.'" "'Hurrah for Nietzsche!' the King shouted and slapped his leg hard" (MTP, journal).

Isabel Lyon professed to have a passion for Mark Twain's "gospel," the philosophical essay "What Is Man?" (which Twain drafted in Vienna). In October 1905, Lyon had written that Twain was "like Nietzsche again," for "his cry is not one of weak pity for the human, but of fierce condemnation for the creator of the devils that war within the human breasts. There are those who think that the King's is a weakening philosophy, but for others it is not so. It can put granite foundations under some feet and show them how to stand alone" (MTP, journal). It is particularly interesting that a Victorian woman would find possibilities for affirmation, strength, and renewal in Twain's later voice. Since Isabel Lyon enjoyed such a close proximity to Twain, it is at least possible that she reiterated the author's own view of his later philosophical ideas submerged beneath her own. In terms of Mark Twain's later fiction, we have stories such as "The Great Dark" that plunges into a nightmare never to return to reality and the unfinished "Mysterious Stranger" manuscripts whose nihilistic and solipsistic pronouncements leave the reader bewildered as to whether Twain saw a way out of the "trap" of existence or believed that man deluded himself about escape and solace. If we consider the ambiguities in these late works within the context of the autobiographical dictations, we begin to see that nostalgia and nihilism function as alternate poles on Mark Twain's search for meaning and significance in his life.

Between 1907 and 1909, Mark Twain began to desire a more private discourse than the autobiographical dictations afforded him. Without perhaps realizing the ways in which his personal life began to infringe on his work, Twain admitted that "Dictating Autobiography has certain irremovable drawbacks" (SMTH, 401). He decided to write letters to friends "and not send them" rather than continue dictating his autobiography. This change from dictating to writing letters came gradually to Mark Twain even though he informed Howells that the idea occurred to him at three o'clock in the morning. Just six months earlier, Isabel Lyon had suffered a "fall" from grace in the Clemens's household—the end result of Lyon's alienation from Albert Bigelow Paine, Mark Twain's official biographer, and her subsequent decision to marry Ralph Ashcroft, Twain's disreputable financial adviser. Rather than focusing on the details of Lyon's demise, which read like a melodrama of misunderstandings, we need to consider the coincidences and connections between Lyon's fall from "the

King's" graces and the rupture in Mark Twain's autobiographical strategy of dictation.

Beginning in 1907, Mark Twain had given Isabel Lyon far more authority over his affairs than his daughter Clara believed was necessary. Isabel had a free hand in the design and management of the construction of the estate in Redding, leading the architect, John Howells, to claim that Stormfield was Isabel's: "'The magic land' that went down into the sea" (MTP, date book, July 21, 1907). In fact, Isabel made as strong an emotional investment in the house as Mark Twain did financially. At Stormfield, Lyon entered a new phase in her tenure at the Clemens home. She began to serve as a blocking figure, shielding Samuel Clemens from undesirable correspondence and meetings, along with unwanted controversies with his daughters. As he had told William Dean Howells, he had gone to Redding to "escape Mark Twain" (*SMTH*, 838).

When Albert Bigelow Paine came into Mark Twain's life, Lyon rejoiced for she believed that Paine was a real "find": "he is doing the very thing that I longed to have some worshipping creature do with Mr. Clemens's papers, letters, clippings, and autobiographical matter. He is bringing the mass into order, reducing the great chaos that I have always longed to be able to touch but have never found time for" (MTP, journal, Jan. 19, 1906). While working for Mark Twain, Lyon frequently lamented about the disarray of the author's work and notes. Lyon wanted to assemble all of Mark Twain's manuscripts, letters, and notes into a meaningful order—partly because she saw more method in the later work than madness and mainly because Twain had indicated that she might publish his letters. That Twain conferred this duty on Isabel is a sure sign of his trust in her because he was protective of his letters throughout his life. But Isabel's all-seeing eye found that several of Twain's letters were missing and that Albert Bigelow Paine had taken them as resources for the biography. Further inquiry proved that Paine had written to William Dean Howells to secure his correspondence with Twain without obtaining the author's permission. The battle lines between Miss Lyon and Paine were drawn, and in retrospect Lyon wrote in the margins of a glowing journal commentary on Paine: "Old Fraud."

As relations between Paine and Lyon became more strained, so too did Isabel's associations with Clemens's daughters Clara and Jean. Increasingly, Stormfield seemed an apt name for the ground upon which tempestuous relationships would play themselves out. Twain grew more interested in playing the role of "King" and testing his daughters and admirers to see who was the more faithful and caring. Because Twain assured Clara and Jean that Isabel Lyon's words and actions should be taken as expressions of his own wishes, and because he asserted that he knew her "better and more intimately than I have ever known anyone except your mother," he effectively gave Isabel the status of a preferred daughter or spouse. Mark Twain's high regard for Miss Lyon, whom Witter Bynner had dubbed the "Lyon of St. Mark," inevitably created a climate of hostility and jealousy between Isabel and the Clemens daughters.

Mark Twain referred to Isabel Lyon as a "scribe" in Florence—a term he preferred over "stenographer," but in 1909, Lyon would be the nameless stenographer whom Mark Twain rejected. Twain's acknowledgment of the breakdown of his autobiographical process obliquely points to the author's feelings of anger and betrayal toward Isabel Lyon. Twain wrote Howells in April 1909, "A stenographer is a lecture-audience; you are always conscious of him; he is a restraint, because there is only one of him, & one alien auditor can seldom be an inspiration; you pay out to him from your own treasury" (*SMTH*, 401). Twain continues to complain to Howells about the "petrified audience-person" who is always there to prevent honest comments in a dictation session. He is particularly irked by the thought of a woman or a religious individual as auditor. Although some of these criticisms may have been made in regard to Josephine Hobby, whom Twain discharged in 1908, most are leveled indirectly at Isabel Lyon, who had disappointed him and lost his trust.

Although Mark Twain continued to tell his stories to Lyon until 1909, he seemed to be working toward the end of something and doing so at an alarming rate. Lyon became wistful about Mark Twain's fiction-making and storytelling powers. The King's talk was like a "dream edifice," for you don't know what is coming next, and his talks build into exquisite towers and pinnacles and when he sits down the wonderful structure he has built fades away and you have only an imperishable memory of a hauntingly beautiful thing that you can never remember and never forget" (MTP, daily reminder, Jan. 2, 1908). Here there are echoes of the "dream edifices" built by Mark Twain's fictional mysterious stranger, but like the stranger, Twain periodically wiped away his joyful creations with a sweep of the hand, and it would be Isabel Lyon's fate to be dismissed in one of these cathartic gestures.

The breakdown in the autobiographical process was at least in part a result of Isabel Lyon's failed attempts to enable Mark Twain to find happiness outside of fiction making. She had heroically tried to focus the author on the modern philosophical aspects of his work and on finding an affirming path through his nihilism. But as Lyon became a preferred companion for Mark Twain, she faced not only the jealousy and wrath of his daughters and admirers, but also the author's unconscious anger at her attempt to replace his wife in the household and as a literary audience. Lyon continually perceived her role as that of a savior who could heal the wounds of loss for Twain and his daughters. Unwittingly, she played the role of a pseudoanalyst by silently listening to Mark Twain's dictations and then urging the author to piece together the disarray in his life and work.

In one of his last letters to Mark Twain on January 18, 1910, William Dean Howells lamented, "You will never be riper for a purely intellectual life again . . . and it is a pity to have you dragging along with a worn out material body on top of your soul" (*SMTH,* 404). Twain's exposure to the new psychological movement in Vienna, his serious study of mind cure, and his acceptance of a Nietzschean worldview made his late works of fiction visionary and experimental, however flawed they might be in terms of narrative and philosophical cohesion. Lacking an official interpreter of his experience and unable to draw on the more life-affirming aspects of his storytelling, Mark Twain found it difficult to manage his own artistic vision, to elicit the meaning behind the free association of ideas and the telling connections between the past and the present. Aptly, Sigmund Freud had believed that one could compare an individual undergoing the talking cure to an artist constructing fictions, yet he had little faith that artists could serve as interpreters of their dreams: "Artists, like the pious cannot really have insight into what they do. No more than religion is art a final resource of judgment; it merely diverts as expression what must be recovered as rational understanding" (*Freud,* 138).

We can enjoy some of the superior prose of the *Autobiography* and the ways in which it tells the story not just of Mark Twain, but also of a vanishing era of faith and optimism, but in doing so, we need to recognize that the *Autobiography* alone could not consistently pull Mark Twain from the nightmare of loss that characterized his life from 1897 to his death in 1910.

The autobiographical dictations had effectively failed as therapy because every story Mark Twain told eventually unraveled rather than affirmed the self. Thoughts had become "vagrant," "forlorn," and "homeless," and Mark Twain wondered what it would be like to be "gradually wasting away, atom by atom, molecule by molecule," until "at last I shall be all distributed, and nothing left of what had once been Me. It is curious, and not without impressiveness: I should still be alive, intensely alive, but so scattered that I would not know it."[17] Ultimately unable to negotiate the paradox between his nihilistic philosophy and nostalgic escapism, the more Mark Twain tried to resurrect the past, the more the past seemed like the stuff of dreams.

17. Twain, "Three Thousand Years among the Microbes," 186.

The Minstrel and the Detective

The Functions of Ethnic Caricature in Mark Twain's Writings of the 1890s

HENRY B. WONHAM

Critical discussion of Mark Twain's approach to ethnic representation has understandably focused primarily on Twain's classic novel *Adventures of Huckleberry Finn*. Since the book's American debut in 1885, readers have expressed both outrage and admiration for Jim's enigmatic image, which remains a flash point for critical disagreement in recent assessments of Twain's racial sensitivities.[1] Jim's advocates note his shrewd irony and shamanistic knowledge of the natural world ("Jim knowed all kinds of signs"), reminding us of the runaway slave's immense dignity and eloquence.[2] Other readers view Jim as less a shaman than a showman, a degraded minstrel caricature whose slack-jawed buffoonery exposes Twain's worst instincts as a writer.[3]

I have argued elsewhere that readers should resist this choice, that the tension generated by Jim's unstable characterization constitutes the essence

1. Some recent discussions of race in *Adventures of Huckleberry Finn* include Jocelyn Chadwick-Joshua, *The Jim Dilemma: Reading Race in Huckleberry Finn*; Jonathan Arac, *Huckleberry Finn as Idol and Target: The Functions of Criticism in Our Time*; and Shelley Fisher Fishkin, *Was Huck Black? Mark Twain and African-American Voices*.

2. Twain, *Adventures of Huckleberry Finn*, 55. Critics who take this position include Fishkin, *Was Huck Black?*; William Dean Howells, *My Mark Twain: Reminiscences and Criticism*; Ralph Ellison, *Going to the Territory*; and David Lionel Smith, "Huck, Jim, and American Racial Discourse."

3. Fredrick Woodard and Donnarae MacCann offer a representative comment in their essay, "Minstrel Shackles and Nineteenth-Century 'Liberality' in *Huckleberry Finn*": "Twain's use of the minstrel tradition undercuts serious consideration of Jim's humanity beyond those qualities stereotypically attributed to the noble savage; and Jim is forever frozen within the convention of the minstrel darky." See James S. Leonard, Thomas A. Tenney, and Thadius M. Davis, eds., *Satire or Evasion: Black Perspectives on Huckleberry Finn*, 141–53.

of Twain's interest in ethnic caricature.[4] In the present essay I want to look beyond *Huckleberry Finn* to Twain's problematic writings of the 1890s in order to understand how his approach to ethnic representation evolved over time. The 1890s were years of professional disappointment, financial disaster, and personal tragedy for Mark Twain, and his uneven literary achievements of that decade have traditionally been viewed through the lens of biography. The financial catastrophes of the early '90s and Susy Clemens's death in 1896 unquestionably shaped Twain's subsequent career, but the 1890s were also years of momentous transition in the production and dissemination of ethnic images, and Twain's evolution as a writer owes something to these events as well. The rise of comic magazines, such as *Puck, Life*, and the *Daily Graphic*, with their generous array of ethnic caricatures, coupled with the displacement of traditional blackface minstrelsy by the more stridently racist "coon shows" of the 1890s, marked a new era in the longstanding tradition of American ethnic stereotyping. Twain's vexed efforts to carry the story of Huck and Jim forward in the writings of this period ran up squarely against a new vocabulary of ethnic misrepresentation, one that could no longer suspend the contradictory impulses of the shaman and the showman in a single figure. With a few strained and problematic exceptions, Twain's ethnic caricatures of the 1890s dismantle the paradox of Jim's complex identity, substituting for Jim's dynamic instability a much clearer and more disturbing account of ethnic identity.

The startling popularity of the "coon song" (of which more than six hundred were published from 1890 to 1900), with its iconology of razor blades, cards, and dice, coincided with the period Rayford W. Logan has labeled the "nadir" of African American history (fig. 1).[5] Twain was by no means immune to the influence of these images, but his writings of the 1890s often resist the popular culture's drift toward an increasingly rigid language of ethnic identity. One strategy of resistance involved turning back the clock in a labored attempt to recover some of the energy and uncertainty Twain associated with an earlier mode of ethnic performance, "the genuine

4. Henry B. Wonham, " 'I Want a Real Coon': Mark Twain and Late-Nineteenth-Century Ethnic Caricature."
5. Logan, *The Betrayal of the Negro from Rutherford B. Hayes to Woodrow Wilson*. See also J. Stanley Lemons, "Black Stereotype as Reflected in Popular Culture, 1880–1920."

Fig. 1. "May Irwin's Bully Song," 1896. Special Sheet Music Collection, University of Oregon.

nigger show," which he eulogized in an infamous autobiographical dictation on antebellum minstrelsy.[6] As Eric Lott and other cultural historians
have explained, the antebellum minstrel show was fraught with ambiguity
and evoked a confusing blend of "loathing and desire in its middle class
white audience."[7] Twain relished such instability for its power to challenge
and readjust racial sensitivities, as in the many minstrel interludes that contribute to Huck's reeducation in *Huckleberry Finn*, including the set pieces
on "King Sollermun" and "You Can't Learn a Nigger to Argue." Anthony
Berret has gone so far as to call the novel a kind of literary minstrel show,
with its three-part structure and formulaic comic exchanges.[8]

But if *Huckleberry Finn* is a literary minstrel show, the novel's staged performances are strangely out of tune with its many fictional audiences, which
have grown impatient with disguises and intolerant of ethnic ambiguity. As
the King and Duke learn when they are ridden on a rail, and as Boggs fatally
discovers, audiences in *Huckleberry Finn* are deadly serious. This may be
why Huck and Jim perform their minstrel dialogues only in perfect seclu-
sion, literally in hiding, where the reader is invited to enjoy a brand of ethnic
comedy that has become utterly irrelevant to the systemic racism of Twain's
Mississippi Valley culture. The novel's controversial final chapters chronicle
the decline of minstrel humor, with its uncertain racial commitments, and
the rise of a different sort of comedy, one better suited to the inflexible racial
categories of the coon era.[9]

In sequels to *Huckleberry Finn*, Twain occasionally returns to this work of
recovery, straining awkwardly to revive what he considers the magical ambivalence of minstrel comedy by removing Huck and Jim from their American context. In *Tom Sawyer Abroad* (1894), for example, Tom, Huck, and
Jim engage in minstrel repartee while traveling over Africa in a balloon.[10]
Dan Beard's first-edition illustration of the three aeronauts dancing above

6. DeVoto, *Mark Twain in Eruption*, 110.
7. Lott, *Love and Theft: Blackface Minstrelsy and the American Working Class*, 142. See
also Dale Cockrell, *Demons of Disorder: Early Blackface Minstrels and Their World*; and David
Roediger, *The Wages of Whiteness: Race and the Making of the American Working Class*.
8. Berret, "*Huckleberry Finn* and the Minstrel Show."
9. I pursue this interpretation in much greater detail in " 'I Want a Real Coon.' "
10. Twain, *Tom Sawyer Abroad and Tom Sawyer, Detective*, 20. Hereafter referred to as
TSA.

Fig. 2. Dan Beard, *Tom Sawyer Abroad* (New York: Charles L. Webster, 1894).

the Sahara in exaggerated evening attire appropriately conveys Twain's conception of the dirigible as a flying minstrel stage, an airborne version of the earlier novel's floating platform (fig. 2). Moreover, the group's incessant discussions replicate the structure of minstrel comedy, as Tom plays the erudite middleman, repeatedly defending abstract principles of representation against the horse-sense naïveté of his interlocutors.

In a typical episode, Tom struggles unsuccessfully to make Jim understand how a painting can be worth more than the thing it represents. As in *Huckleberry Finn*, Jim refuses to accept argument by analogy, rejecting Tom's use of metaphor as a distortion of simple fact. When Jim suggests that the sand they are carrying could be worth five dollars at home, Tom is quick to grasp the symbolic value of their cargo, noting that the sand would sell for thousands if marketed as "genuwyne sand from the genuwyne Desert of Sahara" (*TSA*, 82). This clever scheme links the value of the sand as a "genuwyne" (African) object to its value in the American marketplace as a representation of Africa, resurrecting the oxymoronic logic of Twain's "genuine nigger show" in an unlikely figure. Interestingly, Tom's insistence that the symbolic value of an object often exceeds its intrinsic value leaves Huck as astonished as Jim, despite the fact that Huck, in the earlier novel, has taken Tom's side in essentially the same comic exchange numerous times. Huck attests to the novel's thorough investment in minstrel comedy when he calls Jim "the gratefullest nigger I ever see," adding an unexpected edge to one of the most poignant lines in Twain's 1885 masterpiece: "He was only nigger outside; inside he was as white as you be" (*TSA*, 86).

The comic dividends here are few, in part because *Tom Sawyer Abroad* labors to preserve minstrel caricature by making it unproblematic. By placing Huck's raft beyond the reach of a corrosive American context of performance, Twain finds it possible to enact minstrelsy's racial antics without reference to the social world in which the caricatured ethnic image bears meaning. The performance of ethnic identity—the notion that one might be "only nigger outside"—never complicates the novel's confident management of "real" and "imitation" selves, with the result that *Tom Sawyer Abroad* produces an especially cruel variety of racist comedy for its own sake. Beard's illustrations, which dispense with overt coon symbolism in favor of a quirky evocation of the old minstrel stage, reflect Twain's desire to purge his comedy of its resonance with contemporary racial discourse, so that Jim's exaggerated ethnic poses—"his eyes bugged out," "he lost his head . . . as always"—here emerge as plain fun (*TSA,* 37, 60). Within the fragmented social world of *Huckleberry Finn,* the strong echoes of antebellum minstrelsy always stand in taut contrast to the very different language and imagery of coon caricature. Tom Sawyer's balloon allows Twain to enact minstrel comedy without engaging the earlier novel's internal struggle with evolving forms of racial representation.

Huckleberry Finn's sequels of the 1890s are more often mired in precisely the complexities Twain awkwardly finesses in *Tom Sawyer Abroad.* An unfinished manuscript from 1897, "Tom Sawyer's Conspiracy," again works to recover the elusive energy of minstrel comedy, but this story encounters a variety of obstacles symptomatic of Twain's use of racial caricature in the late writings. As in *Tom Sawyer Abroad,* Huck passively reports the action, while Jim again fails to emerge as anything more than a comic prop. In one episode, as Jim is about to be lynched for a murder he did not commit, Tom introduces a plan for his escape, and Jim immediately grabs his banjo and launches into "a nigger breakdown."[11] The story does nothing to complicate this startling conformity to stereotype, for Twain's interest in questions of ethnic identity has begun to focus squarely on Tom himself.

Bored with life in St. Petersburg at the outset of the story, Tom revives the comic impulse of the "evasion" scene in *Huckleberry Finn*'s final chapters by devising a "conspiracy." As in the earlier novel, he plans to "get the people in a sweat about the ablitionists," although because Jim is not yet falsely imprisoned (as he will be), Tom must first "run off a nigger" (TSC, 142, 145). A problem arises when Jim insists that African Americans in this peculiarly tranquil antebellum world cannot "think up anything to insurrect about," and so Tom determines to black up in order to play the part of the runaway slave himself. Huck reports that "we went up garret and got out all our old nigger-show things . . . and they was better than ever, becuz the shirt hadn't been washed since the cows come home and the rats had been sampling the other things" (TSC, 149).

With this explicit evocation of the old-time "nigger show," Tom prepares to take center stage in his dual capacity as the runaway slave *and* the chief

---

11. Twain, "Tom Sawyer's Conspiracy," 205. Hereafter referred to as TSC.

detective responsible for capturing the fugitive. The joke here recalls Tom's attendance of his own funeral in *The Adventures of Tom Sawyer*, as well as Twain's use of the doubling motif in countless stories of twinship and multiple identity. Minstrel burlesque is in fact one of several devices Twain employs repeatedly throughout his career to activate such dualities, the comic possibilities of which he found endlessly entertaining. Jim's twin roles as wise man and buffoon in *Huckleberry Finn* constitute only one example of Twain's basic habit of employing ethnic caricature to suspend assumptions about identity in a humorous ambivalence. The burlesque disguise makes Tom black and white at the same time, allowing the pretend fugitive to assume the intriguing role of a detective in search of himself.

Yet, if the trope of minstrel performance generally produces such comic opportunities for Twain, "Tom Sawyer's Conspiracy" unravels when Tom's dual roles turn out to be incompatible. The difficulties arise when Tom discovers that his plot has been anticipated by another blackface impostor, a white man who has sold himself to the slave dealer Bat Bradish with the intention of escaping. When that scheme leads to Bradish's murder and disappearance of the purported slave, Tom's detective abilities come into full play. Jim lands in prison as the most likely suspect, and Tom prolongs his incarceration, as in *Huckleberry Finn*, in order to enhance the entertainment value of the adventure. In a courtroom denouement that unfolds like a scrambled rerun of *Huckleberry Finn* and *Pudd'nhead Wilson*, Tom stuns the community by proving that the Duke and King, who have just stumbled into the narrative for the first time, are the true murderers. The text breaks off at this point, with Tom's positive identification of the Duke as the "white nigger" whose minstrel performance led to Bradish's death.

Tom's role in this astounding disclosure is compelling, for his detective work reveals not only the Duke's guilt, but also the truth about the "conspiracy." According to Tom, a conspiracy is carried out by a brotherhood, whose members meet "at night, in a secret place, and plan out some trouble against somebody; you have masks on, and passwords, and all that" (TSC, 141). Jim's charter membership and the group's ostensible abolitionist sympathies only underscore the irony of this veiled allusion to Reconstruction-era vigilante organizations such as the Ku Klux Klan. When it turns out that the Duke and King have anticipated every move in Tom's scheme, the "conspiracy" is revealed for what it has been all along: not an abolitionist uprising, but a child's version of Duke's malicious con game. Moreover, whereas Tom's blackface performance seemed to present a comic opportunity by making him a black fugitive and a white detective at the same time, his courtroom disclosure permanently untangles the web of racial confusion, confirming that no disguise can blur the lines of ethnic identity to a trained eye. The showman's costume is finally no match for the shaman's detective prowess, for Tom knows the signs even better than Jim. As the community's arch detective, he unmasks himself and dismantles the tense arrangement upon which Mark Twain's ethnic humor is based when he lays the story's racial ambiguity to rest.

Tom's detective work restores communal confidence and seals the failure of minstrel comedy by proving that, at some level of analysis, blackface disguise is imperfect. The same tension between competing forms of showmanship, embodied in Tom's contradictory roles as minstrel and detective, animates Twain's most problematic novel of the 1890s, *Pudd'nhead Wilson,* though here Twain's fascination with racial masquerade produces a different threat. In fact, if *Huckleberry Finn* and its sequels owe much of their power to Twain's nostalgic vision of antebellum minstrelsy, *Pudd'nhead Wilson* might be considered his "coon" novel, in that the confusion of racial identities in this story centers on criminal efforts to conceal blackness, rather than on the more traditional motif of blacking up.[12] When the false "Tom" disguises himself with burnt cork before murdering his uncle, he is actually revealing his racial identity, as David Wilson demonstrates in a courtroom climax that combines the emerging technologies of eugenics and fingerprinting to identify "Tom" as black.[13] "Tom's" eastern airs and dandyish clothes, no less than his compulsive gambling and cowardly use of a penknife to stab "Chambers," mark him unmistakably as a "coon," according to the period's rigid vocabulary of racial stereotypes.

12. Eric Lott anticipates this view when he describes *Pudd'nhead Wilson* as "Twain's most sustained blackface production—one that is inspired but ultimately destroyed by the racial contradictions on which blackface rests" ("Mr. Clemens and Jim Crow: Twain, Race, and Blackface," 145).

13. Michael Rogin discusses the role of eugenics in the development of fingerprint technology in "Francis Galton and Mark Twain: The Natal Autograph in *Pudd'nhead Wilson,*" 73–85.

Fig. 3. E. W. Kemble, *A Coon Alphabet* (New York: Russell, 1898).

Moreover, the course of "Tom's" career, from his early success at passing for white to his eventual exposure as a racial impostor, neatly reproduces the narrative logic of countless coon songs, such as Ben Jerome's self-explanatory "Nothin' but a Coon," or Ernest Hogan's popular "All Coons Look Alike to Me." E W. Kemble, who had illustrated *Huckleberry Finn* in 1885, became famous during the '90s for publishing sketchbooks such as *A Coon Alphabet,* in which black characters repeatedly fail, with ridiculous consequences, in their effort to mimic white behavior (fig. 3). The success of Roxy's revolutionary act of racial inversion might at first appear to suggest that for Twain the color line is deceptively fluid, contrary to the reductive logic of Kemble's coon imagery. But the color line reasserts itself even more insidiously than before when Roxy miraculously forgets her act of subversion and accepts "Tom" as her white master, underscoring the fact that, as in "Tom Sawyer's Conspiracy," it simply is not possible to be black and white at the same time in *Pudd'nhead Wilson*. The novel finally embraces coon caricature on its own terms as the period's only available discourse of racial identity.

Fig. 4. C. H. Warren, F. M. Senior, *Pudd'nhead Wilson* (Hartford: American Publishing, 1894).

The novel's first-edition illustrations by F. M. Senior and C. H. Warren make this point with relentless poor taste, firmly locating the "tragedy" of *Pudd'nhead Wilson* in the novel's conformity with conventions of "coon representation."[14] Beverly David and Ray Sapirstein observe that the illustrations often depict African Americans as "blobs of ink," robbing those characters of their individuality in "an extreme miscarriage of the message of Twain's text" (fig. 4). The black-and-white drawings clumsily cancel ethnic ambiguity, "a crucial failure in a text dedicated to undermining notions of racial difference." David and Sapirstein point out that Frank Bliss of the American Publishing Company supervised the artists while Twain

14. In addition to the first-edition illustrations by Senior and Warren, Louis Loeb produced six detailed images for the serial publication of *Pudd'nhead Wilson* in *Century* magazine.

remained out of reach in Europe, with the result that the illustrations substantively contradict the spirit of the novel, informing readers less about Twain's plot than about "prevalent racial stereotypes that his book—with limited success—sought to challenge."[15]

David and Sapirstein aptly describe the quality of Pudd'nhead Wilson's illustrations, but their analysis underestimates the complexity of Twain's engagement with the discourse of late-nineteenth-century ethnic caricature. That discourse provides the machinery for his 1894 novel, just as surely as Pudd'nhead Wilson voices Twain's overt critique of a culture that can see only in black and white. Twain's critics have generally taken sides on the question of the novel's purported racism, but we should not rush to dismiss Twain's problematic association with the logic and conventions of ethnic caricature, any more than we should prematurely condemn his sometimes scandalous treatment of ethnic subjects, for his art depends upon the tension generated by the caricatured image. What we *should* notice is that Twain's problematic fictions of the 1890s work to dispel this very tension. His romantic conception of the "genuine nigger show" animated the relationship between reality and representation in his imagination, balancing his uncertain writerly commitments to realism and burlesque, authenticity and extravagance. As his convoluted and often unfinished fictions of the 1890s demonstrate, the discourse of coon comedy, together with emerging technologies that perform an important role in that discourse, like fingerprinting and eugenics, worked to dismantle the minstrel dialectic, eroding the racial ambiguity that, for Twain, had once made the minstrel performer a study in complex, multiple identity. Pudd'nhead Wilson, with its remarkably appropriate graphic component, is merely his most bitter and most thorough concession to a new order of ethnic misrepresentation.

There was a personal dimension to this concession. Twain's recognition that one cannot be white and black at the same time in late-nineteenth-century America carried important consequences for his own creativity, consequences that may be more clearly discernable in Following the Equator, his 1897 travel narrative. With its lengthy meditations on the nature of "Oriental" bodies and their relation to issues of representation, Following

15. David and Sapirstein, "Reading the Illustrations in Pudd'nhead Wilson," 27, 52.

the Equator offers a unique theoretical account of Twain's perennial interest in ethnic caricatures. The book develops an extended comparison between the physical attributes of Western and non-Western types, consistently favoring the latter in terms that underscore the role of exaggerated ethnic performance in Twain's imagination. After an exuberant account of the "splendid black skin of the South African Zulus," for example, he launches into a series of caricatures "of people whose skins are dull and characterless modifications of the tint which we miscall white. . . . The white man's complexion makes no concealments. It can't." Because of its perfect transparency, white skin is inherently false to itself, according to Twain's analysis, and its wearer is the embodiment of a lie. In order to make his or her skin appear white, the "white" individual must "paint it, and powder it, and cosmetic it, and diet it with arsenic, and enamel it, and be always enticing it, and persuading it, and pestering and fussing at it."[16] To be white, in other words, is to perform an ethnic identity, much as the minstrel entertainer performs in blackface, except that the performance of whiteness involves an attempt to conceal, rather than to expose, the complexity of the performer's identity.

Twain elaborates on this distinction between the expressive potential of Western and non-Western types in his detailed account of clothing styles. "Our clothes are a lie," he notes; "they are insincere, they are the ugly and appropriate outward exposure of an inner sham and a moral decay." Like white skin, somber American clothing is a lie because it exposes the wearer's corrupt intent to conceal "an inner sham and moral decay." As expressions of the disjunction between appearance and reality, sign and referent, our colorless and formal clothes are revolting because they neither mask nor express ourselves, conveying instead "a pretense that we despise gorgeous colors and the graces of harmony and form; and we put them on to propagate that lie and back it up" (*FE*, 2:11).[17]

Like the minstrel's extravagantly theatrical rags and patches, "native" clothing, by contrast, constitutes for Twain a paradoxically sincere disguise, in that it makes no effort to conceal what it covers, when it covers at all,

---

16. Twain, *Following the Equator*, 2:52. Hereafter referred to as *FE*.
17. Gillman comments insightfully about the nature of Twain's "Orientalism" in *Dark Twins*, 97–100.

instead expressing the body naturally and faithfully. Oriental "conflagra-
tions of costume," "smouchings from the rainbow," are not merely beautiful
(*FE,* 2:9, 270); they arrest Twain's attention because of their semiotic value
as visible signs that really do attach to and body forth a hidden referent.
In Ceylon, for example, he contrasts the "frank honesty" of extravagantly
colorful native attire with the "odious flummery in which the little Sunday-
school dowdies were masquerading," pitting the notion of "genuine" ethnic
expression against the bogey man of Western "sham and moral decay" (*FE,*
2:12). Bodily description takes on semiotic overtones again a few pages later,
when Twain describes a Bombay woman whose single article of clothing—
"a bright colored piece of stuff"—"clings like her own skin," revealing a
"slender and shapely creature, as erect as a lightning-rod" (*FE,* 2:15). The
outward sign of native dress, here and throughout Mark Twain's Orient, is
indistinguishable from its referent, the body, and their perfect correspondence clearly arouses both his sexual awareness and his fascination with the
possibilities of transparent representation. "Unconscious of immodesty," as
he puts it, the native bodies of *Following the Equator* operate as privileged
signifiers for the interior self, whereas Twain's Euro-Americans emerge as
irreparable liars or masqueraders, their clothes, like their "bleached out, un-
wholesome" skin, functioning as the "sign of insincerity" (*FE,* 2:8, 51, 11).

Clearly this distinction is powered in part by what Eric Lott calls Twain's
"unexamined exoticism," but Sara Suleri's account of "the great contradiction of the excessive literalism or the excessive metaphoricity of the racial
body" provides a richer sense of Twain's fascination with "native" skin and
clothing.[18] Suleri explains that, to Western eyes, the colonial subject often
appears simultaneously as an uncomplicated extension of nature and as part
of a network of indecipherable cultural signs. Twain's privileging of "native" expressivity hinges on this contradiction, which might also serve as
an economical gloss on the logic of minstrel caricature. The "native" body
in *Following the Equator,* like the minstrel end men Bones and Banjo, expresses itself through, rather than despite, the extravagance of its performative attire. Its paradoxical transparency is not the transparency of white skin
or clothing, which labors ineffectively to conceal identity. It is, rather, the

18. Lott, "Mr. Clemens and Jim Crow," 33; Suleri, *The Rhetoric of English India,* 163.

transparency of blackface performance, minstrelsy's complex representation of an ethnic identity to which "burlesque could have added nothing."[19] The performer's colorful rags and burnt cork, which, according to Twain, can never exceed the extravagance of the slave's actual costume, come very close to repeating the figure of the Bombay woman who is continuous with her colorful clothing. Twain's love of minstrelsy, like his relish for the "utterly tropical" Ceylon, which he calls "Oriental in the last measure of completeness," is the product of his desire to access this model of transparent expressivity, something he almost manages when "a thick ashy layer" of dust turns the narrator of *Following the Equator* "into a fakir, with nothing lacking to the role but the cow-manure and the sense of holiness" (*FE*, 2:8, 153).

Just as important as the expressivity Twain seeks to appropriate by blacking up in this scene is the interpretive ability he attributes to non-Westerners. As we have seen, the equatorial "natives" of *Following the Equator* excel at a form of showmanship that articulates the self naturally, and they also possess the ability to interpret natural signs that elude the comprehension of whites. Like the detectives and mysterious strangers who play such an important role in Twain's late fiction, the aboriginal tracker in *Following the Equator* traces outward signs directly to their interior sources, linking hidden identities to their seemingly ambiguous outward manifestations. Assuming the civic role of Pudd'nhead Wilson or Tom Sawyer, the tracker successfully distinguishes one cow from a large herd with utter certainty by examining a field of apparently identical footprints. The signs that constitute this language are either indecipherable or invisible to the writer's eyes, for the tracker follows a trail over bare rocks "which had to all appearances been washed clear." But to the "native" interpreter these mysterious natural signifiers bear a direct and unambiguous relation to significance. Envious of this idealized interpretive capacity, and of the native's corresponding expressivity, Twain notes that "the aboriginal tracker's performances evince a craft, a penetration, a luminous sagacity, and a minuteness and accuracy of observation in the matter of detective work not found in nearly so remarkable a degree in any other people, white or black" (*FE*, 1:156).

19. DeVoto, *Mark Twain in Eruption*, 111.

The aboriginal tracker, whose "luminous sagacity" is enacted through "performance," is an anomalous figure in Twain's late writing, a hero who deploys the personae of the shaman and showman simultaneously and with equal dexterity. "Tom Sawyer's Conspiracy" achieves a more familiar resolution when Tom's minstrel showmanship is revealed to be perfectly incompatible with his function as a detective. In solving Bat Bradish's murder, the racial sleuth discredits his own ethnic performance, exposing Tom's brand of minstrelsy as nothing more than an art of criminal self-concealment. *Pudd'nhead Wilson* is similarly vexed by its hero's contradictory investments in the performance of racial multiplicity and the affirmation of racial integrity. Throughout the 1890s, Twain found it increasingly difficult to manage these twin impulses toward "performance" and "penetration," terms that coincide above in a rare image of the "native" detective. As an exotic ethnic signifier with immediate access to every conceivable signified, this figure embodies a duality that Twain's fiction could no longer accommodate, except by indulging the boldest forms of fantasy.

Such indulgence produced the mysterious stranger, the omniscient Satan figure of Twain's final years, who again reconciles blackface performance with transcendent detective abilities. In one version of this extended fantasy, Satan appears to August Feldner in the guise of a minstrel performer, dressed in "the loudest and most clownish and outlandish costume," with "fragments of dry bone" "betwixt the fingers of [his] violent hands," a "mouth that reached clear across his face and was unnaturally red," "intensely white" teeth showing through "extraordinarily thick lips," and a "face as black as midnight."[20] This apparition at first terrifies August, but Satan's performance of such minstrel classics as "Buffalo Gals" and "Swanee River" transports the boy "to a cabin of logs under spreading [southern] trees." August's description of the performance is suggestive: That uncouth figure lost its uncouthness and became lovely like the song, because it so fitted the song, so belonged to it, and was such a part *of* it, so helped to body forth the feeling of it and make it visible, as it were, whereas a silken dress and a white face and white graces would have profaned it, and cheapened its noble pathos. Clearly what August Feldner admires in Satan's performance is the

---

20. Twain, *No. 44, the Mysterious Stranger,* 136.

identity of the singer and the song. It is noteworthy that, although Satan has the power to assume any physical form, he appears to August Feldner as a white boy in blackface, his features clearly exaggerated in accordance with the standard minstrel characterization of "Bones," rather than as an actual slave.

Ethnic burlesque in this curious reenactment of the long-defunct "genuine minstrel show" signifies the paradox of authentic representation, the ideal of the singer who "bodies forth" the meaning of his song, much as the "natives" of *Following the Equator* body forth their concealed identities. Satan's "uncouth" costume, for all its extravagance, is an extension and expression of himself, and—like the Bombay woman whose dress "clings like her own skin"—he wears his disguise with transcendent candor. By 1908, the year he quit work on the unfinished "Mysterious Stranger" manuscripts, Twain could imagine such moments of transcendent ethnic performance only under the most fantastic fictional circumstances, in which he managed, if only temporarily, to ignore the dominant ethnic imagery of the late nineteenth and early twentieth centuries. Neither his fading memory of antebellum America's "genuine nigger show" nor the less ambivalent "coon" images of his own era could sustain his final efforts to perform ethnic identity in writing.

Huck, Jim, and the "Black-and-White" Fallacy

JAMES S. LEONARD

A function of logic—from Aristotle to Descartes and on to the present—has been to establish certainty of knowledge. By logical processes we discover what we can possess as knowledge beyond doubt. The function of literature has been somewhat different, as evidenced by its frequently acknowledged recourse to the irrational—by which we usually mean the emotional or otherwise subjective. There are narratives, of course, that evoke a sort of ultrarationality as a means of overcoming the normal fallibility of human perceptions. One thinks, for instance, of the detective stories of Edgar Allan Poe, Arthur Conan Doyle, and Agatha Christie. But overall, literature is more likely to dwell on the human discomforts or anxieties of *living with* doubt than to find ways to dispel it. Mark Twain, though he did dabble occasionally in the genre of the detective story (for example, *Pudd'nhead Wilson* and "Tom Sawyer, Detective"), is not one of those whom we would readily number among the celebrants of logical processes. Yet, he did have his uses for those processes. A notable example is the pervasive presence of logical or pseudological structures in his most admired novel, *Adventures of Huckleberry Finn*. These seem especially prevalent, interestingly enough, when the subject is race.

We are all well acquainted with the moment when Huck Finn resolves his great moral and emotional struggle in chapter 31 of his narrative with the devastating formulation, "All right, then, I'll *go* to hell"—that is, he will accept damnation rather than work against Jim's efforts for freedom.[1] And

---

1. Twain, *Adventures of Huckleberry Finn*, ed. Blair and Fischer, 271. Hereafter referred to as *AHF*.

we recognize that the dramatic force of this decision depends, at least partly, on the way Huck's movingly right conclusion is couched in the terms of a clearly false dilemma: to do what Huck's slaveholding society says he must do, or be damned for his failure to comply. By having Huck lead up to the climactic pronouncement with "I'd got to decide, forever, betwixt two things" (*AHF,* 270), Twain (his pseudonym rhetorically appropriate here) has made certain that we will not miss the logically fallacious structure. It is obvious that the structure of "false dilemma"—also known as the "black-and-white" fallacy—rests on the unwarranted assumption that only two choices are possible. But Huck's dilemma contains a second-order unwarranted assumption: the "hasty conclusion" that societal ethics and legal codes are built on natural law—God's law—and that a crime is thus inevitably a sin. So when we applaud Huck for the moral insight that drives his choice, we are in some sense endorsing the inverse of that proposition. Society's laws are shown, by our appreciation of the fallacious nature of Huck's reasoning, to be unrelated to divine law, or maybe even at odds with it—a subversive notion indeed.

And then there's the conversation with Aunt Sally (in chapter 32) in which Huck is claiming to have experienced a steamboat mishap. Aunt Sally humanely exclaims, "Good gracious! Anybody hurt?" And when Huck replies, "No'm. Killed a nigger," she comments with satisfaction, "Well, it's lucky; because sometimes people do get hurt" (*AHF,* 279). Although Huck's narration gives us no definitive assurance at this point that he disagrees with Aunt Sally's fallacious categorization of blacks as nonhuman—again both technically and literally a "black-and-white" fallacy—we assume that he does disagree. And on that basis we can congratulate him for using Aunt Sally's prejudice to play her like a fiddle. We see him here mastering what his society considers the "right" responses in order to conceal his "wrong" (in that society's view) intentions. Notice the difference between this instance and Huck's "I'll go to hell" soliloquy. In the conversation with Aunt Sally, Huck is in full rhetorical control of the situation. He arrives at the false conclusion knowingly without really giving himself over to it. In the "I'll go to hell" speech, he reaches the "true" conclusion by means of a specious logical process. But both scenes are high ethical moments for Huck.

Let's flash back, though, to consider at somewhat greater length a couple of Huck's ethically lower moments earlier in his narrative. First, the why-don't-a-Frenchman-talk-like-a-man? scene in chapter 14. This is a rich passage, deserving close attention because (1) it is funny, (2) it displays the racial dynamic between Huck and Jim, (3) it demonstrates the importance of Huck's first-person narration, (4) it provides a beautiful example of painstakingly constructed structural logic concealed beneath a burlesque surface, and (5) it's sufficiently self-contained to be appreciated in itself yet vitally connected in terms of theme and character development to the totality of the novel.

The scene consists of a conversation between Jim and Huck that some commentators have taken as a telling example of Jim's "minstrel-show darky" syndrome, but others have seen as a glowing triumph of Jim's native insightfulness over Huck's greater knowledge but lesser shrewdness. The exchange takes place on the raft during the idyllic interlude when Huck and Jim are alone, before they have encountered the troublesome (to say the least) King and Duke. They have escaped for the moment not just from Miss Watson and Pap but from all connection to societal complication—or so it seems. The question at issue in their conversation is why Frenchmen persist in the annoying habit of speaking French when, as Jim says, "Dey ain' no sense in it." Asked by Huck what he would do if someone approached him and said *"Polly-voo-franzy,"* Jim gives a minstrel-show response that not only displays foolishness but also clearly establishes an attitude of subservience to whites: "I'd take en bust him over de head. Dat is, if he warn't white. I wouldn't 'low no nigger to call me dat" (*AHF,* 97).

Which way do the ironies fall here? With Jim's appalling ignorance on one side and his misplaced aggression toward members of his own race on the other, the reader is trapped in an unthinkable bind between pathos and low comedy, which is hardly helped (perhaps aggravated, in fact) by Huck's subsequent rhetorically sophisticated, though somewhat misguided, Socratic interrogation of Jim. Huck begins his logical assault by asking,

> "Looky here, Jim; does a cat talk like we do?"
> "No, a cat don't."
> "Well, does a cow?"
> "No, a cow don't, nuther."
> "Does a cat talk like a cow, or a cow talk like a cat?"

"No, dey don't."

"It's natural and right for 'em to talk different from each other, ain't it?"

"'Course."

"And ain't it natural and right for a cat and a cow to talk different from *us*?"

"Why, mos' sholy it is."

"Well, then, why ain't it natural and right for a *Frenchman* to talk different from us? You answer me that." (*AHF*, 97)

From Huck's insistent appeal to the "natural and right," it is, of course, only a short step to the submerged proposition that slavery—the subservience of the black man to the white man—is likewise "natural and right," based in differences as indisputable as the difference between a cat and a cow. This conclusion is suggested as well by the tone of Huck's explanation, beginning with patient simplicity, in recognition of the "natural" childlikeness of Jim's mind, then suddenly, triumphantly (one might even say viciously), springing the logical trap by which he demonstrates Jim's insufficiency in the realm of adult (which here means "white") logic. Notice, too, how the ratios have shifted. The original comparisons were American-Frenchman and English language–French language. These seem harmless comparisons, relying on the distinction between the familiar and the strange to suggest only difference and not hierarchy—even taking into account Twain's assertion elsewhere that his only prejudice was against the French. But Jim's remark about his possible responses to a speaker of French has shifted the ground to the far more pertinent and potent question of white speaker versus black speaker—for whom Jim uses the conspicuously pejorative term *nigger*. Huck, on the other hand, showing the white man's predilection for taking refuge in abstract analogies, has raised the rhetorical ante but at the same time redomesticated the conversation by changing the subject to cats and cows.

By this time, however, Jim has learned his logical and rhetorical lesson and is ready to show that the black man can play the white man's game with equal or greater adroitness. Tired of serving as Glaucon to Huck's homely version of Socrates, he decides to turn the tables—to rise up, one might say, and overthrow his rhetorical master. Instead of giving in to Huck's demand—"You answer me that"—Jim counters with a Socratic strategy of his own: "Is a cat a man, Huck?" Notice how closely this corresponds in form to the opening of Huck's aggressive interrogation ("Looky here, Jim; does a cat talk like we do?"), including the power play of using Huck's name (as Huck did to Jim) as direct address in the rhetorical question. Just as Jim had to do before, now Huck is forced to respond "No"—to which Jim replies,

> "Well, den, dey ain't no sense in a cat talkin' like a man. Is a cow a man?—er is a cow a cat?"
> "No, she ain't either of them."
> "Well, den, she ain' got no business to talk like either one er the yuther of 'em. Is a Frenchman a man?"
> "Yes."
> "*Well*, den! Dad blame it, why doan' he *talk* like a man? You answer me *dat!*" (*AHF*, 97–98)

What has happened in this latter part of the conversation? First, Jim has trumped Huck's false analogy (cat is to cow as Frenchman is to American) with an unwarranted assumption (a "man" speaks English), complicated by a pointedly thematic equivocation on the word *man* itself. Although Jim's argument is equally fallacious, it is rhetorically superior because it not only successfully appropriates Huck's own rhetorical strategy (in both form and phrasing) but also takes up his carefully contrived analogy and turns the blade, as it were, back against its owner. Second (though it happened at the same time), Jim has done something more remarkable than simply prove himself Huck's intellectual equal (at least within the bounds of this limited engagement). He has come, for the moment, to understand what it means to *be* Huck. Early in the discussion he declared his timidity in the face of a hypothetical confrontation with a white man. After all, Jim is a slave (albeit a runaway) in a slaveholding society; he would be a fool to risk a violent confrontation with a white man—or even a white boy. But he has been a remarkably quick study in his encounter with white—that is, European—logic (and shall we include that cornerstone of rationalism, the Frenchman Descartes, in our equation?). To the extent that such logic defines European and American culture, Jim has shown himself to be more "white" than Huck—foreshadowing Huck's later double-edged declaration (to which I will return later in my discussion): "I knowed he was white inside" (*AHF*, 341). The sense of power from Jim's revelation of inner likeness is apparent in the vehemence of his closing challenge: "You answer me *dat!*" (*AHF*, 98).

In the face of Jim's vehemence and the baffling closure of his logic, Huck attempts no further rejoinder. Instead, he falls back on a different kind of clout, the white man's final refuge in the slaveholding South—his ascribed status. For the slaveholder, or even the nonslaveholding Southerner, this was a legal status. For Huck, reflecting the power of European-American culture generally to justify its domination by force of nonwhite, non-European populations, it is the status of narrator. When he sees no further recourse against Jim's argument, Huck, as narrator, retains the prerogative (a prerogative external to the argument itself) to pronounce the final judgment, including the right to refer to Jim generically as "a nigger." He ends his description of the scene, "I see it warn't no use wasting words—you can't learn a nigger to argue. So I quit" (*AHF*, 98). It is this power—the power of the white man's self-proclaimed status as narrator of the events of American history—that has "colored" our view so as to blind us to the events and (as we see in this scene) the rhetoric that are contrary to his perceived interest. But beyond Huck, the still higher authority of Mark Twain has first limited Huck's reach (by, for a moment, handing the authorial reins to Jim), then has undercut Huck's closing ad hominem by means of conspicuous irony.

Now let's pair this analysis of the Frenchman argument with a look at the incident from the next chapter (chap. 15) in which Huck, after being separated and lost overnight in the fog and then finally reunited with Jim on the raft, immediately plays a trick on him. Here Huck, on returning to the raft, finds Jim sleeping; he pretends to have been asleep himself and, like Jim, to be just waking. Huck then manages to persuade Jim, principally by bald insistence, that in fact they were never separated. Jim has merely dreamed it all. He even suckers Jim into concocting an elaborate interpretation of the supposed dream, drawing on Jim's credentials as dream interpreter established earlier in their relationship. But then on the heels of Jim's gullible acceptance of the fallacious account, Huck turns the tables by questioning Jim's "interpretation": "'Oh, well, that's all interpreted well enough, as far as it goes, Jim,' I says, 'but what does *these* things stand for?' It was the leaves and rubbish on the raft, and the smashed oar. You could see them first-rate, now" (*AHF*, 104). Here Jim's abilities as "interpreter" have worked against him, as he, with Huck's strong encouragement, has made the fatal mistake of believing in his imagination and his white companion's assurances more than he believed his own eyes and memory. He can see the debris *"now,"* but only after Huck has sanctioned its visibility. Jim takes the reversal hard, but he does not take it lying down. As before, he rallies to deliver a blow against his tormentor: "'What' do dey stan' for? I's gwyne to tell you. . . . Dat truck dah is *trash;* en trash is what people is dat puts dirt on de head er dey fren's en makes 'em ashamed" (*AHF,* 105).[2] This is a forceful response that once again demolishes what had seemed to be Huck's ascendancy over Jim. The power lies in Jim's sense of justice and in the depth of feeling he displays. But it also lies once again in cleverness. Although Jim speaks gravely to Huck, he again takes Huck's own argument (just as he did in the Frenchman conversation) and turns it against him. Huck points to the "leaves and rubbish" and smugly asks the rhetorical question, "but what does *these* things stand for?" And just as before, Jim, seeing that he has been abused, refuses to give in to Huck's bullying. He turns the question to his own uses.

This time Huck's major recourse to fallacious logic (other than suppression of the evidence of the "leaves and rubbish") comes at the end of his prank: the inconsistency by which, after luring Jim into belief in his unsupported account of what has happened, Huck disproves the account himself. Jim immediately falls back on his old standby, equivocation, but this time the equivocation is more a literary figure than a logical fallacy. He takes the literal "trash" (the leaves, and so on) and makes it the emblem of figurative "trash"—here, people who humiliate their friends. "Trash" is, of course, a category that Huck is all too prone, as Pap Finn's son, to being placed in. But Jim's point, by no means irrelevant to the novel's moral matrix, is that trash is as trash does. Still, it is not the insult to Huck that is crucial. More important is the facing down (the saying that enough is enough by saying what's what, again momentarily overwhelming, or taking over, the narration) confrontation that includes the use of the word *trash,* Jim's most potent available equivalent for combating his own vulnerability to the term *nigger:* one ad hominem at war with another.

2. Twain's manuscript casts some light on intention here. The large number of revisions he made in writing this scene (especially to Jim's climactic speech), trying evidently to get the articulations in this scene just right, suggests that he considered it a thematically pivotal moment.

This is a dangerous turn for a man in Jim's position, as Huck reminds us in his narration by the racial epithet he uses for Jim and the invocation of the hierarchy that accompanies it. Here Jim is no longer Jim. As at the conclusion of the Frenchman argument, he is "a nigger," the embodiment of a category that signifies disenfranchisement. The "who" has become a "what." However, whereas Huck's closure in the Frenchman argument was dismissive, this time, in the face of Jim's sincerity and the risk taking involved in his man-to-man confrontation with Huck, Huck genuinely recants: "It was fifteen minutes before I could work myself up to go and humble myself to a nigger—but I done it, and I warn't ever sorry for it afterwards, neither" (*AHF*, 105). This bottom line rewrites the one from the previous chapter, "you can't learn a nigger to argue," and in the process redeems Huck, whose credibility has been sagging a bit in these two head-to-head encounters with Jim. This exchange unravels the bitter comedy of the previous encounter and reweaves it thematically, supplying the happy ending withheld from us before and reestablishing the sympathy for Huck that was damaged somewhat by his brutal treatment of Jim in that prior incident.

Twain's mixing of the logical and the rhetorical creates what I referred to earlier as "pseudological" structures. The arguments between Jim and Huck are, in fact, exercises in sophistry—rhetorical push disguised as logic. When Huck, by his example, "teaches" Jim to argue (in the face of his contradictory insistence that it is impossible to do so), what he actually accomplishes is the "sophist-ication" of Jim. For a moment, Huck leaves his role as repository of natural virtue and assumes the role of society at large, and in that capacity his first act is the corruption of Jim. But his creation turns out to be a "Frankenstein's monster" that threatens its creator and (ultimately) society as a whole. The interactions between Huck and Jim graphically illustrate the slaveholding society's need to keep its slave population "ignorant," that is, unsophisticated.

Huck and Jim are "noble savage" figures whose contacts with civilization, in moral terms, work only to undermine their natural virtue. Nonetheless, the progress they make in the art of sophistry is not purely a matter of either moral decline or comic confusion. It is a deftness necessary to deal with society on, and in, its own terms. In the Edenic setting of the raft, it is no accident (both in the usual meaning of the term and in the Aristotelian meaning of "nonessential") that Huck and Jim take healthy (again, in both meanings of the term) bites of the fruit of the tree of knowledge. Instead of the primal simplicity of innocent language use, they learn to put language to uses that bring its more complexly practical (and moral) possibilities into play.

In an earlier scene in the novel, as Jim and Huck grappled with Jim's mystically gifted hair ball and, in the process, with one another, they established a cordial version of the sophistic fencing that is played out more fiercely in the two raft scenes. After the latter two engagements, they have no need for another such confrontation. Although neither says so, they have together learned the art of argumentation, which, putting Huck's heart-versus-conscience dilemma into different terms, is the necessary foundation for articulating one's ethical independence. They are no longer bound by the "logic" of their society's ethical formulations, but can subversively and self-consciously establish an ethical subtext of their own design. Jim can decide for himself what to do about the wounded Tom Sawyer. And though society's highest praise for his action is that he is a "good nigger," Huck has his own formulation: Jim is "white inside."

I earlier referred to this as a "double-edged declaration," by which I meant that although Huck intends it as high praise, it nonetheless retains the degrading assumption that "whiteness" is superior to "blackness." But the ethical dimension is not the only relevant consideration here. Jim has also learned to be "white inside" in terms of his mastery of rhetorical nuance; he is no longer a *slave* to the false assumptions of white society. Among characters in the novel, only Huck is in a position to understand this—thanks to his exchanges with Jim on the raft. But we readers—by virtue of our comprehension of the totality of Twain's narrative, which exposes not only Huck's comprehensions but also those embedded in the ironic space between Huck Finn and Mark Twain—can understand it still better. Twain, by his use of pseudological devices, has forced us to use our own logical powers in sound ways to discover the ironically established premises of his narrative. We see the rhetoric as rhetoric; we are not to be fooled by its disguise as logic. And we see that Jim is, indeed, "white inside"—since his achievement of rhetorical mastery, sophistic though it may at times be, is a major step toward playing society's games on equal terms.

We have seen earlier in the novel that Jim is willing to evoke "black magic" as a force for manipulation of both blacks and whites. It is less clear that Jim himself actually "believes in" the magic in the usual meaning of "belief," but he certainly believes in it as a means for getting what he wants. In his conversations with Huck, he has learned to make similar use of "white magic"—by which I (somewhat equivocally) mean the power of logical forms. Again, the degree to which Jim "believes in" the potency of these forms as representations of truth is unclear. But as he gains power over them, he can believe in them as substantial tools. As I have suggested, he is "white inside" in that he can manipulate argumentation. We might think here of Frederick Douglass, a contemporary of slaves like Jim, who evidently made a strong impression on Sam Clemens. Douglass, an escaped slave, no doubt found acceptance in "white" society partly on the basis of moral uprightness and a devotion to truth. But what really made him "white inside" was his ability to control the rhetorical situation—a more powerful version of what Jim does in *Adventures of Huckleberry Finn.*

In the slaveholding United States the ability to read and write was withheld from slaves not only to limit their ability to communicate and thus conspire but also to prevent their demonstrating humanness by means of language mastery. Jim's gains in his arguments with Huck have little to do directly with learning to read and write, but they have a great deal to do with a demonstration of humanness by the alternative route of rhetorical power—which for Douglass was an important validating adjunct to literacy. In this sense, Jim's accomplishment also points toward the alogical literary art by which Douglass—along with William Wells Brown, Harriet Jacobs, Harriet Wilson, and others (including white writers such as Harriet Beecher Stowe)—moved public opinion in the direction of outrage against slavery.

As for the phrase "white inside" itself, its seeming reinforcement of nineteenth-century assumptions about the inferiority of African Americans is finally outweighed in *Adventures of Huckleberry Finn* by the way it ironically thwarts the straightforwardness of the black-versus-white dichotomy. In the minds of white Southerners (and probably most Northerners as well) and in the eyes of the law of the United States, the difference between European Americans and African Americans was as unproblematic as the distinction between black and white. That is, either one was an African American, and therefore eligible for slavery and the legal restraints it entailed, or one was not. This was clearly an illogical situation since there were by Huck Finn's time many Americans of mixed African and European ancestry. The law dealt with this situation by the still more illogical expedient of maintaining that the presence of *any* African genetic inheritance made an individual "black." This was the equivocal legal and social context within which Twain's narrative was born.

There is nothing in *Adventures of Huckleberry Finn* to suggest that "white inside" had any meaning related to Jim's genetic makeup. He was evidently an African American slave, "pure and simple." But the notion that he could be "black" on the outside and "white" on the inside cannot help entailing a breaking down of the inviolability of the "black" and "white" categories as they were understood in Huck's time. If black and white were not totally separate, unmixable categories established and unchangeable from birth, then the whole foundation of slavery, and of white-versus-black prejudice in general, must rest on insubstantial ground. The white community's first response to Huck's "white inside" exclamation may be agreement: Jim has proved himself worthy of the unqualified approbation of white society. The counterresponse of the reader sensitive to the nuances of the situation is then a reaction against Huck's terminology, leading one to ask, "How is this a compliment, since Jim is obviously morally superior to virtually every white in the novel?" The third level of our response should be to reflect on the sleight of hand by which Mark Twain, through his quicker-than-the-eye prestidigitation, has pulled out of the hat a gem of literary logic—a "rarebit" of magic by which the hidden assumptions are made breathtakingly visible. That "slavery is wrong" is not a conclusion that we find very startling today; it was hardly surprising in Samuel Clemens's time either. But for all the literary-critical sophistication we have gained in recent centuries, there remains an element of truth in Alexander Pope's contention that literature gives us "What oft was thought, but ne'er so well expressed."

As we ponder the arguments on the raft, we should note that they are the two occasions in *Adventures of Huckleberry Finn* when Jim and Huck confront one another with real ferocity. In these arguments, which in terms of plot structure seem mainly a matter of killing time, something extraordinary happens with respect to Huck's narration. Although the episodes are recounted by Huck and from his point of view, it is Jim's point of view— Jim's "narration" vis-à-vis Huck's—that captures us. Jim's responses in both scenes are showcase examples of controlled articulateness, masked by signs of inarticulateness, which Huck does not exceed even in his highest moments. And more generally, does not this blatancy alert us to the tactical mastery of articulation by way of what seems inarticulate, or of textual (or literary) logic by means of what is patently illogical, as precisely the power play Twain uses on us throughout—a principal outcome of his successful employment of a sparsely educated fourteen-year-old boy as narrator?

Throughout Huck's narrative the landscape is littered with rhetorical ploys and logical fallacies. Their prevalence at heated moments such as those discussed here argues for a more thoughtful revision of Huck's crafty question: what does this rubbish stand for? First, and obviously, the ingenious way Mark Twain has brought logical fallacies (and other questionable articulations) to bear in Huck's narrative—varying the degree of self-consciousness with which the characters use them—creates an array of effects that deftly dismantles what for Huck and Jim's society is a simple matter of black and white. The novel's curious magic (in this realm, too, thwarting the distinction between black and white) rests largely on the use of inarticulateness to produce a movingly articulate narrative and on illogic to create a crystalline thematic logic. On a more theoretical (but, for the astute reader, no more remote) level, Twain has brought us face-to-face with the essentially alogical nature of literary narrative.

Humor, Sentimentality, and Mark Twain's Black Characters

DAVID L. SMITH

Questions of race in America are vexed and vexing in every context. We are troubled about racial attitudes, racial realities, and racial representations. Regarding representations, we fret over whether depictions are accurate; and even if they are accurate, we worry over whether honest description will cause offense or encourage attitudes and beliefs of which we do not approve. These are the sort of worries that sometimes get caricatured by the rubric "political correctness," a phrase that often implies that racists and reactionaries are more honest than people who oppose bigoted attitudes. Needless to say, the question of how to interpret racial representations has been one of the most contentious issues in recent Mark Twain criticism. I would like to offer a series of meditations on how Mark Twain presented racial issues, black characters, and black speech.

Let me say now that the "humor and sentimentality" in my title refers to the conventional poles of racial representation in American culture. Thus, in *Uncle Tom's Cabin* we have a comic Topsy and a sentimentalized Uncle Tom. In *Adventures of Huckleberry Finn* we have Jim, the butt of Tom Sawyer's pranks, and Jim, the aggrieved parent, weeping over his deaf child. Though Mark Twain was a comic writer, he did depict some sentimentalized Negroes, such as the blacks in "A True Story." These two modes, which I will also call comedy and melodrama, existed side by side in blackface minstrelsy, and the problematic relationship between the two has been implicitly at issue in the continuing debates over the literary uses of Negro dialect. *Huckleberry Finn* and *Pudd'nhead Wilson,* I want to argue, move beyond these rigidly binary poles of conventional racial discourse, but whether one perceives them to do so depends on how one interprets the texts.

The concluding chapter of Tom Quirk's 1993 book, *Coming to Grips with Huckleberry Finn,* raises the deliberately provocative question, "Is *Huckleberry Finn* Politically Correct?" Quirk's purpose is to challenge various readings of that book that seek, in his view, to domesticate the novel, to "sivilize" it in a manner that would make Huck Finn himself "light out for the territory." He explicitly challenges the central thesis of Shelley Fisher Fishkin's *Was Huck Black?* and also challenges the claim that Huckleberry Finn is an antiracist novel—a central claim of my own work on this novel. Not surprisingly, Quirk's answer to his own rhetorical question is, in effect, no. On the contrary, he insists, "we prize *Huck* for its incorrectness; it is an incorruptibly incorrect book in nearly every particular."[1] Furthermore, he suggests, *Huckleberry Finn* refuses ideology. By this he means that it has no systematic philosophy, no consistent moral or political stance.

Personally, I do not believe that any cultural artifact is ideologically neutral. This, however, is not the point that I wish to argue in this presentation. I also do not want to make this an argument against Tom Quirk's subtle, perceptive, and illuminating book. Rather, I focus on his book because it identifies so acutely some of the fundamental issues regarding how racial attitudes and ideological agendas shape our readings of this great novel. Quirk's reference to "political correctness" is a self-consciously rhetorical gesture, intended to invoke the larger debate within our culture about the acceptable forms and limits of public discourse. Quirk, however, is a serious scholar, not an ideological warrior, and he clearly recognizes that the deeper issue is how our predispositions determine our interpretations. He is not attempting to impose some rigid notion of right and wrong predispositions.

Let me say from the outset that I agree with Quirk on several basic points. Above all, I share his belief that we should not allow our interest in specific aspects of the work, such as its treatment of racial issues, to blind us to other important elements in the work. He chides Fishkin, for instance, for concentrating on Huck's language to the neglect of Huck's "adventures." This I regard to be a constructive and not unfriendly criticism. Similarly,

---

1. Quirk, *Coming to Grips with Huckleberry Finn: Essays on a Book, a Boy, and a Man,* 148. Hereafter referred to as *CGHF.*

he suggests that our concern with the social realities addressed by the book should not blind us to its fundamental character as an imaginative work. This is a simple, seemingly obvious point, but it is one that is too often forgotten. Finally, I agree with him that the actual racial attitudes of Samuel Langhorne Clemens should not be at issue when we interpret the novel. As he puts it, "[T]he imaginative self who created *Huckleberry Finn* ought not be confused with the ordinary self who, on the one hand, wrote abundant racist remarks in letters to his mother, or, on the other, paid a black man's tuition to Yale" (*CGHF*, 158). In other words, an artist might imagine possibilities in his works that transcend the limitations of his day-to-day life. We as readers, critics, and teachers should never forget this fundamental distinction between the artist and his art.

Nonetheless, despite the reasonableness of his arguments, I believe that there are many points on which equally reasonable critics may disagree with Quirk. I am not persuaded, for example, that "incorrectness" is what makes this novel worthy of celebration, though I do appreciate the cogency and force of this view. Certainly it is accurate to say that Huck's honesty, nonconformity, and forthrightness are powerfully appealing and that his comments cut to the heart of our society precisely because his freedom from social proprieties and constraints—his innocence, in other words—allows him to perceive and to speak without distortion. I would not go so far, however, as to call this childish honesty "political incorrectness." Besides, one might argue that *wisdom*, which represents social experience and understanding, is at least as admirable as innocence. The question, then, is how we arrive at such judgments. In order to explore this issue, I want to consider my own writing about this novel. I would like to discuss some of my own unstated concerns and assumptions that informed my particular reading of *Huckleberry Finn*.

In 1984 I published an essay called "Huck, Jim, and American Racial Discourse." It was my contribution to a special issue of the *Mark Twain Journal* that observed the centennial of *Adventures of Huckleberry Finn* with a selection of new essays by black critics. The essays present a spectrum of views ranging from John Wallace's argument that *Huckleberry Finn* "is the most grotesque example of racist trash ever written" at one extreme to my own assertion that "except for Melville's work, *Huckleberry Finn* is without peer among major Euro-American novels for its explicitly antiracist stance."[2] Most of the other essays avoid both extremes and temper their appreciation for the novel's virtues with some degree of uneasiness regarding Twain's handling of racial issues. I want to focus on my own essay not because it is mine and not just because it is the one that I understand best but especially because I want to respond to a pair of criticisms that I find cogent and troubling. Tom Quirk asserts his concern with "protecting Twain from the charge of being a sensitive guy," and Wayne Booth, citing Charles H. Nichols and me, complains that "most critics have talked as if it would be absurd to raise questions about the *racial* values of a book in which the very moral center is a noble black man so magnanimous that he gives himself back into slavery in order to help a doctor save a white boy's life" (*CGHF*, 158).[3] The common thread in these two criticisms is the sense that interpreting *Huck Finn* as antiracist is reductive and ignores countervailing tendencies in the text. For Quirk this implies making Twain into a 1990s politically correct liberal, which he was not, and for Booth it represents the even worse sin of dismissing the moral complexities of the novel in favor of self-satisfied rationalizing. Needless to say, I do not accept either characterization of my position. On the contrary, I share some of the basic concerns that I believe motivate both of these critics. Nevertheless, we do have some fundamental differences of perspective. I believe that difference is illuminating with regard to the practice of criticism and of teaching as well.

My 1984 essay characterizes the novel's treatment of race as follows:

> Twain adopts a strategy of subversion in his attack on race. That is, he focuses on a number of commonplaces associated with "the Negro" and then systematically dramatizes their inadequacy. He uses the term "nigger," and he shows Jim engaging in superstitious behavior. Yet he portrays Jim as a compassionate, shrewd, thoughtful, self-sacrificing, and even wise man. . . . Jim is cautious, he gives excellent advice, he suffers persistent anguish over separation from his wife and children, and he even sacrifices his own sleep so that Huck

---

2. D. L. Smith, "Huck, Jim, and the American Racial Discourse," 16, 104. Hereafter referred to as HJARD.
3. Booth, *The Company We Keep: An Ethics of Fiction,* 463–64.

> may rest. Jim, in short, exhibits all the qualities that "the Negro" supposedly lacks. (HJARD, 105)

Obviously, this passage can be read as portraying Twain to be an earnest, left-leaning social crusader. As Tom Quirk might argue, if he were not so polite, though my discussion sometimes mentions Twain's humor, most of the irreverence and sheer fun of the book is lost in my account. On the other hand, my insistence on Twain's antiracist designs in effect dismisses the racial considerations (stereotypes, demeaning language and jokes, and so on) that lead so many racially sensitive readers of this text to feel offended or at least unsettled. This, I think, is Booth's basic objection.

Even when I was writing my essay, I was quite conscious of these problems with my argument. I decided, for a variety of reasons, that presenting an aggressively antiracist reading of this text, and a reading that credited Twain with antiracist designs, would be the most valuable contribution that I, personally, could make to the special issue and to Twain criticism. I knew that many critics over the years had addressed the book in terms of what they found racially offensive, and I assumed that critics would continue to stress those points. When I read the book, however, and compared it to other pieces of nineteenth-century American writing, especially around the turn of the century, I saw a text that differed in significant ways from other works that addressed racial issues. It seemed important to call attention to these differences, especially because I had just been reading Joel Williamson's profound and troubling book, *The Crucible of Race,* which argued that the post-Reconstruction era was so violently racist and intolerant that he could not identify more than half a dozen liberal voices among the vast multitude of Southerners who wrote or spoke publicly about race during those grim years.

Though I accepted the substantial truth of Williamson's argument, which was consistent with what I had found in my own research into the period, I thought that his pessimism went too far and became, in effect, defeatist. Thus, I was inclined to look for exceptions. I wanted to show that even in the worst of times, the capitulation to racism has never been total in this country. Good motives, however, do not justify dishonest or inaccurate interpretations, and the challenge for me was to read the textual evidence in ways that even critics who did not share my premises would find persuasive.

With this in mind, I decided to reconsider some of the scenes that had most frequently been discussed by critics in terms of their racial implications. Many critics have complained, for instance, that Twain portrays Jim as a comically superstitious darky.

Here is part of what I said about Tom Sawyer's first prank against Jim, which occurs in chapter 2:

> When Jim falls asleep under a tree, Tom hangs Jim's hat on a branch. Subsequently Jim concocts an elaborate tale about having been hexed and ridden by witches. The tale grows more grandiose with each repetition, and eventually Jim becomes a local celebrity, sporting a five-cent piece on a string around his neck as a talisman. "Niggers would come miles to hear Jim tell about it, and he was more looked up to than any nigger in that country," the narrator reports. Jim's celebrity finally reaches the point that "Jim was most ruined, for a servant, because he got so stuck up on account of having seen the devil and been rode by witches." That is, no doubt, amusing. Yet whether Jim believes his own tale or not—and the "superstitious Negro" thesis requires us to assume that he does—the fact remains that Jim clearly benefits from becoming more a celebrity and less a servant. . . . By constructing a fictitious narrative of his own experience, Jim elevates himself above his prescribed station in life. By becoming, in effect, an author, Jim writes himself a new destiny. (HJARD, 108–9)

One may read this scene and laugh at Jim and the other slaves for being superstitious and gullible. The point of my interpretation is not to dismiss the possibility of such laughter but rather to challenge our habit of seeing stereotypes and nothing more. My argument is intended to enable a different way of understanding the scene, and it is based on a careful reconsideration of the textual details. A reading that focuses on stereotypes, by contrast, stresses only the most superficial details. For me, the scene actually becomes *more* funny when read my way because, in addition to the minstrel-show foolishness, my reading sees Jim enjoying a self-serving joke at the expense of his master and being one up on Tom Sawyer. This view allows for a more complex response to this scene, and it also complicates our understanding of the last section of the novel where Jim again rises above Tom's cruel pranks.

I will not continue to stand here and shamelessly rehash my own work, but I disagree that my or Fishkin's kind of argument makes Mark Twain into a "sensitive guy." On the contrary, I believe that to find new ways of reading the details of texts and of understanding the historical and cultural derivations of texts is a fundamental and very traditional responsibility of literary critics. *Political correctness,* as I understand the term, suggests a kind of opportunist conformity: adopting certain language and attitudes in order to avoid offending anyone and to fit in with the prevailing fashions. By that standard, I do not see how readings that challenge the standard interpretations of this childhood favorite and cultural icon can be called "politically correct." On the contrary, my interpretation of Twain, and Fishkin's as well, is that he was *not* politically correct. The political correctness of his era was, after all, strident racism. To understand this point, we must turn for a moment to the racial discourse of the turn of the century.

When Mark Twain's contemporaries wrote about race, they defined *Negro* as a natural and inherently problematic identity. The concern of racial discourse was solutions to "the Negro Problem": industrial education, emigration, castration, lynching, and so on. Mark Twain is a radical writer because he treats blacks and whites as morally equal human beings, and he sees the problem not in the so-called Negro but rather in the cruelty and unfairness mandated in American social relations governed by notions of race. This distinction sounds trivial, yet it has profound implications that most Americans reject even today. Most of us still think racially, seeing black and white identity as distinct, natural phenomena. We are likely now to advocate racial "tolerance," but we still believe that race exists and entails fundamental differences among human beings. Inevitably, then, we continue to have a Jim Crow view of the world, though we dress it up politely. We believe in a single human species but not a single human race. Twain cynically offers us a glimpse of unity: one damned human race.

In order to make an adequate assessment of Mark Twain's racial views, we need to think of him relative to the discursive norms of his own time. At the turn of the century, even benevolent comments on African Americans were often demeaning. To take a conspicuous though not benevolent example, Theodore Roosevelt commented in 1895: "A perfectly stupid race can never rise to a very high place. The Negro, for instance, has been kept down as much by lack of intellectual development as by anything else." Six years later, in a letter to the novelist Owen Wister, he declared: "I entirely agree with you that as a race, and in the mass, the [blacks] are altogether inferior to the whites."[4] These are harsh words, yet Roosevelt was in most respects a liberal on racial issues.

Another self-declared friend of the Negro, George T. Winston, president of the North Carolina College of Agriculture and Mechanic Arts (later renamed North Carolina State University), wrote in a 1901 address to the annual meeting of the American Academy of Political and Social Science: "The Negro race is a child race and must remain in tutelage for years to come; in tutelage not of colleges and universities, but of industrial schools, of skilled and efficient labor, of character building by honest work and honest dealing, of good habits and good manners, of respect for elders and superiors, of daily employment on the farm, in the household, the shop, the forest, the factory and the mine" (*Negro,* 118).

This echoes Booker T. Washington's prescription from his "Atlanta Exposition Address" of 1895. If it sounds like a blueprint for resurrected slavery, perhaps that is because, as these eminent educators both point out, slavery was a school of civilization. Indeed, Thomas Nelson Page stated this idea succinctly: "[T]o the Negro [slavery] was salvation. It found him a savage and a cannibal and in two hundred years gave seven millions of his race the only civilization it has had since the dawn of history" (*Negro,* 285). Even W. E. B. Du Bois, arguably the greatest advocate black Americans have ever had, finds African Americans sadly deficient. As he remarks in *The Souls of Black Folk,* "I should be the last one to deny the patent weaknesses and shortcomings of the Negro people."[5] I will spare you the comments of those who really did not like Negroes. In any case, Mark Twain sounds very enlightened compared to the discursive norms of his time.

As a commentary on race, *Pudd'nhead Wilson* is a very odd book for the 1890s. It is deeply and very explicitly concerned with the social fictions that people construct to justify their own behavior—usually stupid, deluded, or mean-spirited behavior. The first such fiction is the folkloric recasting of David Wilson as Pudd'nhead Wilson—a cautionary tale about the dangers

4. Quoted in Page, *The Negro: The Southerner's Problem,* 387–88. Hereafter referred to as *Negro.*
5. Du Bois, *The Souls of Black Folk: Essays and Sketches,* 329, 387–88.

of failed irony. Roxy's subterfuge, her well-intentioned but ill-fated switching of babies, is yet another misbegotten fabrication. As the author puts it, "by the fiction created by herself, [her son] was become her master." Race, too, is treated as a fiction. Clemens makes this point explicitly in chapter 2 when he notes regarding Roxy's son, "[H]e, too, was a slave, and by a fiction of law and custom a negro."[6] Throughout this work, the fictions of race are exposed and ridiculed as absurd in the face of specific human realities.

This novel attacks the fundamental racial notion that differences in appearance entail fundamental differences in behavior or character. Of course, just as in American reality, the definition of race in this novel has nothing to do with appearance. In stressing this point, Clemens deviates from other writers of the period. In Thomas Dixon's novels, for instance, Negroid traits are always discernible: a slight kink of the hair or fullness of the lips. And even the most refined (that is, white) of mulatto behavior eventually gives way to Negroism: irrationality, emotional excess, superstition, uncontrolled lust, and so on. The only differences between black and white characters in *Pudd'nhead Wilson* are clearly the results of social experience. We see this in the portrayal of Roxy, but the role reversal of the two babies makes the point most forcefully. The white boy develops into a perfect, stereotypical Negro servant: docile, loyal, long suffering, physically adept. Roxy's own son develops into a stereotypical, sociopathic white aristocrat. Their behaviors reflect their social positions, not the clichés of racial character.

In one of the scenes most often analyzed by critics, Roxy lambastes Tom for his cowardice in failing to seek a duel with Luigi, who has insulted him. "It's de nigger in you!" she declares (*PW,* 70). Here, the novel leans heavily on traditional racial ideology. Placing this condemnation in the mouth of Roxy, however, is the irony that subverts the cliché. One-sixteenth-part Negro, she is *twice* as black as her son. If Negro ancestry led to cowardice, Roxy ought to be a coward. In fact, despite her dubious ideas and decisions, she exhibits exemplary physical and moral courage throughout the novel. Still, she is not infallible, as the content of her tirade shows. Like any other human being, she is a product of her culture. Belonging to the oppressed social group does not guarantee that Roxy will have an adequate critique of racial discourse.

6. Twain, *Pudd'nhead Wilson and Those Extraordinary Twins,* 9, 19. Hereafter referred to as *PW.*

In certain respects, she is a racist herself. Twain does not commit the liberal error of exempting black characters from normal human foibles.

On this question of inherited behavioral traits, we must also remember that the mythology works both ways. If the "Negro blood" supposedly engenders cowardice, then the white, aristocratic Essex blood supposedly engenders bold vengefulness: the instinct to fight duels. (I hope, however, that I need not remind anyone that blood is not the medium of heredity. This dead metaphor reflects the premodern, discredited assumptions of race thinking.) Valet, who actually possesses this white, aristocratic lineage, does not retaliate against tormentors, nor does he display cowardice. Finally, Tom exhibits an endless supply of vices but not one of the appealing traits that racial discourse attributes to the Negro. In this novel, Twain thoroughly repudiates racial explanations of behavior.

One other aspect of supposedly racial behavior deserves comment. Common racial discourse holds Negroes to be thieving as well as cowardly by nature. In chapter 2, Mr. Driscoll confronts four of his slaves regarding the theft of some petty cash. Only Roxy is innocent, and even she passed up the money reluctantly. Such theft is stereotypical, but Twain subverts the stereotype in two ways. First, he explains that slaves steal because "they had an unfair show in the battle of life, and they held it no sin to take military advantage of the enemy" (*PW,* 11). They steal small amounts, however, and the slave thief steals "perfectly sure that in taking this trifle from the man who daily robbed him of an inestimable treasure—his liberty—he was not committing any sin that God would remember against him" (*PW,* 12). With these remarks, Twain redefines the moral issue, reminding us that factors of power and social standing must be taken into account when we judge people's behavior.

Second, when Driscoll threatens to sell all four slaves down the river, the three guilty parties confess—presumably to spare the innocent from their own hideous fate. Such honesty in the face of dire consequences is not the behavior of stereotypical Negroes. By contrast, Tom robs indiscriminately to pay his gambling debts. Even worse, whereas these slaves save Roxy from being sold by accepting the consequences of their acts, Tom seeks to escape the consequences of his misdeeds by selling Roxy—his own mother—down the river. Roxy's declarations notwithstanding, Tom is despicable not because of his black fraction but because he is, in the author's words, "like any other miscreant" (*PW*, 12, 82). The moral universe of *Pudd'nhead Wilson* depends upon individual character, social conditioning, and personal choice, not upon biological determinism. This novel insists that we judge the characters on the basis of their personal behavior, not their pedigree. Unfortunately, its insistence is not sufficient to break our habit of thinking in racial terms.

Like the concluding episode of *Huckleberry Finn, Pudd'nhead Wilson* makes careful and sensitive readers profoundly uncomfortable because it challenges our fundamental values and assumptions. The humor of these works troubles us, and many of us would prefer conclusions that leave us feeling virtuous. This is the appeal of melodramatic fiction. By arousing uncomplicated sentiments of sympathy and outrage, melodramatic works such as Twain's early sketch "A True Story" allow us to feel virtuous by identifying easily with the victim while at the same time opposing an unambiguous evil. Twain's humor, on the other hand, is deeply ironic, and it unsettles us because it subverts our desire for easy virtue and instead implicates us in the moral contradictions that it exposes. In my view this is a virtue, not a flaw, of Mark Twain's art.

Mark Twain's art also depended upon his ability to create and construct appropriate and consistent dialect. Dialect writing, which emphasizes deviations from standard English, is a standard comic convention in American literature. But since many Americans do in fact speak dialects, realism demands some use of dialects. Thus, the relationship between realistic depiction and comic distortion is often problematic. Furthermore, because dialect has often been used to depict African Americans as comical and inferior, Negro dialect has been an especially problematic convention. At the beginning of *Adventures of Huckleberry Finn*, Mark Twain attached an explanatory note regarding the use of dialects in the novel. The note declares:

> In this book a number of dialects are used, to wit: the Missouri negro dialect; the extremest form of the backwoods South-Western dialect; the ordinary "Pike-County" dialect; and four modified varieties of this last. The shadings have not been done in a haphazard fashion, or by guess-work; but pains-takingly, and with the trustworthy guidance and support of personal familiarity with these several forms of speech. I make this explanation for the reason that

without it many readers would suppose that all these characters were trying to talk alike and not succeeding.[7]

Two things interest me about this statement. First, I find it curious that of all the potentially controversial elements in this novel, Twain chose to single out dialect for such authorial quibbling. Of course, this "Explanatory" follows his so-called "Notice," a tongue-in-cheek disclaimer of motive, moral, or plot. Nevertheless, he delivers his remark about dialect in a tone that at least sounds serious. The second point of interest is that he begins his list with Missouri Negro dialect. That, too, seems odd, since the book is narrated by Huckleberry Finn, who does not appear to be a Missouri Negro. Then again, perhaps it is not so odd if, as Fishkin so persuasively argues, Huck really is linguistically black.

Mark Twain's "Explanatory" declares the authenticity of his dialect. In this, the most original American writer of his generation was being utterly conventional. At the end of the nineteenth century, virtually everyone was writing dialect, especially Negro dialect, and insisting on its authenticity. In 1880, five years before the American edition of *Huckleberry Finn,* Joel Chandler Harris had published *Uncle Remus: His Songs and Sayings.* In his introduction Harris asserted that his Negro dialect, unlike that of the minstrel stage and popular darky fiction, was "at least phonetically genuine." In his characteristic, self-effacing manner, Harris went on to suggest that his work was poor indeed if phonetic accuracy was all that he accomplished:

> [I]f the language of Uncle Remus fails to give vivid hints of the really
> poetic imagination of the negro; if it fails to embody the quaint
> and homely humor which was his most prominent characteristic;
> if it does not suggest a certain picturesque sensitiveness—a curious
> exaltation of mind and temperament not to be defined by words—
> then I have reproduced the form of the dialect merely, and not the
> essence, and my attempt may be accounted a failure.[8]

The racial condescension implicit in Harris's remarks is obvious, but his sincerity ought to be equally obvious. The literary vogue of Negro dialect

---

7. Twain, *The Adventures of Huckleberry Finn,* ed. Bradley et al., 2. Hereafter referred to as *AHF.*
8. Harris, *Uncle Remus: His Songs and Sayings,* 39.

that began in the early 1880s with Harris, Twain, and Thomas Nelson Page continued in the next decade with the works of Paul Laurence Dunbar and Charles Chesnutt. It resurged in the twenties with Dubose Heyward, Julia Peterkin, and others, and culminated in the thirties with the novels and folklore collections of Zora Neale Hurston. All of these writers were serious about rendering African American language accurately, and all of them, including Harris and Page, held "dialect writing," the sort of writing that merely stereotypes black speech, in contempt.

The classic argument against dialect writing was articulated by James Weldon Johnson in the preface to *The Book of American Negro Poetry:* "Negro dialect is at present a medium that is not capable of giving expression to the varied conditions of Negro life in America, and much less is it capable of giving the fuller interpretation of Negro character and psychology. That is no indictment against the dialect as dialect, but against the mold of convention in which Negro dialect in the United States has been set."[9]

In his preface to the second edition, Johnson elaborates this latter point by explaining that he sees minstrelsy as the culprit in reducing dialect to stereotypes. By exaggerating certain aspects of African American appearance, speech, and behavior, minstrelsy established a set of narrowly comic conventions that degenerated rapidly into tiresome clichés.

To many Americans, however, including Samuel Clemens, these clichés were an inexhaustible source of pleasure. Johnson's complaint, in any case, is that conventional representations of dialect had become an impediment to the expression of anything other than minstrel foolishness. I want to stress Johnson's distinction: the problem was conventions of dialect, not dialect as such. All expressive modes work through conventions. Thus, we as critics must be mindful of the limitations that specific conventions entail; we should not delude ourselves that any form of representation or dialect can be a simple mirror of reality, devoid of convention and artifice. The choice of conventions is in itself meaningful and is likely to be more revealing of authorial design than the mere fact of sociolinguistic accuracy.

I am using the terms *black dialect, Negro dialect,* and *black English* pretty much interchangeably in part to signal my own skepticism regarding no-

9. Johnson, *The Book of American Negro Poetry,* 19.

tions of racial or cultural "authenticity." Though valid issues may be raised regarding criteria of authenticity, I would prefer to focus on the rhetorical function of authenticity claims. From this point of view, whether a given utterance is authentically African American or not is a less interesting question than why and how the appearance of authenticity matters. After all, it is not self-evident that fiction writers ought to be so concerned to make the language of individual characters typical of, for instance, "Missouri Negro dialect." There is a profound cultural logic to this impulse, however, and I will return shortly to this point. Obviously, the representation of dialect in American culture is always closely linked to our consciousness of class status, racial identity, and caste distinctions. Less obviously, but equally important, the use of dialect often functions as a nostalgic gesture that romanticizes the past or sentimentalizes dialect speakers as vestigial synecdoches, representing a defunct mode of life. Such nostalgia is not always benign.

Let us set aside for the moment this question of whether a particular author's use of dialect is authentic and consider instead what is at stake rhetorically in authors' authenticity claims. First, the author's authority is at stake. Dialectical accuracy signifies the author's intimate knowledge of a given culture and mode of life. Whether this synecdochal equation is valid or not—dialect represents a culture; knowledge of dialect entails knowledge of culture; therefore, the author's mastery of a dialect represents his mastery of that culture—it has great rhetorical force. Thus, when Mark Twain asserts that *Adventures of Huckleberry Finn* deploys several precisely rendered variants of a regional dialect, he is implicitly establishing his qualifications to be a chronicler of that culture. When Joel Chandler Harris states his aspiration to render through his use of dialect not just the speech mannerisms but also the sensibility of the Negro, he is urging us to accept the equation between his dialectical accuracy and his profound cultural knowledge.

The long tradition of critical responses to dialect suggests that we have generally accepted this equation. Critics who regard *Huckleberry Finn* as a racist book have often challenged the authenticity of Jim's speech, comparing it to the conventions of minstrelsy. The defenders of the book have felt obligated to claim validity for Twain's depiction of Jim's speech. The most detailed and impressive reading of the latter sort is Shelley Fisher Fishkin's *Was Huck Black? Mark Twain and African-American Voices.* Fishkin surveys more than a century's worth of ethnolinguistic scholarship in order to demonstrate that both Jim and Huck use vocabulary and grammatical constructions that linguists have identified as distinctively African American. Fishkin's work is especially pertinent in this context, because it addresses so clearly the entailments of the debate over dialectical authenticity.

Fishkin describes her designs as follows: "My goal is to foreground the role previously neglected African-American voices played in shaping Mark Twain's art in *Huckleberry Finn*. Given that book's centrality in our culture, the points made implicitly illuminate, as well, how African-American voices shaped our sense of what is distinctively 'American' about American literature."[10] Her case is built upon both circumstantial and linguistic arguments. The former consists of Twain's own testimony regarding African American speakers whose style had influenced him; the latter comprises her listing of distinctively African American linguistic traits and her identification of these traits in the language of Jim and Huck. If Huck is at least in part linguistically black, and the book that according to Hemingway, Faulkner, and others constitutes the foundation of modern American fiction is therefore also black (and here, I follow our standard American practice of defining blackness by a "one-drop" standard), then it follows that American literature is also black. I do not intend to oversimplify Fishkin's argument to the point of parody. Quite the contrary, I want to insist that she has identified correctly the issue that has always simmered beneath the surface of debates about black dialect. One of the most brilliant and delightful accomplishments of her book is its use of the most conventional scholarly tools to demolish the conventional view of dialect as a marker of inferiority and difference. In Fishkin's account, black English is the identity that Huck and Jim most fundamentally share.

What her argument achieves seems to me not a reversal but rather the public exposure of a truth that was always embarrassingly present. Mark Twain took great pleasure in disconcerting statements of truth, so it should not surprise us that his greatest novel tweaks our racial sensibilities so aggressively. The more pertinent point, however, is this collapse of difference into identity on the site of black English. In most works of fiction that use black dialect, the dialect serves to exemplify difference, and the collapse of

10. Fishkin, *Was Huck Black?* 9.

such distinctions indicates a failure of authorial designs. In *Huckleberry Finn* this transgression is an integral part of the narrative design. This subversive use of dialect, I want to argue, reflects Twain's own rebellion against the conventions of American racial discourse.

We can see this distinctly when we compare *Huckleberry Finn* to the stories of Harris and Page. Both of these latter writers often construct narratives in which a black man speaks dialect, telling his story to a white person who does not speak in dialect. Whether it is one of Page's faceless white narrators who meets some garrulous old Negro on a country road or Harris's Uncle Remus entertaining a white child, dialect serves as a strict marker of difference between the black and the white, the young and the old, the antebellum and the modern. Though Twain uses the same narrative devices and even the same basic time frame as Harris and Page, his choice of a narrator who speaks dialect rather than standard English ultimately emphasizes commonality rather than difference. At the end of *Adventures of Huckleberry Finn,* Huck remarks: "I reckon I got to light out for the Territory ahead of the rest, because Aunt Sally she's going to adopt me and sivilize me and I can't stand it. I been there before" (*AHF,* 229). This proposed flight from civilization is a continuation of what Huck has done throughout the novel, not a new resolve. Linguistically speaking, civilization is the realm of proper English, and the territory is the realm of dialect. Huck does not want to become another Tom Sawyer, and he is quite content to talk like a Negro. This latter is a common American impulse and one that is usually gratified through means less dangerous than striking out for real frontiers. Indeed, part of the appeal of the Uncle Remus tales is that they allow adults to slip into dialect and out of civilization—perhaps nightly, if they are parents who read to their children—without the risk of being trapped in dialect or treated like Negroes. We might gain some useful insights into our culture if we would ask ourselves honestly why it is that we so greatly enjoy slipping into dialect, the verbal equivalent of blacking up.

As a final reflection on dialect, let us consider a recurrent image from Zora Neale Hurston's *Their Eyes Were Watching God.* Again and again, Janie, the protagonist of that novel, yearns to join the storytelling and the talk of the black folk community around her. Even when Janie returns home at the end of her adventures—this occurs at the beginning of the novel—the narrator tells us that she is driven by the oldest of human urges: the need to tell one's own story. Yet, contrary to her impulses earlier in the novel to join the talkers on the porch, when she returns home after her adventures, she spurns them and retreats into her kitchen, where she tells her story to just her friend Pheoby.

Though the issue for Janie is posed in terms of audience, not dialect, I believe that Janie's dilemma is essentially the same as Huck's. They both identify with vernacular culture, yet they also yearn to be the authors of narratives regarding their own experiences, which is essentially a literary aspiration. Talking and writing are quite different. Huck declares, "[I]f I'd a knowed what a trouble it was to make a book I wouldn't a tackled it and ain't agoing to no more" (*AHF* 229). Writing, after all, is a quintessentially civilized activity. To reject writing is, in effect, to light out for the territory. Janie, by contrast, lights out for the territory—"The Muck" in Hurston's novel—and elects to return home. This is the difference that I want us to consider.

Janie has concluded that you have to go there to know there, but having had the experience, she decides not to stay among the folk. Instead, she leaves The Muck and returns to her Big House. Like Huck, she has money in the bank, which buys her the freedom to choose her social location. Unlike Huck, she remains ambivalent about her future options. The novel ends with the narrator's voice in standard English, not Janie's dialect, describing the moving picture of memories cast against the screen of Janie's own subjectivity. The passage marks a startling turn inward, a gesture of self-sufficiency that incorporates folk culture even as it signifies Janie's having transcended the limitations of folk culture. *Their Eyes Were Watching God* embodies this dual yearning to slip into and slip out of dialect at will—a privileged kind of social mobility that is possible only for those who have already moved up the social ladder from folk culture.

In this respect, *Their Eyes Were Watching God* is an ideal novel for the alienated intellectuals of our own time. It particularly reflects the conflicted social position and yearnings of African American academics who find themselves ensconced in positions of privilege that they would not relinquish yet yearning for the folkish community of which dialect is so compellingly seductive a synecdoche. This novel invites its readers to slip into dialect and provides a gratifying narrative that ultimately celebrates the transcendent gesture of slipping out again. Representing a total participatory immersion in the world of folk life, *Their Eyes Were Watching God* offers a far more intimate vicarious experience than the works of Harris and Page, which invite one only to be a spectator and perhaps a performer of dialect but not to cast off one's social status and plunge headlong into a folk identity. By contrast, *Adventures of Huckleberry Finn* represents the embattled urge to remain uncivilized forever.

Dialect, obviously a synecdoche of folk life, necessarily entails inscriptions of social hierarchy, precisely because it is defined in contrast to the language of a dominant class. Not surprisingly, then, it reminds listeners of their own social position and social attitudes. For this reason, discussions of dialect are always politically charged. Furthermore, authors who write dialect are likely to have a nostalgic relation to it, since their being authors almost invariably means that they have acquired fluency in the dominant form of the language. Thus, dialect is likely to be associated with the Old South, lost youth, one's roots, or whatever good old days. As critics, we should be attentive to how dialect is used and, more fundamentally, to the values that it appears to entail. What attitudes does it encourage us to take toward the people and modes of life that it represents? Does it highlight or obfuscate the ambiguous relationship of the highly educated to vernacular culture?

If *Adventures of Huckleberry Finn* is a nostalgic work, it is nostalgia of a highly qualified sort. If we identify with Huck's desire to spurn "sivilization" and "light out for the Territory," we might do well to remember Pap Finn's tirade against the educated Negro and his disgust with a government that would let such a man vote. Pap swears off voting in such a country and, in effect, lights out for the territory. For different reasons, father and son reach the same conclusion. Mark Twain may be right about the accuracy of his dialects, but I believe that the book offers us a deeper truth than sociolinguistic verisimilitude. It calls to our attention the profound ironies and ambiguities, the troubling uncertainties, that are embedded in our deployments of language. Mark Twain reminds us that civilization is more dialectical than we like to believe.

Black Genes and White Lies

Twain and the Romance of Race

ANN M. RYAN

Adventures of Huckleberry Finn is not, particularly, a "good" book, in the moral sense of the term, nor is it particularly well written, according to conventional, novelistic standards of style and structure. Although sensitive to the fact that "human beings can be awful cruel sometimes," Twain ends his novel with a grotesque practical joke at the expense of Jim, the most "human" being in the narrative.[1] And though Hemingway hailed *Adventures of Huckleberry Finn* as "the best book we've had. All American writing comes from that," he also claims that the closing chapters were "just cheating." At its best, then, *Huckleberry Finn* seems to be what Herschel Parker would characterize as a "flawed text," divided against its best intentions and unsteady in its expression of them.[2]

Yet, as Jonathan Arac demonstrates in *Huckleberry Finn as Idol and Target: The Functions of Criticism in Our Time,* despite these apparent failures, and in some cases because of them, literary critics, teachers, journalists and even American presidents continue to insist that *Huckleberry Finn* represents the nobility of the American character, and does so beautifully. According to Arac, critics since the 1940s have self-consciously engaged in an interpretive process that equated Huck with tolerance and love, Twain with Huck, and America with Twain. Reacting to a longstanding history of self-serving criticism on the part of a white literary establishment, Arac

1. Twain, *The Adventures of Huckleberry Finn,* ed. Bradley et al., 182. Hereafter referred to as *AHF.*
2. Hemingway, *The Green Hills of Africa,* 22; Parker, *Flawed Texts and Verbal Icons: Literary Authority in American Fiction,* 1.

represents *Adventures of Huckleberry Finn* as a novel with a mean spirit, and Twain as an author with a hard heart.

I want to suggest that it is precisely this raw quality, in both the book and its author, that makes *Adventures of Huckleberry Finn* a valuable asset in contemporary racial discourse. Certainly, Twain evades political entanglements, yet he intentionally represents this evasion. Clearly, the novel operates on racist assumptions and privileges, yet it unflinchingly illustrates how both are expressed and defended. Finally, I hope to demonstrate the extent to which critics are troubled by humor—Twain's sense of humor in particular—as an imaginative response to our racist history. If Twain imagines that race is a joke, he does not necessarily mean that we should not take it seriously.

Over the course of the twentieth century, *Adventures of Huckleberry Finn* has become both a racial text and a racial test, differently valenced depending upon the reader's ethnic and racial identity. David Smith describes "the work of Mark Twain" as being "an especially fraught topic" for black critics, which demands a "gesture of self-declaration." Smith argues that whereas white critics can choose to evade or embrace the racial politics of *Adventures of Huckleberry Finn,* "black critics who discuss this novel without addressing the portrayal of Jim and the racial issues posed by the novel risk appearing personally deficient, ashamed to admit their own racial identity."[3]

On the other hand, according to Arac's understanding of the ideology that has produced and continues to support the "hypercanonization" of Twain's masterpiece, for white critics either to argue that *Adventures of Huckleberry Finn* belongs in the secondary-school curriculum or to suggest that it undermines racist perceptions and behaviors is to participate in a distortion and an evasion of America's racist history. It is difficult for readers—black or white—to disagree, unless, that is, we are willing to risk being associated with both a text and an interpretive history that have allowed African American children to be demeaned under the guise of being uplifted and afforded white readers and academics the opportunity to feel good while doing nothing. By the end of Arac's argument, his readers are left wondering why anyone should read or teach the book at all.

---

3. D. L. Smith, "Black Critics and Mark Twain," 123, 126.

The politics most informing Arac's study are those of the civil rights era. This was a time when the color line was dramatized at lunch counters and picket lines and where consequent racial politics appear, at least from a historical distance, equally uncomplicated; however, though the color line continues to be as determinant as it was in the 1960s and '70s, it is also significantly more anxious. Racial minorities, and black men in particular, continue to be the objects of extreme hate crime—in Texas, a black man was chained to a pickup truck and dragged to his death; in New York, a Haitian immigrant was sexually brutalized by police officers. Yet, this racialized violence is occurring and possibly even escalating at the same time when some of the most basic assumptions of racial identity are being dismantled and redefined.

We also live in a historical moment when one may represent one's racial and ethnic identity in multiple terms for the census bureau. Checking the "identity box" has become as much a metaphor as a political gesture, and both are as difficult to read. The term *nigger* is a convention in rap and hip-hop music, an ironized noun that rejects its own historical context and a totem for wannabe white boys—director Quentin Tarantino foremost among them—who imagine that speaking the word transfigures their whiteness and makes them "boys from the hood." If "our" students are traumatized by Twain's use of the word *nigger,* and clearly many of them have been, they are also living in a culture that variously fetishizes the word, glamorizes its usage, and obscures its history.

Finally, if reading *Adventures of Huckleberry Finn* seems to invite white readers away from the political and social battlefield, it may be that, as a metaphor at least, "battle" no longer represents the complicated interactions presently defining racial politics and identity. The political worth of imagined white heroes and villains, black martyrs and victims, is being undermined by an increasingly diverse American landscape. This is not to suggest that the oppression of or violence against African Americans has decreased, but that at the present moment we seem less to be fighting a battle than caught in a riot where identities are blurred and objectives are confused. It may be that *Adventures of Huckleberry Finn,* a novel that at once fears, despises, and maintains the privileges of white masculinity, is particularly relevant now as we anticipate a century where white people in America will no longer determine the nature of race or control readings of it.

I would suggest that, despite the dangers inherent in reading this "flawed text," *Adventures of Huckleberry Finn* speaks specifically to the shifting nature of contemporary identity politics. Implicit in this process of debunking national literary heroes is the substitution of a superior narrative for the inadequate original. At the end of his essay on James Fenimore Cooper, Twain concludes that *The Deerslayer* is "simply a literary *delirium tremens*," clearly positioning himself as—curiously enough—the sober alternative to Cooper:

> If Cooper had any real knowledge of Nature's ways of doing things, he had a most delicate art in concealing the fact. For instance: one of his acute Indian experts, Chingachgook (pronounced Chicago, I think), has lost the trail of a person he is tracking through the forest. . . . Chicago was not stumped for long. He turned a running stream out of its course, and there, in the slush in its old bed, were that person's moccasin-tracks. The current did not wash them away, as it would have done in all other cases—no, even the eternal laws of Nature have to vacate when Cooper wants to put up a delicate job of woodcraft on the reader.[4]

Twain invites comparison, encouraging the reader to accept "Huckleberry" as a more realistic name, and Huck as a more acute observer of nature, and of the workings of rivers in particular: "and by and by you could see a streak on the water which you know by the look of the streak that there's a snag there in a swift current which breaks on it and makes that streak look that way" (*AHF,* 96). Twain reconstructs not only the reader's vision of Cooper, but the reader's critical eye as well. Although Twain complains predominantly about Cooper's style, by arguing for accuracy in language and consistency in tone, Twain is also advocating a type of realism and all the values that it implies—foremost among them, a credible relationship to history and an accurate representation of individuals within that history.

As a corrective to "hypercanonization," Arac suggests the sublime as defined by Longinus, especially because it seems to preclude unitary readings: "The sublime does not depend on fancy language, and it does not arise from the unity of a work; like a 'whirlwind' it tears up any established pattern

---

4. Twain, *Tales, Speeches, Essays, and Sketches,* 381. Hereafter referred to as *Tales.*

or texture, so as to stand out from the context or work in which it occurs." In order to avoid the hegemonic readings of mid-twentieth-century critics and consequent "fruitless and ultimately offensive hyperbole about the excellence of the work as a whole," the reader is pointed toward the most antipolitical of literary experiences, the sublime.[5] It is unclear how this will make for a more politically effective reading of *Adventures of Huckleberry Finn,* but it will at least ensure a less disturbing reading. If a sublime encounter with the text allows the reader to frame the meaning of the novel within his or her own experience and perception, it seems likely that students will not be troubled by *Adventures of Huckleberry Finn* or by canonical sermons about its goodness. Of course, it is also less likely that students will encounter the inherent divisiveness of the novel, the racial "civil war" present both within the text and within the already divided "Mark Twain."

By introducing the sublime as an ideological value, highly individualistic, even fragmentary, readings of the text are privileged. The sublime is preconditioned, at least within an American context, by an aggressive rejection of people and politics. Emerson, the representative man of American transcendentalism, aspires to this whirlwind effect specifically because it prevents the kind of coherence that forms identity and oppresses individuals: "I become a transparent eye-ball; I am nothing; I see all. . . . The name of the nearest friend sounds then foreign and accidental; to be brothers, to be acquaintances,—master or servant, is then a trifle and a disturbance. . . . In the wilderness, I find something more dear and connate than in the streets or the villages."[6]

Twain anticipates the interpretive struggles Arac highlights between politics and aesthetics or, more accurately for Twain, between conscience and comfort. Throughout his career as a fiction writer, and later in his life as public moralist, Twain wavered, wanting both to preach and to please. Hamlin Hill makes this point about the last ten years of Twain's life. Hill argues that the "jeremiad strain in his voice" was, in part, a conscious development: "What is significant is that Mark Twain, an author more sensitive than most of his image in the eyes of his audience, was becoming persuaded

5. Arac, *Huckleberry Finn as Idol and Target,* 36.
6. Emerson, "Nature," 10. Hereafter referred to as Nature.

that a vocal dissident minority was respectable and even proper."[7] There-fore, even in works such as "To the Person Sitting in Darkness," in which Twain appears to be in a full-blown rant against the most basic operations of American culture (its missionary politics and its redemptive identity), he is also anxious to maintain his currency within that culture.

In *Adventures of Huckleberry Finn* this anxiety surfaces in the interpretive frame that surrounds the novel. As the beginning and the ending of the novel demonstrate, Twain can only imagine two interpretive responses to his work: either the novel will be overread (hypercanonized) and forced into some representative function alien to Twain's comic impulses, or the text will be enjoyed and dismissed, a victim of these same comic practices. Aware that his is a dangerous text, Twain underscores that fact by heightening the consequences of reading it. Twain wants his work to be taken seriously, but he also intends it to be misunderstood. At the beginning of the novel Twain notes, "Persons attempting to find a motive in this narrative will be prosecuted; persons attempting to find a moral in it will be banished; persons attempting to find a plot in it will be shot" (*AHF*, 2).

Twain draws a line in the sand and dares literary critics to cross it, know-ing full well, as he has demonstrated in "The Literary Offenses of James Fenimore Cooper," that they will do so with abandon, generating readings and misreadings that are political, moral, and social in nature. Twain invites serious readers to violate his text and translate it into something meaning-ful. However, at the end of the novel Huck aborts his own incipient career as an author, suggesting Twain's frustration with the meaning-making busi-ness: "[T]here ain't nothing more to write about, and I am rotten glad of it, because if I'd a knowed what a trouble it was to make a book I wouldn't a tackled it and ain't agoing to no more" (*AHF*, 229). If he warns the reader against finding too much meaning in his narrative, Huck expresses Twain's fear of authorial emptiness, that "there ain't nothing more to write about." Here Twain seems playfully to be suggesting that "the rest is silence," that his own desire to bring the novel—perhaps *any* novel—to some meaningful closure is pointless.

In essence, Twain has orchestrated an all-or-nothing game. If Twain

7. Hill, *Mark Twain: God's Fool*, 39, 21.

intentionally evades the efforts of sentimental literalists such as Miss Wat-son and the hyperbolic misreadings of Tom Sawyer, he also anticipates the impressionistic readings of posttranscendentalists. Although Twain will end his career by claiming to be nothing more than a "jack-leg" author, and though he would certainly agree that Huckleberry Finn was not "doing cultural work comparable to Stowe's with regard to racial issues," Twain does not seriously intend the reader to embrace the void that he himself has constructed. To agree that the novel has no meaning, no moral, and no plot is to suggest that the humor is itself meaningless, or that it is just a stimulus within the highly personal experience of the sublime. If the sublime has any value in Twain's fiction, it may be in what Bruce Michelson character-izes as "the wildness" of Twain, "his uncontainable humor, rambunctious barbarism, spontaneity, changefulness, insouciance, and anarchy."[8]

For Twain's audience, this wildness emerges at the moment of laugh-ter, yet even this apparently sublime release occurs within a social context. Twain's fiction, which depends upon the privatized experience of reading, nonetheless reflects the aesthetic sensibilities of a stand-up comic working a crowd: an overall episodic structure, marked by lengthy setups, shock-ing revelations, and an emphasis on tone and presentation. Twain "excites the laughter of God's creatures" by violating social norms and the collective conscious, as much as by disrupting individual expectations.[9] The sublime may allow for open-ended, fragmentary possibilities, but it is a necessarily private encounter and almost undoubtedly serious.

The concept of the sublime is imbued with notions of spiritual purifi-cation and religious conversion, as well as with romantic notions of truth and beauty. Yet, if Twain's sense of humor inspires his audience, it is more often with guilty pleasure and the thrill that accompanies his transgressive wit. At no point is Twain's comedy pure. Although—once again returning to an American context for the sublime—Twain's sense of humor frequently makes his audience "glad to the brink of fear" (Nature, 10). In his essay "How to Tell a Story," Twain describes both a comic technique and an ob-jective: "If I got it the right length precisely, I could spring the finishing

8. Arac, *Huckleberry Finn as Idol and Target*, 96; Michelson, *Mark Twain on the Loose: A Comic Writer and the American Self*, 3.
9. Cox, *The Fate of Humor*, 6.

ejaculation with effect enough to make some impressible girl deliver a star-
tled little yelp and jump out of her seat—and that was what I was after"
(*Tales*, 394).

Twain enacts this principle during a performance at Bryn Mawr, where
his daughter Susy was a student. Susy begged Twain not to tell "The Golden
Arm" at this particular reading, and he promised not to do so. In this short
story, Twain mimics black dialect while narrating the tale of a husband
who is haunted by his dead wife after he robs her grave and steals her
"golden arm." When Twain closed his performance with this ghost story,
Susy jumped from her seat, "ran up the aisle and out of the room, weeping";
Twain got what he was after (*MC&MT*, 310). Twain's performative values
seem to parody sexual intercourse, where the audience is metaphorically,
and in this case perhaps literally, a collective virgin, and Twain a kind of
stranger in the night. In addition, the performance is also a violation of
paternal bonds and notions of racial purity: Twain promises to be a good
white father, and instead, he becomes an angry and haunting black woman.

Twain lies to his daughter and excites his audience; they laugh and she
cries. Embedded within the white man's comic performance is a "Negro
Ghost story" about a "monsus mean man" who steals his wife's treasure.
Twain's sense of humor confuses the comic and the tragic, laughter and
cruelty, and it also tensely arranges black both within and against white.
Twain enacts the same type of comic performance in *Adventures of Huckleberry Finn,* where the heroic fantasies of Tom Sawyer are punctuated by the
death of Buck and where the playful teasing of Jim at the beginning of the
novel seems to license caging him at the end. The structure of *Adventures
of Huckleberry Finn* approximates the long setup to a joke. In this case the
punch line is neither satisfying nor funny.

Rather than transporting us "into a new state or position," Twain's sense
of humor haunts his readers with their own subversive desires and repressed
fears. Twain inverts the sublime structure (wherein the individual is uplifted
beyond the boundaries of time, place, and identity) and exposes his readers
to the comic grotesque both within their own lives and within the normative
values and practices of American culture. In a letter to his brother Orion,
Twain admits that he had a "call to literature, of a low order—i.e. humorous" (*MTL1*, 322). Twain draws upon the language of religious calling and
conversion; however, as a preacher whose medium is humor, Twain often

leads his audience to question faith and to believe exclusively in the fiction of his own comic performance.[10] Twain recounts an episode from one of his early experiences as a lecturer that is emblematic of these conversions: "San Francisco had been persecuted for five or six years with a silly and pointless and unkillable anecdote which everybody had long ago grown weary of— weary unto death. It was as much as a man's life was worth to tell that moldy anecdote to a citizen. I resolved to begin my lecture with it and keep on re-peating it until the mere repetition should conquer the house and make it laugh." The gamble ultimately pays off as the audience, after many tense and confused moments, "recognized the sell and broke into a laugh. It spread back, and back, and back, to the furtherest verge of the place."[11] Twain was determined to make the audience see that he was "working a delicate piece of satire," the target of which is the entire process and context in which they were collectively engaged. It was a metajoke aimed at the audience's own desire to be entertained. The point is that if Twain could get the members of his audience to laugh at nothing, he could get them to laugh at anything. Twain's comic theory and practice are based upon deceit, upon his ability to encourage readers to see what is not there and possibly to laugh at what is not funny. While the rest of America in the nineteenth century searched for truth, Twain developed an aesthetic based upon the beauty of a lie.

10. Twain imagines himself, perhaps not incorrectly, as a corrupting influence: within a year of her marriage Olivia, from a strictly religious and proper New England family, was drinking beer before bedtime and "drinking cocktails of Scotch, lemon, sugar, and Angostura bitters before breakfast" (*MC&MT*, 80). By the end of their marriage, originally supposed to be a vehicle of Twain's reformation, Olivia Clemens had come to doubt organized religion and faith. After the death of their second child, Susy, Twain both reinforces and regrets his wife's doubts: "He had long ago undermined Livy's religious faith, another thing he could claim guilt for. Now, when she looked for comfort in orthodox notions of a just or purposeful deity, he told her that the universe was governed by some sort of malign thug. He raged on and on, but when his storm subsided he stroked her hair and said shortly, 'Don't mind anything I say, Livy. Whatever happens you know I love you.' And then he took his daughters by the Thames and told them how vile the human race was" (*MC&MT*, 338). The reader discovers that, like Olivia Clemens, we are being asked to represent the very standards and beliefs that Twain is about to assault. Like any good comedian—the term perhaps an oxymoron—Twain replaces the conventional with the personal, the institutional with the intimate; Twain's "I love you" fails to signify, and has all the effect and purpose of a practical joke. Within Twain's marriage he offers intimacy as a substitute for all the standards that he assaults: "God is dead, the text is meaningless, but I love you."

11. Twain, *The Autobiography of Mark Twain*, 144, 146. Hereafter referred to as *AMT*.

Twain's sense of humor is at the heart of the controversies surrounding *Adventures of Huckleberry Finn.* Often apologists suggest that since the novel is a work of humor, its racist language and content need not trouble the reader: they are historical lapses in an otherwise harmless book. Critics also evade the racist vocabulary of the novel, claiming that it works in the service of irony: because the subtext is humanitarian and the goal is satire, the offensive nature of Twain's language is only superficial. Finally, would-be censors argue that the humor is racist, and, therefore, the novel is both oppressive and dangerous, nothing more than "racist trash." These conventional readings elide the relationship that Twain cultivates between race—particularly whiteness—and humor by making his use of humor incidental to the meaning of the narrative.

In *Adventures of Huckleberry Finn* there is very little that is idyllic about the humor Huck encounters: from the laughter of Colonel Sherburn, "not the pleasant kind, but the kind that makes you feel like when you are eating bread that's got sand in it" (*AHF,* 118); to the pranks of the all-male mob, "There couldn't nothing wake them up all over, and make them happy all over, like a dog-fight—unless it might be putting turpentine on a stray dog and setting fire to him, or tying a tin pan to his tail and see him run himself to death" (*AHF,* 113); or even the highly orchestrated con games of the Duke and the King, "We never showed a light till we was about ten mile below that village. Then we lit up and had supper, and the king and the duke fairly laughed their bones loose over the way they'd served them people. The duke says: "Greenhorns, flatheads!" (*AHF,* 123).

If Twain invites his reader into nostalgic reveries, and if the ending of *Adventures of Huckleberry Finn* is both a literal and a figurative evasion of racist America, it is also humor that discomfits the reader, that assaults our pleasure even as it seems to create it. The novel begins with a boy's sense of escape and pleasure as expressed in Tom Sawyer's games and Huck's white lies, and it ends with a kind of practical joke—a sense of humor that is, for Twain, exclusive to men and dangerous in adults. As an evasion, the humor of *Adventures of Huckleberry Finn* fails to "transport" the reader to some "new state"; instead, it causes the reader to long for some more complete and absolute escape from the South of Twain's memory.

Through *Adventures of Huckleberry Finn,* Twain explores not only his own identity as a humorist—and the moral as well as interpretive endgame it encourages and avoids—but also a sense of humor that is the privilege of being white and male. Of course, the question remains as to the value of representing this laughter and the particular relevance it holds in current racial discourses and practices. In 1885 the triumph of white racial politics was absolute, a comic closure to the tragic losses of the Civil War. Yet, as Twain represents this victory in *Adventures of Huckleberry Finn,* the closure is unstable and violent, like the punch line to a bad joke or like the freeing of an already free man. Mark Twain does not—and perhaps cannot—narrate the tragedy of slavery, or its haunting presence in American history; instead, through *Adventures of Huckleberry Finn,* he explores the unconvincing comic fiction of Reconstruction and the enormous practical joke of race in America.

Twain's conception of race as a joke is echoed by W. E. B. Du Bois in several of his autobiographical works. First, in *The Souls of Black Folk* (1903), he describes being rejected as a child by a fellow classmate: "Then it dawned upon me with a certain suddenness that I was different from the others; or like, mayhap, in heart and life and longing, but shut out from their world by a vast veil."[12] Du Bois frames his racial awakening, as would many turn-of-the-century black writers, as a humiliation, as if he had been the target of a practical joke. Later, in his autobiography, *Dusk of Dawn* (1940), he describes the experience of being black as something like being in a cave where the opening is sealed by glass:

> One talks on evenly and logically in this way, but notices that the passing throng does not even turn its head, or if it does, glances curiously and walks on. It gradually penetrates the minds of the prisoners that the people passing do not hear; that some thick sheet of invisible but horribly tangible plate glass is between them and the world. They get excited; they talk louder; they gesticulate. Some of the passing world stop in curiosity; these gesticulations seem so pointless; they laugh and pass on. They still either do not hear at all, or hear but dimly, and even what they hear, they do not understand. Then the people within may become hysterical. They may scream and hurl themselves against the barriers, hardly realizing in their bewilderment that they are screaming in a vacuum unheard

12. Du Bois, *The Souls of Black Folk,* 8.

and that their antics may actually seem funny to those outside
looking in.[13]

Here Jim's prison is described from the inside, exposing the reality that
makes him seem to be a clown and the ideology that perceives his suffering as comedy. Du Bois links white laughter and black pain as a primary
illustration of the forces that organize race.

Twain makes a similar connection from a radically different perspective. *Adventures of Huckleberry Finn* pointedly explores the humor of the
master as it anxiously, yet absolutely, expresses the ideology of a master
race. Throughout the novel Twain represents jokes—telling them, repeating them, and aiming them—as a privileged function of white masculinity.
One of the advantages of being a white man in the novel is the ability to
orchestrate the comic stage, to determine the target of the joke, the content
of the humor, and the audience who will enjoy it and profit from it. Twain
illustrates this dynamic in a nightly exchange early in the novel among three
men "talking at a ferry landing":

> [O]ne man said it was getting towards the long days and the short
> nights, now. 'Tother one said this warn't one of the short ones, he
> reckoned—and then they laughed, and he said it over again and they
> laughed again; then they waked up another fellow and told him, and
> laughed, but he didn't laugh; he ripped out something brisk and
> said let him alone. The first fellow said he 'lowed to tell it to his old
> woman—she would think it was pretty good; but he said that warn't
> nothing to some things he had said in his time. (*AHF,* 33)

Only the most unfortunate of readers (those who presumably have not
spent enough time on front porches or in bars) can fail to appreciate the
pleasure of sharing an inside joke. The humor of the speaker's remark is
determined by the context and not by the extreme wit of his statement. In
effect, the two initial jokers form a kind of hermeneutic circle where the humor derives primarily from their own arbitrary and insistent experience of
the moment *as* humorous: whereas their brisk companion illustrates what
the speaker's wife will surely discover, the circle is closed, available to only

---

13. Du Bois, *Dusk of Dawn,* 650.

these privileged two. The inside joke functions as discursive capital. It operates as if it were private property and establishes boundaries and social hierarchies. Huck, like the reader, experiences the humor as an outside observer, recording the humor rather than participating in it: "I heard what they said too, every word of it!" (*AHF*, 33). The scene recalls Twain's San Francisco performance where the source of the humor is not in the originality of the joke but in Twain's willingness and determination to include the audience in his humor.

As the novel progresses, the exclusivity of the inside joke is paired with the violence of the practical joke. Twain represents the practical joke as a fundamental abuse of power, employed to humiliate an innocent victim and to please the joker. Twain often locates the practical joke within a social landscape that makes it a part of the shared history and discourse of some dominant community. Tom Sawyer clearly aspires to master this public stage by orchestrating a comic masterpiece. As Tom will later admit, he plans Jim's fate "from the start, in his head." Only Tom knows that Jim is already free, and that his elaborate plan of escape is a kind of practical joke:

> Only I couldn't believe it. Tom Sawyer a nigger stealer!
> "Oh, shucks," I says, "you're joking."
> "I ain't joking either."
> "Well, then," I says, "joking or no joking, if you hear anything said about a runaway nigger, don't forget to remember that you don't know nothing about him, and I don't know nothing about him."
> (*AHF*, 178)

Once again Huck and the reader are in the same situation: trying to decide if the end of the novel is "joking or no joking."

The power to organize the terms of a joke mirrors the power of the master, as Tom Sawyer's treatment of both Jim and Huck demonstrates:

> And he said, what he had planned in his head, from the start, if we got Jim out all safe, was for us to run him down the river, on the raft, and have adventures plumb to the mouth of the river, and then tell him about his being free, and take him back up home on a steamboat, in style, and pay him for his lost time, and write word ahead and get out all the niggers around, and have them waltz him

into town with a torchlight procession and a brass band, and then he
would be a hero, and so would we. (*AHF*, 228)

Jim's freedom and safety—"if we got Jim out all safe"—are in service
to Tom's desire to be a hero, just as Twain suborns the historical reality
suggested by running slaves and burning torches to the imaginative comic
parade that Tom has authored. As both white master and practical joker,
Tom chooses the victim and enjoys the process and product of his choice.
The practical joke, according to Twain, assaults the humanity of the target:
it awakens a sense of their own contingent physicality, and it causes them to
doubt their perceptions of truth. For example, Jim is bitten by snakes and
rats, convinced that he has been stolen by witches and fooled by Huck in the
fog. Yet, Jim expresses his anger only once: "En all you wuz thinkin' 'bout
wuz how you could make a fool uv ole Jim wid a lie. Dat truck dah is *trash;*
en trash is what people is dat puts dirt on de head er dey fren's en makes
'em ashamed" (*AHF*, 72). Although Jim's anger is a pale reflection of the
slave's legitimate fury, he nonetheless highlights the inherent betrayal and
humiliation at the core of the slave experience. Jim exposes Huck's white
identity to the reader, and the abusive power inherent in it, when he calls
practical jokers "trash."

The most significant aspect of the ending is not that Jim is treated like
a slave, or targeted as the butt of a white boy's joke, but that Twain fails to
make the ending pay off. Tom Sawyer lets loose with what is effectively a
punch line, that Jim is, in fact, "as free as any cretur that walks this earth";
however, no one seems to get the joke. Aunt Sally wonders, "Then what
on earth did you want to set him free for, seeing he was already free?"
(*AHF*, 226). In this case, Twain's comic performance collapses: the pro-
tracted chapters leading up to Jim's escape do not result in an explosive
laugh; he is not able to "sell" us on the redemptive or humanitarian possibilities of the ending; nor do we—unlike the ferryman—want to repeat
the experience at some future date for a new audience. Huck exits the novel
by asserting multiple endings: he will not return to civilization, he will not
write another book, and he will not join Tom Sawyer in his adventures. "I
reckon I got to light out for the Territory ahead of the rest, because Aunt
Sally she's going to adopt me and sivilize me and I can't stand it. I been
there before" (*AHF*, 229). Twain admits, through Huck, that the ending

does not bear repeating, either as the punch line of a joke or as the moral of the story.

To suggest that the ending is merely ironic ignores the enormous disappointment of these final chapters. Hemingway correctly describes the end of the novel as "cheating." In this case, however, Twain is not taking the short cut to the easy laugh, as Hemingway supposes; instead, he is refusing to complete his comic performance, exposing the desire of the reader to, at all costs, have the last laugh. As a comic performer, Twain understands the problematic morality of his audience's comic appetite. If he so desires, he could make the caging of Jim seem comic, and it is entirely possible that the audience would laugh. Instead, Twain exposes Tom Sawyer's sense of humor and the white privilege that makes it possible.

The real question is whether Twain chooses not to be amusing in this ending. Does his genius fail, as numerous critics and biographers have suggested, or does he intentionally betray our expectations? In any event, like Susy running from the stage or Huck lighting out for the territory, readers tend to reject the ending of the novel. They are disturbed by its "sense" of humor, particularly because they have been so implicated in it. Twain aligns the reader, via Huck, with the supposed good humor of Tom's adventures, and in so doing, he exposes the reader as part of Du Bois's "passing throng," and makes Jim's fate both visible and unpalatable.

Twain's own relationship to practical joking dates back at least to his early adolescence. He chronicles in his autobiography a childhood spent orchestrating practical jokes, an activity he connects with his desire to be in the spotlight. At one point Twain admits: "[B]ut they were all cruel and barren of wit. Any brainless swindler could have invented them. When a person of mature age perpetrates a practical joke it is fair evidence, I think, that he is weak in the head and hasn't the heart to signify" (*AMT*, 50).

Although Twain seems to associate practical joking with the world of children, he himself continues to be a practical joker "as a person of mature age," and in *Adventures of Huckleberry Finn* he narrates a series of practical jokes that are primarily the work of adult men: the loafers outside Sherburne's store, the locals waiting to pelt the "Royal Nonesuch" with rotten eggs, and the Duke and the King as they in turn work over the locals.

Even Pap, though not exactly a practical joker, still manages to humiliate and threaten his targets: "And to see the cool way of that nigger—why, he wouldn't a give me the road of I hadn't shoved him out o' the way" (*AHF*, 27). Pap personifies violence and cruelty, which he expresses in a bullying sense of humor that contrasts his feeling of alienation with his sense of entitlement and his masculinity with Huck's effeminacy: "Ain't you a sweet-scented dandy, though? A bed; and bedclothes; and a look'n-glass; and a piece of carpet on the floor—and your own father got to sleep with the hogs in the tanyard. I never see such a son. I bet I'll take some o' these frills out o' yu before I'm done with you" (*AHF*, 22).

In the initial encounter with Pap, Huck records not only his own surprise and fear, "my breath sort of hitched—he being so unexpected," but also Pap's grotesque appearance: "His hair was long and tangled and greasy, and hung down, and you could see his eyes shining through like he was behind vines. It was all black, no gray; so was his long mixed up whiskers. There weren't no color in his face, where his face showed; it was white; not like another man's white, but a white to make a body sick, a white to make a body's flesh crawl—a tree-toad white, a fish-belly white" (*AHF*, 20). Twain focuses the reader's critical eye through Huck and makes Pap's whiteness a visible property. In several of his works, Twain explores the nature of race, contrasting a biological definition with a cultural one. Implicit in these theories—both of which Twain finds inadequate—is the prejudice that "white" is not a color or a race. In Pap Finn, Twain belies both notions. Pap is a mixture, a tangle: his whiteness is invisible—"there warn't no color in his face"—but it is also apparent. He is the embodiment of whiteness but also morally "blackened." Pap is deadly serious throughout his encounters with Huck, but he leaves the child feeling frightened and wary, like the victim of a practical joke.

Twain opposes the masculine sense of humor in the novel to the child's sense of pleasure. Unlike the "little man" Tom Sawyer, who begins the novel wanting to "tie Jim to the tree for fun," Huck has only a limited concept of humor (*AHF*, 10). In general, Huck chooses comfort over laughs: "We catched fish, and talked, and we took a swim now and then to keep off sleepiness. It was kind of solemn, drifting down the big still river, laying on our backs looking up at the stars, and we didn't ever feel like talking loud, and it warn't often that we laughed, only a little kind of a low chuckle" (*AHF*, 55).

The ending of the novel punctuates this tension between the man's sense of humor and the boy's sense of joy. Despite the ultimately compensatory qualities of humor, Twain understands what Freud will eventually theorize: that it is a shadow of the joy available to the uncivilized child. The nostalgia of the novel effectively resists humor and the implicit losses it represents. Without a sense of humor an adult man could become neurotic; however, without a sense of guilt or pain, the boy child has no need to laugh. When Huck makes a fool of Jim, he reveals himself as "no more than trash," the legitimate heir of Pap Finn. In fact, Huck is never so unattractive to us as when he is trying to act like a grown-up man: judging, being ethical, and, most of all, joking.

Although Twain represents the power of the joker as essentially masculine, he imagines the audience as inherently feminine. Twain represents the desires of the father (for power and glory) and the desires of the mother (for pleasure and sympathy) as underpinning his experience both as a comic and as a white man. Immediately following Twain's reflections on being a practical joker, he describes the arrival in Hannibal of a traveling mesmerist, and his own faked hypnotic performance: "I was fourteen or fifteen years old, the age at which a boy is willing to endure all things, suffer all things short of death by fire, if thereby he may be conspicuous and show off before the public; and so when I saw the 'subjects' perform their foolish antics on the platform and make the people laugh and shout and admire I had a burning desire to be a subject myself" (*AMT*, 51).

Twain's first appearance on a comic stage is a disappearing act where he at once asserts his identity and belies that assertion. This tension is at the core of Twain's identity as a humorist: he wants both to please his audience and to betray their expectations, to represent himself as a subject but to play with the significance of his own performance. In response to his mesmeric impersonation, Twain notes that his mother, Jane Clemens, "refused to believe that I had invented my visions myself; she said it was folly: that I was only a child at the time and could not have done it. . . . And so the lie which I played upon her in my youth remained with her as an unchallengeable truth to the day of her death. Carlyle said, 'A lie cannot live.' It proves he did not know how to tell one" (*AMT*, 57). Part of the humor of this incident is that Jane Clemens never gets the joke. Another part is that Twain remains unknown—a performer only—to his family and his community. The joke is on Twain as well.

Ultimately, Twain connects his comic persona to his identity and experience as a white man. As a comic performer, Twain controls his audience: he is effectively the master of the house, making young girls leap from their chairs and audiences buy his moldy old jokes. However, as in the case of his mesmeric performance in Hannibal, he is essentially an imposter, powerful and false and, most important, bound by the expectations of his audience. Twain's relationship to the white community is represented by his interaction with his mother: the only way to please her is to maintain her illusions, and the only way to retain control is to continue to perform a lie. In his autobiography, Twain illustrates his mother's compassion for "people and other animals" by suggesting that she could find redeeming qualities in Satan:

> Satan was utterly wicked and abandoned, just as these people had
> said; but would any claim that he had been treated fairly? A sinner
> was but a sinner; Satan was just that, like the rest. What saves
> the rest?—their own efforts alone? No—or none might ever be
> saved. To their feeble efforts is added the mighty help of pathetic,
> appealing, imploring prayers that go up daily out of all the churches
> in Christendom and out of myriads upon myriads of pitying hearts.
> But who prays for Satan? (*AMT,* 26)

Although Twain's description of his mother is overwhelmingly sympathetic, he makes a point to demonstrate the moral implications of defending Satan. Jane Clemens embodies for Twain the moral relativism at the heart of white ideology and the rhetorical processes that ensure its dominance:

> Yet, kind-hearted and compassionate as she was, I think she was
> not conscious that slavery was a bald, grotesque and unwarrantable
> usurpation. She had never heard it assailed in any pulpit but had
> heard it defended and sanctified in a thousand; her ears were fa-
> miliar with Bible texts that approved it but if there were any that
> disapproved it they had not been quoted by her pastors; as far as her
> experience went, the wise and the good and the holy were unanimous
> in the conviction that slavery was right, righteous, sacred, the pecu-
> liar pet of the Deity and a condition which the slave himself ought to
> be daily and nightly thankful for. Manifestly, training and association
> can accomplish strange miracles. (*AMT,* 26)

More so than the violence of Pap Finn or the honor of Colonel Granger-ford, Jane Clemens expresses the absolutism of white mastery in her re-fusal to imagine the world in anything other than redemptive terms. Slavery, through her eyes, appears to be a sentimental fiction where suffering is re-warded, where goodness triumphs, and, in this case, goodness is colored white. Twain confuses this racial equation. He inverts moral "blackness" with genetic whiteness and mixes moral purity with the stain of various racial markers. Jim is white on the inside, whereas white Roxana is black "by fiction of law and custom." Despite these provocative assaults on white hege-mony, Twain remains a kind of ideological mama's boy: he fails to dismantle the illusions of his audience, just as he failed to convince his mother that his performance was a lie. Still, Twain exposes the mask of his own comic identity, thereby exposing the fiction of whiteness itself. Twain paints Jim as a sympathetic clown, whereas he represents himself as a white minstrel, playing a role, signifying nothing.

James Cox has characterized Twain's comic persona as a fate, suggesting that Twain had no other way to negotiate the oedipal tensions embedded in his personal experiences or his cultural moment. Jonathan Arac rejects such a formulation and represents Twain's comic mythmaking as a conscious choice that is both morally evasive and self-promoting. And Twain agrees. Twain consistently illustrates his own capitulation to humor and the moral consequences of his choice. Twain narrates his own failure to signify. In the end of *Adventures of Huckleberry Finn,* Twain chooses to be a practical joker, and he represents that choice as both the privilege and the crime of being white.

In the summer of 2000, *Harper's* pictured on its cover Mark Twain and Tom Wolfe, two white men in their signature white suits, beneath the cap-tion, "Celebrating 150 Years of Literature: 1850–2000." It would seem that the interpretive practice Jonathan Arac describes is still framing American fiction and fueling critical traditions surrounding it. We are still celebrating Twain rather than exposing his politics. The critical traditions and popular perceptions that surround Mark Twain and *Adventures of Huckleberry Finn* help to create an idyllic image of race in America. Yet, I would suggest that this cultural practice extends beyond the reading of *Adventures of Huckle-berry Finn.* Everywhere—in film, in fiction, in politics, and in education—

white Americans want to believe that racism is either no longer an issue, that it is easily resolved, or that their role in the history of race has been heroic. Surely, it is possible for white instructors to celebrate and redeem white history in Harper Lee's *To Kill a Mockingbird,* and certainly it is possible for African American students to be offended by the painful representations of black masculinity in *Native Son.*

The difference between these texts, standard in many secondary-school curriculums, and *Adventures of Huckleberry Finn* is that in Twain's fiction the heroic potential of the main character is complicated and undermined by the humor of the author. The white characters in *Adventures of Huckleberry Finn* can appear transcendently heroic only by virtue of extreme critical denial. Yet, even in such instances, as the combative critical tradition has demonstrated, it is a struggle to keep faith either with Huck or with Mark Twain. Making white people "feel good" about being white may be one of the intentions of the author, but he is only variously successful in the effort. The mean spirit of Twain's humor assaults black pride and disconcerts the possibilities for white heroism.

Several recent films imagine the possibilities for white heroism by condensing racial politics into a single, decisive gesture (walking a picket line, sitting at a lunch counter, taking a freedom ride) and by allowing these symbolic and heroic gestures to be written "white." In films such as *Mississippi Burning, Ghosts of Mississippi, The Long Walk Home,* and *Driving Miss Daisy*—to name a few—screenwriters and directors romanticize the struggles of the '60s by positioning fictionalized white characters at the center of the battle for civil rights and then narrating their gradual racial awakening and eventual sainthood. It may be relevant that white women drove their black maids to and from work, or that thirty years after Medger Evers's murder a white prosecutor convicted the assassin, or that black domestics and white employers occasionally developed bonds of love and friendship. It may even be worth noting that the FBI managed to find the murderers of three civil rights workers. But surely these white fragments do not wholly or centrally represent this history.[14] All of these narratives radically personify

14. This romantic notion of race relations informs films that claim to represent our present historical moment. In *A Time to Kill,* a southern town is taken over by the Klan as the fabulously white Matthew McConaughey defends the murdering black father of a

racial ideology, suggesting in the process that the real problem in American race relations is, either literally or figuratively, the Klan. They do not explore a corporate or cooperative racism, nor do these narratives explore its familial and cultural sources.

Rather than representing heroes and villains in his narratives, Twain blurs the lines between the two. Racists in Twain's fictions do not wear white hoods. They often wear white suits, clerical collars, and kitchen aprons. They are radically sympathetic characters (Twain states in his autobiography, "there were no hard-hearted people in our town") who believe in the moral value of a "mild domestic slavery" (*AMT,* 30–31). At the beginning of *Adventures of Huckleberry Finn,* Miss Watson and the Widow Douglass "fetched the niggers in and had prayers," and they do both with a clear conscience (*AHF,* 8). Huck is willing to go to hell to save Jim, but he is not willing to defy Tom Sawyer. Aunt Sally puts Jim in prison when she thinks he is a runaway but "made a heap of fuss over him" and "give him all he wanted to eat" when he seemed to be a hero (*AHF,* 228). Twain invites us to forgive, to explain, and to ignore the racist attitudes and actions of these characters, but he makes it enormously difficult to do so. Novels such as *Uncle Tom's Cabin* and films such as *Mississippi Burning* personify racism, but Mark Twain makes it personal: racism is in the work of friends and family, layered within the memories of childhood, expressed in our prayers and our jokes.

Teaching *Adventures of Huckleberry Finn* is a risk. Many black students will be offended, and white students may remain wholly ambivalent to the novel and to its controversies or, worse, charmed by its hero and its author. However, these risks—black pain and white complacency—are inherent in almost any discussion of race in an American context. The virtue of reading *Adventures of Huckleberry Finn* as a racial text is that it makes these options clear. Twain opposes black pain to white pleasure throughout the novel and refuses to provide a moral to the story or to package its politics in simplistic terms. Unlike the *After-School Special,* preferred by parents and teachers alike, *Adventures of Huckleberry Finn* complicates racial ideology

---

rape victim while helping this same man overcome his own latent racism. Or better yet, in *American History X* a buff neo-Nazi experiences a racial awakening while in prison after having befriended a lovable black inmate.

and confuses our responses to it. Twain brings into view the hateful language of the racist and the casual racism of white culture, and he frames it all with a smile. Twain reproduces exactly the terms of racial oppression in this country—where white people are sure that they are not so bad and where many black Americans remain effectively imprisoned anyway.

There are other racial romances at work today, many of them presenting white people as victims and white men as redeemers or avengers. Whereas these fictions are being played out in cultural and political arenas (in resistance to hate-crime legislation, in the dismantling of Affirmative Action, or even in battles over the meaning of the Confederate flag), the romance of white victimization is particularly powerful in our schools. Tom Sawyer is alive and well and planning his next big adventure. His dreams of glory, however, are no longer comic fantasies; they are instead violent melodramas. In *Adventures of Huckleberry Finn*, Mark Twain makes visible the transparent operations of white ideology as embodied by Tom Sawyer. Like Twain's mother, Tom defends the myths and traditions of white culture, and in so doing, he exposes their inadequacies. Tom longs to be applauded by "all the niggers all around" (*AHF*, 228); Jane Clemens believes that slavery is the particular "pet of the Deity." Twain's sense of humor in this novel flirts with madness and brutality, yet it has come close to convincing generations of white Americans that there was such a thing as "mild domestic slavery."

Given the power of Twain's humor to manipulate the audience, it is not possible to guarantee that readers of *Adventures of Huckleberry Finn* will be safe; nor is it possible to ensure that teachers who assign the novel will confront its racial content honestly. It is possible to say only that the sense of humor Twain fears and employs, rejects and relishes, continues to organize race in America as an absolute practical joke. Now may be the time to bring this humor into the classroom and to figure out what it all signifies.

Mark Twain in Large and Small

The Infinite and the Infinitesimal
in Twain's Late Writing

TOM QUIRK

Mark Twain and his creations are always getting lost. They lose their identities; they lose their fortunes; they lose their minds. They get lost in caves, in the fog, in snowstorms, even in the darkened room of a German inn. They get lost on the river and on the ocean; they get lost in time and in space. They get lost on rafts, on mules, on foot, on icebergs set adrift in the sea; they get lost beneath the surface of the earth and above it in a hot air balloon. There is nothing very original in this. Thoreau observed that if you turn around once you are lost, which ironically is a step in the right direction. Ishmael, in a drowse at the tiller, turns his back on the prow and compass, and is lost metaphysically. The experience prompts him to advise: "Look not too long in the face of the fire, O man! Never dream with thy hand on the helm! Turn not thy back to the compass."[1] But Twain seems to get lost not so much in moral or spiritual terms as just plain lost. And a compass, or a map, does not seem to do much good.

In *Tom Sawyer Abroad,* Huck complains that the balloon he, Jim, and Tom Sawyer are in is moving mighty slowly because the land beneath them is still green. Tom asks him to explain. Everyone knows that Illinois is green and Indiana is pink, just like on the map, he answers. Tom corrects this misapprehension, and Huck rejoins that it appears a map is supposed to teach you facts but instead teaches you lies. The reason mapmakers make every state a different color, Tom explains, "ain't to deceive you, it's to keep

---

1. Melville, *Moby-Dick; or, The Whale,* 424.

you from deceiving yourself."[2] Huck and Jim remain unconvinced. And so should we. Given Twain's preposterous "Map of Paris" or Colonel Sellers's improvised map of the Pacific Railroad, or the less-than-reliable maps in "The Private History of the Campaign That Failed," maps appear rather to be invitations to self-deception than otherwise. Besides, Twain evidently liked the prospect of getting lost because it afforded him ample comic and dramatic opportunities—as for example in the high resolutions and teary forgiveness of the miners lost in a snowstorm in *Roughing It,* who wake up to find themselves fifteen yards from a comfortable inn but annoyingly saddled with their good intentions. In a rather different way, Twain found himself lost when he returned as an adult to his hometown, Hannibal, Missouri: "I presently recognized the house of the father of Lem Hackett. . . . It carried me back more than a generation in a moment, and landed me in the midst of a time when the happenings of life were not the natural and logical results of great general laws, but of special orders, and were freighted with very precise and distinct purposes—partly punitive in intent, partly admonitory; and usually local in application."[3] But those great "general laws" (particularly the laws of astronomy and geology) were disorienting in their own way, and one might say that a whole generation, afflicted by the findings of nineteenth-century science, was lost in the cosmos. At any rate, Twain spent a good deal of imaginative energy domesticating imponderables and humanizing the incomprehensible.

In April 1896, Twain recorded in his notebook, "[A]ll world distances have shrunk to nothing. . . . The mysterious and the fabulous can get no fine effects without the help of remoteness; and there are no remotenesses any more."[4] Only a few years later, Twain understood that remoteness was near at hand and that he could get lost in his easy chair, assisted only by a basic sort of arithmetic and a couple of mind-boggling facts. Sometime in 1909, for example, he sat down to compute in miles the actual length of a light-year. Twain's biographer, Albert Bigelow Paine, recalls coming in one morning to find Twain sitting before several sheets of paper

2. Twain, *The Complete Short Stories and Famous Essays of Mark Twain,* 12.
3. Twain, *Life on the Mississippi* (Penguin ed.), 375.
4. John S. Tuckey, ed., *"Which Was the Dream?" and Other Symbolic Writings of the Later Years,* 87.

with "interminable rows of ciphers" on them and his face aglow with self-satisfaction. According to Paine, the "unthinkable distances of space" (and one might add the great reaches of what we now call "deep time" as well) threw Twain into a sort of "ecstasy" (*MTB*, 4:1509–10). He did not, at any rate, appear to share in the modern dread that the vastness of space is terrifying and that one cowers, rather insignificantly, on the abyss of the unfathomable. Instead, he delighted in trying to make the unthinkable vivid, even palpable.

Twain indulged himself in the sort of imagining I am describing in the sardonic little essay "Was the World Made for Man?" (1903). His announced answer to the question he posed there was yes, but his comic explanations imply an emphatic no. It takes time for God to prepare the world for man, he argues, for he has to do some experimentation meantime. The Creator must first prepare the world for the oyster, because man will want to eat oysters when he arrives upon the scene. And it will take 19 million years to get things set up for that tasty morsel:

> You must make a vast variety of invertebrates, to start with—
> belemnites, trilobites, jebusites, amalekites, and that sort of fry,
> and put them to soak in a primary sea, and wait and see what will
> happen. Some will be a disappointment . . . but all is not lost, for
> the amalekites will fetch the home-stake; they will develop gradually
> into encrinites, and stalactites, and blatherskites . . . and at last the
> first grand stage in the preparation of the world for man stands
> completed, the Oyster is done.[5]

However, the oyster, vain little bivalve that he is, is apt to mistake that the long background to his debut signifies the world was made for the oyster. And so it goes through the ages—the pterodactyl, 30 million years in the making, likewise thought the world was made for him, as did all the other saurians. But look about you, and you will see that the only saurian to survive in our time is the lonely Arkansawrian. Twain concludes the essay with a figure that makes the 100-million-year preparation of the world for man both comprehensible and absurd: "If the Eiffel tower were now

---

5. Twain, *Collected Tales, Sketches, Speeches, and Essays,* 573. Hereafter referred to as *CTSSE.*

representing the world's age, the skin of the paint on the pinnacle-knob at its summit would represent man's share of that age; and anybody would perceive that that skin was what the tower was built for. I reckon they would, I dunno" (*CTSSE*, 576).

Twain was as fascinated with space as he was with time. In "Extract from Captain Stormfield's Visit to Heaven," he played with the same sort of comparisons that amused him in idle hours. When the story opens, Captain Eli Stormfield has been sailing his vessel through space for some thirty years and at a considerable clip. We are not told how fast he is going, but we know he likes to race comets traveling two hundred thousand miles a minute. There is really no contest, however: "it was as if the comet was a gravel train and I was a telegraph despatch." But then he comes across a real comet so big that when his ship approaches he feels like a "gnat closing up on the continent of America." This comet, it so happens, is tearing through space in order to deposit its cargo of lost souls in hell. When Stormfield thumbs his nose at the captain, he realizes he has woken up a pretty ugly customer. The captain of the comet gives the command to jettison his entire cargo— "Eighteen hundred thousand billion quintillions of kazarks." A "kazark," we learn, is exactly the *"bulk of a hundred and sixty nine worlds like ours!"* (*CTSSE*, 831)—and he leaves Stormfield in his dust.

Twain goes on in this vein. Stormfield's ship arrives at one of the many thousand gates of heaven, though he rather suspected he was bound for the other place. The gate he arrives at is the wrong one, however, and he has to identify his point of origin: "Why the world of course." "*The* world," replies the clerk. "H'm! there's billions of them! . . . Next!" (*CTSSE*, 831) Eventually, they pull out a map the size of Rhode Island and locate the earth, a fly speck locally known as "the Wart." One is tempted to describe Twain's fanciful rendering of the sheer magnitude as hyperbolic, except that the distances that astronomers invite us to contemplate are no less fantastic.

If Twain delighted in conveying a sense of infinite space, it seems to me that he is even better at rendering a sense of eternity. Stormfield checks out a harp and a pair of wings and heads for the nearest cloud. He sits beside a kind old gentleman and launches into a tune. After about sixteen or seventeen hours, his neighbor asks:

"Don't you know any tune but the one you've been pegging at all day?"

"Not another blessed one," says I.

"Don't you reckon you could learn another one?" says he.

"Never," says I; "I've tried to, but I couldn't manage it."

"It's a long time to hang to the one—eternity, you know."

(*CTSSE*, 837)

I suspect that not even Thomas Aquinas himself could have given a more eloquent accounting of eternity, but those who doubt it are invited to sing a few choruses of ninety-nine-billion bottles of beer on the wall.

There is another sort of infinity, however—the infinitesimal. Here, too, Twain tried his hand at comprehending the incomprehensible, notably in "The Great Dark" (1898) and in "Three Thousand Years among the Microbes" (1905). From a philosophical and mathematical point of view, the infinitesimal is a much more significant problem than the infinite. In outlining the history of this problem, I am principally relying on a review essay in the *New York Review of Books* by Jim Holt.[6] In that essay, Holt reviews four books that deal, at least in part, with the infinitesimal. Only one of those four have I read, however; the other three I am incapable of reading because they deal heavily with what was once known as "the Calculus." I am not proficient in the calculus, but, then, so far as I know, neither was Twain. Twain and I had to settle for a humbler science—the arithmetic.

Nevertheless, the conundrum of the infinitesimal antedates calculus, and in fact constituted one facet of a general disagreement between and among pre-Socratic philosophers. Monists and pluralists haggled over the issue, and the debate has continued to our own day. This question is not exclusively tied to how small a unit of matter may be without being susceptible to further subdivision. More important, from a philosophical point of view, is whether space might be infinitely subdivided. Space is that arena where the molecule, the atom, the quark, or some yet-to-be-discovered subatomic particle is allowed to move and thus to permit change—and change is the chief instrument of time.

6. Holt, "Infinitesimally Yours." Hereafter referred to as IY.

For Parmenides the universe was a plenum, and thus change was illusory. In the nineteenth century, German and French mathematicians introduced highly complicated notions of limits that effectively exiled the infinitesimal from scientific and philosophical thinking. Without some notion of the infinitesimal, however, the world lacks continuity; it does not hang together in any rational way, and according to William Everdell, "the heart of Modernism is the postulate of ontological discontinuity."[7] That recognition, in its turn, so he argues, prompted such diverse artistic innovations as the pointillist paintings of a Seurat or the prose style of a Joyce.

In Twain's day, however, philosophers such as Charles Saunders Peirce and Henri Bergson clung fast to notions of the infinitesimal, for without it neither temporal change nor even the concept of the "now" was possible. William James, too, held to such a worldview, though in rather different terms, terms that, because they were less intricate, were perhaps closer to the ways Twain thought about the subject. More than once, Peirce chided James for his friend's relative ignorance or indifference to mathematics. James could unhappily imagine a discontinuous universe, nonetheless: "The world is One just so far as its parts hang together by any definite connexion. It is many just so far as any definite connexion fails to obtain." Pragmatism, as it does with most oppositional arrangements, stands squarely between absolute postulates of the One or the Many. Of all the possible universes, however, "The lowest grade of universe would be a world of mere withness, strung together by the conjunction 'and.'"[8]

Perhaps William James was, as Everdell says he was, the "last continuarian," something of an antique from the modern and postmodern point of view (*First*, 352). At all events, the modern world of mere "withness" may not be constituted of such low-grade ore as he imagined. In the realm of art, for example, we have since become accustomed to the techniques of the disparate and the discrete—of collocation and montage of juxtaposition and fragment, of cubist disassembling and pointillist synthesis. The techniques differ in other arenas, but the principle is the same. We are on easy terms with deconstruction and know how to read one text with another. We

---

7. Everdell, *The First Moderns: Profiles in the Origins of Twentieth-Century Thought*, 351. Hereafter referred to as *First*.

8. James, *Pragmatism and Four Essays from the "Meaning of Truth*," 105.

typically think of "decentering" as a state to be achieved, not a condition to be lamented. We speak casually of multiversities, diasporas, or antifoundationalism. We know our computer images down to the last pixel and call it virtual reality, and we accept as meaningful but not particularly related such phrases as "centers of power," "zones of opportunity," and "pockets of poverty." We pluralize with impunity ("outcomes," "behaviors," "impacts," and the like), hooking things together with an implicit *and*. We accept the idea of "social construction" as an explanatory principle that renders ineffectual those pesky claims that a common, transhistorical humanity and a continuous universe might otherwise have upon us. We reject the idea of pluralism in favor of multiculturalism, only to claim in turn the authority of "culture" for such random collections of people as stamp collectors, truck drivers, and Harvard MBAs. These are but specimens of the grammatical, analytic, and anthropological maneuvers that permit us to negotiate a world that we have come to believe is essentially discontinuous. If things have fallen apart, the modern world has devised a multitude of coping strategies. However, our contemporary methods of thought may themselves be outdated.

In the 1960s, the logician Abraham Robinson single-handedly rehabilitated the idea of the infinitesimal when he established what is known as "nonstandard analysis" and, according to Holt, brought about "one of the great reversals in the history of ideas." Robinson added to ordinary number theory a new symbol that was by definition smaller than any finite number but not yet zero. The result was an "enriched" theory of numbers that does not contradict the system of ordinary numbers and is consistent with it so long as that number system is itself consistent. This new calculus was "nonstandard" according to Holt because it contains all sorts of exotic entities in addition to the ordinary finite numbers. What is more, this method, though it does not alter the properties of ordinary numbers, nevertheless "yields proofs that are shorter and more insightful" (IY, 66–67).

Not everyone has joined in this great reversal, however; several current theories hold to certain absolute minimums, or limits. The minimum length, it is believed, is 10^{-33} centimeters and the minimum time 10^{-43} seconds (exactly the amount of time, says Holt, it takes for a New York cabby to honk after the light turns green). Whether mathematicians and physicists will continue, a bit nostalgically, to cling to notions of minimums that dominated their thinking between 1900 and 1960 remains to be seen.

Perhaps, more nostalgically still, they will embrace the infinitesimal and, with it, a continuous universe, a vision somewhat closer to the nineteenth century than our own. "If ontological continuity should ever come back into fashion," Everdell observes, "the story will have begun with Robinson" (*First*, 352).

It is an even question whether the infinitesimal will reclaim its tiny but supremely consequential place in the scheme of things. Robert Kaplan notes, "The battle still rages, because if Leibnitz's infinitesimals were ghosts of departed quantities, Robinson's seem to be ghosts of what aren't even quantities but linguistic expressions." Nevertheless, such a transformative vision might have real effects upon our thinking: "It is as if you have decided that the connectives of our language ('and,' 'or,' 'but' and so on) were also names of things and in the fresh world enriched by these creatures, found that previously opaque notions suddenly became transparent. You might be loath to forgo these insights just because some dubious intermediaries brought them about."[9] Of course, William James's continuarian view of the universe was precisely of this sort, for he firmly believed that the relations between and among things were given in experience and were therefore as real as the things themselves.

But this new story, if it is ever told, will have more to do with nonstandard analysis than it will with pragmatism. One accidental by-product of Abraham Robinson's restoration of ontological continuity to the world might be to resuscitate our interest in the stories Twain wrote on this theme. And because the foundational idea of continuity necessarily carries with it political, moral, and artistic implications, we may well turn to his late fictions with a more vital and practical attention than we have in the past. In a word, when and if methods of critical inquiry catch up to what is known about the physical universe, we may find that Twain is cordially waiting for us at the end of our difficult intellectual trek.

By supplying this brief context for the infinitesimal, I do not for a moment mean to suggest that these heady intellectual and scientific difficulties occurred to Mark Twain, at least not in the fashion I have been describing them. Nor was he likely to have been aware of the enormous implications

9. Kaplan, *The Nothing That Is: A Natural History of Zero*, 173–74.

that might be heaped on the back of such a tiny and unpretentious Atlas. Nevertheless, it is interesting to note, and curious too, that, by whatever means, Twain was often able to arrive at conclusions that were congruent with scientific fact and philosophical understanding. Sherwood Cummings remarks, for example, that in *What Is Man?* and "without being directly familiar with most of the speculations about and experiments with human behavior during the preceding two and half centuries, Mark Twain presents the salient ideas of the tradition in chronological order." Twain's imaginative apprehension of behavioristic science was founded on a "few seminal books, read years before, on private thoughts, and on an exquisite sensitiveness to ideas in the air." In 1913, Paul Carus, the editor of the respected philosophical journal *Monist,* reached a similar conclusion—that Twain's "philosophy" was in essential agreement with the facts of science and psychology and that his argument was a sound one.[10]

That said, I do not wish to insist that we must take Twain seriously as a thinker. His thinking, taken as a whole, is riddled with contradictions; humor is not logical rigor, and flights of fancy are no substitute for controlled experiment and scientific observation. Instead, I merely want to observe that contemplation of the infinitely small should not be dismissed as trivial, and the ruminations of an infinite jester, however accidentally, may dramatize potent human and humanizing truths. Besides, during the last decade of his life, there were personal reasons Twain might have wanted the world to hang together, so broken and fragmentary was his own life. The bankruptcy of his publishing company in 1894; the deaths of his daughter Susy in 1896 and his wife, Olivia, in 1904; his own illness; and other factors surely contributed to his philosophical speculations late in his life. That philosophical vision is unmistakably expressive of his own despair and bitterness, but it may have been therapeutic as well, restoring a certain perspective to his life. In point of fact, at least part of Twain's intent in both "The Great Dark" and "Three Thousand Years among the Microbes" is moral not philosophical— to install within his readers (and perhaps within himself as well) some accurate and respectful sense of the nevertheless absurd proportions of things and the modest position human beings occupy in the world.

10. Cummings, *Mark Twain and Science,* 208, 210; Carus, "Mark Twain's Philosophy."

In "The Great Dark," Mr. Henry Edwards and his family, through the mysterious intervention of the Superintendent of Dreams, find themselves aboard a ship that is lost in a drop of water beneath a microscope. The captain of the ship, though he is loath to admit it, is helplessly lost—Greenland is not where it is supposed to be; there is no gulf stream; they are pursued by some monstrous spider squid; and the sky is in perpetual semidarkness. Edwards is confounded: "Were *all* the laws of Nature suspended?" he asks himself.[11] Those laws are intact, but the conditions of his natural environment have changed enormously.

Edwards is no longer certain whether his present situation is dream or reality. He takes stock of this new understanding of the human condition: "[W]e see that intellectually we are really no great thing; that we seldom really know the thing we think we know; that our best built certainties are but sand-houses and subject to damage from any wind of doubt that blows" (GD, 125). A character from Tom Stoppard's *Arcadia* makes a similar observation but with greater satisfaction:

> It makes me so happy. To be at the beginning again, knowing almost
> nothing. Relativity and quantum looked as if they were going to clean
> out the whole problem between them. A theory of everything. . . .
> [However, w]e're better at predicting events at the edge of the galaxy
> or inside the nucleus of an atom than whether it will rain on auntie's
> party three Sundays from now. . . . It's the best possible time to be
> alive, when almost everything you thought you knew is wrong.[12]

Stoppard ends his philosophical drama by having two characters respond to the chaotic uncertainty of things in most human terms; they begin to waltz, and the curtain closes. Twain's lost sea captain concludes "The Great Dark" a bit differently: "I don't know where this ship is. . . . If it is God's will that we pull though, we pull through—otherwise not. We haven't had an observation for four months, but we are going ahead, and do our best to fetch up somewhere" (GD, 150).

"Three Thousand Years among the Microbes" is more rambling than "The Great Dark," but it is more incisive, too. After a failed biological exper-

11. Twain, "The Great Dark," 111. Hereafter referred to as GD.
12. Stoppard, *Arcadia,* 47–48.

iment, the narrator finds himself transformed into a cholera germ and in the blood of a tramp named Blitzowski. This fanciful point of view permitted Twain to make comments on the relativity of beauty, time, class, currency, and many other things, but I am chiefly interested here in his ruminations on the infinitesimal.

The narrator, who later dubs himself Huck, sees with a microbe eye and now knows for a certainty, "Nothing is ever at rest—wood, iron, water, everything is alive. . . . [T]here is no such thing as death, everything is full of bristling life. . . . Heaven was not created for man alone, and oblivion and neglect reserved for the rest of His creatures. Man—always vain, windy, conceited—thinks he will be the majority there. He will be disappointed. Let him humble himself."[13] The vision of the world Twain articulates here is known as hylozoism (a two-dollar word for an indiscriminate pantheism), but he has added his humorous touches to the picture. His moral purpose is to deride human vanity and expose the human tendency to look down on lower life forms. "Well, it's a picture of life," he says. "The king looks down upon the noble, the noble looks down on the commoner," and so on all the way to the bottom, "the burglar looking down on the house-renting landlord, and the landlord looking down upon his oily brown-wigged pal the real estate agent—which is the bottom, so far as ascertained" ("Three," 528).

Huck knows that Blitzowski is merely a tramp, but for the microbes he is the entire and sacred universe. A sleeping sickness germ called the "duke" knows something Huck does not know, however, for he has a microbe microscope. Within the blood of microbes known as "Sooflasky" are other microbes, known as "Swinks":

> Then the inexorable logic of the situation arrived and announced
> itself: . . . there being a Man, with a Microbe to infest him, and for
> him to be indifferent about; and there being a Sooflasky, with a Swink
> to infest him and for the said Sooflasky to be indifferent about . . .
> and it also follows, of a certainty, that below that infester there is yet
> another infester that infests him—and so on down and down and

13. Twain, "Three Thousand Years among the Microbes," 447. Hereafter referred to as "Three."

> down till you strike the bottomest bottom of created life—if there is
> one, which is extremely doubtful. ("Three," 527)

So what, if anything, are we to make of Twain's playful contemplation of the infinite and the infinitesimal? For one thing, Twain extended the reach of his fundamentally democratic imagination outward to the fringes of the universe and inward to the single-celled world teeming with class-conscious life's anxious sense of self-approval. Twain the determinist might conceive of a microbial world regulated by a desire for approval, but Twain the democrat railed against self-satisfaction and smugness in the human animal. Clive James once remarked that Twain was "democratic all the way down to his metabolism," but perhaps that is something of an understatement.[14] He seems to have been democratic all the way down to his subatomic particles. For another thing, the world Mark Twain imagines hangs together; it has a fine sense of connectedness. Every particle of atomic dust participates on equal terms with the angels in some as-yet-undetermined purpose. Everything has a "mission," he declares, and our duty is clear: "let him do the service he was made for, and keep quiet." Huck the microbe perceives the folly of human ways and the value of an inquisitive mind: "We live to learn," he says, "and fortunate are we when we are wise enough to profit by it" ("Three," 448). Finally, the universe itself teaches us to be humble in our station and not to indulge in feelings of superiority, not to lord it over any living creature . . . except, perhaps, the real estate agent.

14. James, "The Voice of America."

Mark Twain Studies and the Myth of Metaphor

JOHN BIRD

A flood of books and articles on Mark Twain appears every year and shows no sign of subsiding. That outpouring demonstrates the robust health of Twain studies, but the volume can be somewhat overwhelming, even bewildering for those who conscientiously try to keep up. Enlightening as the work generally is, how do we make sense of it all? It is important now and then to take a step back and try to make sense of trends, try to find out where we are and where we are going. The annual chapter on Mark Twain in *American Literary Scholarship* does that, of course, as did Alan Gribben's 1980 *ESQ* article, "Removing Mark Twain's Mask: A Decade of Criticism and Scholarship." My aim here is not to replicate that work; instead, I wish to examine some of the book-length critical studies that have appeared in the last decade or so, with a goal perhaps larger than the usual overview.[1] I will examine these studies not so much for their content or argument but for the metaphors that underpin them. Metaphor, since it is so fundamental to language, has a power to reveal much that might otherwise remain hidden, and I think it can do the same about critical ideas, as well about the direction of Mark Twain studies in general. I will use two metaphor critics, one widely known, one much lesser known, in an overview that will not only comment on the direction of Mark Twain studies but also point out some of its distortions, past and present. By recognizing distortions, we do not necessarily

---

1. Coverage includes only book-length studies, and is not comprehensive. The earliest book cited is 1986, the most recent 1997, providing roughly a decade of criticism, however selectively.

get any closer to the truth, but we at least become aware that we are in the midst of distortion, and thus do not mistake the distortion for the truth.

The lesser-known critic is Colin Turbayne, who published in 1962 a study of the history of metaphor in science, particularly optics. His *Myth of Metaphor* is rarely cited in the voluminous scholarship on metaphor, yet I have found it to be one of the richest and most suggestive metaphor studies I have encountered. Turbayne's ideas, I think, prove very illuminating, both for Mark Twain and for his critics.

Turbayne begins by tracing the way metaphor passes through several stages. He uses a metaphor to define metaphor; after Max Black, he calls it a "screen" or "filter," both of which change the way we look at the world. A metaphor inevitably changes, Turbayne argues, "[w]hen the pretense [of the metaphor] is dropped either by the original pretenders or their followers, what was before called a screen or filter is now more appropriately called a disguise or mask. There is a difference between using a metaphor and being used by it, between using a model and mistaking the model for the thing modeled. The one is to make believe that something is the case; the other is to believe it." If we are used by the metaphor, if we "mistak[e] the model for the thing modeled," if we believe the metaphor, we become what Turbayne calls a "victim of metaphor": "The victim of metaphor accepts one way of sorting or bundling or allocating the facts as the only way to sort, bundle, or allocate them. The victim not only has a special view of the world but regards it as the only view, or rather, he confuses a special view of the world with the world. He is thus, unknowingly, a metaphysician. He has mistaken the face for the mask."[2] This idea has implications for Mark Twain's characters, for his readers, and for Mark Twain himself.

What, then, are the metaphors that have governed Mark Twain studies? There are many, but clearly the most dominant and persistent have been the metaphors of doubling, of twinness, of the split. The metaphor is so firmly ingrained in our critical vocabulary that some of us may be unable to see it as a metaphor; after all, we are talking about Mr. Clemens and Mark Twain, the river versus the shore, a sound heart and a deformed conscience, reality and dream, white and black, male and female. No doubt these paired phrases bring specific articles and books to mind. But do we see these splits

2. Turbayne, *The Myth of Metaphor,* 21, 22, 27. Hereafter referred to as *Myth.*

and oppositions and divisions because they are there, in both the writer and his texts, or because that is the metaphor we have embraced so fully that we do not even recognize it as a metaphor anymore? Thus, as victims of the metaphor, is the split all we can see?

To illustrate the point, let's suppose that instead of splits the metaphorical way we perceived Mark Twain and his works was triangles. We would then see what we formerly saw as oppositions, but with a third, mediating element: Samuel Clemens, constructed persona, Mark Twain; the river, the raft, the shore; sound heart, language conflict, deformed conscience; reality, perception, dream; white, mulatto, black. Given such a formulation, Mark Twain studies would have a very different history and content.[3]

I am sure that an immediate response to my questioning of these splits and oppositions in Mark Twain studies is that the splits and oppositions came originally from Mark Twain (or Samuel Clemens) himself. Turbayne has an answer for this: "A great metaphor made by a genius, and treated as metaphor, always tends to pass into a later stage in its life. The more effective it is in the realm of make-believe the more seriously it comes to be believed until it is taken literally, by posterity, or by the great man's contemporaries, or even by himself. It awaits an iconoclast from a later age who will explode it as myth" (*Myth*, 60). The metaphor becomes a myth.

Mark Twain's metaphor has been taken literally by all three groups Turbayne mentions—posterity, his contemporaries, and, to some extent, himself—and a number of iconoclasts have attempted to explode the myth. Rather than begin with recent critics, I find that I must go back to the two original iconoclasts in our debates: Van Wyck Brooks and Bernard DeVoto. As we shall see, several recent critics also begin with them and are very consciously engaged in the ongoing debate these two set up so long ago.

To quote Brooks is to recognize how early (1920, ten years after Mark Twain's death) he stepped forth to try to challenge the myth of metaphor:

> [Mark Twain] seems to exhibit himself, on the one hand, as a child
> of nature conscious of extraordinary powers that make all the world

---

3. Tom Quirk makes a similar point in his annual review of Mark Twain criticism: "If Samuel Clemens had taken as his alias the name 'Mark Multiplicity' or 'Mark Monad,' I wonder whether the character and emphasis of Twain criticism might have been different" (Mark Twain chapter in *American Literary Scholarship: An Annual, 1994*, 99).

and even the Almighty solicitous about him, and, on the other, as a humble, a humiliated man, confessedly second-rate, who has lost nine of the ten talents committed to him and almost begs permission to keep the one that remains. A great genius, in short, that has never attained the inner control which makes genius great, a mind that has not found itself, a mind that does not know itself, a mind that cloaks to the end in the fantasy of its temporal power the reality of some spiritual miscarriage![4]

The metaphor of division is clear here, but even more so in another quotation. Note the string of metaphors as Brooks attempts to describe and define Mark Twain:

From his philosophy alone, therefore, we can see that Mark Twain was a frustrated spirit, a victim of arrested development, and beyond this fact, as we know from innumerable instances the psychologists have placed before us, we need not look for an explanation of much of the chagrin of his old age. He had been balked, he had been divided, he had even been turned, as we shall see, against himself; the poet, the artist in him, consequently, had withered into the cynic and the whole man had become a spiritual valetudinarian. (*Ordeal*, 40–41)

Brooks's title itself, *The Ordeal of Mark Twain*, announces its own metaphorical emphasis, as titles often do whether the authors recognize it or not; figuring Mark Twain's life and career as an ordeal, his book set the tenor for the debate that has continued to this day. In Turbayne's terms, Brooks is both the iconoclast who tries to explode a myth as well as the creator of a new metaphor that itself becomes a myth.

That metaphor, of course, was answered in 1932 by Bernard DeVoto in his book *Mark Twain's America*. Rather than a metaphorical emphasis, DeVoto's title seems to emphasize a metonymic connection, as the following quotation shows:

Somewhere in the person of Mark Twain . . . must have been an artist—as American.

---

4. Brooks, *The Ordeal of Mark Twain*, 38, 40–41. Hereafter referred to as *Ordeal*.

> The artist's career is worth a summary. More widely and deeply than any one else who ever wrote books, he shared the life of America. Printer, pilot, soldier, silver miner, gold-washer, the child of two emigrations, a pilgrim in another, a sharer in the flush times, a shaper of the gilded age—he, more completely than any other writer, took part in the American experience.[5]

DeVoto's metonymic focus finally amounts to a metaphor that directly challenges Brooks's: the artist as American and, finally, the artist as America. Consider this string of metaphors in DeVoto's description of Mark Twain's move east: "He was the frontier itself"; "He was, that is, a savage;" "He was anarchy."[6]

I realize I am treading very well-worn ground in reviewing the Brooks-DeVoto debate, but I think my emphasis on the metaphorical nature of the debate makes the review worthwhile. In using the terms *metaphor* and *metonymy*, I am of course referring to the influential theorist Roman Jakobson, whose 1956 article "Two Aspects of Language and Two Types of Aphasic Disturbances" has been very important in a number of fields, including both structural and poststructural literary theory. Jakobson found that aphasics, those who had suffered speech loss through brain damage, made meaning either by connecting words or by substituting them, but they were incapable of the opposite operation. From this he postulated that aphasics were operating according to a principle either of metaphor or of metonymy. Further, he postulated that these two poles are in opposition to one another in people with normal speech and that we are all constantly shifting between the two.

The thrust of Jakobson's article was mainly an attempt to diagnose speech dysfunction linguistically, but what has proved important for literary study are his brief but suggestive comments in his final pages in which he looks at the way metaphor and metonymy divide and underlie all forms of discourse. Jakobson proposes that all discourse is structured either metaphorically, by similarity, or metonymically, by contiguity. He applies the distinction to literature, painting, film, psychoanalysis, and anthropology, showing how the language of each is structured either by similarity or by contiguity,

---

5. DeVoto, *Mark Twain's America*, 321.
6. Ibid., 192, 193, 195.

by metaphor or by metonymy. For example, poetry, romanticism, and dream symbolism are structured metaphorically, whereas prose, realism, and dream condensation are structured metonymically. As an editor of Jakobson's work summed it up, "With one stroke he defined a fundamental polarity of language, culture and human thought in general."[7] That "fundamental polarity of language" can apply even to critical approaches. Thus, we might make the quick distinction that because of Brooks and DeVoto, Mark Twain studies have been founded on a conflict between metaphor and metonymy, and we might then be able to chart subsequent studies as being either predominantly one or the other. Such a distinction breaks down somewhat when we recognize that DeVoto's metonymic study gradually emerges as metaphoric, but at least the preliminary distinction is helpful in categorizing various critical responses.

I see several trends in recent criticism, especially in regards to metaphoric underpinning. These breakdown not only by metaphor-metonymy but also by an attempt to deal with Mark Twain's doubleness and identity, as well as by an attempt to define him and his work in new ways. A number of studies examine Mark Twain and his works in connection with a specific topic or idea; the titles make their metonymic focus clear: Henry B. Wonham, *Mark Twain and the Art of the Tall Tale;* Anthony J. Berret, *Mark Twain and Shakespeare;* David Sewell, *Mark Twain's Languages;* Sherwood Cummings, *Mark Twain and Science;* Peter Stoneley, *Mark Twain and the Feminine Aesthetic;* J. D. Stahl, *Mark Twain, Culture, and Gender;* Laura E. Skandera Trombley, *Mark Twain in the Company of Women;* Susan K. Harris, *The Courtship of Olivia Langdon and Mark Twain;* Andrew Jay Hoffman, *Twain's Heroes, Twain's Worlds;* and Jason Gary Horn, *Mark Twain and William James.* Each work makes a metonymic connection between Mark Twain and the particular topic in question, and the connection forces a metonymic shift in our understanding of Twain. For example, Stoneley gives this explanation of why he uses a man to study a feminist issue with language that highlights the metonymic shift:

> Mark Twain is a representative example of a man who tried, with
> a variety of techniques, to both enforce and moderate the cult of

7. Roman Jakobson, *On Language,* 17.

femininity. He can be used to suggest the extended integration of masculine and feminine values, the uses that the feminine aesthetic had for men, and to illustrate the threat that "excessive" femininity contained. For although Twain is usually associated with a boyish, picaresque world, he returned throughout his career to the questions raised by the role and nature of the feminine aesthetic. (*MTFA*, 8)

Similarly, Susan K. Harris recounts the usual metaphoric representation of Twain to argue for a reappraisal of Olivia Langdon's importance, a reappraisal that forces a metonymic shift in our perception of Twain:

Mark Twain may have been as saintly or as devilish, as sane or as neurotic, as passive or as manipulative, as he has been painted by the various biographical camps that have tackled him, but he cannot be assessed without genuine attention to the people with whom he daily interacted—and the emphasis here must be on interaction. Perhaps because it was composed of women, the family that most of Twain's early biographers portray is flat, a collective background for Mark Twain's angst and antics.[8]

If such a metonymic approach is successful in convincing the reader of its validity, the approach finally becomes metaphoric, as the writer makes us see Mark Twain anew.

Similar metonymic shifts are always occurring with any writer, and we can see from the list above the other kinds of shifts occurring in Mark Twain studies as critics turn their attention to various matters. A number of other works, however, are more metaphoric in approach, but note that their subtitles often reveal a metonymic connection: Shelley Fisher Fishkin, *Was Huck Black? Mark Twain and African-American Voices;* Victor Doyno, *Writing Huck Finn: Mark Twain's Creative Process;* Gregg Camfield, *Sentimental Twain: Samuel Clemens in the Maze of Moral Philosophy;* Randall Knoper, *Acting Naturally: Mark Twain in the Culture of Performance;* and Bruce Michelson, *Mark Twain on the Loose: A Comic Writer and the American Self.* Still others are fully metaphoric: Tom Quirk, *Coming to Grips with*

8. Harris, *The Courtship of Olivia Langdon and Mark Twain,* 9–10.

Huckleberry Finn; Jeffrey Steinbrink, *Getting to Be Mark Twain;* and Andrew Jay Hoffman, *Inventing Mark Twain.* I will return to some of these, but I want now to turn to two studies of the late '80s by Forrest G. Robinson and Susan Gillman. We can see from their titles, *In Bad Faith* and *Dark Twins,* respectively, the predominantly metaphoric nature. Significantly, however, in both their subtitles is embedded a metonymic reference to DeVoto's work: Robinson's *Dynamics of Deception in Mark Twain's America* and Gillman's *Imposture and Identity in Mark Twain's America.* Robinson makes metaphoric connections between America's bad faith over what he calls "race-slavery" and *Tom Sawyer* and *Huckleberry Finn;* thus, *Huckleberry Finn* becomes, metaphorically, "a direct, anguished meditation on the affliction itself [*sic*], the environment through which it spreads, and the tortuous pattern of its operation in the minds of its agents and victims and witnesses."[9] As Turbayne says, "A new theory, even one not metaphysical, like a new pair of spectacles, changes the facts. . . . New theories not only save the appearances; they change them, and even create new ones" (*Myth,* 66). Critics try to change our metaphoric relation to the text or author, in Robinson's case to make us read a text we have formerly read as a comic masterpiece or as a coming-of-age adventure story or as a satire on society's shams as "a direct, anguished meditation." Part of the resistance many readers may have to such an interpretation comes from the distance between such a new reading and our previous metaphoric stance toward the novel. When a critic tries to change our metaphoric stance so radically, he or she takes on an even greater burden of proof.

Gillman's study demands a smaller metaphoric shift in the reader, examining as it does what she calls the "critical language of twinning, doubling, and impersonation [that] has . . . developed around" Mark Twain. I would argue, of course, that it is not merely a critical language of twinning, but a metaphor that shapes the way we form our critical language about the writer. Gillman posits that "Mark Twain presses his investigations of twinness to the point where coherent individual identity collapses," and that includes the Clemens–Mark Twain split. A few pages later, she goes even further (and I would propose that she begs the question), referring

---

9. Robinson, *In Bad Faith: The Dynamics of Deception in Mark Twain's America,* 114.

to "Mark Twain's own unstable personal identity." This leads to her thesis: "My approach to the subject that might be called by its nineteenth-century name of 'duality' is to (re)create the dialogue between Twain's language of identity and the cultural vocabularies available to him." This sentence is full of metaphorical implications, but I find especially intriguing the central metaphorical term *re-create,* which Gillman further complicates by putting "re" in parentheses. As she no doubt intends, this gives the term a double meaning, but when we consider the word(s) as metaphorical, that move becomes somewhat troubling. Which is it: create or re-create? Gillman seems to recognize that she is creating rather than re-creating when she admits that "it will be my Mark Twain and my nineteenth-century that emerge."[10] Both Gillman and Robinson seem to be appropriating DeVoto's metonymic phrase and stance—"Mark Twain's America"—but with a complete reversal, so that their argument shares more in spirit with Brooks's.

Clearly, we remain engaged in the same debate Brooks and DeVoto were engaged in seventy-five years ago, over not just our metaphorical vision of Mark Twain but also our vision of America. In fact, I am struck by the number of recent studies that begin with a discussion of the Brooks-DeVoto argument, showing not only how central the debate remains, but also how aware Mark Twain critics generally are of our critical history. Guy Cardwell's controversial 1991 book *The Man Who Was Mark Twain* not only begins with the debate, but also highlights the debate's metaphorical nature. His opening chapter is basically a reprint of his 1977 article "Mark Twain: The Metaphoric Hero as Battleground," in which he uses the terms *metaphor* and *synecdoche* (often considered interchangeable with *metonymy*). Curiously, he never mentions Jakobson directly. In fact, even though he seems aware of the metaphoric nature of his approach, he seems not to be aware of some of its implications. For example, early on he states that "[a]n obvious step toward ordering the chaos is to attempt to disentangle Samuel Clemens from his metaphoric roles." It is good to use and recognize metaphor, but it is impossible to "disentangle Samuel Clemens from his metaphoric roles": as Turbayne shows, all we do is get enmeshed in another metaphoric role. Cardwell's stated intention is "to undermine

10. Gillman, *Dark Twins,* 1, 3.

superstitiously devised memorial statues that have been cherished as acceptable likenesses," but every act of undermining is actually the erection of another statue, even if the undermining critic does not recognize that.[11] The challenge to Cardwell's book developed in part because his metaphorical presentation of Mark Twain as a masturbating, impotent pedophile with a gambling problem is so far from our shared metaphorical image. We need to be metaphorically aware so we can avoid work such as Cardwell's (or to go back, such as Brooks's, or even DeVoto's). It is a temptation for a critic or biographer to attempt to strip away the metaphorical myth and arrive at "truth." But what he or she is really doing is substituting one metaphor for another. Turbayne makes this point emphatically: "The attempt to reallocate the facts by restoring them to where they 'actually belong' is vain. It is like trying to observe the rule 'Let us get rid of the metaphors and replace them by the literal truth.' But can this be done? We might just as well seek to provide what the poet 'actually says'" (*Myth*, 64). As critics and biographers, we do seem so often to be trying to do just this; we all seem to be engaged in "an essay in the creation of ideas," as DeVoto calls his book on his dedication page.

That impulse combined with our own metaphors can lead us into some interesting places. Consider this example from Laura Skandera Trombley's introduction:

> Past criticism by both men and women has wrongly dismissed Twain as being anti-female and has come to portray Twain almost as a caricature of the "man's man," far removed from the realm of women. I find this view fallacious.
>
> Some feminist critics have responded to this conception of Twain by repeatedly attacking and finally dismissing him, yet it is questionable whether critics have been responding to the man or to an invention of past biographies. Thus, central to my work is the challenge of distinguishing the person from the plethora of published opinion. My intention is to dynamite this hollow creation and reveal Twain as he really was, an author so dependent upon female interaction and influence that without it the sublimity of his novels would have been lost. (*MTW*, xvi)

11. Cardwell, *The Man Who Was Mark Twain: Images and Ideologies*, 5, 7.

Skandera Trombley has reacted to a metaphorical definition of Mark Twain as a "man's man" with the metaphorical act of dynamiting. But what has she replaced that hollow image with? If we accept Turbayne, not with "Twain as he really was." Does this mean, then, that we cannot make any point, that we cannot write anything? Turbayne offers this answer:

> I have said that one condition of the use of metaphors is awareness. More accurately speaking, this means more awareness, for we can never become wholly aware. We cannot say what reality is, only what it seems like to us, imprisoned in Plato's cave, because we cannot get outside to look. The consequence is that we never know exactly what the facts are. We are always victims of adding some interpretation. We cannot help but allocate, sort, or bundle the facts in some way or another. Thus the second level of analysis which purported to reveal process and procedure purged of metaphysics was at best an approximation. (*Myth*, 64–65)

Rather than show "Twain as he really was," Skandera Trombley has made a very convincing new metaphor of Mark Twain as a "woman's man," a metaphor arising from her metonymic examination of Mark Twain in the company of women. She, Stoneley, Stahl, and others are engaged in a new metaphoric creation of Mark Twain as regards his relations with women, a new metaphoric creation that is already changing our image of Mark Twain.

All I am arguing is that it is better that we be aware of the metaphoric nature of that image rather than fall into the trap of thinking we are finally getting at "the real Twain." In fact, my examination of recent Mark Twain studies reveals the extent and the number of ways that metaphoric image is being changed. By metaphorically seeing, or rather hearing, Huck as black, Shelley Fisher Fishkin is, like others, changing our view of Mark Twain and his works in their metonymic relation to African American issues. Such a radical metaphoric shift makes her claim hard for many readers to accept, and at least part of the reluctance of some to accept her theory that Sociable Jimmy provided Mark Twain the voice for Huck Finn lies embedded in the metaphorical language of her claim: "as an engaging black child he encountered in the early 1870s helped him reconnect Twain to the cadences and rhythms of black speakers from Twain's own childhood, he inspired him to liberate a language that lay buried within Twain's own linguistic repertoire and to apprehend its stunning creative potential."[12] The metaphors *reconnect, liberate,* and *buried* seem to lie at the heart of some readers' objections to Fishkin's assertion because they suggest that this particular encounter somehow reconnected Mark Twain to a language that many of us would argue he had never lost touch with in the first place. But even if the Sociable Jimmy theory fails to win over everyone, Fishkin's other, broader claims about African American influence will no doubt prove enduring and image altering, especially coupled with her continuing work on race, as well as the work of other scholars and critics. As on the question of women, we are in the midst of a dramatic metaphoric shift in Mark Twain and race. The Mark Twain of the twenty-first century will likely be very different from the Mark Twain of the nineteenth, or even the twentieth.

To me, an exciting area of recent inquiry goes back to that question of doubles and identity, the metaphor that has proved the most persistent and shaping throughout the history of Mark Twain studies. In *Mark Twain on the Loose,* Bruce Michelson uses the controlling metaphor of wildness to recover Twain from the domestication Michelson sees him undergoing at the hands of critics and biographers. But rather than using wildness as a defining term, Michelson warns against any attempts at definition: "To try to define or confine Mark Twain ideologically is therefore a risky business, for the range and reflexivity of his own work can easily outrun—or overthrow—discourse about economic and political configurations of the self." His metaphor for Mark Twain's humor is its "absolute fluidity," the same metaphor Don Florence uses throughout *Persona and Humor in Mark Twain's Early Writing.* Rather than an evasion, I see this metaphor as one that will allow us to take a new look at Mark Twain, a new look not defined by or limited by oppositions and dualities. Michelson poses this question: "Is it possible that this 'self' that Mark Twain seems to exemplify in American culture, this literary-mythological identity with such stubborn appeal, defines itself by how it refuses and evades, rather than by how and what it affirms?"[13]

In a similar vein, we have J. D. Stahl announcing that he is "not attempting to 'invent' a new text or a new author. I am simply trying to see,

12. Fishkin, *Was Huck Black?* 4.
13. Michelson, *Mark Twain on the Loose,* 2–4, 8.

without some of the preconceptions which it is easy to bring familiar—and unfamiliar—texts, what is there in the texts that is not necessarily easy to see."[14] Or we have Gregg Camfield questioning the oppositions that Henry Nash Smith and others set up, asserting that such "polar oppositions [as 'democracy versus elitism, freedom versus constrain, pragmatic realism versus sentimental idealism'] . . . begin to collapse if put under pressure."[15] Andrew Jay Hoffman explains why a decade ago he refused to use the biographical approach (he has used a biographical approach in his recent full-length biography, of course), saying that the idea of a "divided Twain" has "stalled" Twain criticism: "Twain's bifurcated self has been made to account for so much in Twain's fiction that the fiction itself risks being lost in this simplistic code. The skeleton key of 'divided Twain' threatens to turn the wonder of entering the maze of Twain's work into a walk down a well-lit corridor."[16]

Such moves are, of course, themselves metaphorical. But clearly there is a metaphoric battle being waged over Mark Twain, a battle in many ways like the battle between Brooks and DeVoto earlier in the century. Critics such as Robinson and Gillman present us with a Mark Twain who is metaphorically bound by his culture, his race, his gender; critics such as Michelson counter with a metaphorically more loose writer and person; critics such as Skandera Trombley and Fishkin are altering the metonymic representation of Mark Twain. The stakes in this battle are high: the result will be our new Mark Twain, or at least the new way we perceive him. We must always remain aware of the metaphorical nature of the battle.

A number of recent critics do explicitly acknowledge the metaphorical nature of their approaches. For example, Richard S. Lowry, in *"Littery Man": Mark Twain and Modern Authorship*, discusses Europe as a metonymic series and the metaphors of *Life on the Mississippi;* Maria Ornella Marotti in *The Duplicating Papers* traces the space-time and writing-printing metaphors

---

14. Stahl, *Mark Twain, Culture, and Gender*, x.
15. Camfield does not, however, deny the presence of oppositions; he is trying "to relocate the site of that opposition from between conflicting world-views, to within the rather multiform and paradoxical ideology of American liberalism" (*Sentimental Twain*, 17–19).
16. Hoffman, *Inventing Mark Twain: The Lives of Samuel Langhorne Clemens*, 14.

in the "Mysterious Stranger" manuscripts, as well as calling "duplication" the central metaphor of Twain's late work; and Susan K. Harris, in *The Courtship of Olivia Langdon and Mark Twain*, figures the courtship as a series of tropes, rightly reading Mark Twain's letters as centered around various metaphors—the language of material possession as one example.[17]

At this moment of revision, it is vitally important that we all constantly remain metaphorically aware; otherwise, we will remain, in Turbayne's terms, "victims of metaphor." Turbayne sums up his argument this way:

> We are now at the final level of analysis where, having become
> to some degree aware of the metaphors involved, we proceed to re-
> use them instead of being used by them. But need we use the same
> ones? If we are aware, we can stop and think. We can choose our
> metaphors. We are no longer the duped citizens of the city-state of
> Oz but the wizard of Oz himself.
>
> Perhaps the best way to avoid being victimized by a metaphor
> worn out by over-use is to show that it is expendable. The best way
> to do this is to choose a new one. If the operation, just described,
> of presenting the literal truth is naïve, this one is sophisticated.
> (*Myth*, 64)

I think it is clear that we are engaged in choosing a new metaphor for Mark Twain. Turbayne says that "a new metaphor changes our attitude to the facts" (*Myth*, 214). That is what happens with a new critical metaphor, especially one we accept. The metaphor does not change the text, or change Mark Twain. It does change our attitude (and note that attitude is itself a metaphor). And that attitude is important, not only for us as scholars and critics and teachers, but for the culture at large as well. Tom Quirk comments on this point: "Somehow our attitude toward Twain and Huckleberry Finn matters—matters as a response to a cultural property, to be sure, but it matters as well because the novel [and I would add the author as well] challenges our tepid commitments and false assurances and promotes values we do not as yet own" (*CGHF*, 152).

---

17. Harris has long been aware of the metaphorical implications of Mark Twain's work; her *Mark Twain's Escape from Time: A Study of Patterns and Images* (Columbia: University of Missouri Press, 1982) is one of the most metaphorically aware books in Mark Twain studies.

I am not proposing myself as either the genius or iconoclast, to use Turbayne's labels, who makes the new metaphor. Instead, I propose as our iconoclastic genius Louis Budd, with these words from *Our Mark Twain:*

> My insisting on his success [in creating a persona] does not mean
> to concede Twain's dishonesty with or about himself. His moods
> of self-accusation often plunged to the edge of irrationality, and he
> regularly warned the public that his character was flawed. He also
> warned it that he was posturing.
>
> At the risk of sounding like Twain's official biographer, Albert
> Bigelow Paine, I proceed in the tone of gratitude that his posturing
> worked and gave us both his writings and his public personality.
> We would not have these writings as they now stand if he had
> shaped a substantially different life; biographers once understood
> that principle better than does the guild today. Within and beyond
> his books Twain reinforced qualities crucial to the happiness and
> perhaps survival of humankind: delight in experience, emotional
> spontaneity, and irreverence toward pomposity, petrified ideas,
> injustice, and self-pride. The function of a humorist centers in a
> liberating aggression that can spin toward tedious venom or anarchy.
> But effective naysaying carries over into affirmation. Twain reinforced
> some old and some modern values: courage in the face of dishonest
> or carping criticism, candid self-judgment that humbles the delusion
> of being able to gauge interpersonal reality without error, flexibility
> of mind and response (when his career is perceived as it happened
> rather than simplified to suit some theory), respect for the integrity
> of others, concern for the common welfare, and rapt awareness
> sweeping from the submicroscopic to the cosmic. While holding
> no monopoly on those values, Twain embodied them uniquely.
> My analysis tries to catch that rounded uniqueness, which serves
> us better than the flattened models that the mass or elitist media keep
> manufacturing.[18]

"Rounded uniqueness." There is a new metaphor, one we can build on in
interesting and fruitful ways.

---

18. Budd, *Our Mark Twain: The Making of His Public Personality,* xiv–xv. His next sentence, however—"I hope to make sure that we can enjoy and emulate the quintessential
Twain"—would of course contain some of the same problems as those mentioned above (xv).

"Who Killed Mark Twain?" Long Live Samuel Clemens!

LAURA E. SKANDERA TROMBLEY AND GARY SCHARNHORST

Contemporary literary studies, in particular scholarship on Mark Twain, remain rooted in an outworn philological tradition that sometimes (too often) rewards pedantry and tortured prose. (Philology: the art of slow reading.) A generation ago, Hamlin Hill warned in his essay "Who Killed Mark Twain?"[1] that literary scholarship seemed destined to devolve into "flavorless, objective historical introductions, collations of variants, and tabulations of end-of-the-line hyphenation." He cautioned that critics were missing the big picture because of their fondness for minute, trivial observations and failed to appreciate innovative work by Leslie Fiedler and Justin Kaplan (and of course Hamlin Hill). As it turns out, he was right.

Hamlin wondered if some of the current obsession with "the mathematical discipline of descriptive bibliography" was fallout from the Brooks-DeVoto controversy over the question whether Twain tamed and domesticated his boisterous style under the influence of his wife, his editors, and others. Certainly, Hamlin concluded, after watching the "scholarly ranks" close to "defend" Twain after the Brooks-DeVoto clash decades earlier, some politically savvy researchers would avoid any controversial topics, if only to defend their scholarly investment. That observation is still timely. What we propose to do here is to respond to whether Hamlin's venting was at all successful.

Has Twain scholarship published over the past generation begun to fill the gaps Hill identified? A large part of the problem, of course, is that "Mark

1. Hill, "Who Killed Mark Twain?" 119–24.

Twain"—make no mistake about it—is a major scholarly and commercial industry. Even during his life "Mark Twain" was recognized as a brand name as well as a pseudonym. Books about Mark Twain sell, much like books about the Civil War, Abraham Lincoln, fly-fishing, and vintage wines. Our challenge as scholars is to find a way to discuss Twain without pandering to his circle of devotees or merely exploiting his commercial appeal.

Almost three decades ago Hamlin railed that it was time to challenge and change the entrenched trademark "Mark Twain" though wondering if it was not already too late. After all, people who mess with the folk savior who wrote "both a best-seller and an accepted masterpiece" and is still revered as "a hero, a prophet, a legend, a demigod" present an awfully tempting target. The result to scholarship nearly thirty years later is like Penelope at her loom, with some (too many) critics weaving fine fabric by day and ripping out their stitches by night, indefinitely frustrating the expectation they will eventually reach a conclusion. Others are so eager to win a reputation in a debased academic culture that promotes celebrity that they become "experts" whose real contribution is confined to appearances on *Nightline* or C-SPAN. Yes, as much as we hate to admit it, because we know he would welcome a quarrel, Hamlin Hill many years ago bewailed the state of a scholarly industry that sometimes (too often) blinds readers behind a thick wall of smoke and dry-as-dust prose. Hamlin was right then and he is right now because for still too many people "[Mark Twain] is Hal Holbrook."

It is probably not a stretch to interpret Hamlin's essay as his venomous reply to the critical hammering that greeted his biography *Mark Twain: God's Fool*, published just one year earlier in 1973. In *God's Fool*, Hamlin wrote a biography strikingly different from previous studies in its scope, tone, and subject matter: first, it was a period study, in stark contrast to Justin Kaplan's chronological *Mr. Clemens and Mark Twain*, and its focus was the last decade of Twain's life; second, Hamlin included archival sources that previous scholars had either deemed unimportant or ignored; third, and perhaps most important, he openly challenged established scholars to dust off their constructions of Twain and make way for his version. To put it mildly, critics were unkind to Hamlin and his biography.

In his *American Literary Realism* piece Hamlin continued his brazen challenge to the Twain establishment, and he dished out his contempt for his critics' comments in ample quantity as made clear by his statement that criticism published during the early 1970s was "written by humorless, dull pedants whose prose style alone would be enough to petrify an unwary reader as comprehensively as Ice-9." This gem was deposited in the opening paragraph. Hamlin's charge was not well received (no surprise there), and we can say with authority that there are people who are still mad as hell about that article and who are still angry about his biography. To assert that scholars were responsible for producing dull, pedantic, self-important prose is a gutsy rhetorical strategy indeed. Hamlin's no-holds-barred approach was a clever tactic to underscore his concerns regarding Twain scholarship in addition to giving the individuals who criticized his work a whopping Bah.

What probably was unintentional on his part, yet nonetheless quite effective, is that the piece also inspired people considering entering the field. (Laura—I remember with crystal clarity where I was when I first read Hamlin's article. It was 1985, and I was a graduate student living and teaching in Bavaria. I came across the piece while I was thumbing through an old copy of *American Literary Realism* looking for an article for a paper I would never write on feminism [actually the lack thereof] in *Sometimes a Great Notion*. I stood in the deathly Saturday-morning silence of the Eichstaett University library, reading "Who Killed Mark Twain" in slack-jawed, guffawing astonishment. Hamlin's charge at his peers was so far outside the rules of scholarly engagement I had been taught that I felt as though I had been hit with a brick. I was stunned, yet in a good way. I liked this brick because for the first time since entering graduate school I felt that I had read something authentic: it was real and it was exciting. Hamlin convinced me on the strength of that essay to sign up for duty, and in a very real sense I have continued to follow his lead.)

In his *American Literary Realism* article, Hamlin clearly dared critics to examine areas previously overlooked or ignored either for personal or political reasons (such as dealing with Clara Clemens's legacy) or because the topics seemed too "marginal" to warrant serious scholarly scrutiny. For the record, to be sure, Hamlin omitted a few items from his list of Twain-related topics ripe for investigation. (Gary—for example, his complex and conflicted relationship with Bret Harte. He once lamented what he called in a subsequent review "the strong odor of whitewash" that marred Margaret Duckett's *Mark Twain and Bret Harte*. Ironically, Duckett subsequently complained about the "strong opposition from defenders of Mark Twain, who charged that my purpose was to denigrate Twain" in her book. That is, Hamlin indicted Duckett for publishing precisely the brand of scholarship he called for in his earlier essay. And, for the record, let me add here that she told the truth, mainly. There may have been some stretchers, but all in all the book was well done, as angry as it made some Twainians.) (Laura—Hamlin did not recognize the importance of the personal papers Isabel Lyon left and wrote her off as Twain's sycophant, which pushed her off the stage for the next twenty years. He also should have more strongly outlined Clara's utterly pivotal role in establishing the icon Mark Twain that the scholarly community accepted and venerated, the same one that Hamlin was determined to deconstruct.)

To his credit, however, Hamlin worried a generation ago that Mark Twain had been killed and buried "under a Procrustean bed" of trivia. He particularly bemoaned the emphasis some individuals gave to errata. There exist dozens of articles covering such minutiae as "Did Mark Twain's Laziness Cost Him a Fortune?" "Mining Days Sweetheart of Mark Twain," and "The Truth about That Humboldt Trip." We wonder, ninety years after Twain's death, whether he has been so varnished by silly speculation and bad critical writing that he is frozen like a fly in amber, victim of a brand of scholars who share a footnote fetish. An apt illustration might serve to underscore our point. (Gary—a few years ago I received a submission to *American Literary Realism*, which I edit, from a Twain "specialist," an old hand at the publication game. In a breathless tone, he announced in his article a likely literary source, never before identified, for the river chapters in *Adventures of Huckleberry Finn*—an obscure narrative about a trip on the Mississippi by a German travel writer published a decade or so before the novel. The ostensible source alluded, for example, to the dangers of a river fog reminiscent of the one that Mark Twain described in chapter 15. It had apparently never occurred to the essayist that the author of the novel, who had worked as a riverboat pilot on the Mississippi for more than two years while in his midtwenties, would not have required a literary source to inspire his description of fog.) Everyone who is anyone in American literary scholarship feels obliged, sooner or later, to add her or his two cents worth on Twain, much as every actor aspires to play Hamlet. The latest MLA bibliography includes no less than thirty-three column inches of citations to Twain scholarship, up from twenty-three column inches the year before. Do we really NEED two or three feet of scholarly citations to Twain every year? How many careers have been built on the literary landscape Twain surveyed? The self-appointed Twain specialist Charles Neider has made a good deal of money over the years either reediting trade books that did not need to be reedited *(Plymouth Rock and the Pilgrims and Other Speeches, The Complete Travel Books of Mark Twain)* or editing trade books that would need to be *(The Autobiography of Mark Twain, The Selected Letters of Mark Twain)*. It takes a determined editor to ruin Twain, and Neider almost succeeded.

On the one hand, the quickest way to earn a reputation in the current climate of academic scholarship is to propose a radically new thesis, the more controversial the better. In recent years literary critics have suggested that Emily Dickinson had an abortion, that Melville was a wife beater. Twain has been variously portrayed by biographers as the damaged son of a castrating mother, a split personality, a womanizer, a gay man, an impotent man, a child molester, a hypochondriac, a gold digger, an abusive spouse, a neglectful father, a misogynist, and an alcoholic. On the other hand, to paraphrase Fitzgerald's Nick Carraway, we beat the same horses against the current, borne back ceaselessly into the past. The ready market for books and articles on Twain, his centrality to the American literary canon, and the rewards for inspiring academic controversy in fact inhibit our ability to read him—yea, even enjoy him!—from a fresh (unbiased, nonideological) perspective.

There are exceptions. Hamlin himself hailed (pardon the alliteration) the publication of Guy Cardwell's controversial book *The Man Who Was Mark Twain:* "Rambunctious, iconoclastic, radical revisionist, Guy Cardwell gallops into Mark Twain Territory like e. e. cummings' Buffalo Bill and sets out to 'break onetwothreefourfivemythsjustlikethat,' assaulting all the various clichés that surround the legend called Mark Twain." As Hamlin wrote in *Studies in American Fiction*, "This will no doubt disturb the conservative Twain faction."[2]

With the publication of Bruce Michelson's *Mark Twain on the Loose*

---

2. Hill, "Review of *The Man Who Was Mark Twain.*"

in 1995, Twain studies came full circle from Brooks's controversial thesis some seventy-five years ago that Twain was chastened by the custodians of eastern culture and respectability. Such an "opposed-forces model" of his career has survived in various forms in Twain studies since the 1920s, as in Kaplan's *Mr. Clemens and Mark Twain* and Henry Nash Smith's *Mark Twain: The Development of a Writer*. In his book, however, Michelson offers a fresh critical perspective on Twain's writings, one that emphasizes their maniacal, heretical, and outrageous comedy, their irrepressible and sometimes irrational war against convention. In Michelson's view, Twain was scarcely a literary realist, not primarily (or even incidentally) a social satirist, but an anarchic humorist whose tales and sketches resist closure and subvert neat conclusions. To his considerable credit, in short, Michelson does not so much discover a "new Twain" as he recovers an old one by dissolving years of grease that have dulled Twain's writings. Like Twain "on the loose," Michelson unsettles our assumptions and reintroduces us to a writer we thought we knew, which is exactly what Hamlin had hoped. Perhaps it can be taken as a sign of Michelson's success that there is already a scholarly reaction to it, namely, Leland Krauth's *Proper Mark Twain*.

(Gary—I want to plug a couple of other recent Twain studies—if I may be permitted to use the term *other* in the sense of *additional,* and not as a verb. In *Mark Twain and the Art of the Tall Tale,* Henry B. Wonham reminds us that, on the page no less than on the stage, Twain was a raconteur, a rhetorician if not a careful craftsman of "tall humor." The tall tale became the organizing principle of his work, according to Wonham, and "continued to provide a structural and thematic pattern that he would return to throughout" his career. Thus, *The Adventures of Tom Sawyer* becomes a "contest for narrative authority" among the hero, the narrator, and the author, and *Adventures of Huckleberry Finn* becomes a type of collaborative fiction epitomized by the raftsman's passage now restored to chapter 16 of many recent editions of the novel. Wonham's argument has inspired dissent, most notably a spirited exchange with Forrest G. Robinson over the basic [or even primal] issue of authorial intention in *Nineteenth-Century Literature.* Robinson regards Twain as something of a "jackleg" writer rather than the skilled raconteur Wonham considers him—see the articles and rejoinders in the December 1995 and June 1996 issues of the journal.³ But is not this brand of discussion and debate finally a sign of vitality, an indication that SOMEONE is listening, unlike the myopic self-promotion of the type Tom Sawyer called "the authorities"?

I also want to recommend *Mark Twain in the Company of Women* by Laura Skandera Trombley, my collaborator on this essay, not because I am inclined to pander shamelessly but because it too fills a glaring void in Twain scholarship. Rather than a feminist defense or apology or attack, Laura offers a straightforward and refreshing feminist reading of Twain's relations with women, especially his immediate "female community"—his wife, Olivia; their daughters, Susy, Clara, and Jean; and his personal secretary, Isabel Lyon. His interactions with these and many other women "helped define his boundaries." Laura argues persuasively that "what fed Clemens's propensity for pessimism" and "robbed him of his creative voice" toward the end of his life was the disintegration not of his personality [as in the old Van Wyck Brooks thesis] but of his "charmed circle" of familial and female readers. He desperately tried to refashion such a circle in his "Angelfish," to little avail. Like a prospector who assiduously works a claim, Laura opens a provocative but unfortunately neglected field to Twain scholars.)

(Laura—I have two recommendations of my own that I'd like to include here. *Getting to Be Mark Twain* by Jeffrey Steinbrink, is a superb period study of Twain's Buffalo years. Steinbrink carefully traces how Twain's move to the East, his marriage to Olivia, and his growth as a writer all contributed to his evolution from the Wild Humorist of the Pacific Slope to a well-established author of books. Until Steinbrink's biography, this period, 1868–1871, went largely unremarked by critics, and the typical scholarly view was that during this time Twain's writing was fallow, his editorial venture was unsuccessful, and his marriage was off to a decidedly rocky start. What Steinbrink presents so effectively is that these four years really determined the course of the rest of Twain's writing and life, and without understanding the events of this time we cannot hope to realize the remainder of Twain's career.

Ron Powers's *Dangerous Water* is another insightful period study of Twain's early years. What is so appealing about this work is that Powers does

---

3. Robinson, "An 'Unconscious and Profitable Cerebration': Mark Twain and Literary Intentionality."

a fine job of describing how the rich chaos of Twain's early years reflected and refracted in "his very best works, [which] were nearly always pastiche." There is a lyric quality to Powers's writing that is a fine match with his subject. Powers has done his homework, he graciously acknowledges Dixon Wecter as "the greatest scholar of Twain's boyhood," and his discussion of the genesis of southwestern humor is very well done. The end of the book leaves the reader with a clearer vision of Mark Twain as a boy and young man—certainly no simple feat.)

Hamlin ended his essay by observing that "there is everything yet to be done with both Samuel Clemens the man and Mark Twain the artistic creation; the next generation of Mark Twain scholars and critics ought to take nothing for granted and should be able to reassess practically every facet of their subject's life and work." Once again we agree. Currently there is an openness to the field that has never previously existed. Although factions and excesses certainly are still present, there is fine scholarship being done that has resulted in Twain being viewed in radically different ways than Clara, Paine, Howells, Brooks, or DeVoto would have approved. So much for the good. It is imperative that this careful, bold work be encouraged and that it continue.

Lou Budd commented at the 2000 American Literature Association Conference that "Mark Twain has become an American Rorschach test," a comment that Twain would have willingly endorsed. Twain wanted to remain an enigma, to remain the focus of critical attention, and he wanted to influence (even from the grave) outcomes in the endless effort to see him more clearly. Perhaps it is best to let Twain have the last word here. When researching and writing on Twain it is probably helpful to keep in mind one of his comments about his autobiography: "I like criticism, but it must be my way."

Works Cited

Publications by Mark Twain

Adventures of Huckleberry Finn. 1885. Reprint, Berkeley and Los Angeles: University of California Press, 1985.

Adventures of Huckleberry Finn. Ed. Sculley Bradley et al. 2d ed. New York: W. W. Norton, 1977.

Adventures of Huckleberry Finn. Ed. Walter Blair and Victor Fischer. Berkeley and Los Angeles: University of California Press, 1988.

"Adventures of Huckleberry Finn": A Case Study in Critical Controversy. Ed. Gerald Graff and James Phelan. Boston: Bedford Books, 1995.

The Adventures of Tom Sawyer. Foreword and notes by John C. Gerber. Berkeley and Los Angeles: University of California Press, 1980.

"Around the World." *Buffalo Express.* (Oct. 16, 1869–Jan. 29, 1870).

The Art of Authorship: Literary Reminiscences, Methods of Work, and Advice to Young Beginners. London: J. Clarke, 1890.

The Autobiography of Mark Twain. Ed. Charles Neider. New York: Harper and Row, 1959.

Collected Tales, Sketches, Speeches, and Essays, 1891–1910. New York: Library of America Press, 1992.

The Complete Short Stories and Famous Essays of Mark Twain. New York: P. F. Collier and Son, 1928.

Europe and Elsewhere. With an appreciation by Brander Matthews and an introduction by Albert Bigelow Paine. New York: Harper and Bros., 1923.

Extract from Captain Stormfield's Visit to Heaven. New York: Harper, 1909.

Following the Equator. 2 vols. New York: Harper, 1897.

The Gilded Age: A Tale of Today. With Charles Dudley Warner. New York and Oxford: Oxford University Press, 1996.

"The Great Dark." In *Mark Twain's "Which Was the Dream?" and Other Symbolic Writings of the Later Years,* ed. John S. Tuckey. Berkeley and Los Angeles: University of California Press, 1967.

The Innocents Abroad. Hartford: American Publishing, 1869.

The Innocents Abroad; or, The New Pilgrims Progress. New York: Signet, 1966.

Life on the Mississippi. New York: Penguin Publishers, 1984; New York: Oxford University Press, 1996.

Mark Twain Papers. Bancroft Library. University of California–Berkeley.

Mark Twain's Autobiography. Ed. Albert Bigelow Paine. 2 vols. New York: Harper and Bros., 1924.

Mark Twain's Letters. Vol. 1, *1853–1866.* Ed. Edgar M. Branch, Michael B. Frank, and Kenneth A. Sanderson. Berkeley and Los Angeles: University of California Press, 1988.

Mark Twain's Letters. Vol. 2, *1867–1868.* Ed. Harriet Elinor Smith and Richard Bucci. Berkeley and Los Angeles: University of California Press, 1990.

Mark Twain's Letters. Vol. 4, *1870–1871.* Ed. Victor Fischer, Michael B. Frank, and Lin Salamo. Berkeley and Los Angeles: University of California Press, 1995.

Mark Twain's Own Autobiography: The Chapters from the North American Review. Ed. Michael J. Kiskis. Madison: University of Wisconsin Press, 1990.

Mark Twain's Works. Hartford, Conn.: American Publishing, 1900.

Mark Twain to Mrs. Fairbanks. Ed. Dixon Wecter. San Marino, Calif.: Huntington Library, 1949.

No. 44, the Mysterious Stranger. 1969. Reprint, Berkeley and Los Angeles: University of California Press, 1982.

Plymouth Rock and the Pilgrims and Other Speeches. New York: Harper and Row, 1984.

The Prince and the Pauper. Ed. Victor Fischer and Lin Salamo. Berkeley and Los Angeles: University of California Press, 1979.

Pudd'nhead Wilson and Those Extraordinary Twins. Ed. Sidney E. Berger. New York: Norton, 1980.

"A Record of Small Foolishnesses." Clifton Waller Barrett Collection, University of Virginia–Charlottesville.

The Selected Letters of Mark Twain. New York: Harper and Row, 1982.

The Signet Book of Mark Twain's Short Stories. Ed. with an introduction by
    Justin Kaplan. New York: Signet, 1985.
Tales, Speeches, Essays, and Sketches. Ed. Tom Quirk. New York: Penguin
    Books, 1994.
"Three Thousand Years among the Microbes." In *Mark Twain's "Which Was
    the Dream?" and Other Symbolic Writings of the Later Years,* ed. John
    S. Tuckey. Berkeley and Los Angeles: University of California Press,
    1967.
Tom Sawyer Abroad and Tom Sawyer, Detective. 1894, 1896. Reprint, Berke-
    ley and Los Angeles: University of California Press, 1982.
"Tom Sawyer's Conspiracy." In *Huck Finn and Tom Sawyer among the Indi-
    ans and Other Unfinished Stories.* Berkeley and Los Angeles: University
    of California Press, 1989.
"A True Story." In *The Unabridged Mark Twain.* Ed. Lawrence Techer. Phil-
    adelphia: Running Press, 1976.
"The Turning Point in My Life." In *"What Is Man?" and Other Essays.* 1917,
    Reprint, Freeport, N.Y.: Books for Libraries Press, 1972.
"What Is Man?" and Other Essays. With an appreciation by Brander Mat-
    thews and an introduction by Albert Bigelow Paine. New York: Gabriel
    Wells, 1923.
"What Ought He to Have Done?" *Christian Union* 32 (July 16, 1885): 3, 4–5.

Other Sources

Adams, Henry. *History of the United States of America.* 9 vols. New York:
    Scribners, 1889–1891.
Anderson, Frederick, William M. Gibson, and Henry Nash Smith, eds. *Se-
    lected Mark Twain–Howells Letters, 1872–1910.* New York: Atheneum,
    1968.
Arac, Jonathan. *Huckleberry Finn as Idol and Target: The Functions of Criti-
    cism in Our Time.* Madison: University of Wisconsin Press, 1997.
Baetzhold, Howard G. "Mark Twain on Scientific Investigation: Contempo-
    rary Allusions in 'Some Learned Fables for Good Old Boys and Girls.'"
    In *Literature and Ideas in America: Essays in Memory of Harry Hayden
    Clark,* ed. Robert Falk, 128–54. Athens: Ohio University Press, 1975.

Bennett, William J., ed. *The Book of Virtues: A Treasury of Moral Stories.* New York: Simon and Schuster, 1993.

Berret, Anthony. "*Huckleberry Finn* and the Minstrel Show." *American Studies* 27 (fall 1986): 37–49.

Bleiler, Everett F. "Dime Novel Science-Fiction." *Cite AB* (Oct. 23, 1995): 1542.

Booth, Wayne C. *The Company We Keep: An Ethics of Fiction.* Berkeley and Los Angeles: University of California Press, 1988.

Branch, Edgar M. "Newspaper Reading and the Writer's Creativity." *Nineteenth-Century Fiction* 37 (Mar. 1983): 576–603.

Brooks, Van Wyck. *The Ordeal of Mark Twain.* London: William Heinemann, 1922; New York: E. P. Dutton, 1933.

Brown, Gillian. *Domestic Individualism: Imagining Self in Nineteenth-Century America.* Berkeley and Los Angeles: University of California Press, 1990.

Budd, Louis J. *Our Mark Twain: The Making of His Public Personality.* Philadelphia: University of Philadelphia Press, 1983.

Camfield, Gregg. *Sentimental Twain: Samuel Clemens in the Maze of Moral Philosophy.* Philadelphia: University of Pennsylvania Press, 1994.

Cardwell, Guy. *The Man Who Was Mark Twain: Images and Ideologies.* New Haven: Yale University Press, 1991.

———. "Mark Twain: The Metaphoric Hero as Battleground." *ESQ* 23 (1977): 52–66.

Carus, Paul. "Mark Twain's Philosophy." *Monist* 23 (Apr. 1913): 181–223.

Chadwick-Joshua, Jocelyn. *The Jim Dilemma: Reading Race in Huckleberry Finn.* Jackson: University Press of Mississippi, 1998.

Cockrell, Dale. *Demons of Disorder: Early Blackface Minstrels and Their World.* Cambridge: Cambridge University Press, 1997.

"Commentary: An Exchange between Henry B. Wonham and Forrest G. Robinson." *Nineteenth-Century Literature* 51: 1 (June 1996): 137–42.

Cox, James M. *Mark Twain: The Fate of Humor.* Princeton: Princeton University Press, 1966.

Cummings, Sherwood. *Mark Twain and Science: Adventures of a Mind.* Baton Rouge: Louisiana State University Press, 1988.

Curtis, Anthony. Introduction to *The Aspern Papers and the Turn of the Screw.* Middlesex, England: Hammondsworth, 1984.

David, Beverly R., and Ray Sapirstein. "Reading the Illustrations in *Pudd'n-head Wilson*." In *The Tragedy of Pudd'nhead Wilson and the Comedy of Those Extraordinary Twins*. 1894. Reprint, New York: Oxford University Press, 1996.

Delaney, Wesley A. "The Truth about That Humboldt Trip as Told by Gus Oliver to A. B. Paine." *Twainian* 7 (May-June 1948): 1–3.

DeMause, Lloyd. *The History of Childhood*. New York: Psychohistory Press, [1974].

DeVoto, Bernard. *Mark Twain at Work*. Cambridge: Harvard University Press, 1942.

———. *Mark Twain's America*. Boston: Little, Brown, 1932.

———, ed. *Mark Twain in Eruption: Hitherto Unpublished Pages about Men and Events by Mark Twain*. New York: Harper, 1940.

Dickinson, Leon T. Review of *Mark Twain Abroad*, by Dewey Ganzel. *Modern Philology* 68:1 (1970): 117–19.

Dolmetsch, Carl. *Our Famous Guest: Mark Twain in Vienna*. Athens: University of Georgia Press, 1992.

Doyno, Victor. *Writing Huck Finn: Mark Twain's Creative Process*. Philadelphia: University of Pennsylvania Press, 1991.

Du Bois, W. E. B. *Dusk of Dawn*. Cambridge: Library of America Press, 1986.

———. *The Souls of Black Folk: Essays and Sketches*. Chicago: A. C. McClurg, 1903; Cambridge: Library of America Press, 1986.

Duckett, Margaret. *Mark Twain and Bret Harte*. Norman: University of Oklahoma Press, 1964.

Ellenberger, Henri F. *The Discovery of the Unconscious: The History and Evolution of Dynamic Psychiatry*. New York: Basic Books, 1970.

Ellison, Ralph. *Going to the Territory*. New York: Random House, 1986.

Emerson, Everett. *Mark Twain: A Literary Life*. Philadelphia: University of Pennsylvania Press, 2000.

Emerson, Ralph Waldo. "Nature." *Essays and Lectures*. New York: Library of America Press, 1983.

Everdell, William. *The First Moderns: Profiles in the Origins of Twentieth-Century Thought*. Chicago: University of Chicago Press, 1997.

Fairbanks, Mary Mason. "The Cruise of the 'Quaker City,' with Chance Recollections of Mark Twain." *Chautauquan* 14 (Jan. 1892): 429–32.

————. *Emma Willard and Her Pupils; or, Fifty Years of Troy Female Seminary, 1822–1872.* New York: Mrs. Russell Sage, 1898.

Fiedler, Leslie. *Love and Death in the American Novel.* New York: Dell, 1966.

Fishkin, Shelley Fisher. *Was Huck Black? Mark Twain and African-American Voices.* New York: Oxford University Press, 1993.

Florence, Don. *Persona and Humor in Mark Twain's Early Writing.* Columbia: University of Missouri Press, 1995.

Freeman, Mary E. Wilkins. *Selected Stories of Mary E. Wilkins Freeman.* New York: W. W. Norton, 1983.

Galbraith, John Kenneth. *Money: Whence It Came, Where It Went.* Rev. ed. Boston: Houghton Mifflin, 1995.

Ganzel, Dewey. *Mark Twain Abroad: The Cruise of the "Quaker City."* Chicago: University of Chicago Press, 1968.

Gay, Peter. *Education of the Senses.* Vol. 1, *The Bourgeois Experience: Victoria to Freud.* New York: 1984.

Gillman, Susan. *Dark Twins: Imposture and Identity in Mark Twain's America.* Chicago: University of Chicago Press, 1989.

Grant, Thomas. "The Artist of the Beautiful: Mark Twain's Investment in the Machine Inventor." *Publications of the Missouri Philosophical Association* 4 (1979): 59–68.

Gribben, Alan. "Removing Mark Twain's Mask: A Decade of Criticism and Scholarship." *ESQ* 26 (1980): 100–103, 149–71.

Gribben, Alan, and Nick Karanovich, eds. *Overland with Mark Twain.* Elmira, N.Y.: Center for Mark Twain Studies at Quarry Farm, 1992.

Grinspoon, Lester, and James B. Bakalar. *Cocaine: A Drug and Its Social Evolution.* Rev. ed. New York: Basic Books, 1985.

Harris, Joel Chandler. *Uncle Remus: His Songs and Sayings.* New York: Appleton, 1895.

Harris, Susan K. *The Courtship of Olivia Langdon and Mark Twain.* Cambridge: Cambridge University Press, 1996.

Headrick, Mrs. C. L. "Mining Days Sweetheart of Mark Twain." *Twainian* 15 (May-June 1956): 1–2.

Hemingway, Ernest. *The Green Hills of Africa.* New York: Simon and Schuster, 1935.

Herndon, Lt. William L., and Lardner Gibbon. *Exploration of the Valley of the Amazon . . .* 2 vols. Washington, D.C.: R. Armstrong, 1853–1854.

Hill, Hamlin. *Mark Twain: God's Fool.* New York: Harper and Row, 1973.

———. *Mark Twain and Elisha Bliss.* Columbia: University of Missouri Press, 1964.

———. "Mark Twain and His Enemies." Review of *Mark Twain and Bret Harte. Southern Review* 4 (spring 1968): 520–29.

———. Review of *The Man Who Was Mark Twain. Studies in American Fiction* 20:2 (fall 1992): 226–27.

———. "Who Killed Mark Twain?" *American Literary Realism, 1870–1910* 7 (1974): 119–24.

Hoffman, Andrew. *Inventing Mark Twain: The Lives of Samuel Langhorne Clemens.* New York: William Morrow, 1997.

———. *Twain's Heroes, Twain's Worlds: Mark Twain's "Adventures of Huckleberry Finn," "A Connecticut Yankee in King Arthur's Court," and "Pudd'nhead Wilson."* Philadelphia: University of Pennsylvania Press, 1988.

Holt, Jim. "Infinitesimally Yours." *New York Review of Books* (May 20, 1999): 63–67.

Horn, Jason Gary. *Mark Twain and William James: Crafting a Free Self.* Columbia: University of Missouri Press, 1996.

Howells, William Dean. *My Mark Twain: Reminiscences and Criticism.* Ed. Marilyn Austin Baldwin. New York: Harper and Bros., 1910; Baton Rouge: Louisiana State University Press, 1967.

Hunter, Louis C. *Steamboats on the Western Rivers.* 1949. Reprint, New York: Octagon Books, 1969.

Hurston, Zora Neale. *Their Eyes Were Watching God.* Philadelphia: J. B. Lippincott, 1937.

Jakobson, Roman. *On Language.* Ed. Linda R. Waugh and Monique Monville-Burston. Cambridge: Harvard University Press, 1990.

———. "Two Aspects of Language and Two Types of Aphasic Disturbances." In *Fundamentals of Language,* ed. Roman Jakobson and Morris Halle. 2d ed. The Hague: Nouton, 1971.

James, Clive. "The Voice of America." *New Yorker* (June 14, 1993): 81.

James, William. *Pragmatism and Four Essays from the "Meaning of Truth."* Cleveland and New York: Meridian Books, 1955.

Jewett, Sarah Orne. *The Night before Thanksgiving: A White Heron and Selected Stories.* St. Clair Shores, Mich.: Scholarly Press, 1979.

Johnson, James Weldon. *The Book of American Negro Poetry.* New York: Harcourt, Brace, and World, 1958.

Johnston, William M. *Vienna: The Golden Age, 1815–1914.* New York: Clarkson N. Potter, 1980.

Kaplan, Justin. *Mr. Clemens and Mark Twain: A Biography.* New York: Simon and Schuster, 1966.

Kaplan, Robert, *The Nothing That Is: A Natural History of Zero.* Oxford and New York: Oxford University Press, 1999.

Knoper, Randall. *Acting Naturally: Mark Twain in the Culture of Performance.* Berkeley and Los Angeles: University of California Press, 1995.

Kolodny, Annette. "Dancing through the Minefield: Some Observations on the Theory, Practice, and Politics of a Feminist Literary Criticism." In *Falling into Theory: Conflicting Views on Reading and Literature,* ed. David H. Richter, 278–85. Boston: St. Martin's Press, 1994.

Krauth, Leland. *Proper Mark Twain.* Athens: University of Georgia Press, 1999.

Kuhn, Thomas S. *The Structure of Scientific Revolutions.* 2d ed. 1962. Reprint, Chicago: University of Chicago Press, 1970.

Lauber, John. *The Inventions of Mark Twain.* New York: Hill and Wang, 1990.

Lears, T. J. Jackson. *No Place of Grace: Antimodernism and the Transformation of American Culture, 1880–1920.* Chicago: University of Chicago Press, 1981.

Lee, Judith Yaross. "Anatomy of a Fascinating Failure." *Invention and Technology* (summer 1987): 55–60.

Lemons, J. Stanley. "Black Stereotype as Reflected in Popular Culture, 1880–1920." *American Quarterly* 29 (spring 1977): 106.

Leonard, James S., Thomas A. Tenney, and Thadius M. Davis, eds. *Satire or Evasion? Black Perspectives on Huckleberry Finn.* Durham: Duke University Press, 1992.

Lewis, Richard Warrington Baldwin. *The American Adam: Innocence, Tragedy, and Tradition in the Nineteenth Century.* Chicago: University of Chicago Press, 1955.

Logan, Rayford W. *The Betrayal of the Negro from Rutherford B. Hayes to Woodrow Wilson.* New York: Oxford, 1965.

Lorch, Fred W. "Mark Twain in Iowa." *Iowa Journal of History and Politics* 27 (1929): 408–58.

Lott, Eric. *Love and Theft: Blackface Minstrelsy and the American Working Class.* New York: Oxford University Press, 1993.

———. "Mr. Clemens and Jim Crow: Twain, Race, and Blackface." In *Criticism and the Color Line: Desegregating American Literary Studies,* ed. Henry B. Wonham. New Brunswick, N.J.: Rutgers University Press, 1996.

Lowry, Richard S. *"Littery Man": Mark Twain and Modern Authorship.* New York: Oxford University Press, 1996.

Marotti, Maria Ornella. *The Duplicating Imagination: Twain and the Twain Papers.* University Park: Pennsylvania State University Press, 1990.

Melville, Herman. *Moby-Dick; or, The Whale.* Evanston and Chicago: Northwestern University Press and the Newberry Library, 1988.

Michelson, Bruce. *Mark Twain on the Loose: A Comic Writer and the American Self.* Amherst: University of Massachusetts Press, 1995.

Neider, Charles. *The Complete Travel Books of Mark Twain.* New York: Doubleday, 1966.

Page, Thomas Nelson. *The Negro: The Southerner's Problem.* New York: Scribner, 1904; New York: Johnson Reprint, 1970.

Paine, Albert Bigelow. *Mark Twain, a Biography: The Personal and Literary Life of Samuel Langhorne Clemens.* 4 vols. New York: Harpers, 1912.

———. *Mark Twain: A Biography.* Vol. 3. New York: Chelsea House, 1980.

Parker, Herschel. *Flawed Texts and Verbal Icons: Literary Authority in American Fiction.* Evanston: Northwestern University Press, 1984.

Powers, Ron. *Dangerous Water: A Biography of the Boy Who Became Mark Twain.* New York: Basic Books, 1999.

Quirk, Tom. Mark Twain chapter in *American Literary Scholarship: An Annual, 1994.* Durham: Duke University Press, 1996.

———. *Coming to Grips with Huckleberry Finn: Essays on a Book, a Boy, and a Man.* Columbia: University of Missouri Press, 1993.

Rafferty, Jennifer L. "Mark Twain, Labor, and Technology: *A Connecticut Yankee* and *No. 44, the Mysterious Stranger.*" *Over Here* 15 (1995): 20–33.

Rieff, Philip. *Freud: The Mind of the Moralist.* Garden City, N.Y.: Anchor Books.

Robinson, Forrest G. *In Bad Faith: The Dynamics of Deception in Mark Twain's America.* Cambridge: Harvard University Press, 1986.

————. "An 'Unconscious and Profitable Cerebration': Mark Twain and Lit-
    erary Intentionality." *Nineteenth-Century Literature* 50:3 (Dec. 1995):
    357–80.

————, ed. *The Cambridge Companion to Mark Twain.* New York: Cam-
    bridge University Press, 1995.

Roediger, David. *The Wages of Whiteness: Race and the Making of the Amer-
    ican Working Class.* London: Verso, 1991.

Rogin, Michael. "Francis Galton and Mark Twain: The Natal Autograph
    in *Pudd'nhead Wilson.*" In *Mark Twain's "Pudd'nhead Wilson": Race,
    Conflict, and Culture,* ed. Forrest G. Robinson and Susan Gillman.
    Durham: Duke University Press, 1990.

Schorske, Carl E. *Fin-de-Siècle Vienna: Politics and Culture.* New York: Al-
    fred A. Knopf, 1980.

Sewell, David R. *Mark Twain's Languages: Discourse, Dialogue, and Linguistic
    Variety.* Berkeley and Los Angeles: University of California Press, 1987.

Singer, Alan. *A Metaphorics of Fiction: Discontinuity and Discourse in the
    Modern Novel.* Tallahassee: University Presses of Florida, 1983.

Skandera Trombley, Laura E. *Mark Twain in the Company of Women.* Phil-
    adelphia: University of Pennsylvania Press, 1994.

Smith, David Lionel. "Black Critics and Mark Twain." In *The Cambridge
    Companion to Mark Twain,* ed. Forrest Robinson. Cambridge: Cam-
    bridge University Press, 1995.

————. "Huck, Jim, and American Racial Discourse." *Mark Twain Journal*
    22 (fall 1984): 4–12.

Smith, Henry Nash. *Mark Twain: The Development of a Writer.* Cambridge:
    Harvard University Press, 1962; New York: Atheneum, 1974.

Stahl, J. D. *Mark Twain, Culture, and Gender: Envisioning America through
    Europe.* Athens: University of Georgia Press, 1994.

Steinbrink, Jeffrey. *Getting to Be Mark Twain.* Berkeley and Los Angeles:
    University of California Press, 1991.

Stoneley, Peter. *Mark Twain and the Feminine Aesthetic.* New York: Cam-
    bridge University Press, 1992.

Stoppard, Tom. *Arcadia.* London: Faber and Faber, 1993.

Suleri, Sara. *The Rhetoric of English India.* Chicago: University of Chicago
    Press, 1992.

"To the Editor." *Christian Union* 34 (June 11, 1885): 24.

Turbayne, Colin Murray. *The Myth of Metaphor.* New Haven: Yale University Press, 1962; Columbia: University of South Carolina Press, 1970.

The Victor and Irene Muir Jacobs Collection. Sale catalog. Items 210, 221. New York: Sotheby's, 1996.

Warner, Susan. *The Wide, Wide World.* New York: Feminist Press at the City University of New York, 1987.

Webster, Samuel C. *Mark Twain, Business Man.* Boston: Little, Brown, 1946.

Williamson, Joel. *The Crucible of Race: Black-White Relations in the American South since Emancipation.* New York: Oxford University Press, 1984.

Wonham, Henry B. "'I Want a Real Coon': Mark Twain and Late-Nineteenth-Century Ethnic Caricature." *American Literature* 72 (Mar. 2000): 117–52.

———. *Mark Twain and the Art of the Tall Tale.* New York: Oxford University Press, 1993.

Woodard, Frederick, and Donnarae MacCann. "Minstrel Shackles and Nineteenth-Century 'Liberality' in *Huckleberry Finn.*" In *Satire or Evasion? Black Perspectives on Huckleberry Finn,* ed. James S. Leonard, Thomas A. Tenney, and Thadius M. Davis, 141–53. Durham: Duke University Press, 1992.

Zelizer, Viviana A. *Pricing the Priceless Child: The Changing Social Value of Children.* New York: Basic Books, 1985.

Contributors

JOHN BIRD is Associate Professor of English at Winthrop University. He has published articles on Mark Twain, and is working on a book about Mark Twain and metaphor. He is currently executive coordinator of the Mark Twain Circle of America.

VICTOR DOYNO is Professor of English at the State University of New York at Buffalo. His works include *Adventures of Huckleberry Finn: The Growth from Manuscript to Novel in One Hundred Years of Huckleberry Finn*, *Mark Twain: Selected Writings of an American Skeptic*, and *Writing "Huckleberry Finn": Mark Twain's Creative Process*. He is now working on a two-disk CD-ROM of the newly rediscovered "Huck Manuscript."

MICHAEL J. KISKIS is Professor of American Literature at Elmira College. He is editor of *Mark Twain's Own Autobiography: The Chapters from the North American Review*. He is past president of the Northeast Modern Language Association and the Mark Twain Circle of America. He is past editor of *Studies in American Humor* and is currently the editor of *Modern Language Studies*.

JAMES S. LEONARD is Professor and Chair of the Department of English at the Citadel. He is the coauthor of *The Fluent Mundo: Wallace Stevens and the Structure of Reality*; coeditor of *Satire or Evasion? Black Perspectives on Huckleberry Finn* and *Authority and Textuality: Current Views of Collaborative Writing*; editor of *Making Mark Twain Work in the Classroom*; and editor of the quarterly *Mark Twain Circular*.

TOM QUIRK is Professor of English at the University of Missouri–Columbia. His books include *Coming to Grips with Huckleberry Finn*, *Mark Twain:*

A Study of the Short Fiction, the Penguin edition of *Selected Tales, Essays, Speeches and Sketches of Mark Twain,* and, most recently, *Nothing Abstract: Investigations in the American Literary Imagination.*

ANN RYAN is Assistant Professor of English at Le Moyne College in Syracuse, New York. In addition to her work on Twain, she has written about Edith Wharton and Ralph Waldo Emerson. She is currently coediting a book on the photography of Rita Hammond to be published by Syracuse University Press.

ROBERT SATTELMEYER is Professor and Chair of the Department of English at Georgia State University. Coeditor of *One Hundred Years of Huckleberry Finn,* he also writes about Thoreau and transcendentalism. In his spare time he is working on a light opera based on "Experiences of the McWilliamses with Membranous Croup."

GARY SCHARNHORST is Professor of English at the University of New Mexico, editor of *American Literary Realism,* general editor of the monograph series *Studies in American Literary Realism and Naturalism* published by the University of Alabama Press, and editor in alternating years of the research annual *American Literary Scholarship.*

DAVID LIONEL SMITH is the John W. Chandler Professor of English at Williams College. His scholarly interests include African American writing, southern writing, Mark Twain, nature writing, and literary theory. He is coeditor, with Jack Salzman and Cornel West, of the *Encyclopedia of African American Culture and History.*

J. D. STAHL is the author of *Mark Twain, Culture, and Gender* and articles about Mark Twain in *American Literature* and other journals. He teaches in the Department of English at Virginia Tech in Blacksburg, Virginia. He is particularly interested in cross-cultural representations by and about Mark Twain, as in Twain's travel writing and in his translation of Heinrich Hoffman's *Struwwelpeter* (Slovenly Peter).

JEFF STEINBRINK teaches American literature and creative writing at Franklin and Marshall College, where he is Alumni Professor of English and American Belles Lettres. He has spoken on Mark Twain in venues from Hartford to Manila, and his published work includes the book *Getting to Be Mark Twain,* a critical account of the writer's most formative years. He is an occasional commentator on National Public Radio's *Morning Edition* and on *Maine Things Considered* from Maine Public Radio.

LAURA SKANDERA TROMBLEY is Professor of English, Vice President of Academic Affairs, and Dean of the Faculty at Coe College. She is President of the Mark Twain Circle of America. She has been elected to the board of the American Conference of Academic Deans and as a member of the International Association of University Professors of English. Her books include *Critical Essays on Maxine Hong Kingston, Mark Twain in the Company of Women,* and *Epistemology: Turning Points in the History of Poetic Knowledge.* She has lectured internationally on Mark Twain, Chinese American women's literature, and information literacy.

HENRY WONHAM is Associate Professor at the University of Oregon and the author of two books, *Mark Twain and the Art of the Tall Tale* and *Charles W. Chesnutt: A Study of the Short Fiction.* He is currently at work on a study of ethnic caricatures in American literary realism.

JENNIFER ZACCARA is an independent scholar and has taught at the University of Connecticut, Trinity College, and the Winsor School. Beginning in the fall of 2001, she will be teaching at the Taft School in Watertown, Connecticut. Jennifer has written journal articles for *Over Here* and the *Mark Twain Journal.* Most of her work and research on Twain explores issues of strangers and estrangement in Twain's late fiction, in particular, issues of productivity, mechanization, and literary creation.

Index

Aboriginal tracker, 136–37

Acting Naturally: Mark Twain in the Culture of Performance (Knoper), 209

Adam and Eve, 22, 25, 27, 87

Adams, Henry, 91

Adventures of Huckleberry Finn (Twain): Arac's view of, 11; Aunt Sally's response to steamboat mishap in, 140; "black magic" evoked by Jim in, 147–48; as collaborative fiction, 223; criticisms and scholarship on, 10–11, 15, 151–55, 169–73; dialect in, 161–62, 164–66, 213–14; "false dilemma" or "black-and-white" fallacy in, 10, 139–50; family relationships and children in, 9, 15–20, 26, 31, 47; feminist criticism of, 15; as flawed text, 169–72; Frenchman argument in, 141–44; Huck and Jim as survivors in, 18–19; Huck's contemplation of patricide in, 17–18; Huck's "I'll go to hell" soliloquy in, 139–40; Huck's innocence in, 153; Huck's self-exile in, 19, 166, 168, 182–83; Huck's voice and point of view in, 29; humor in, 141, 151, 161, 176, 178–83; interpretive frame surrounding, 174; and intimate talk between Huck and Jim, 19; and Jim as "white inside," 143, 147–49, 187; Jim's characterization in, 122–23, 122n3, 129, 139–51, 154–56, 187; logical fallacies in, 10, 139–50; and minstrelsy, 125, 141; moral lesson of, 19–20; "noble savage" figures in, 146–47; Pap Finn in, 17–20, 168, 183–84; practical jokes against Jim in, 144–46, 145n2, 156, 169, 181–82, 184, 185; racial issues in, 10, 11, 16, 17, 122–23, 122n3, 125, 129, 139–56, 161–62, 164–66, 169–90, 210; students' familiarity with, 13; and Twain's

experiences, 88, 221; violence and human cruelty in, 17–20, 100

Adventures of Tom Sawyer (Twain): doubling motif in, 129; family relationships and children in, 24, 25–26, 47; narrative authority in, 223; racial issues in, 210; students' familiarity with, 13; and Twain's experiences, 88; writing process for, 85

Africa, 80, 81, 134

African Americans. *See* Race and ethnicity

"Age of Anxiety," 103

Alta California letters (Twain), 64

American Academy of Political and Social Science, 158

American Adam (Lewis), 4

American History X, 189n14

American Literary Realism, 219–20, 221

American Literary Scholarship, 203

American Literature Association, 225

American Publishing Company, 132–33

American Yankee in King Arthur's Court (Twain), 25

Angina, 48

Animal tales, 26

Arac, Jonathan, 11, 122n1, 169–73, 187

Arcadia (Stoppard), 200

"Around the World" letters, 79, 79n7

Art of Authorship (Bainton), 82, 82n9

Ashcroft, Ralph, 117

"Atlanta Exposition Address," 158

Atlantic Monthly, 53, 65n15, 88

Australia, 91

Austria, 101, 102, 103–5, 108, 115–16, 117, 120

Autobiography of Mark Twain (Twain): on autobiographical method, 4, 8, 105; character sketches of friends in, 114; coca trade and cocaine in, 94, 100; on critics and criticism, 1, 225; dates for composition of, 101; deaths of Twain's family and friends in, 21–23; dictation of, by Twain, 10, 101, 106, 108–9, 111–14, 117–18, 120, 121; family relationships in, 9, 21–27; on farm, 24, 114; fifty-dollar-bill story in, 97–99, 100; and free association, 105–6, 120; Howells's cautions on, 106; as life story of a persona, 107–8, 113; and Lyon, 10, 101–2, 111–14, 119–20; on mother, 185–86; and nihilism, 115–17, 120–21; nostalgia and recollection in, 112–15, 117, 120–21; on practical joking, 183; process of composition of, 101, 105–6, 108–9, 111–14, 117–21; on slavery, 189; and "talking cure," 101–2, 120–21; and technology, 10; truth of, 106–7, 113; and Twain's interest in psychology, 10, 101–21; on Twain's own death, 22–23

Baetzhold, Howard G., 73n2
Bainton, George, 82, 83
Bakalar, James B., 96n12
Beach, Emma, 51, 52–53, 56
Beach, Moses, 51
Beard, Dan, 125–27
Beecher, Henry Ward, 51–52
Bennett, William, 16
Bergson, Henri, 196
Berret, Anthony J., 125, 208
Bird, John, 11, 203–17
Bixby, Paul, 90, 93
Black, Max, 204
Black dialect. See Dialect
Blacks. See Race and ethnicity
Bleiler, Everett F., 73–74, 73–74n3
Bliss, Elisha, 74, 77, 78, 79–80, 89n5
Bliss, Frank, 132–33
Boats. See Steamboats
Book of American Negro Poetry (Johnson), 163
Booth, Wayne, 154, 155
Borgia, Lucretia, 62
Bowen, Will, 33
Branch, Edgar M., 82n8
Breuer, Josef, 104n10
Brooks, Van Wyck, 13, 23, 56, 205–6, 211, 212, 215, 218, 223, 224, 225
Brown, Gillian, 14–15, 27
Brown, William Wells, 148
Budd, Louis, 217, 217n18, 225

Buffalo Express, 53, 76, 79, 79n7
Bynner, Witter, 119

California gold rush, 91
Camfield, Gregg, 209, 215, 215n15
Cardwell, Guy, 211–12, 222
Caricatures. See Race and ethnicity
Carus, Paul, 199
Cather, Willa, 24
Century magazine, 132n14
Chadwick-Joshua, Jocelyn, 122n1
"Chapters from My Autobiography" (Twain), 27
Charcot, Dr., 102–3
Charles L. Webster and Co., 89
Chesnutt, Charles, 163
Childbirth, 30–31
Children: deaths of, 31–32, 34, 48, 97; discipline of, 40–46; nineteenth-century views of, 28–29; as orphans, 15–16, 30; in Twain's fiction generally, 29, 47–48; whipping of, 41–42, 44–46
Christian Science, 102
Christian Union, 35, 40–46
Christie, Agatha, 139
Civil War, 93, 99–100
Clemens, Benjamin, 31
Clemens, Clara: childhood of, 34–38, 40; father's protectiveness of, 46, 48; and Isabel Lyon, 118–19; and Jean's death, 21; marriage of, 20; and move to Europe, 20, 26; study of piano by, 104; survival of, to full adulthood, 31; and Twain studies, 220, 221, 224, 225
Clemens, Hannibal, 31
Clemens, Henry, 30, 31, 90, 92, 97
Clemens, James, Jr., 90
Clemens, Jane Lampton, 29–31, 53, 54, 62, 185–87, 190
Clemens, Jean: childhood of, 38, 39; death and burial of, 9, 20–23, 26, 31, 32; and epilepsy, 21, 31, 46–47, 103; and Isabel Lyon, 118–19; and philosophy, 116; relationship with father, 21, 26, 46, 48, 224
Clemens, John Marshall, 29, 31, 69
Clemens, Langdon, 31, 33, 34, 36, 97
Clemens, Margaret, 31
Clemens, Mollie, 76
Clemens, Olivia Langdon (Livy): in Buffalo, 33–34, 76–77; as censor and editor of Twain's works, 109–11; children of,